W9-CKE-887

TRAPPED BY DANGER

"Move out of my way if you please."

"But I don't please."

He began to grin, the arrogant smile of a man who knows he has a woman at a disadvantage. Flaring with anger over his impertinence, I drew my skirts tight and tried to circle around him to get to the lift, but he kept stepping back and forth to block my path.

"I will thank you to stop looking at me and to let me go by."

"You're a treat for the eyes. We don't get young beautiful female guests here much anymore."

"I can certainly understand why."

At last I managed to dart past him into the lift. I peered at him through the grillwork. But before I could speak the lift shuddered and began to move.

"Henry, I didn't push the lever!"

The lift moved inexorably upward with a rattle and a whine. Henry's startled face vanished from sight.

I stepped backward and huddled against the wall of the cage. Heart pounding, I kept my eyes fixed on the view through the bars as the second floor hallway glided past and I was borne upward toward the third floor—and whoever or whatever awaited me there. . . .

THE MISTS OF MILWOOD

CHILLING GOTHICS
From Zebra Books

MIDNIGHT HEIRESS   (1933, $2.95)
by Kate Frederick

Aunt Martha's will held one stipulation: Barbara must marry the bastard son that Martha never acknowleged. But her new husband was tormented by secrets of the past. How long could Barbara hope to survive as the . . . *Midnight Heiress*.

HEATH HALLOWS   (1901, $2.95)
by Michele Y. Thomas

Caroline knew it was wrong to go in her cousin's place to Heath Hallows Abbey; but the wealthy Hawkesworths would never know the difference. But tragedies of the past cast a dark and deadly shadow over Heath Hallows, leaving Caroline to fear the evil lurking in the shadows.

THE HOUSE OF WHISPERING ASPENS   (1611, $2.95)
Alix Ainsley

Even as the Colorado aspens whispered of danger, Maureen found herself falling in love with one of her cousins. One brother would marry while the other would murder to become master of the HOUSE OF WHISPERING ASPENS.

THE BLOODSTONE INHERITANCE   (1560, $2.95)
by Serita Deborah Stevens

The exquisite Parkland pendant, the sole treasure remaining to lovely Elizabeth from her mother's fortune, was missing a matching jewel. Finding it in a ring worn by the handsome, brooding Peter Parkisham, Elizabeth couldn't deny the blaze of emotions he ignited in her.

THE HOUSE AT STONEHAVEN   (1239, $2.50)
by Ellouise Rife

Though she'd heard rumors about how her employer's first wife had died, Jo couldn't resist the magnetism of Elliot Stone. But soon she had to wonder if she was destined to become the next victim.

Available wherever paperbacks are sold, or order direct from the Publisher. Send cover price plus 50¢ per copy for mailing and handling to Zebra Books, Dept. 2074, 475 Park Avenue South, New York, N.Y. 10016. Residents of New York, New Jersey and Pennsylvania must include sales tax. DO NOT SEND CASH.

THE MISTS OF MILWOOD

MONIQUE HARA

ZEBRA BOOKS
KENSINGTON PUBLISHING CORP.

ZEBRA BOOKS

are published by

Kensington Publishing Corp.
475 Park Avenue South
New York, NY 10016

Copyright © 1987 by Monique Hara

All rights reserved. No part of this book may be reproduced
in any form or by any means without the prior written
consent of the Publisher, excepting brief quotes used in
reviews.

First printing: May 1987

Printed in the United States of America

To the memory of my parents,
Blanche and Lester Fisher
And to Hill Wheatley, that "Grand Old Man"
of Hot Springs, Arkansas

Chapter 1

My first view of the Milwood Hotel, pale in the moonlight with plumes of vapor drifting on the wind, struck me with such fear, such foreboding, that I would have turned back then had it been within my power. Trying to cover my reaction, I said with a shaky laugh, "It looks haunted."

"It is," Simon Hampton replied, glancing over his shoulder toward me from the driver's seat. "Didn't your aunt tell you?"

My great-aunt Alice, huddled beside me in the carriage, gave a disdainful snort.

"Nonsense, Simon! Come, Joanna, act your age."

She spoke to me as though I were two years old rather than twenty-three. I bit my lower lip while reminding myself to respect *her* age, which was seventy-four.

"But there is a ghost," Simon insisted. "A Spanish conquistador, complete with sword and clanking armor. If you see him, say, 'Peace be with you,' or he'll lop off your head."

That announcement did not reassure me.

"You're joking, of course."

He shrugged. "Who knows? Folks say they've seen some mighty strange things around here. Some say the ghost of an Indian, and some say a woman, but most say they've seen a Spanish soldier. De Soto and his troops did camp near here over three hundred years ago, so maybe it's one of them. I once found a Spanish coin down near the old mill."

"Well, *I've* never seen a ghost at Milwood," said my aunt. She thumped her cane on the carriage floor to show that the matter was settled. I'd long since learned not to argue with her once that cane came down.

Simon flicked the reins and the horse speeded up, bouncing the carriage along the rough lane. I grabbed at my bonnet to keep it from sailing off into the night. Although we were well into June, there was a clamminess to the air, a damp musty smell that made me think of country cemeteries. Perhaps the odor came from the hot springs, I thought, carried aloft by the drifting steam.

It was my aunt who had come to "take the waters," both to drink the scalding liquid and to soak in the mineral-laden baths. She'd been traveling to Arkansas for her health each summer for over thirty years, but this was my first visit. I hadn't wanted to come, for I felt my family back in St. Louis needed me near at hand; but since my aunt had recently employed me as her private nurse, I had no other choice but to accompany her on this journey.

"Don't offend her," my mother had begged. "Go along with her whims and keep her happy. You know how much I need the money she gives me."

I did indeed know. My widowed mother, with six other children still at home to clothe and feed, teetered always on the edge of financial disaster. Although I helped her all I could, she still depended on handouts from Great-aunt Alice, given grudgingly and accompanied by lectures on frugality.

During the two-day train journey from St. Louis, I'd told myself that the summer might be difficult but I'd just have to make the best of a bad situation. I had not counted on a hotel that housed a haunt.

The moon, a lopsided pearl hanging over the bluffs behind the hotel, highlighted the rising mists, while the building itself, lavish with towers, verandahs, and stained glass windows, could have been an illustration from a book I'd read as a child,

8

a story filled with giants and goblins. Although beautiful, the hotel still seemed sinister to me, as though it might have been conjured up by a mad genie, who could send it vanishing back into the underworld at any time, taking all its occupants with it. I did know, of course, that appearances can be deceiving. Who has not met a cold woman whose aloofness, viewed as conceit, proved to be caused by timidity, or a gruff man whose porcupine coat, protection against a threatening world, actually covered a soft heart? On the other hand, a beautiful face may sometimes conceal an evil nature, and the same thing can be true of houses as well.

I shivered, overcome by reluctance to go any closer. Had my aunt noticed my reaction, she would have asked in her usual imperious way, "Who walked over your grave?"

During my months in her service, I had experienced all too often the lash of her tongue and the capricious nature of her demands. Now she said, using the snappish tone of voice I'd come to expect, "For goodness sakes, Joanna, let Simon drive. Don't bother him with foolish talk."

While clucking his tongue at the horse, Simon glanced toward me again, his eyes flashing with amusement. I noted the way his curly hair sprang back from his face in the wind set up by the horse's pace. His hands, clutching the reins, appeared firm and capable.

Eyes and hands—those are the indicators I look at when forming first impressions of people. My impression of Simon Hampton when I'd first glimpsed him waiting for us at the train station back in Hot Springs had been, and remained, favorable indeed.

"What do you really think of it?" he asked, again indicating the hotel.

"It rivals any hotel I saw in town," I replied.

Since he was one of the owners of Milwood, I didn't wish to offend him by revealing my true feelings; but as we jolted closer down the bumpy lane, I became increasingly disturbed by the signs of decay, not visible at the greater distance: a loose gutter, a boarded-up window, a missing length of gingerbread trim along the front verandah.

"Why have you let it run down like that?" I finally burst out, then bit my lip in embarrassment at the impertinence of such a question, directed toward a man I'd known for less than three hours.

"Lack of funds, what else? Most of our old clientele now prefer the glamour of Hot Springs itself. Racing, gambling, dancing every night. How can we compete with that? Last January the rest of the world entered the Twentieth Century, but at Milwood we're still stuck in the Dark Ages."

Although he continued to smile, a line deepened along one side of his mouth, giving his expression a bitter cast, a cloud to shadow my initial bright impression. For one brief moment he looked almost menacing.

"Stuff and nonsense, Simon!" my aunt exclaimed briskly. "It's clamour, not glamour, in Hot Springs now, all those infernal clanging trolleys and people everywhere! The quiet of Milwood is much to be preferred." She thumped her cane upon the floor, disturbing the quiet she extolled.

As the carriage rolled inexorably forward, the hotel seemed to swell against the curtain of drifting mist until it loomed over us, a bird of prey with extended wings. Simon circled the carriage to a halt before a flight of flagstone steps that swept up to the front verandah. Double doors stood open into the house, revealing a spill of light from the lobby beyond. A figure appeared and paused there, a tall male figure silhouetted against the light. Then he stepped out onto the porch and held up a lantern, and I saw a lean man whom I judged to be in his late twenties. He marched solemnly down the steps and extended his hand to my aunt to help her from the carriage.

"Be careful . . . her arthritis," I began, but my aunt cut across my words with a sharp command. "Be quiet, Joanna! Henry knows about my arthritis after all this time."

This, then, was Simon's older brother. For years, following each of her summer sojourns, I'd listened to tales of the

Hampton family from my aunt. I had cried as a little girl when I'd learned how Henry's puppy had been crushed under the buggy wheels, and I had shuddered at the story of Simon's broken arm, injured when he'd attempted to fly with canvas wings from the stable roof. Now, grown to maturity, we were meeting for the first time.

I climbed down quickly without assistance and circled to join the others. Looking back and forth between the two men, Simon short and stocky, Henry as thin as a pole, yet both with the same wide-set eyes and dark curly hair, I saw them as old friends, men I could trust without question. Then my earlier thought about appearances being deceiving flashed into my head. I tried to dismiss it, but a persistent uneasiness nagged at the back of my mind. There was no reason, I told myself sternly, to have any doubts where these two men were concerned. Nevertheless, I shivered again, struck by a nameless fear. I am not usually given to premonitions, but this one would not go away. What did I sense here? I wondered. Why did I want to turn and run? I felt as though something heavy hung over my head, ready to fall and crush me.

While I stood there fighting against my fear, Henry finished helping my aunt from the carriage. One of her knees creaked and she let out a groan.

"Careful . . . careful now, Aunt Alice," he said.

Simon had called her that, too, back in Hot Springs, although she was not related to either of them. My aunt did not often permit such liberties of address outside the family, but then she'd known both Henry and Simon since they were born. Perhaps the rigid rules by which she usually lived back in St. Louis were relaxed during these summer vacations. After all, her last name, McPherson, might have been hard for these men to say when they were small, and so she had made allowances.

With my aunt safely on the ground, Henry turned his gaze toward me. Simon introduced me, and I saw Henry's eyes narrow as he took my measure. But he said, civilly enough, "You must be hungry."

11

"We ate supper in town," I replied, grateful for his concern.

Along with the stories of their boyish escapades, my aunt had also told me other stories of the family: how Henry and Simon's grandfather, Rhodes Hampton, had left St. Louis and traveled with his ailing mother to Arkansas back in 1843, during Hot Springs's early days, and had uncovered his own hot springs strictly by accident in this valley six miles from town where no springs had previously been suspected. "Accident," indeed: Having heard that there were gems in the area, Rhodes had set off a dynamite charge in a hillside and had been rewarded by a rift in the rock through which poured a spate of hot water and steam. He'd laid claim to the land at once and begun building his own hotel, a simple log lodge to start with, the "baths" mere gravel-lined pools surrounded by canvas walls. Following his mother's death, he had married a local girl and together they had improved their property, replacing the lodge, after the war between the states, with this sprawling hotel and continuing through the years to improve the resort with the help of their sons and now their grandsons. Although old Rhodes had finally died not so long ago, my aunt had told me that his widow Nell still watched over the operation with an eagle eye.

Her eye must no longer be so sharp, I thought now, glancing at a hole in the verandah railing where a round was missing.

"Where's Jeremy?" my aunt asked in an eager voice.

I whipped my head about in surprise to see a smile soften her usually stern features. For one moment, in the magic of the moonlight, I glimpsed the girl she had once been.

Why, she must have been pretty! I thought in startled amazement, realizing that to me she had always just been "Aunt Alice," born old and forbidding, an iron-corseted ogre who made my mother cry. Even while telling those stories to me, back when I was young, she had kept her distance, constantly finding things in me to criticize. "Pull your skirts down, Joanna, and keep your feet together. You are a girl, not a boy, and you must learn to deport yourself accordingly." Or,

12

when I would ask a question about her latest story, "Speak clearly, Joanna! Do not slur your words. A slovenly tongue is the sign of a slovenly mind."

I had decided when I was ten that I must tolerate Aunt Alice for my family's sake, but I did not have to love her. In these past few months that I'd worked for her, I'd seen no reason to change my mind.

"Jeremy? He's mooning about somewhere with his notebook," Henry said.

I detected sarcasm in his voice, but Aunt Alice didn't seem to notice. She turned shining eyes upon me and exclaimed, "Such a sensitive soul, Joanna! Mark my words, he's this country's next Longfellow."

I continued staring at her, struck dumb by her change of manner. Never had she responded to my younger brothers and sisters or to me with such enthusiasm, or to anyone else that I could recall.

"Still so young, Joanna, yet already so gifted," she went on.

I knew Jeremy to be at least twenty-seven years old, which didn't seem all that young to me, considering the fact that the poet Shelley had died at the age of thirty. Henry and Simon exchanged a look, their expressions smooth, yet their glance told me plainly that they, too, did not share my aunt's opinion about their cousin's "gift."

"There he is! Jeremy, Jeremy . . ." My aunt pulled away from Henry's grip, stumbling forward in her eagerness, as a pale young man stepped into the moonlight from among the shadows near the porch. I leapt forward and grabbed my aunt's arm while Henry did the same on the other side. Together we kept my aunt from falling. She shook us off impatiently and continued her forward progress, her attention still riveted upon the newcomer.

"Ah, Aunt Alice, you are here!" Jeremy exclaimed, his soft high voice floating toward us on the wind. "I have composed a poem in honor of your arrival."

He advanced into the light flaring from the lantern, where

he struck a pose, chin lifted and head tilted slightly to one side, notebook held at arm's length, and proceeded to read aloud:

O carriage blest, that brings so fair a guest!
Hark, how lark and wren proclaim their joy.
No need to seek beyond, for friendship's quest
Ends here. Weep with envy, Helen of Troy.
When once you walked the earth, you reigned supreme
In beauty and in grace, the legends tell.
Now you are gone, and in your place, this queen
Of grace and beauty comes to dwell
Within our humble walls. Peel forth, O bell,
Our welcome and our joy the world to tell.

My aunt clasped her hands over her breast. "Jeremy, it's beautiful! Isn't it beautiful, Joanna?"

How could I say, in the face of such enthusiasm, that I thought it the worst poem I'd ever heard?

"Yes, Aunt Alice. Beautiful."

She laid a tentative hand on his arm, almost as though she were afraid he would break. "Is your book finished, Jeremy? Oh, tell me that it is!"

"No, dear lady, not yet. I want my poems to be perfect . . . to be strong and ready to live on their own before I release them into a hostile world. There are those, you know, who won't understand what I'm trying to say . . . critics, frustrated poets themselves no doubt, who will go out of their way to wound someone new. I must make sure my poems are above reproach."

"Yes, my dear, you're right, of course. Now come and meet my niece Joanna. I've told her much about you over the years."

What she had told me I didn't like: how Jeremy had stayed in the house when the other boys were out playing; how he'd cried and had to go to bed whenever they'd teased him.

"Because he's so much more sensitive than the others, you

know," my aunt had explained.

Jeremy, in my opinion, was a toad.

He linked his arm now with my aunt's, smiling down at her fatuously, and together they moved toward us. Jeremy's hair, fair and fine, stirred in the wind like cobwebs, while his face shown so pale in the moonlight that I knew he must still spend much of his time inside. What a contrast to his virile cousins! Even his clothing seemed affected: soft trousers, a white shepherd's shirt with dropped shoulders and bloused sleeves, a silk scarf tied loosely about his neck. When my aunt introduced us, he sighed wearily and took my hand for just a moment in his soft grasp, as though he were too spent from his creative efforts to do more.

"Joanna is a nurse," my aunt explained to them all. "My personal nurse now, since I paid for her training so she could attend me in my old age."

"A nurse!" Henry exclaimed, his eyes lighting with interest.

I smiled at him in a brief moment of camaraderie, knowing that he had, for a time, attended medical school before giving up his studies to come back and work at the hotel.

"And now, Jeremy, if you'll help me inside?" my aunt asked.

She beamed at him while he replied, "Of course, dear lady," and led her toward the steps.

I could only follow in dismay, staying close behind them as my aunt struggled up the steps with little help from Jeremy, hoping I could catch her or at least break her fall should she topple backward. How much better had she chosen Simon or Henry for support, yet she'd had eyes for no one but Jeremy since he'd arrived upon the scene. It made me wonder suddenly about her girlhood. Had she once been in love with a simpering fool like this one? Was that why she had never married, fossilizing at an early age into the dragon I must now attend under the threat of seeing my mother and brood of younger brothers and sisters tossed out into the street should I defect?

I felt for a moment the chill of my own mortality. To wither

15

and harden like my aunt, unwed, childless, attended by relatives only out of duty or fear . . . what a sad fate.

We managed to arrive inside the front lobby without mishap. It was a spacious but shadowed place, dimly lit by two brass chandeliers and furnished with a wooden desk, throw rugs, potted plants, and wicker chairs. Near the desk a carved wooden staircase angled up toward the second floor.

Simon and Henry followed us in, carrying our smaller bags. My aunt's heavy brass-bound trunk, stowed in the boot of the carriage, would take their combined efforts to lug inside, I felt sure.

"You have reserved my favorite suite?" my aunt asked now.

"Yes, indeed," Simon said. "East wing. Third floor front. Bay window."

"The stairs—" I protested, only to have my aunt interject harshly, "Don't be a fool, Joanna. Of course there's a lift."

"But so far from town—"

"We make our own electricity," Henry said.

Simon furnished the explanation. "We're on a branch of the Ouachita River, you see, and we've got a waterfall and an old mill on our property. The fall generates just enough power to run the lift and to light the lobby. As for the rest of the fifty rooms . . ." Again a cloud passed over his countenance, and his mouth took on the bitter twist I'd seen before. "Old-fashioned, that's us . . . lamps with wicks. How can we compete with the hotels in town if we don't modernize?"

"Oh, for the days long past!" Jeremy sighed. "Knighthood and chivalry, castles and tapestries—"

"Disease and fleas," Simon snapped.

Jeremy gave him a wounded look, his large brown eyes as limpid as a doe's.

"Alice. Here you are again."

The raspy voice sounded mocking and none too pleased. I turned to see an old woman, her white hair piled high in a coronet, come sweeping into the lobby from a back hallway, her black silk skirt rustling like a snake through autumn

16

leaves. My aunt released Jeremy's arm and planted her cane with a thump directly in front of her body, clasping the top with both hands and straightening her arms in stiff support as she reared back, chin held high, to greet the newcomer.

"Yes, Nell, I made it through another winter, and here I am."

Nell came to a halt in front of my aunt, and they eyed each other, animosity crackling between them like lightning leaping from one cloud to another in a summer storm. I almost expected to see them attack each other, two old cats with extended claws, hissing and tearing, but Henry stepped into the breach before the fight could begin.

"Grandmother, this is Joanna Forester, Aunt Alice's grand-niece. Miss Forester, I'd like to present our grandmother, Nell Hampton."

Old Rhodes's widow, then, the woman who had helped build this resort. I gave her a slight bow while murmuring, "Mrs. Hampton."

All around us the potted palms, stirred by an errant breeze, threw flickering shadows upon the walls. Multi-fingered, the shadows gestured toward us like so many greedy hands. In my agitated state, I started with fear when I heard a strange creaking sound echo down one of the darkened corridors nearby. I whirled and watched two forms materialize from the shadows: a mousey woman in a long gray skirt and white shirtwaist pushing a gray-haired man in a wheelchair. I realized then that I'd allowed Simon's story about the Spanish ghost to affect my nerves.

"Here's the rest of the welcoming committee," Henry announced.

He introduced them as his parents, Charlotte and Amos Hampton. Charlotte smiled at me timidly and ducked her head in a gesture of welcome, but I couldn't help noticing how tense her face was when she darted her eyes back and forth between the two older women, obviously fearing what they might do next. It was her husband she should have been watching. He

17

fixed me with a murderous glare and demanded harshly, "Where have you hidden the trunk?"

"What?"

"You're a thief, I can see it." To the others he said, "Ask her! Ask her what she's done with the trunk. Ask her where she's hidden the money."

Charlotte's hands fluttered in the air as though to take back her husband's words.

"Dad, that's enough!" Simon said sharply, while Henry gave me a pointed look and shook his head.

I examined their father with a professional eye, noting the way one of his eyelids drooped in a face which bore, on that side, a slight grimace. My aunt had told me that Amos had been thrown by a horse the year before and had struck his head on a rock. The accident seemed to have caused symptoms similar to those of a stroke, she'd reported, and I could see that she was right.

The tension bristling in the air could not be ignored. My skin prickled with the force of it, and I eyed each of the people I'd just met, trying to discover, from an inadvertent gesture or expression, what was going on here. Charlotte placed a trembling hand on her husband's shoulder but he shook her off with an impatient shrug. Simon glowered at his father, while Henry glanced away from me, his brows drawn together in a studied frown. Nell snapped, "Amos, control yourself," and even Jeremy looked nonplussed.

I decided to end the scene by asserting my authority as a nurse.

"Come, Aunt Alice, you've had a tiring trip. You must get to bed now, or your knees will swell up."

She flicked me an angry look. "I feel perfectly fine, thank you."

I could see, by the curl of triumph on Nell Hampton's lips, that I had placed my aunt at a disadvantage in this unspoken war by referring to her infirmity.

"I'm glad you feel fine, but I'd like to rest now," I said,

18

taking a different tack.

My aunt huffed through her nose in disdain. "Because *you're* tired, Joanna, doesn't mean that others are as well. Oh, all right, if you insist."

As we proceeded toward the lift situated at the far end of the lobby, I caught Henry's eye now fixed upon me with sardonic humor. He raised one eyebrow and nodded slightly to show me that he'd understood my ploy. One of the doctors I'd worked with during my training had given me a number of hints on how to deal with difficult patients, and I felt sure, seeing the expression on Henry's face, that he, too, had had instructions along that line. I wondered how often each day he had to use such tactics on his father.

The lift, an ornate bird cage made of brass, was so narrow that it could carry only three people at once. Jeremy rode up with us, holding a lamp in one hand and operating the levers with the other, while I clutched the walls and prayed we wouldn't plummet suddenly to earth. The rattle of chains and pulleys, echoing through the shaft, made me think once more of Simon's clanking conquistador, and I wrinkled my nose, again aware of a musty smell in the air. We finally arrived at the third floor with a shuddering jerk.

"Someone needs to oil the mechanism," my aunt announced with a thump of her cane.

We proceeded to the right down a long, dark hallway. I counted the doors from the top of the stairs until we reached our assigned room, having been trained to do that during hospital fire drills. The purpose of such a practice is to ensure that one can feel one's way to safety even when a corridor is filled with smoke. Seven doors. Seven doors from the head of the stairs. While Jeremy fumbled with the lock, I peered into the shadows of the corridor beyond, struck by the unreasonable feeling that we were being watched. I felt decidedly relieved when Jeremy finally got the door open and admitted us to a large sitting room, which glowed a welcome from lamps already lit. I pushed past the others and turned full circle in the middle of the carpet, taking in the elegant furnishings, then darted to a bay window on the opposite side of the room, where I rested one knee on the padded window seat while I leaned forward to peer toward the grounds three floors below. I found myself looking into a courtyard where a fountain splashed a shower of diamonds in the moonlight. Even as I watched, a ghostly shape appeared behind the fountain and I let out a faint cry, feeling the hairs lift on my arms. Then I saw the wraith twist and vanish, and I knew I was once more seeing the drifting mists of Milwood. I turned back into the room, brushing past the leaves of a fern that stood on a small wooden table in one corner of the bay. The ruffled curtains, a filmy white, bellowed gently in the moist breeze that wafted through the screens.

"Joanna, you're acting childish again," my aunt said in a querulous tone. "Here's my cape. Please hang it up."

As I moved to obey, I glanced again about the room. A mahogany fireplace with brick lining and marble mantel stood against one wall, with comfortable-looking upholstered chairs arranged in front. Between the chairs was a low marble-topped table holding a kerosene lamp with a pink glass base. Other tables and chairs were arranged about the room, while family portraits on the walls added a homey touch. An open door to one side led into a large bedroom. I entered there to see a four-poster bed against one wall where my aunt would sleep, with a cot in one corner for me. A handsome dresser with lyre mirror, reflecting the light from the other room, occupied another wall, while two additional doors gave access to a clothes closet and to a water closet, which proved to be a marvel in tile and brass, with a claw-footed tub, marble sink, and a flush commode.

I hung up the cape and returned to the sitting room to find Jeremy finishing the recitation of another poem:

> . . . and never can we now regain
> Those pleasant days of yore.

20

"Lovely!" sighed my aunt. "Jeremy, repeat it for Joanna."
Dutifully he began:

> *I often think, 'ere break of dawn,*
> *Upon those wondrous times now gone . . .*

I was saved by the arrival of Simon and Henry with our smaller bags.

"Please put the bags in the bedroom," I directed, and bustled after the two men to occupy myself there, hoping that Jeremy would leave. But it was Simon and Henry who left, saying, "We'll be back with the trunk."

"Come out, Joanna. Jeremy is going to recite for us again," my aunt called.

I poked my head through the bedroom door to say, "We really must rest," but my aunt interrupted me, indicating the chairs before the fireplace.

"Here, sit beside me," she said. "These chairs are quite suitable for resting."

With a sigh I joined her, forcing a smile to my lips in response to Jeremy's own smile. For the first time I noticed the shyness beneath his arty facade, an appeal in his eyes that was almost touching. Had he exhibited some self-awareness at that moment, any hint that he realized his poetry was bad, I could well have liked him. Instead, he leaned dramatically against the fireplace, one hand over his heart, and rewarded us with ten minutes of trite sentiment in singsong verse. I kept my ears tuned for the lift and relaxed at last when I heard the clang of its arrival. Shortly thereafter Simon and Henry carried in the trunk, and now I had a legitimate reason to excuse myself from the poetry session by reminding my aunt that her dresses needed to be unpacked at once and hung up to let the wrinkles fall out.

"Come along, Jeremy, the ladies must be tired," Henry said.

I could tell that he was rescuing us on purpose, and I felt a surge of gratitude.

"Mother says she'll send up a tray with some sandwiches and a pot of tea," he added.

"Oh, that will be marvelous!"

"Now remember," Simon put in, "beware of the ghost."

"I'll remember."

"You told her that old story?" Henry said, shaking his head at his brother in reproval, but Jeremy, his face pale, blurted out, "I've seen it, you know. It's horrible, surrounded by a blue glow—"

"That's enough. You'll give them nightmares," Henry interrupted. He took Jeremy's arm and propelled him, none too gently, through the door.

As soon as they were gone, I carried the lamp into the bedroom and began unpacking while my aunt came in and sat down in a chair to supervise.

"Be careful, Joanna. Don't handle that gown so roughly. The lace is very delicate."

"Yes, Aunt Alice."

"And watch that jet bead collar. You'll snag the silk underneath."

"Yes, Aunt Alice."

"And you really must curb your impetuous behavior, running to the window like that a while ago in front of Jeremy. Such abrupt movement is unladylike."

"Yes, Aunt Alice."

I answered automatically, having long since learned to turn my thoughts elsewhere during her tirades. Now I was thinking about Simon and Henry and trying to decide who was the more attractive. True, Henry was the taller, a point in his favor, yet Simon was neatly built, strong, and compact, a man bursting with energy and ideas. On the other hand, Henry's medical training gave us something in common, and I looked forward to asking him questions about his training. . . .

". . . so I think it's time you married."

Aunt Alice's words penetrated at last. I turned toward her,

a bed jacket clutched in my hands, and said, "I beg your pardon?"

"Well you might! You've been woolgathering, as usual." She fixed me with a disapproving frown.

"I—I'm sorry, my thoughts were elsewhere. What is this about my getting married?"

"You're still immature, I know, but I will be there to guide you. You and your husband will live with me, of course, for you'll both need my help. . . ."

"Aunt Alice, what are you talking about?"

"Your marriage. Are you still not paying attention?"

I dropped the bed jacket back into the trunk and stepped toward the chair where my aunt now sat bolt upright, both hands planted upon her cane.

"What husband? What marriage?"

"You *are* an addlepated fool! What have we been discussing these past five minutes? Your marriage to Jeremy, of course!"

With that, she thumped her cane upon the floor.

Chapter 2

My first inclination was to laugh. Then I saw that Aunt Alice wasn't joking. I should have known that, of course. She was not one for levity.

"Marry *Jeremy?*" I said, unable to keep my revulsion from my voice.

But she took it differently. "I can understand your doubts. You feel you are unworthy, of course, of a man who is a genius, but I told you that I will help you, and I will. You may certainly depend on that."

"Aunt Alice, I—I don't love Jeremy. I've only just met him."

"You'll allow time for a proper courtship, of course, that's only right. But it won't take long for you to fall in love, as young as you are."

"Then why not Simon or Henry? Why Jeremy?"

"Simon or Henry!" She glared at me, as though the suggestion were obscene. "They're common, Joanna. Jeremy is a rare person, the kind you may meet once in a lifetime. But he isn't strong. He'll need the care of a nurse at an early age, I fear, and you are already trained. Yes, you will marry Jeremy and live with me, and then you can care for us both."

She thumped her cane again, more emphatically than before. Such a prospect for my future might have tumbled me headlong into despair had I taken her seriously. But I didn't *have* to marry Jeremy, I told myself, no matter what plans my aunt might have. My initial shock began to dissolve. That's when Aunt Alice presented me with the proverbial carrot designed to lead the donkey forward.

"On your wedding day to Jeremy I will give your mother twenty-five thousand dollars."

My knees went weak and I sank down on the edge of the bed. With a fortune like that, my mother could support and educate all my brothers and sisters and still have enough left over to open the millinery shop she'd always wanted.

I turned my thoughts to Jeremy. There *had* been that look of appeal in his eyes, a hint of underlying sweetness, which might mean he was not so bad as I'd first thought.

"We'll have two months here," Aunt Alice reminded me. "Plenty of time for love to bloom."

I put aside my daydreams of Simon and Henry and tried to concentrate on Jeremy's pale, delicate features. I rose and moved to the mirror, picturing us together: me, with my auburn hair and brown eyes, skin tanned to match . . . (*"Where* is your parasol, Joanna? Do you want to look like a gypsy?"* my aunt had demanded a dozen times this spring) . . . beside Jeremy, soft and soulful. It was not a picture that appealed to me. In my daydream, I substituted first Henry's lean-jawed face with the glint of sardonic humor in his gaze, then Simon's rugged features, green eyes dancing, with just a touch of bitterness around his mouth. Neither of those faces belonged to men who were startlingly handsome, but then, my face was not so handsome either, with a mouth too large to be a rosebud, cheekbones too prominent for the soft dewy look of women's faces in the society section of fashionable magazines. A creamy brow, rosy cheeks, and a dimpled chin . . . that's what I needed to be considered beautiful. Lacking those, I would have to concentrate on character.

Would a woman of charcter marry a man she didn't love? I

asked myself, and answered that it would depend upon the circumstances. I didn't love Jeremy, but I did love my mother, a brave but frail woman who had adored my father and who had never blamed him for his lack of business sense, which left his family penniless when he died.

For it was Great-aunt Alice who had inherited the family fortune, made in shipping and fur-trading back in St. Louis. Her brother, my grandfather, had been disowned by their Union-supporting family when he chose to fight for the South during the war. I never knew my grandfather, but I'd often heard my father talk about him.

"Papa did *not* like slavery," he said, "but it was the issue of states' rights which concerned him. He felt the national government was assuming too much authority and that we had to get back to our original constitutional ideas."

The issue was still a tender one, both in Missouri and in Arkansas, and I did my best to avoid political discussions, particularly if Aunt Alice was around.

"Staring in that mirror will not improve your appearance," she said now. "Are you going to finish unpacking or not?"

"Yes, I am, but first I'm putting you to bed."

She grumbled while I helped her out of her clothes and into her voluminous flannel nightgown, but I noticed that she sighed with relief when her head touched the pillow. Soon her mouth fell open and she began snoring gently. I saw, observing her now with the eyes of a nurse, how shrunken and defenseless she looked in sleep. She was, after all, an old woman, despite her efforts to hold back the years through iron-willed control. Indeed, it was probably her irascibility that kept her going, I thought. Her anger energized her and gave her purpose as she created victims around her upon whom to vent her ire. I remembered that old saying, "Only the good die young."

I straightened the summer quilt over her bony body, then finished unpacking. Usually an ordinary task like that would have calmed me, but not this time. The feeling of dread that had come over me at the first sight of Milwood still hung about my shoulders like a damp cloak. Perhaps what I'd sensed, approaching the hotel, had been this proposal of my aunt's, I thought, this settlement of my fate in the form of Jeremy. That was undoubtedly part of it, yet there was more, too, something I couldn't put my finger on, a feeling of pending danger like a dark shadow lurking in the mists.

A distant clang echoed through the walls, giving me a start and causing me to glance quickly over my shoulder. Common sense told me I'd heard the lift, but I still shivered, struck by the sudden fantasy that something evil was even now making its way toward our rooms. As I stood frozen to the spot, shuffling footsteps paused outside and I heard three low raps at the door. For a moment, I couldn't move.

Then Henry's voice called, "Joanna," and the spell was broken. I darted into the other room and flung open the door to see him standing there with a large tea tray.

"I'd forgotten about the tea!" I exclaimed. "Aunt Alice is already asleep."

"She did look exhausted," he said. "Do you want me to take this away?"

"No, no, come on in."

He entered and placed the tray on the table in front of the fireplace, then straightened to look me in the eye with disconcerting directness.

"She'll eat you alive, you know."

When I didn't reply, surprised by such a forthright statement, he continued, "It's hard having one's life ruled by a tyrannical invalid."

"Are you speaking of me or yourself?"

He lifted one eyebrow with that mocking look I'd already seen downstairs. "You're a sharp one."

A current seemed to flow between us, an exchange of energy that ignited my body. It was a surprising sensation, which momentarily took my breath. I would never, I knew, have a reaction like this to Jeremy. With difficulty I forced my eyes away from his and motioned toward a chair.

"Please, sit and drink some tea with me."

While he folded his lanky body into one of the upholstered chairs, I sat opposite him and poured out two cups of tea. Wisps of steam rose from the amber brew, reminding me of the drifting vapors outside.

To cover the confusion I felt in his presence, I said, "The steam behind the hotel . . . I assume that comes from the springs?"

"Yes, the waters are very hot. It makes one wonder if we're perched over the gateway to hell."

I remembered my earlier fantasy about the mad genie who might have conjured up Milwood and who could send it sinking back into the ground with everyone in it. The idea of a fiery pit beneath us was not reassuring.

Nevertheless, I said, "If we're headed for hell, then I'm going to eat first."

Henry laughed and saluted me with his cup. I saw his glance slide in frank appraisal over my body, and I felt a rush of heat through my veins. Trying to pretend I hadn't noticed his surveillance, I lifted away the napkin covering the sandwiches. The smell of sweet fresh bread wafted into the air, along with the tang of strawberry preserves, much more appealing than the musty smell that had haunted me since my arrival. I offered the plate first to Henry, but he shook his head. It had been a long time since dinner in town, so I ate with good appetite while Henry leaned back in the chair and stretched his long legs toward the empty fireplace. As he sipped the tea his smile vanished, to be replaced by a moody, withdrawn look.

"Has Aunt Alice talked much about this place?" he asked at last. There seemed to be more implied in his question than just idle curiosity.

"She's told me so many stories about you and Simon that I feel we've grown up together," I replied.

"Has she ever mentioned . . . a trunk?"

Shock washed through me, bringing me upright in my chair.

"What? . . . Your father said—"

"It's an obsession with him."

"Henry, what are you talking about?"

"Then she didn't mention it?"

"What trunk?"

He opened his mouth as though to speak, then shrugged. "No matter. If she didn't mention it, then she knows nothing of it." He swilled the tea and plunked down the cup on the table. "You're tired, I'm sure. I'll leave you alone now."

"But surely—" I began, wanting to hear more.

He interrupted, saying, "It's not important. I'll see you in the morning. Breakfast is at eight, but the bell rings fifteen minutes before that to give you a little time to get downstairs."

He rose and headed for the door. I followed him, puzzled by the whole conversation. "Henry, about that trunk—"

"Forget it, please. I should never have mentioned it. Sleep well."

And with that he was gone.

I returned to my chair and tried to drink a second cup of tea, but it seemed to have lost its flavor. Finally I blew out the lamps, then tiptoed into the other room and managed to get into bed without disturbing my snoring aunt. I lay awake for some time, thinking about Henry, Simon, and Jeremy, before drifting into a nightmare where a snoring Spanish ghost pushed me into a pool of fire.

I awoke in the morning to a pink sky and the trill of birds. My nightmare demons vanished, chased back into the earth by the rising sun. I leapt from bed and hurried into the water closet to complete my toilette before having to contend with my aunt. The water that gushed from the bathtub faucets sparkled like faceted crystal. I'd read that the waters at Hot Springs were the purest in the nation—an advertiser's story, no doubt. Still, when I climbed into the steaming bath to scrub away the grime from the former day's trip, I felt so refreshed I could well

29

believe the claims.

Back in the bedroom, I donned clean chemise and drawers but decided not to wear a corset. Had my aunt been awake to notice, she would have been scandalized. As I slipped into my long petticoat, then into my dark blue nurse's uniform with white collar and cuffs, I mentally thanked my mother for giving me such a small waist. I felt sure that no one would notice the omission of the corset, which was, in my opinion, an instrument of torture designed by some Puritan with a morbid yen for martyrdom.

I brushed my waist-length hair, dampened by the bath, and repinned it in a coil on the back of my head. Despite my efforts to make my coiffure smooth, a few tendrils escaped to curl about my face.

My aunt stirred and pushed herself up on her elbows.

"What time is it?"

I looked at the small watch on a ribbon I wore pinned to my uniform. "Almost seven. I understand breakfast is at eight."

"Yes, it is, and I don't want to be late. Why didn't you wake me, Joanna, instead of simpering before that mirror?"

"Sorry, Aunt. Here, let me help you."

The process of bathing my aunt and getting her dressed for the day went much slower than usual, for she seemed driven to look her best.

"Nell thinks she's going to outlive me, but I'll show her!" she said emphatically. "The day Nell Hampton gets the better of me will be a long day in hell."

Again I thought of the fires burning beneath our feet, evidenced by the steaming springs. All these references to hell seemed to me to be tempting fate. I quickly changed the subject by saying, "Your good green silk, then? Is that the dress you'd like to wear?"

"Of course not. That green color makes me look bilious and feel that way, too. Why I let you talk me into buying that material, Joanna, I'll never know."

I pressed my lips together, refraining with difficulty from

reminding her that she was the one who had insisted on the fabric over my protests. Aunt Alice often rewrote history to suit herself.

At last she settled on a gold and mauve silk gown with leg-of-mutton sleeves and a shirred bodice trimmed with crystal beads. I brushed her thin gray hair around a padded gray roll to make it look thicker, then disguised my efforts by pinning into place a Spanish comb trimmed with beads and feathers. She eschewed face paint, of course, but did permit me to soften her wrinkles with powder.

"There, Aunt Alice, you look quite elegant."

She rose with the aid of her cane and turned before the mirror. "Perhaps the blue voile would be better. . . ."

We were interrupted by the clang of the dinner bell.

"Come, Aunt Alice, you look just fine, and you said you don't want to be late."

I led her to the end of the hallway and pushed the button to call the lift from below. I would personally have preferred the stairs, but I knew Aunt Alice could never manage. The ride in the shuddering lift took only a few moments but seemed long to me. I was relieved when we groaned to a stop at last. I opened the door and helped my aunt out into the lobby, only to meet the glowering eyes of Amos Hampton.

"There she is again!" he shouted. "Henry, there's the thief!"

Henry hurried around the desk while flicking an apologetic glance in my direction.

"Now, Father, we told you last night, remember? This is Miss Forester, Aunt Alice's niece."

"You did *not* tell me. No one tells me anything," John protested in a petulant tone.

"Now, Dad—"

"Ask her what she's done with Father's money."

"She doesn't have the money, Dad."

"She does. I see the guilt in her eyes."

Henry's face flushed a dull red. I could not tell whether his reaction was caused by anger or embarrassment. Ignoring his father, Henry asked, "How are you feeling this morning, Aunt Alice?"

"I'm doing quite well," she said belligerently. "What did you expect?"

Henry's and my glances met and held in one brief moment of unspoken understanding over our difficult charges. Then Amos broke in to demand that Henry bring in the police to have me arrested, and the moment was gone.

"Amos, you're acting like a fool," my aunt now said with a total lack of compassion. "You must try to pull yourself together."

Amos turned his gaze upon her. I saw a flicker there of intelligence, of sanity peeking out from behind the ruined face, which held me transfixed with a sudden realization: *He's not as daft as he makes out.*

There was something else behind those eyes, just a brief fierce flash and then gone, yet I recognized that, too: *It was hatred.*

Fear crawled along my arms like damp worms. Something *was* going on here, I thought. Amos was playing a game, and playing it well. But why? Did Henry know what his father was up to?

Even as I thought those things, Amos's eyes dulled into an unfocused stare.

"It's raining," he said petulantly. "I hate rain."

I glanced toward the lobby windows, which framed a vista of sunlit trees and flowers. Henry followed my gaze, then looked back at me and shook his head.

"Perhaps the weather will clear soon," I said to Amos in a soothing tone. "Meanwhile, we're going to have breakfast now. Would the two of you like to join us?"

"The family eats in the kitchen," Henry told me. "Guests are served in the dining room."

With a slight bow, he gestured toward doors beyond the lift, doors that had been closed the night before. Now they stood open, revealing a large dining room streaming with light.

"Stuff and nonsense, Henry," my aunt huffed. "I want Jeremy to eat with us."

"But, Aunt Alice, if those are the rules—" I began. One person I did not wish to spend time with at this moment was Jeremy.

She thumped her cane on the floor. "Jeremy will eat with us, that's all there is to it."

"I'll send him out," Henry assured her. "Come, Dad, time for a little ride."

Without further adieu, Henry pushed the wheelchair down the corridor that extended beyond the dining room toward the back of the hotel. There was nothing for me to do but follow my aunt into the dining room, which proved to be a huge place with tables and chairs for at least a hundred people. Only two tables were laid with cloths and cutlery, both of them near a large bay window through which blew a cool morning breeze. A man was already seated at one of the tables, a middle-aged man, very fat, with a fringe of brown hair surrounding his gleaming bald pate. His right foot, wearing a large, soft slipper, rested on a pillow on a chair beside the table, while a pair of crutches lay on the floor nearby.

"Good morning, ladies," he boomed, his florid face lighting with an unctuous smile that carried the flash of a gold tooth. "Forgive me for not rising, but you see how it is." He gestured toward his foot. "I'm Albert Lock from Little Rock, and I'd be at your service if I could."

With that voice and smile, he had to be a used buggy salesman, I thought.

"How do you do, Mr. Lock?" my aunt said coolly. I knew she didn't expect an answer, but he replied, "Rather poorly, ma'am. Got a touch of the old gout and decided to see if the springs are as magical as folks say."

My aunt looked him up and down, taking in the plaid suit

33

and bulging waistcoat with such obvious contempt that I felt a pang of sympathy for Mr. Lock. All she said was, "Yes, the waters are most beneficial."

She maneuvered about so that her back was to him when she sat down. Although I cared little for Mr. Lock myself, I gave him a nod and a smile, trying to soften the effect of my aunt's rudeness. That proved to be a mistake. He seemed to see my nod as permission to go on.

"So why are you here, little lady? Worn out from too many parties and balls, I'll wager, and needing a rest before the fall social season begins?"

I'd never been to a ball in my life, but I didn't care to reveal how limited my social engagements were, particularly to Mr. Lock. Since I knew that my aunt would not appreciate my discussing her infirmities in public, I said, "We, too, have heard of the wonders of the water."

"Hope it heals up the old foot soon," he said. "I need to get back on the road. I'm a drummer for the Perkins Company. You know, Perkins Products? Salves, soaps, syrups, condiments, things like that. Good line. Yes indeed." He nodded at me vigorously, his face a smiling moon.

My aunt cleared her throat and gave me a hard look that showed she wished me to discontinue the conversation. I was willing to do so but didn't want to appear ungracious. Distraction came in the form of Jeremy, who drifted into the room in tan trousers and velvet jacket, his soft blond hair swept back from his high forehead in a Byronic wave.

"Hi, there, sonny!" shouted Mr. Lock. "How's the versifying?"

My aunt tried to freeze Mr. Lock with a haughty look, but the man was grinning once more at me and didn't seem to notice.

"Sonny, here, writes damned . . . er, pardon me, ma'am . . . crackee good poems, and that's a fact!"

Jeremy reached our table and swept us a low bow. I peered from beneath lowered lashes, reassessing him by daylight. He looked just as insipid as he had the night before. If I'd been like my old roommate at school, a dreamy girl given to the reading of cheap novels, I might have considered Jeremy a romantic figure. But I'd always been a tomboy all my life, preferring to romp outdoors with my little brothers when I was young and progressing to the doctoring of all the neighborhood pets when I'd gotten a little older. The nursing profession had been a natural choice for me, and I was grateful to Aunt Alice for paying for my training, although I wished I could work in a hospital instead of spending all my time taking care of one person. If I married Jeremy and spent the rest of my life doctoring him and my aunt together, I would lose my mind, I told myself grimly. But surely my aunt would have forgotten her pronouncement from the night before. It had to be just as obvious to her as it was to me that marriage to Jeremy was out of the question.

"Sit down, dear boy," said my aunt. "Have you written anything new?"

Jeremy brushed his hair back from his face with a weary gesture and said, "I tried to sleep, but the verses kept coming—"

"Genius," whispered my aunt to me behind her napkin. To him she said in a louder tone, "A hearty breakfast, that's what you need. Something to revive you and help you face the day."

"Hear, hear," said Mr. Lock.

Jeremy sighed and placed one hand limply on his notebook. "What is food for the body compared to food for the soul?"

My aunt shook her head at him in fond reproof. "You must keep up your strength so you can finish your book."

"Well . . . perhaps some tea and toast," Jeremy conceded.

What he really needed, I thought, tightening my lips to keep from speaking out, was meat, potatoes, and a romp in the sun.

The squeaking sound of unoiled wheels drew my attention toward the doorway. I turned in my chair to see a tea cart being pushed by a young woman of no more than eighteen. She wore a maid's black uniform covered by a long white apron. A

35

ruffled dust cap covered most of her hair, but a few unruly golden curls had escaped to frame her face, complementing her blue eyes and pink cheeks. When she passed through a shaft of sunlight, she was briefly surrounded by a nimbus, which flared and softened the edges of her body, making her appear for one moment to be a part of the light, an apparition in gold. She passed through the light and became once more a pretty young lady with a shy smile.

"Who are you?" my aunt asked bluntly. "Where is Mrs. Bennett?"

"Granny's busy in the kitchen," the girl replied softly. "Please, ma'am, I'm Maybelle. Don't you remember?"

"You can't be Maybelle. Maybelle is a little girl."

"I've grown up now."

"I'll say you have, little lady," boomed Mr. Lock. "And you're quite a beauty, too."

"Maybelle works here now," Jeremy explained to my aunt. "She helps her grandmother in the kitchen and also attends our lady guests in the bathhouse."

"Lucky ladies," said Mr. Lock.

A tide of pink suffused the girl's face at Mr. Lock's suggestive tone, and I saw her glance sideways toward Jeremy. My aunt swiveled about and fixed Mr. Lock with an outraged glare, but he just smiled blandly back. I really do not believe he thought he'd said anything out of place.

The tea cart proved to be loaded with food: rashers of bacon, a platter of fried eggs, fresh-baked biscuits, butter, jam, a large bowl of strawberries frosted with sugar, a pot of coffee, a pot of tea. I noticed that Jeremy gave in to Maybelle's gentle urging and took some of everything, after all. She stood to one side while we ate, darting quickly forward to refill the cups or to offer more food as we cleaned our plates. While my aunt and Jeremy discussed the weather, the upcoming Fourth of July celebration in Hot Springs, and the nature of God, covering well the first two issues but leaving the third unresolved, I watched Mr. Lock watching Maybelle. It was a good thing he couldn't walk, I decided, or the girl might well have found herself with a problem.

Soon I discovered that she did indeed have a problem, but not the one I'd first imagined. All through the meal she kept her eyes fixed on Jeremy, ready to meet his every need. A tiny smile played about her lips whenever he spoke, while her eyes softened with yearning. Hard as it was for me to believe, I had to accept the proof before my eyes: Maybelle was in love with Jeremy. He seemed totally oblivious to the fact, however, directing all his attention toward my aunt and me. When my aunt told him that I'd written a little poetry, too—an exaggeration that was prompted, I felt sure, by her desire to make a match between us—he lifted my hand to his lips, then presented me with a rose from a vase on the table. The pain in Maybelle's eyes at that moment was as raw as an open wound.

"Yes, Jeremy, my dear Joanna will make someone a fine wife someday," my aunt said, beaming back and forth between us.

The pain in Maybelle's eyes vanished, replaced by a dark glare. When she'd first walked through the light, Maybelle Bennett had looked to me like a haloed angel. I now realized that her innocent exterior concealed a passionate nature capable of strong feelings and rash action.

Watch out, Jeremy! I thought.

But when Maybelle turned that baleful glare in my direction, chilling me to the core, I knew I'd been warning the wrong person.

Chapter 3

After breakfast my aunt took her daily constitutional, choosing the front verandah as the place where she could walk and still be out of the sun. I strolled up and down with her, holding her arm whenever I sensed a wobble in her balance, a move on my part she did not appreciate. "Let go of me, Joanna. I'm managing perfectly well on my own."

When I finally accepted her at her word and moved away to stand by the railing, she was equally displeased. "What are you going over there for? I can't talk to you when you're so far away."

The sound of a galloping horse echoed through the trees. I soon saw Simon come flying around a bend in the lane on the back of a large brown stallion. His muscular body melded with the horse so well that they could have been one unit. I remembered how the early Indians had thought that the Spanish soldiers on their horses were centaurs. It was easy to see how such a mistake could be made. I pictured de Soto and his soldiers entering this valley three hundred years before and wondered if they had been riding horses. In my mind I dressed Simon in Spanish armor, giving him a plumed helmet and a banner blowing in the wind. He would have made a dashing soldier, I could see.

"Hello there!" he called when he neared the hotel.

I turned from my aunt to give him a wave. He slowed the horse as he drew near, stopping with a flourish at the hitching post beside the front steps. He slid nimbly from the saddle and wrapped the reins about the post, then mounted the steps and walked briskly along the verandah toward my aunt and me. His riding boots thumped with a hollow sound against the wooden floorboards, keeping time with the idle *slap, slap* of his riding crop against his right thigh. I saw a sheen of perspiration below the hollow in his neck, revealed by the open collar of his white shirt. With his brown hair tumbling about his tanned face, he made a handsome picture, and I felt a flutter in my pulse at the sight of him.

"Beautiful day," he announced with a grin, "although it will probably get hot later on. Well, Aunt Alice, have you taken the waters yet?"

"Not yet. Is that little flibbertigibbet really going to attend me in the bathhouse?"

"You mean Maybelle? She's very good. Her grandmother has been training her not only to give baths but also to give massage. I think she can help you."

"Humph! I'll let Joanna help me, thank you. Maybelle is nothing but a child."

I saw a look of amusement flicker across Simon's face. "Hardly a child, not any more," he said dryly.

His voice carried an undercurrent of admiration for Maybelle's budding womanhood, and I felt a moment of jealousy, wondering how I compared with her in his eyes.

I made myself suppress the feeling and picture Jeremy, instead. *Twenty-five thousand dollars,* I reminded myself firmly. *Think what your mother and brothers and sisters can do with that money. . . .*

But with that thought came another. *You'll be selling yourself. What does that make you?*

My aunt's preoccupation with Jeremy seemed unnatural to me. I couldn't understand how an intelligent woman—and I knew her to be quite intelligent despite her quirks—could be so blind to Jeremy's faults. Why should she want him to live with her for the rest of her life? Yet she seemed quite besotted with him, beyond all reason.

But then, so did Maybelle. There *had* to be more to Jeremy than I was seeing. I wondered suddenly about William, Jeremy's father, who had been Nell's and Rhodes's adopted son. What had William been like, and what had been his wife's character? I remembered that William had died many years ago in a buggy accident, leaving Jeremy to be reared at Milwood by his mother; but she had died, too, of pneumonia when Jeremy was in his early teens, and then Jeremy had been under the care of Charlotte and Amos. Considering how rowdy both Simon and Henry must have been at that time, I felt a surge of sympathy for the orphaned Jeremy, a kitten who'd been brought up with a couple of lions. He'd undoubtedly suffered some hard knocks because of it. Perhaps my aunt's preoccupation with him had begun at that time; perhaps she'd felt sorry for him and had tried to become a mother substitute, although such a picture seemed totally out of character.

"You'll be taking the waters, too no doubt?" Simon's smile to me was friendly and engaging. Perhaps he would explain to me about the trunk if I asked him. I resolved to do so whenever I could manage to meet him alone.

"Yes, of course, but our main purpose here is to treat my aunt's arthritis."

"My arthritis is not as bad as you make out," my aunt said in an injured tone.

I had to admire her spunk, for I knew she often suffered agonies from her swollen hands and knees. There were days when she got around on sheer willpower alone. But that, I realized, was to be our secret, kept at all costs from reaching the ears of Nell. In such an endeavor I suddenly found myself to be my aunt's ally. It is difficult to have someone lord it over you in the condescending way I'd already observed Nell Hampton do. I would have hated to have been her daughter-in-law, I told myself, no longer wondering at Charlotte's mousey frightened look.

As though called by my thoughts, Nell Hampton came sweeping through the front doors and out onto the verandah. She looked regal in a high-necked dress of lavender silk trimmed with black lace. From the stiff way she carried herself, I knew she wore a corset tightly laced. Her chin was high, her white hair flawlessly coiffed. My aunt straightened at once, holding her own head high.

"Good morning, Nell. You certainly look stifled by the heat this morning," she said, getting in the first blow.

Even as I inwardly cheered, I wondered at such enmity between two women who had spent every summer together for over thirty years. One would have expected them to be like sisters by now, yet the same tension I'd felt the night before again fried the air between them.

"And you look peaked," retorted Nell. "Perhaps you should go back to bed. At your age, one can't be too careful."

"I'm younger than you," snorted my aunt.

"That's hard to believe," said Nell, lifting one eyebrow in an exaggerated look of astonishment. "I could have sworn you were at least ten years older. I suppose it's the cane . . . it gives you such a look of decrepitude."

"The cane is strictly for show," I put in quickly. "You'll find, if you check the society pages of the newspapers, that carrying a cane is now the latest fashion."

The lie fell from my mouth like a dark insect. I felt sure the others would know I'd just made that up. Still, I'd been overcome by the sudden urge to give my aunt some moral support.

"Yes," echoed my aunt. "All the women in St. Louis now carry canes, but fashion trends of that sort take time to filter down to backwoods areas such as this."

"In that case, where is *your* cane?" Simon asked me with a twinkle in his eye.

I should have remembered that lying is a profitless venture. The more one prevaricates, the deeper one gets mired.

"I'm not a fashionable person," I said. "Aunt Alice, isn't it time I saw the bathhouse and learned what 'taking the waters' is all about?"

She agreed with alacrity, welcoming the chance, I could see, to get away from Nell. She circled around Nell as one would circle a dangerous animal, putting as much distance between them as possible. Then she led me back into the hotel and down the corridor past the dining room. Before we reached the kitchen, however, my aunt opened a door to one side. I followed her out into a pleasant courtyard with benches and pots of flowers. A stone path angled from the courtyard toward the two long bathhouses back by the bluffs. Built of wood and painted white, with gingerbread trim and little towers at either end, the bathhouses reflected the architecture of Milwood itself. One bore a sign over the front door reading MEN, the other a sign reading WOMEN. There was a small stream flowing between the hotel and bathhouse row. Vapor wafted off the surface of the water, while plumes of steam issued from vents in the bluffs, reminding me once more of Henry's allocation that we sat over the gateway to hell. When my aunt and I tapped across a wooden bridge, I felt warmth rising from the stream below, along with the musty smell that had bothered me the night before. Green and yellow slime rimmed the edges of the stream, while the bluffs beyond glistened with mineral deposits left by the dripping water.

"Wasn't it clever of me to remember?" my aunt asked me with satisfaction in her voice.

"Remember what?" I asked.

"That canes are now the fashion in St. Louis. When I told her that, you could just see Nell Hampton writhe! What's the matter, Joanna, weren't you paying attention again?"

I bit my lower lip and took a deep breath before responding, "Yes, Aunt. You were very clever."

Maybelle emerged from the front door of the women's bathhouse.

"I'm all ready for you, Miss McPherson," she called, and I

heard now a cheerful friendly note in her voice. Either she was dissembling or she'd gotten over her pique.

"Joanna will give me my bath," my aunt retorted.

"But I don't know the proper procedure," I reminded her. "Let me watch this morning how Maybelle does it, and then I'll know better what to do."

"Humph!" she said. "Well, all right, this once. I don't know why I can't have Mrs. Bennett attend me."

Maybelle came forward to meet us at the foot of the bridge. "Granny's getting old," she explained. "She can't lift the way she used to."

My aunt snorted indignantly. "Old? Nonsense. She started here when she was just a young woman, and that wasn't all that long ago."

"Hello there!" Henry's voice boomed across the stream. I looked back to see him pushing Mr. Lock in a wheelchair along the path toward the bridge. Mr. Lock groaned when the wheelchair hit a bump and jostled his foot.

I knew that gout could be quite painful, although some people consider it a laughable disease and show little sympathy for the sufferer. Perhaps that's because gout is often associated with overindulgence in wine and rich food, causing people to judge the victim and say he brought it on himself—an unfair judgment, in my opinion, since gout can be caused by other things, too. Henry VIII suffered from gout. Maybe his wives laughed and that's why he had them killed. Henry VIII . . . and Henry Hampton. The similarity in name, coupled with that thought about the murdered wives, suddenly made me uncomfortable.

Nevertheless, I waited while Henry maneuvered Mr. Lock across the bridge.

"Look at all these pretty ladies, Henry!" bellowed Mr. Lock. "Let's forget the baths and have a lawn party instead."

"Not this morning, I'm afraid. We've got to soak that foot." As Henry spoke, he threw me a conspiratorial smile, belying the haunted look I'd seen on his face the night before, and I put

43

aside all thoughts of Henry VIII as I noticed how handsome Henry looked at that moment. He proceeded with the wheelchair toward the men's bathhouse while Mr. Lock blew kisses in our direction.

I turned away from Mr. Lock's ardor and swept my gaze over the rear of the hotel and the grounds on either side. One thing I've always noticed about buildings—the front is usually dressed up for show, but it's the view from the back that reveals the true character of an establishment. I saw now that the back was a hodgepodge of architectural afterthoughts. The general shape of the hotel, when one looked past the towers, verandahs, and bay areas, was that of an E, with the three arms extending toward the rear. The arms at either end were the full three stories tall, but the central arm, containing the dining room and the corridor through which we'd just passed, rose only one story. It ended in the kitchen, where a broad brick chimney, blackened at the top, emitted a wispy gray plume. A smokehouse was connected to the kitchen by a covered breezeway, while a root cellar lifted the earth nearby like a buried animal trying to break free. A laundry shed could be identified by the washtubs turned upside down beside the door and by clotheslines marching in parallel rows with sheets already flapping like flags in the wind. A path led away from the kitchen toward a garden near the woods. Beyond the garden was a chicken house with a fenced yard, where noisy leghorns discussed the day while a rooster stretched his neck toward the sky to peal his lordship over the hen yard. I saw through the trees the silhouette of barn and stables, heard the whinny of horses, the low of cows. I felt overwhelmed by the amount of work necessary to keep such an establishment running. Three paying guests could not possibly provide enough money to meet Milwood's bills.

I thought again about Simon's bitter look when he'd mentioned Milwood's deterioration, about Henry's strange questions the night before concerning the elusive trunk, about Amos Hampton's demand that I give up the money and that one flash of hatred on his face when he'd looked at my aunt and me.

Despite the warmth drifting from the slimy stream, I shivered, feeling suddenly vulnerable and alone in the middle of a situation that seemed to carry too many threatening undercurrents. At that moment, with my nerves already exposed, I got a second shock: I saw a pale face peering toward me from behind the filmy curtains of a second-floor window in the west wing. I could not determine whether the face was that of a man or a woman, but I knew I didn't like what I saw. There was something about the stillness of the figure, the way the face, partially obscured by the curtain, seemed to direct its gaze toward me, that froze my blood.

"Look—up there!" I cried out to Maybelle. "Who is that in the window?"

Even at that moment the figure melted away into shadow.

"Where?" asked Maybelle. "I don't see anyone."

I pointed with a shaking finger. "That window on the second floor, there to the west . . . I saw a face."

"You couldn't have. All the rooms in that wing are closed off now. The Hamptons didn't have guests to fill them so they locked those rooms up."

"But I did see someone."

Maybelle laughed. "Maybe you saw that ghost."

I had to laugh, too, at the absurdity of such a suggestion. There were several logical explanations as to why someone might be in one of the locked rooms. Perhaps it was Charlotte or Nell or Mrs. Bennett, someone with access to the hotel keys, checking to make sure that mice were not nesting in the beds, that the windows hadn't started to leak. My reaction showed me that I was letting my imagination run rampant, an unprofessional way for a nurse to behave. I'd been taught by stern Miss Steel, the head nurse in charge of my training, that I must keep calm in all situations and draw my conclusions about a patient's condition based upon evidence carefully evaluated. In this case, Milwood was not my patient, but neither was I behaving logically.

With the resolve that I would indeed get myself under control, I turned to face my aunt and Maybelle just as my aunt burst out impatiently, "Joanna, what *is* the matter with you this morning? Come, you're wasting time."

Henry and Mr. Lock had already disappeared into the men's bathhouse. Now I followed Maybelle and my aunt through the door of the women's bathhouse into a front lobby with a desk and a large open-faced cupboard with shelves holding folded towels and bath mitts. Maybelle took several large towels and one of the bath mitts from the cupboard, then led the way down a corridor to a large dressing room with curtained alcoves, tables, chairs, and a large mirror on one wall.

"Do you wish to bathe nude?" Maybelle asked my aunt.

"Certainly not! I will use my regular bathing costume."

"Just a minute, then, I'll get it."

Maybelle hurried away while my aunt grumbled, "Bathe nude, indeed! To appear without clothing before a stranger— how uncivilized. In the old days such a thing would never even have been considered. Everyone covered themselves with flannel suits, the way God intended for decent people to behave."

"Do the Hamptons keep your bathing costume here, then, from year to year?"

"Of course. They do that for all their regulars."

Not so many regulars now, I thought.

Maybelle returned with a large bag labeled with my aunt's name. From the bag she removed a blue flannel suit with short-sleeved blouse, knee-length drawers, and an overdress in blue with red piping. For my aunt, this would be a daring costume, indeed.

I entered one of the alcoves with her and helped her into the suit. She had finally overcome her sense of modesty with me, now viewing me truly as a nurse, but when I'd first begun to serve her, she had found it hard to let even me see her unclothed. Her body itself was still soft and youthful-looking, providing sharp contrast with her gray hair, wrinkled face, and gnarled hands and feet. I'd noticed much the same thing with the other elderly patients I'd treated during training: flesh protected by clothing does not seem to age as fast as the flesh exposed to the sun. Why that should be so, I don't know. Perhaps that's one of the reasons a woman of breeding is supposed to wear gloves and carry a parasol whenever she goes out, even on a hot summer day. But I like the feel of the sun on my skin and I'd long since decided to take my chances on developing early wrinkles.

When my aunt was ready, I helped her out into the dressing room where Maybelle was waiting for us.

"The first step in the treatment," said Maybelle to me, "is to soak in a tub of hot spring water and to drink the water at the same time."

She led us to another large room containing sheet-draped tables and individual tile-lined bath cubicles, each with a curtain that could be pulled across the door for privacy, and each containing a tub, a tin teapot, and a bench for the attendant. Maybelle filled one of the tubs with steaming water. I stuck in my hand and hastily withdrew it, finding the water much hotter than in the hotel bathroom, although the flow from the spigot was just as crystal-clear. A vapor rose from the surface of the water to condense on the walls and flow downward in tiny rivulets.

"The spring waters as they bubble from the depths are pure and have no odor," Maybelle told me.

"But the smell outside—"

"—is the slimy mud in that hot stream," she explained, confirming my earlier guess.

With Maybelle's help, my aunt gradually eased into the tub. Her hands and feet turned pink almost at once from the heat, and I imagined that her submerged body must be sweltering in that heavy flannel suit. Maybelle adjusted a padded board behind my aunt's back for her to rest against. There was even a tiny pillow at the top for her head. She relaxed against it with a sigh and closed her eyes. While Maybelle filled the tea kettle from the spigot, my aunt took several deep breaths, inhaling the vapor. When Maybelle handed her the small tin pot, she took a long drink from the spout.

The very thought of drinking plain hot water made me gag. When I said so, Maybelle laughed.

"I told you this water is pure," she said. "You can drink it hot and enjoy it as you would the finest tea."

She got another teapot from an adjoining cubicle and filled it for me. Tentatively I took a sip, then another and yet another. She was right. There was absolutely no flavor, just a crisp clean feel against my tongue combined with the sensation of heat expanding through my system. I took several deep swallows, trying to capture in words the strange quality of the water, but I couldn't pin it down. Finally I decided just to enjoy it without further question.

Maybelle now sat down on the bench beside the tub. She let me feel the bath mitt before she put it in the water. It was made of a substance as abrasive as bark.

"This stimulates the skin and gets the blood to flowing," she explained.

She dipped the mitt into the water, then gently bathed the exposed surfaces of my aunt's body: her face, her neck, her arms and hands, her legs and feet, including the soles.

I heard my aunt sigh, saw her body relax even more as she lay back against the supporting board.

"Now the patient soaks in the water for twenty minutes while sipping the water," Maybelle explained to me. "Any longer than that, and the person may begin to feel dizzy from the heat. If I have more than one patient to bathe at a time, I keep coming back to check each one at regular intervals to make sure she's all right."

"I'll be fine," my aunt interjected in a lazy drawl. "Just leave me alone for a few minutes so I can rest and enjoy the water."

Maybelle turned to me. "If you'll wait here in the room and

look in on your aunt every five minutes or so, I'll go on out and feed the chickens. I'll be back in time for the next step in the treatment."

"All right."

"Stop the chattering, you're bothering me," came my aunt's drowsy voice.

"In that case, I'll wait right outside the curtain and peek in from time to time," I told her.

Maybelle left and I sat down on one of the sheet-covered tables to wait. I looked in on my aunt after a few minutes and saw her take a sip from her teapot. I was about to resume my vigil when I heard a voice outside urgently calling my name.

"Joanna! Joanna, come and help me!"

The cry seemed to come from behind the bathhouse. The voice was so hoarse with strain I didn't recognize it. It could have been either a woman's or a man's. Still, I thought, the voice must be Maybelle's, and she sounded in serious trouble.

"Maybelle's calling me," I said to my aunt. "I'll be right back."

"You don't have to hurry, I'm fine," she answered through the curtain.

But I did hurry, concerned by the urgency which had filled that voice. As soon as I got outside, I glanced in both directions, thinking the person who had called me might have come by then to the front of the bathhouse, but I saw no one. I ran around to the back where a low cloud of steam temporarily obscured my view.

"Maybelle? What's the matter?"

A gust of wind was my only answer. The wind scattered the steam, revealing only bluffs and bushes. I darted around to the side of the bathhouse and looked toward the chicken yard, but Maybelle was not in sight. Puzzled, I circled to the front again, thinking perhaps Henry had called my name from over by the men's bathhouse. The door there was closed. In fact, I seemed to have the whole backyard to myself. Involuntarily, I glanced toward that second-story window where I had seen the face, but the curtains did not reveal any shadow standing behind. Finally I reentered the bathhouse and hurried to the tub room.

"Aunt Alice, I'm back."

When she didn't answer, I went to her cubicle and drew back the curtain. She lay slumped forward in the tub, her face beneath the water.

Chapter 4

I darted forward and grabbed my aunt by the shoulders, heaving her head out of the water. Her face was blue, her eyes half open. I screamed for Maybelle while struggling to get my aunt's limp body out of the tub. The skirt of the bathing costume dragged in the water and pulled against my efforts. I took a deep breath, willing strength into my arms while bracing my feet on the slippery floor. At last I was able to drag my aunt over the lip of the tub and onto the floor. I turned her on her face and lifted her up by the waist, then gave her a hard shake, causing a stream of water to pour from her throat. Quickly laying her down once more, I rolled her over and tilted back her head, then pulled her mouth open while pinching off her nose. I leaned forward and blew into her mouth, trying to force air into her lungs. I sat back and yelled again for Maybelle, then resumed my efforts to get my aunt to breathe.

"What is it, what's happened?" Maybelle's frightened voice broke into my concentrated effort to keep up a regular rhythm.

"You called from outside . . . I went out to see why . . . came back and found her underwater," I explained between breaths.

"I didn't call you."

I blew into my aunt's mouth, then gasped out, "Someone did."

51

"Are you sure?"

"Yes. . . . Someone called my name. They sounded . . . in trouble. . . ."

I felt a convulsion shake my aunt's frame and drew back as she spewed forth a mixture of water and vomit. As I wiped the mess from her mouth, she took a shuddering breath and then another, settling at last into a regular pattern of breathing on her own. Her color began to return.

"Thank God!" I sighed, sitting back on my heels. "I thought at first that she was gone."

"Oh yes, thank God," Maybelle echoed. "The heat . . . it can make old folks dizzy, and they faint and slip under the water. That's why I'm careful not to leave them alone."

The reproach in her voice twisted like a knife inside me.

"I feel terrible about this. You did warn me, Maybelle, so it's my fault. But I was gone such a short time. . . ."

My aunt's eyelids fluttered open and she peered up at me, looking dazed. "Wh—what happened?"

"You fainted and fell into the water."

"My head . . ."

I looked at her closely and saw that her pupils had contracted. "What about your head?"

"Hurts. It hurts." Her voice was small, the voice of a tired child.

I lifted her carefully, ran my hand over the back of her head, and found a swelling the size of an egg. I knew I'd handled her roughly but I didn't remember dropping her on her head. I looked toward the tub to see if she could have struck her head before falling into the water. The backrest still floated there with its padded pillow. If she'd fainted, she should simply have slumped down into the water without getting a bump.

While I continued to study the tub, frowning in bewilderment, I noticed something dark poking out from behind one of the claw feet, something I couldn't remember having seen there when my aunt had first started her bath. I reached down and pulled it out, and found myself holding a stout stick, broken off at both ends, like the limbs one often sees lying about on the ground, debris torn from trees during storms.

A suspicion, almost too horrible to countenance, began to form in my mind.

"Aunt Alice, did someone come in here while I was gone?"

"I—I don't know."

"Did you hear a noise? Anything strange you can remember?"

"My head hurts."

"Try to remember."

"I'm so dizzy."

"Could? . . ." I paused, finding it hard to form the words. "Could someone have struck you from behind?"

I heard Maybelle gasp. From the corner of my eye I saw her draw back and clap her hand over her mouth.

"Look," I said in a low aside to Maybelle, "someone did call me outside. If not you, who was it? When I got back in here, my aunt was in the water, and now I find a bump on her head and a stick on the floor. What if—what if it wasn't an accident? What if someone sneaked in here and hit her?"

"But that's terrible!"

"Yes, it is. Go get Henry, will you?"

"You want me to go in the *men's* bathhouse?" She sounded scandalized.

"This is no time to be prudish. Hurry."

She darted a quick look about the room, her face frightened. That caused me to wonder, too, where the assailant might be hiding. My heart began to pound while I found my mouth had gone suddenly dry.

"Hurry, Maybelle. Please!"

She rose and dashed away, her skirts flying behind her.

"Head . . . hurts," said Aunt Alice again.

"You may have a concussion," I told her. "Just lie still. I've sent for Henry."

"Send for . . . William. Let William come," she said.

I knew then that she was wandering in her mind. The

53

possibility of concussion became even stronger.

"William can't come," I told her quietly, not wanting to remind her that he was dead. "Henry will be here soon."

"Henry . . . is just a little boy. Send for William."

"All right, we'll send for William, too. Now rest."

I grabbed a towel from the bench and folded it under her head. I wrapped the other towel about her body, then drew the stick closer to use as a weapon should the attacker return. I picked up one of my aunt's cold hands and began to massage it vigorously, trying to bring warmth back into her body.

Why would anyone want to harm my aunt? I knew she had a sharp tongue, but that seemed no reason to try to kill her. It was true, Amos Hampton had seemed to look at her with hatred, and there was certainly no love lost between my aunt and Nell. Then, too, there'd been that glare from Maybelle in the dining room. Still, as one of the few paying guests in the hotel, surely my aunt was someone whom not only the Hampton family but also their employees would want to coddle so she'd stay a long time and pay out a lot of money.

No, it didn't make sense.

Maybelle rushed back in, her breath coming in gasps from her exertion.

"Henry wasn't there."

"You're sure? Did you go in?"

"Yes. Mr. Lock is there soaking his foot, but Henry left him a while ago, saying he'd be back soon."

"Then run to the house and bring someone, anyone, and also bring a wheelchair. We must get my aunt into bed."

Maybelle rushed off again and I went out into the other room and snatched some sheets from the tables. I wrapped my aunt up as warmly as I could and sat down on the floor, cradling her in my arms. When she started to drift off, I began questioning her again to keep her mind working, not wanting her to slip into shock. Again she said she couldn't remember what had happened, that she didn't think she'd heard any strange noises. She also said she hadn't heard anyone call my name.

"But you must have! Whoever it was called from behind the bathhouse and said they needed my help."

I began to shake with chill, both from a delayed reaction to my aunt's narrow escape and from fear at being alone with her in this bathhouse when a potential murderer might be on the loose. I remembered that strange face I'd seen watching us from the second-story window.

Although it couldn't have been more than a few minutes, it seemed an hour before Maybelle returned with a wheelchair and with the "someone else" I'd requested without being specific.

"Look who I found!" she said brightly. "He'll be able to help us now."

I knew who it was without looking, just from the lilt in her voice. The next moment proved me right.

"Oh my, oh my," murmured Jeremy.

"Help me lift her into the chair," I told him brusquely. "We've got to get her into the house and into some dry clothes."

He stepped gingerly into the tub room and I glanced up to see him staring with dismay at the mess on the floor. Disgust with him made me brutal.

"She almost drowned. Sometimes people throw up when they've swallowed that much water."

"Oh my," he repeated.

But he did help me wrest her off the floor and into the chair, despite his squeamishness, and he seemed genuinely concerned about her concussion.

"She *will* be all right?" he asked me for the third time as we wheeled her down the corridor.

"Yes, I think she will, but it was a narrow escape."

It occurred to me then that the high voice I'd heard could have been Jeremy's.

"Did you call to me a while ago?"

"Call to you? No, of course not."

55

"Where were you about twenty minutes ago?"

"Inside working on my poetry. Why?"

"Someone called me to come outside. When I got back to the tub room, my aunt was facedown in the water."

"You didn't find the person who called you?"

"No."

"That's very odd."

A decided understatement, I thought. My aunt emitted a faint groan, and I bent over her, saying, "We'll soon have you back in your room."

We emerged into the sunlight to see Henry crossing the bridge from the direction of the house. I called to him at once, saying there'd been an accident and asking him to accompany us inside to help me check my aunt's vital signs. He loped forward and took over with the wheelchair while dispatching Jeremy to collect Mr. Lock. As we proceeded toward the house, Henry asked me to run through the whole story in detail. I held nothing back, including the voice that had drawn me away from the bathhouse and the stick I'd found on the floor. As Henry listened, the color drained from his face.

"My God," he said. "But who . . . did you recognize the voice?"

I shook my head. "I don't even know if it was a man's or a woman's."

"But attempted murder . . . no, it can't be. No one around here would . . . Look, if Aunt Alice tried to get out of that tub by herself, and she slipped and fell . . . well, she could have hit the back of her head then."

"What about that stick?"

"It could have been in there a long time. We have so few guests now, the stick might have been overlooked in the cleaning. Maybe you finally nudged it accidentally and pushed it out into view while you were working on Aunt Alice."

I flared with anger over his attempt to explain everything away. "What about that voice?"

"Could you have imagined it? The wind sighing around the

eaves can play strange tricks sometimes."

"I tell you, someone called me out of that bathhouse!"

"Heard . . . no one," muttered my aunt. "Heard no voice."

Henry drew his brows together and shot me a warning look while indicating my aunt with a jerk of his chin.

"Maybe we'd better talk about this later," he said in a low tone.

He was right, of course. If I continued this argument in my aunt's presence, I would just upset her and endanger her more. Right now my main concern should be to get her into dry clothes and then into bed.

Simon came bounding from the hotel into the courtyard, followed by Charlotte.

"What is it, what has happened?" he demanded.

Prompted by another warning look from Henry, I merely stated that my aunt had collapsed in the water and nearly drowned. Simon turned a stern face on Maybelle.

"You know you don't leave older people alone in the tub rooms!" he said fiercely.

"Don't blame her, it was my fault," I put in quickly. "Maybelle left me in charge and I—I went outside for a minute."

Simon turned a surprised look in my direction. "You? A nurse? I would think you'd know better."

I felt sorry to lose stature in his eyes, but now was not the time to worry about that. I said no more but concentrated on getting the wheelchair into the house and up to the third floor. Henry started to help me strip the bathing costume from my aunt, but she was alert enough to protest such invasion of her privacy.

"I've studied doctoring," he reminded her, but she would have none of it.

Therefore, Henry waited outside while Maybelle and I took off the bathing suit and vigorously toweled my aunt dry. We dressed her in her flannel gown and got her into bed. Henry came in then and helped me check her over. We found her pulse to be steady, her breathing back to normal.

When I showed Henry the knot on the back of my aunt's head, he nodded at me soberly but said to her in a cheerful voice, "You took quite a knock there, Aunt Alice. Did you slip and fall in the tub?"

"Maybe. I—I don't remember."

Henry then examined each of her eyes while I peered over his shoulder. I was relieved to find that her pupils had returned to normal size.

"I don't believe it's a bad concussion," he said to me at last, "but I do think she should stay in bed for the rest of the day."

"Yes, I'd already decided that."

I sent Maybelle to the kitchen for a pot of tea and then Henry and I went into the sitting room, out of my aunt's hearing, to discuss once more the events in the bathhouse.

"The person did call for help," I insisted. "Called for me by name. I want to know who it was."

Henry pursed his lips, considering the problem. "All right, I'll ask everyone in the house if they saw or heard anything."

"And if the guilty one lies?"

His face sobered, taking on the haunted look I'd seen the night before. "Joanna, I can't believe that anyone here would want to hurt Aunt Alice. Nevertheless, I'll do everything I can to get to the bottom of this. But you've got to look at the fact that you've had a scare and you may be overreacting."

"Don't patronize me. For all I know, you could be the one who called me out of that bathhouse."

I hadn't really meant that statement until I said it. Suddenly it struck me that it could be true. Henry had been nearby; he'd had the time and the opportunity. The "why" I couldn't fathom, but there was much going on in this house I couldn't fathom. Henry's face went cold and still.

"You don't believe that, do you?"

"I don't know what to believe. What I do know is my aunt almost died."

"Joanna, I've got something to say you may not want to

58

hear. . . ." He hesitated, surveying me quizzically.

"Go on."

"The mind . . . well, it can indeed play tricks on a person."

"I know that."

"You left Aunt Alice alone, and she almost drowned. That's a heavy burden for you to bear."

I stared at him for a moment, considering the implication in his words.

"You think I'm trying to fix the blame on someone else in order to absolve myself?" I finally asked.

"It's possible. You may well have dreamed up that voice after the fact."

"Now just a minute—!"

"Hear me out. While you worked trying to bring Aunt Alice back, your guilt was more than you could bear. You then fabricated that voice. . . ."

"But I didn't!"

"You might not remember it now even if you did. The mind really is that powerful. There's another thing. . . ."

The look on his face was sympathetic, but I didn't like the tone in his voice. It had the sound of a pending revelation that would not be to my credit.

"What other thing?"

"Working with a demanding invalid can be very trying."

"As you well know."

"I do know. There are times when I wish my father were dead."

I stared at him in horror as I followed his train of thought.

"You think—!"

"That you noticed your aunt was dizzy and so you went outside and left her on purpose? Could be. Or maybe, just maybe, you knocked her on the head yourself."

I rose to my feet, my face burning with anger. "How dare you say a thing like that!"

"I don't know you, Joanna, any better than you know me. What I do know is that there are times when I'm tempted to push my father's wheelchair down the stairs. You can't tell me you've never been angry with Aunt Alice and wished she'd vanish from the face of the earth."

He was right, of course.

"But I didn't try to kill her," I insisted.

"Neither did I," he responded, looking at me steadily.

I turned and paced the room. "Henry, what am I going to do?"

"First, you've got to face the fact that you may have been wrong, that there was no voice calling you, and that no one, other than yourself, has tried to harm Aunt Alice."

I nodded my head miserably, not wanting to look at him.

"Next, you must be very careful, both for yourself and Aunt Alice, just in case you're right and there really is someone at Milwood who wants to hurt you, maybe even to kill you both."

Chapter 5

I tried to get Henry to say more, but he refused to speculate any further.

"I'll go now and ask around," he said, "to see if anyone heard or saw anything suspicious. I'll be back in about an hour to tell you what I've learned."

He left then, and I sat with Aunt Alice to watch for any change in her condition. Henry returned, true to his word, about an hour later.

"Well?" I asked.

He shrugged. "I've spoken with every person here, even my father. No one knows anything about the accident. None of them called to you from outside the bathhouse, and no one heard a voice."

"That's what they say," I commented flatly, "but someone is lying."

"Maybe," he replied.

Once more I could see he believed I'd dreamed the whole thing up. Fury flamed through my body.

"You made me doubt my senses a while ago, but I know what I heard, and *something* is going on here I don't like," I snapped. "As soon as she can travel, I'm packing Aunt Alice up and taking her back to St. Louis."

His mouth tightened into a thin line that made the muscles

on either side of his jaw stand out like ropes. "That might be a good idea," he replied.

He then mumbled something about getting back to work and strode away, shutting the door none too gently behind him.

I returned to my vigil with Aunt Alice. She stayed in bed most of the day, but by late afternoon she grew restless and insisted on getting up and dressing for dinner.

"Just because I felt a little faint this morning doesn't mean I'm sick," she announced emphatically.

But she winced when I tried to brush her hair. I ran my fingers lightly over the knot on her head and found it somewhat diminished in size. I decided she was strong enough to risk some questions now.

"Try to remember, Aunt Alice. Was someone with you in that bathhouse just before you . . . fell?"

"You were."

"Yes, but I went outside for a minute."

"And left me alone when Maybelle told you not to!" She fixed me with an accusing glare.

"I'm sorry about that, but I told you, I thought I heard someone calling to me from outside."

"You said something else, too, don't think I don't remember! You asked if someone could have hit me on the head."

You rascal, I thought. *You don't miss a thing.*

"Well, it's the most ridiculous thing I ever heard of!" she went on. "These are my friends, Joanna. I've known all of them since before you were born. Hit me on the head, indeed! I got dizzy, that's all, and fell against the tub. And *you* weren't there to watch out for me."

"Why does Nell Hampton hate you?" I asked bluntly.

Her eyes wavered and shifted away from mine, but her voice kept its sharp tone. "I don't know what you're talking about."

"And Amos . . . he hates you, too."

She whipped back toward me. "Oh no, not Amos. In that you are mistaken."

62

"He seems angry."

"Wouldn't you be if you couldn't walk?"

"He mentioned a trunk . . . a missing trunk that seems to have had money in it. Henry mentioned it, too. Do you know anything about some missing money?"

"Of course not!" But again her eyes dropped and she looked away.

"There's a mystery here, Aunt Alice, something I don't understand. Someone did call me out of that bathhouse this morning, and then you were attacked. . . ."

Her indignant "humph" interrupted me, but I ignored her and repeated, "You were attacked and almost killed. I think we should leave here first thing in the morning and go home."

"I know what you want." Again she faced me, and now she used the stern stare she seemed to consider intimidating. "You want to get back to that mealymouthed mother of yours, and you'll use any excuse to get your way."

Don't cross her, Joanna. My mother's words echoed in my mind, and a good thing, too, for I was sorely tempted to use strong language.

"I'm thinking of you. . . ."

"You're thinking of yourself! This whole story you've dreamed up is nonsense. We are staying here, that's all there is to it!" She grabbed her cane and thumped it on the floor. "Don't forget, you owe everything—your training, your family's support—to me."

How could I forget, when she reminded me of it almost every day? I swallowed the pride that must be, I thought, the food of most beggars. It leaves a bitter taste.

"I do remember, and I'm grateful. . . ."

"Besides, you've only just met Jeremy. You are to marry him before the summer ends, and you can't do that if you're back in St. Louis. Twenty-five thousand dollars, Joanna, to your mother on the day you wed Jeremy."

The pride became an indigestible lump that stuck in my throat. If we'd been back in that bathhouse, I might have pushed my aunt's head under the water myself. I realized, with a shock, that that was the very impulse of which Henry had accused me. My hands trembled as I finished arranging Aunt Alice's hair. To keep from speaking out, I rummaged busily through her jewelry case for the proper hair accessory. I finally chose a jet comb to go with the jet bead collar on her wine silk dress. I had long since changed my damp nurse's uniform from that morning for a simple pink muslin with pearl buttons and leg-of-mutton sleeves. Again I tried to force my hair into a severe knot but errant tendrils insisted on curling about my ears.

My mind whirled with indecision. I couldn't force Aunt Alice to leave if she continued to refuse to do so, and I certainly couldn't run away and abandon her if she really were in danger.

"You dozed off and dreamed that voice," she told me, "just as I dozed off and slipped into the water. It was hot in there and steamy, and that makes a person drowsy."

Between her arguments and Henry's, I once more began to waver. My imagination had been stirred up, I admitted, by my sense of fear when we'd first arrived, combined with that story about the ghost. Those things could have led me to look for danger where none existed.

"You may be right," I finally conceded.

"I'm always right," she replied.

What a burden, having always to be right, I thought.

"Bring me my writing case," she now demanded. "I wish to address a letter to my lawyer back home."

I brought the black lacquer box decorated with Japanese-style painted flowers, which we'd carried with us from St. Louis. My aunt unlatched the case and opened it to reveal paper and envelopes, an inkwell with a screw top lid, and several steel-nibbed pens. I saw that she had already covered a page of paper with her decisive handwriting. She quickly folded the sheet and slipped it into an envelope, then uncapped the inkwell and wrote the address. As I watched the way she

64

jabbed her pen point into the ink and then attacked the paper with slashing strokes, I remembered another example of her handwriting I'd seen not too long before, handwriting so different I would never have believed it could have been done by the same person.

What had happened was this: While straightening her desk for her one day back in St. Louis I'd come across an essay she'd written as a girl in school, and she'd given me permission to read it. Her thoughts regarding the beauty of nature had been sentimental, while her handwriting had also been sentimental . . . flowing and delicate, with little circles instead of dots over her *i*'s. She'd signed her name with a flourish, swirling the tail of her first initial in the Spencerian style to form a tiny bird with outstretched wings. Somewhere through the years she had lost the romanticism evidenced by that essay to become this harsh old woman. I found it interesting that her handwriting reflected the change.

She sealed the envelope with a drop of wax and announced that she was ready for dinner. I wanted to lock our door, but she said she'd never locked her door at Milwood and she didn't intend to start now. I bit my lip over her stubbornness but saw there was no use to argue. We walked together to the lift and made our usual shaky descent. Before we reached the lobby, I became aware of angry voices echoing through the shaft from below.

"Look, Simon," I heard Henry bellow. "How the hell do you expect us to pay for advertising when we can't even meet our bills?"

"But that's the point! Advertising will bring in more guests, and then we'll have the money we need to fix up this place."

The voices broke off abruptly as the lift clanged to a halt. When I opened the door and helped Aunt Alice out, I saw both men standing by the desk, their faces still congested with the force of their argument.

Again Aunt Alice seemed oblivious to any problem except her own need. She advanced upon them with the letter extended in her hand.

"I'd like to have this posted in Hot Springs," she said. "Will one of you be going into town tomorrow?"

Simon took the letter from her. As he glanced at the address, I saw him stiffen. But his voice, when he spoke, was genial enough. "I hadn't planned to, but I'll be happy to do so for your sake."

"Good, then, that's settled," said my aunt, as though rearranging Simon's life for him was her prerogative.

Jeremy did not join us for dinner, which I found to be one blessing in this otherwise terrible day. My aunt's tirade against my mother had filled me with yearning for my family, and I decided to ask Simon to post a letter for me, too. Consequently, I welcomed the chance to deposit my aunt, per her request, on the front verandah after dinner to chat and drink tea with Charlotte, for this gave me the opportunity to seek out Simon.

While I'm at it, I'll ask him about that trunk, I thought.

I hurried down the corridor to the kitchen, hoping to find him lingering over his supper. What I found, instead, was a wizened old woman with gray hair and eyes clouded with cataracts who stood beside a sink filled with soapy water. She turned and leaned toward me, her eyes squinted into slits, as she peered through steel-rimmed glasses that she kept adjusting back and forth on the end of her nose in an obvious attempt to improve her vision.

"You'll be Miss Joanna," she stated without a question in her voice.

"That's right, Granny," Maybelle said, emerging from the pantry nearby. To me, she said, "Granny's the one who used to give your aunt her baths. Now she's teaching me the bath business."

I smiled at the older woman, although I wasn't sure she could distinguish expressions. "Then you'll be Mrs. Bennett."

Maybelle hurried forward to give the woman a fond hug. "Granny's lived in these hills most of her life. Everybody around here just calls her Granny, and you can call her that,

66

too, if you want."

"You told her yet?" Granny asked Maybelle in a demanding tone, which took me by surprise. From my initial impression of her, I'd expected a gentler nature.

Maybelle slid her eyes toward me nervously and said, "Hush, that's not important now."

"Tell her."

"It's foolishness."

"It ain't. You been right too many times before. Tell her."

"What is it?" I asked. "Tell me what?"

"I had a dream. . . ." Maybelle began, and then stopped, glancing toward her grandmother.

"Maybelle's dreams come true," the old woman said.

"Sometimes. Sometimes they come true," Maybelle amended.

A chill slid over my flesh. I sensed that the dream was not going to be pleasant. "When did you have this dream, and what was it?"

"Last night. I told my Granny—"

"She told me *before* breakfast."

I caught the significance of Granny's emphasis. All my life I'd heard that if you tell a dream before breakfast, it will come true. I'd been told that applies even to those of us who don't have the gift of prescience. If Maybelle really was able to see the future through dreams, and if she told one of those dreams before breakfast, then there were those who would feel she had conspired with the Fates to ensure the realization of her vision.

Of course I knew such belief to be nonsense. Nevertheless, I felt the skin on the back of my neck crawl with apprehension.

"What was your dream?" I repeated.

"It—it was a dream about death," she said, and paused again.

"Go on."

"I saw a coffin . . . a coffin draped in black."

"That's not so unusual. Other people dream of death, and nothing comes of it," I said.

Her eyes took on a misty look. "There was a spray of white

67

roses on the black cloth. Roses mixed with mushrooms."

"Mushrooms?"

"Those white ones called the Death Angel."

"What happened?"

"I didn't want to go near that coffin. But something drew me closer, as though I had no will of my own. Someone wearing a black robe with a hood pulled over the face stepped forward and took away the spray and the cloth. And then the lid began to open. Slowly. Slowly . . ."

I held my breath, mesmerized by the hypnotic tone that had crept into Maybelle's voice.

"Oh so slowly. I didn't want to look. But I had to."

She stopped, her eyes fixed ahead. I could bear the suspense no longer, for I feared I knew what was coming.

"Who did you see in that coffin?" I asked.

I was so sure she was going to say Aunt Alice that I went weak in the knees when she replied, "I don't know. The body was wrapped in a white sheet. The black-robed figure held out a bony hand and sprinkled more mushrooms over the body, then said in a deep voice, 'Someone at Milwood will soon die.' And then I woke up."

A shudder ran through her body and she blinked a couple of times before looking back at me. I saw that her face had gone as white as her ruffled dust cap.

"'Someone at Milwood will soon die,'" she stated again. "That's what the voice said. And then this morning . . . when your aunt—" Her voice broke, and she inhaled sharply before going on. "You said you heard a voice. Was it a deep voice? A voice . . . like Death?"

The question brought me back to my senses. I'd heard no supernatural voice from beyond the grave but rather a high-pitched voice filled with stress, the voice of a human being in trouble . . . or pretending to be in trouble.

"The voice I heard was real enough," I said. "Someone here called out to me, and now they won't admit it. I'd like to know why."

"Somehow I feel the whole thing is my fault," Maybelle said. Her face twisted with misery, and I remembered how I'd felt when Henry advanced his theory about my own guilt.

"I don't think you should worry about it anymore," I said, touching Maybelle gently on one arm. "My aunt is going to be all right. Your dream didn't come true, after all, so you've nothing to worry about."

"Maybelle's dream has all the signs," Granny put in sharply. "There'll be a death here soon, you mark my words."

"But I don't know whose," Maybelle continued. "If I could just have seen that face. . . ."

Such speculation seemed pointless to me. I had to admit that Maybelle's dream had been eerie, but of course there could be no meaning to it other than a reflection of her own worries. With that thought came the memory of Maybelle's abrupt change in manner at the breakfast table when my aunt had suggested me to Jeremy as good marriage material. Yes, I told myself, Maybelle was a girl seething with hidden emotions, which disturbed her sleep. Of course her dream had come before she'd had any reason to be jealous of me. But then she'd probably feared for some time that her position as a servant in the household precluded any fulfillment of an alliance with Jeremy, and indeed it might. That would be enough, I thought, to cause nightmares in any young girl in love with the wrong man.

Jeremy. How could she possibly love Jeremy! Now if her choice had been Henry or Simon . . .

Which reminded me of my reason for coming to the kitchen in the first place.

"Do you know where Simon is?" I asked.

"He's down at the stable," Maybelle replied.

I wished them a good evening and went out through the kitchen door into the backyard. The descending sun burned through the trees, a molten disk near the horizon. A warm breeze ruffled my hair and filled my nose with a dank moldy odor. Pillars of mist, tinted by the evening light, drifted above the bathhouses, while a wispy curtain floated over the surface of the stream. I paused in the center of the bridge and looked back toward the hotel, searching the windows of the west wing for another glimpse of that strange face I'd seen that morning. Had the face appeared, I think I might have bodily snatched up my aunt and fled Milwood that very evening. All I saw, however, were mirrored golden panes catching and reflecting the setting sun.

I continued on across the bridge and along the path past the women's bathhouse. My skin prickled as I glanced from the corner of my eye toward the bushes that fronted the bluffs. Perhaps the person who'd lured me from the bathhouse that morning had hidden there. Feeling suddenly defenseless, I swept my eyes over the ground, seeking a stout stick from the many that lay scattered about. With the stick clutched in one hand, I continued on my way down the path toward the stable.

I rounded a bend in the path and saw Simon ahead in the stable yard, oiling a saddle that was flung over a sawhorse. His white shirt sleeves were rolled high around biceps that bulged with strength as he worked. The top three buttons of his shirt hung open, exposing a gleam of perspiration on his chest, while his hands and arms bore an oily film, which caught the light and emphasized his muscles. His tight black trousers molded the outline of his strong thighs, his feet were encased in boots. In the reddish light he looked like a hero from a Norse myth, a man capable of flinging thunderbolts if riled. As I watched his hands slide over the oily leather, I found myself responding with a sensuous shiver, imagining those hands sliding over my body. The carnal thought made me blush with shame. I took an involuntary step backward and snapped a twig beneath my shoe.

At the sound, Simon's head whipped up from his work. I saw that his jaw was clenched, his brows drawn together in a fierce expression; but when he recognized me, his face relaxed.

"Oh, it's you."

I wondered who he'd been expecting, to have caused that

first ferocious look on his face.

As I advanced into the clearing, Simon glanced toward the club in my hand and his mouth twisted wryly.

"I see you're now afraid to walk around here without protection," he commented.

Again a tide of warmth flooded my face. I tossed the stick into the bushes at the edge of the clearing.

"Today has set my nerves on edge," I replied.

"Mine, too. Is Aunt Alice really going to be all right?"

"She's made up her mind the whole thing was an accident."

"But you're still not sure."

"No."

He nodded as though he shared my doubts. "I went into the women's bathhouse after Henry questioned everyone," he said.

"What were you looking for?"

"That stick you mentioned, for one thing."

He glanced toward the bushes where I'd just flung my cudgel, then brought his eyes back to my face. There was no reason for my guilty reaction, yet I found myself shifting about uneasily under his gaze, as though my having had the second stick implied I might also have been the one who'd carried in the first stick with which to strike my aunt. I decided to take the offensive.

"You found that stick? What did you do with it?" I demanded.

"I did nothing. There was no stick."

"What!" I flashed with shock. "Then that means whoever used it came back and got it. To destroy the evidence, don't you see?"

"You still think someone struck Aunt Alice?"

"Don't you?"

"I don't know. People do sometimes faint in the baths." He stared down at the ground, his face drawn in a troubled frown. "Why anyone would want to harm her . . . it's hard to imagine."

71

"Your grandmother doesn't seem to like her, and neither does your father."

He looked up with a wry grin. "There's been bad blood between Grandmother and Alice for years."

"Bad enough for Nell to try to kill her?"

"No, no. Just tension between two strong women, that's all. I think maybe it's envy on my grandmother's part, the fact that your aunt is so wealthy when Nell's had to scrimp all her life. Pinching pennies—"

"—can lead to a pinched soul," I interrupted, finishing the statement for him. I realized, too late, that there had been a bitter edge to my voice.

Simon scrutinized me for a long moment. "Doesn't she pay you well?"

I wasn't about to admit the paucity of my income.

"I'm doing all right," I said. "It's my mother . . . she's so poor, you see, and she depends on Aunt Alice. . . ."

"So Alice rules you by threatening to withdraw support from your mother?"

I laughed ruefully at the accuracy of his insight. "Right now I'm worried about Aunt Alice's safety. I tried to get her to leave here, but she refuses to go."

"If you do leave, you'll be withdrawing support from us," he stated while one corner of his mouth quirked in a wry smile. "That's why I don't think anyone here would try to hurt her. She's the goose that lays the golden egg."

I'd read that fairy tale. In the story, the man who owns the magic goose kills it, thinking it will be filled with gold. Instead, he is left with a plain dead goose, now rendered incapable of producing any eggs at all.

"Who was it said money is the root of all evil?" Simon went on.

"It's in the Bible," I replied, "and you've misquoted. It says *love* of money is the root of all evil. There's a difference."

He grinned. "I'd *love* plenty of money right now. I'd make Milwood the showplace of the whole Ouachita valley, and then

I'd advertise in Little Rock and St. Louis and maybe even Chicago. No more closed-off rooms—"

"Simon," I interrupted, "who's staying on the second floor of the west wing?"

His grin dissolved as he fixed me with a startled frown. "Those rooms are empty."

"I saw someone behind a curtain up there this morning. Whoever it was watched my aunt and me go into the bathhouse."

"Well, well, someone else is looking, then," he muttered.

"Looking for what?"

"The trunk."

"Simon, what is this trunk?"

He wiped his hands on a rag that was draped over the back of the sawhorse, then led the way to a pine bench near one wall of the stable. While I settled myself beside him, he ran one hand through his errant locks, pushing his damp hair back from his forehead.

"We've been in a real mess here ever since Granddad died nine months ago. He's the one who handled the finances, and he never explained where the money came from."

"It came from your guests, didn't it?" I asked, puzzled by his statement.

He shrugged. "We haven't had enough guests the last few years to support a tearoom, let alone a full-sized hotel. Still, old Rhodes always managed to come up with cash whenever we'd start to go under. It's been a mystery through the years how he did it. Henry and I used to joke around, pretending the black trunk Granddad kept locked up in his private office was filled with treasure. We made up all kinds of stories, you know how kids are. Once we decided maybe Rhodes really did find a diamond mine when he set off that dynamite that uncovered the springs. Another time we thought maybe he'd found an old Spanish sword covered with jewels and that he'd been selling the jewels one by one on those trips he sometimes took to Little Rock or St. Louis by himself. But when he died and we broke into his office—broke in, because his key had disappeared—we found the trunk was gone, too. Locating that trunk is all my dad talks about."

"He thinks I stole it."

Simon sighed and I saw his shoulders sag. "He accuses everyone who visits the hotel. That doesn't help business, either. He also accused Albert Lock, if that makes you feel any better."

I had to laugh, picturing gouty Mr. Lock trying to run off with a heavy trunk.

"I've been trying to find that trunk," Simon went on, "and it looks now as though someone else at Milwood is trying to find it, too."

"Well, I'm glad to know the ghost isn't the one who looked at me through the window."

Simon joined me in laughter. "Don't be too sure. I've never seen the ghost myself, but Jeremy swears he has."

"Poor Jeremy. Has he ever written a poem about it?"

"I don't know. I try to avoid listening to Jeremy's poetry."

We grinned at each other in sudden camaraderie. For the first time I saw, beneath his adult veneer, the adventurous youth who had tried long ago to fly from the stable roof with canvas wings, the visionary who now dreamed of turning Milwood back into a showplace. I became aware of the heat radiating from his body in the warm evening air. My own body tingled as though my very skin had taken on a life of its own. The sun had set during our talk, and I realized that dusk was upon us, turning the stable yard with its surrounding walls of timber into an intimate trysting site, an enclosed room separating us from the rest of the world. My breath quickened. I knew that I should leave at once, before my reputation was compromised. On the other hand, I wanted to prolong the moment and used my original reason for seeking him out as my excuse.

"When you go into Hot Springs tomorrow, could you post a letter for me, too?"

"Of course. But I'm going to ask for something in return."

For a moment I thought he might actually try for a kiss. I felt my lips soften in anticipation.

"Wh—what is it you want?" I asked, scarcely able to breathe.

I was both disappointed and intrigued when his answer took a totally different direction from the one I'd expected. "I want you to help me find that trunk."

Chapter 6

Simon walked me back to the house through the warm dusky evening. Secure in his company, I was able to relax and appreciate the beauty of the rising mists, which wreathed and curled above the bathhouses like disembodied spirits.

"I'll ride into town first thing in the morning," Simon said. "Then, when your aunt takes a nap, we'll do some searching. A real treasure hunt, just like in the stories."

I laughed, both from the pleasure of his nearness and from a spurt of excitement at the thought of the upcoming adventure.

"As soon as I get back to my room, I'll write my letter and bring it down to the desk for you," I said. "That way, you won't be held up in the morning waiting for me."

We parted company in the front lobby. Simon headed back toward the kitchen while I tiptoed forward and peeked around the edge of the front door. There I saw my aunt still comfortably ensconced on the front verandah in a cushioned wicker chair and now engaged in conversation with Jeremy. Quickly I ducked back out of sight before she could call to me to join them and hurried toward the lift to go upstairs to write my letter.

A chill draft wafted through the door of that rickety brass cage and stopped me in my tracks. Suddenly I could not force myself to climb into that cell for the shuddering ride to the third floor. Instead, I turned and headed up the stairs, glad to be able to step out quickly without having to suppress my energy to match my aunt's slow movements. The light from the lobby glowed around me until I reached the turn at the landing, but once I passed beyond that, the illumination diminished rapidly, so that the steps toward the top of that flight were swallowed up by the yawning darkness of the second-floor corridor beyond.

For the first time I felt a quiver of doubt at the wisdom of my action. If there really were a potential murderer loose in this hotel, then what was I doing, headed alone toward the second floor where I'd seen that strange face? I hesitated, tempted to go back downstairs again; but then I scolded myself for letting my nerves get the better of me. I couldn't give in to this fear, I told myself, or I'd end up crippled by it.

Nevertheless, my steps slowed until, by the time I had mounted the stairs to the second floor, I felt as though I were trying to push my shoes through molasses. My feet had taken on a will of their own, telling me as clearly as though they possessed voices, "Stop; don't go any farther."

The round stained glass window above the lower landing blocked most of the light that might have filtered through from the dusky sky outside, revealing itself only as a dim patch against the dark wall, robbed of all color by the absence of the sun. I trailed my fingers along the polished wooden bannister, forcing myself to walk through the darkness toward the next flight of steps leading toward the third floor.

Your rooms aren't that far away, I told myself. *You'll be there in just a minute or two, and then you can laugh about this.*

I started up the steps toward the next landing, marked by another dim round window. The air behind me seemed to thicken and take on substance. I had the feeling that someone had stepped from the shadows below and was even now treading up the steps behind me. The skin prickled between my shoulder blades and intensified into an itch. I envisioned a hand reaching toward me through the darkness to touch me on

77

the neck. I gasped, my heart pounding in my throat, and quickened my steps. I heard no sound, yet I felt that the thing was increasing its own speed, moving inexorably in my direction. I gathered up my skirts in one hand and broke into a run, using my other hand on the bannister to propel me faster up the steps. I fled across that landing and bounded up the last flight, sobbing with fear.

You're imagining this, I told myself fiercely.

But when I glanced back over my shoulder, I saw a dark form glide in front of the pale window, a shapeless thing that picked up speed even as I watched.

"Oh!"

The sound tore from my throat, a high-pitched cry. I darted down the hallway in the direction of our suite. Unable to see the doors in the dark, I ran one hand along the wall, trying to keep count.

One, two, three . . .

Behind me I heard a swishing rush of sound, like autumn leaves sliding over a bare patch of earth in the wind.

. . . four, five . . .

The sound grew closer, seeming to bring with it a drop in temperature, a wintry blast. I couldn't tell whether the cold was real or just my fear freezing my blood.

. . . six, seven.

Our door. I twisted the knob and pushed, planning to throw myself inside and slam the door behind me. My shoulder thudded up against hard wood, which held fast against my efforts. I cried out, frantically rattling the knob. Behind me I heard a low chuckle. The evil in that sound lifted the hair on my head. With my breath burning my throat, I once more hiked up my skirts and fled on down the hallway through the darkness, pursued by that rustling sound of dry leaves. The chuckle floated after me, a throaty whisper.

"Go away!" I cried. "Leave me alone."

I ran full tilt into the solid wall at the end of the corridor and bounced back, almost losing my balance. I turned and flung myself down the side corridor toward the back of the hotel, fleeing mindlessly with no goal except to stay ahead of that unknown thing behind me. I saw a pale rectangle in the space ahead, a window outlined against the gloom. It looked lighter than the stained glass windows had, and I realized, drawing closer, that the panes were of clear glass, revealing the bright edge of the rising moon just peeking over the tops of the bluffs outside. Now I could pick out the shapes of the doors on either side and, ahead, the barred outline of another bannister. A side staircase, I realized with sudden hope. A way down, out of this trap.

But I wasn't safe yet. My body burned with the malice radiating from whatever it was that bounded along behind me. The contact came just as I reached the top of the stairs, two hands flat against my back, pushing so hard that my neck popped with the force of the blow. I flailed my arms, grabbing wildly at the air as I tumbled forward down the steps. I caromed off the wall and bounced back across the bannister, teetering for one heart-stopping moment headfirst over the stairwell before toppling back onto the steps and rolling in a tumble of skirts to sprawl on the landing. I scrambled to my knees, glancing fearfully up the stairs where I expected to see my attacker leaping toward me. The moonlight that filtered through the window above illuminated an empty hallway. I grabbed hold of a baluster and pulled myself to my feet, testing for broken bones. My muscles were sore, but otherwise I seemed to be all right. For once I thanked the puritanical fashion designers who seemed determined to encase women's bodies in multiple layers of clothing, for it was my long, full skirt and underlying petticoat and bloomers that had cushioned my fall, protecting me from serious injury.

I staggered down the stairs into the darkness below, preferring to face whatever lay ahead rather than confronting once more the sure danger that lurked above. When I reached the ground floor I brushed up against a door with a small window in the middle showing the glow of moonlight. I pushed the door open and emerged into the warm June night, where a chorus of tree frogs sang praises to the columns of mist curling toward the sky.

I inhaled a deep lungful of the moldy air and slowly released it, trying to still my racing heart. Now that the immediate danger was over, my body shook with the release of tension. I made my way awkwardly over the mist-dampened grass, pulled by the light that fell from the kitchen windows to spill across the ground. Light meant people; light meant safety.

In the kitchen I found Granny setting a pot of lima beans to soak.

"Have you been here ever since I left earlier?" I asked brusquely.

She squinted toward me through her cloudy eyes, her expression matching my unfriendly tone. "Yes."

"How many staircases does this place have?"

Granny's frown grew even tighter. "Why?"

"It's a big hotel. I was just wondering."

"Three sets of stairs. The grand staircase going up from the lobby, and a side stairs at the end of either wing."

Which meant anyone could have slipped upstairs ahead of me without being observed.

"Where's Maybelle?"

"Folding the laundry in the wash shed."

An ember of rage flickered inside me, heated up, exploded into flame.

"Where's the dinner bell?"

"Outside." She gestured toward the kitchen door.

"Is that the fire bell, too?"

"Yes, but what do you—"

Not waiting for her to finish, I strode out through the door, onto the porch and down the steps, where I saw a brass bell the size of a bucket suspended from a pole. I grabbed the rope and began ringing the bell with all my might. Its harsh peal splintered the night.

"Don't do that!" Granny cried, limping out onto the porch.

"They'll think the place is burning down."

"Good!" I rang the bell even harder.

Henry was the first to arrive, dashing out through the kitchen door.

"Where's the fire?" he shouted, glancing wildly about.

"There is no fire. I want to see how long it takes the people to get out here and where they come from."

"Have you lost your mind?"

"You'd like to think that, wouldn't you?" I snarled while continuing to ring the bell.

Footsteps pounded through the yard, coming from the east wing of the hotel where I had just escaped. That would be my attacker, I thought grimly. By ringing the fire bell, I'd flushed him or her from hiding. I peered through the moonlight, trying to determine the identity of the person. My heart turned over in my chest when Simon dashed into view, his hair disheveled, his shirt tail flying.

"What's on fire?" He sounded just as frantic as Henry had a few moments earlier.

"Nothing. Joanna's gone crazy!" Henry exclaimed.

Simon stepped forward and struggled with me for possession of the rope. The rhythm of the bell's cry changed to a wild syncopated dance.

"Get away," I shouted. "Don't touch me!"

"What do you think you're doing?"

I countered with a question of my own. "What were you doing over on that side of the hotel?"

"What? . . ." He let go of my arms and took a step backward. His face, highlighted by both the moon and the glow streaming through one of the kitchen windows, stared at me in bewilderment. "My bedroom's over there on the ground floor. All the family bedrooms are over there. What's the matter with you?"

Charlotte now appeared from the same direction, panting with the exertion of pushing her husband's wheelchair over the rough ground.

"Is the hotel on fire?" she cried. Her voice, strained by fear, emerged a high-pitched squeak.

"False alarm," Henry shouted in response.

I let go of the rope. The bell clanged a few times more, then wavered to a stop. My plan to flush out my attacker lay around me in shambles.

Henry came forward and grabbed my arm, giving me a shake as though I were a recalcitrant child.

"Explain yourself!" he demanded, glaring down at me. His face was distorted with anger.

I held his gaze while my own anger flared, subsided, flickered again, then died away into ashes. The others now appeared, one by one: Maybelle from the direction of the laundry shed; Great-aunt Alice hobbling with her cane from the kitchen courtyard, and Mr. Lock struggling along on his crutches, both assisted by Jeremy; Nell stalking over the grass from the back of the east wing, a gaunt figure in the moonlight. Everyone gathered around me, their faces accusing, their questions a babble of overlapping sound.

"All right, all right!" I called, holding out my hands to quiet them. "You're asking why I rang this bell? This morning my aunt almost drowned, and I don't care what any of you say to the contrary, I don't think it was an accident. Now, just now, someone pushed me down the stairs. Over there. On the third floor." I pointed an accusing finger toward the rear of the east wing.

"Did you see who it was?" Simon's voice sounded hoarse, as though he'd suddenly contracted a cold.

"No, it was dark up there. Someone followed me up the stairs. . . ."

"Why didn't you use the lift and carry a lamp?" Henry asked.

I laughed without humor. "I'm now asking myself that same thing. All I know is I told Simon I was going upstairs to write a letter, and then I decided to take the stairs. I hadn't realized how dark it was going to be up there in those hallways, all those

82

closed doors, with only the stained-glass windows over the landings. I'd started from the second floor to the third when someone came out of the shadows. . . ."

"The ghost!" Jeremy gasped.

"There was no blue light," I said, "and the hands that pushed me down the stairs were real enough, I can tell you. Someone . . . one of *you* . . . is trying to kill my aunt and me."

I swept my glance around the circle, searching each face for a guilty reaction. All I saw were looks of disbelief or puzzlement.

"Joanna, you're making a fool of yourself!" Aunt Alice's remark cut through the air like a sword.

"We're leaving here," I told her firmly. "We're leaving here first thing in the morning."

"I am not leaving," she responded in a tone equally firm. "You're just making these things up because you want to go home. I came here to take the waters, and that's what I intend to do. I'm staying here, and so are you." She thumped her cane on the ground.

Ignoring her, I looked around the group. "I want to know where each of you was during the last fifteen minutes."

"This is ridiculous," Nell huffed, glaring down her nose at me with a look obviously intended to quell.

"I think we should answer her," Simon said firmly.

But when they did answer, not a one of them other than Jeremy and my aunt, who had been together on the porch, could prove their whereabouts. All the others had been off pursuing their own interests, and while each of them claimed not to have been in the upstairs corridors, there was no way to verify those claims. I circled on one heel, surveying each of them closely. I saw anger or dislike on several of the faces, but nothing I could pinpoint as guilt.

"You are an unpleasant young woman," Nell said. "I'm going back to my room."

She turned and stalked off across the grass toward the back door of the east wing. Her skirts made a swishing sound, like dry leaves blowing across the ground in the autumn, I thought, chilling with shock.

Simon stepped forward and touched my arm. "You don't strike me as a liar. Tell us again what happened up there."

I repeated my story, and those who were left listened with varying degrees of attention, evidenced by their small sounds of response: "Uhmmmm" or "Oh!" or "Ah," uttered in small explosions of breath throughout my tale.

"But you saw nothing," Henry said when I finished.

"I saw that shadow in front of the window. And I heard a chuckle."

"You seem to be good at hearing things," Charlotte commented flatly.

"It's those ghost stories!" my aunt burst forth in disgust. "You got frightened in the dark and ran from shadows. Honestly, Joanna, you're beginning to sound mentally unstable."

I flicked a glance toward Henry and saw, from the solemn look of appraisal on his face, that he agreed with my aunt.

"Well, I, for one, think you're telling the truth," Simon said, still holding my arm. "And I don't intend to let you go back upstairs without an escort."

As I felt the tightening of his fingers on my arm, I heard a tiny voice in the back of my mind whisper, *Don't trust him. He's the one who knew you were going to your room a while ago. He could have taken the side stairs and been waiting for you.*

I stepped aside, pulling out of his grasp.

"We could leave here now and not wait until morning," I said to Aunt Alice. "I can pack our bags, and we can go into Hot Springs for the night and catch the train out tomorrow."

"I told you, we're not leaving!"

I clenched my teeth together in frustration as I looked at her set face.

Henry chuckled, a deep throaty sound. "This is certainly a melodramatic scene, all of us out here in the moonlight. I suggest we go back inside."

"A good idea," Charlotte agreed. To me, she added, indicating Amos, "If he comes down sick from all this to-do over nothing, it will be your fault, young lady. Ringing the fire bell! I can't believe it."

"Ask her where the trunk is," Amos demanded. "Ask her what she's done with the money."

A look of pain tightened Charlotte's face. She patted Amos gently on the shoulder. "Don't worry yourself over that, dear. Things will work out, you'll see."

She disengaged the brakes on the wheelchair and pushed her husband off across the yard. They passed through a horizontal wisp of steam, which had floated sideways off the stream. For one instant they seemed to be suspended above the ground, supported only by clouds, a ghostly pair in the moonlight. The squeak of the wheels added a shrill counterpoint to the frog chorus.

I walked with my aunt and Jeremy back into the hotel, not wanting at that moment to have anything more to do with the others. My bruised muscles had begun to throb, while my stomach burned with anger over the whole situation. My aunt was the fool, I thought, to try to argue away two such overt acts of violence. Surely she didn't believe that I'd made all of this up. Surely Henry didn't believe that, either, despite his efforts to analyze me.

Perhaps he was a student of that doctor in Europe I'd read about, that Freud, who was coming up with such strange ideas about why people behave the way they do. I'd read an article about Freud, about the way he used dreams to analyze people's innermost fears and aversions. A strange way to try to heal people, I'd thought, but interesting. I wondered, thinking of those white roses and mushrooms, how he would analyze Maybelle's dream.

When we reached the lobby, I found that the lift now seemed like a haven of safety. Accompanied by Jeremy with a lighted lamp, we once more rode to the third floor to the squeaking music of the unoiled gears and chains.

"What a scene, Joanna!" my aunt complained during the ride. "You've embarrassed me twice today."

But Jeremy turned a look upon me so filled with sympathy that I felt quite disarmed. Beneath his gaze my anger melted away to be replaced by a stinging of tears behind my eyelids, brought on by my gratitude at receiving support from this unexpected source.

"This has been a terrible day for you," he said quietly. "I'm afraid that what you've claimed is all too true. I've known for some time that there's a malignancy at Milwood, forces at work I don't understand but have come to fear. I think you're right. I think you and Aunt Alice should leave."

The affectation was gone from his voice. His speech was simple and direct, his concern sincere.

"Thank you, Jeremy," I murmured, truly touched. Turning to Aunt Alice, I continued, "Did you hear that? Jeremy thinks we should leave, too."

"Nonsense, dear boy," Aunt Alice said with a bright smile. "We can't leave yet. We have the whole summer ahead of us here."

The clanging arrival of the lift at the third floor put a stop to our conversation.

"I'll step out first and take a look around," Jeremy said firmly, then suited actions to his words.

My respect for him shot up at that display of bravery. There was good metal in him, I decided, if the false gold could be distilled away. He returned to announce that the coast was clear. We followed him down the hallway, and I automatically counted off the doors as I had before: *One, two, three . . .*

When we reached the seventh door, Jeremy started to reach for the knob.

"It's locked—" I began.

"No it isn't," Aunt Alice interrupted. "I told you, I never lock my room here."

Sure enough, when Jeremy tried the door, it swung open at once.

"But it *was* locked!" I cried. "When that . . . thing . . . chased me, I couldn't get into our room."

"You must have miscounted the doors," Aunt Alice replied.

That was possible, I thought. But it was also possible that my pursuer had wanted to make sure I'd no place of refuge at hand and had locked the door, then unlocked it again afterwards. My head began to ache, a throb behind my eyes that blurred my vision, and I found that I was suddenly so weary I was tempted to fall into bed without undressing.

Jeremy escorted us inside and lit the lamps, then checked the rooms before taking his leave. I followed him to the door where he murmured in a low tone, "Don't pay attention to her. Lock this door behind me."

"There still might be something out there. Jeremy, be careful."

"Yes, I will. Try to get some sleep. You look worn out."

"All right."

He shot me a sweet smile before stepping out into the hallway and drawing the door firmly shut behind him. Following his instructions, I locked the door, then leaned my ear against the wood, listening to his retreat down the corridor. I breathed a sigh of relief when I heard the lift door slam and the mechanism begin its complaining rumble.

But it was Aunt Alice who had the last word.

"Dear Jeremy, so thoughtful, so kind. He'll make you a fine husband, Joanna."

Her smile of satisfaction, beaming at me from across the room, reminded me of a well-fed cat. I blinked against the pain behind my eyes.

"Come, Aunt Alice, let me help you get to bed."

For once she went cheerfully and without argument. She was still smiling when she fell asleep.

Chapter 7

I awoke before dawn the next morning. Unable to sleep any longer, I got up and quietly slipped into my long white wrapper, then put on my embroidered slippers and tiptoed into the other room, where I curled up in the window seat while staring out at the slowly brightening sky. The night before, while getting Aunt Alice ready for bed, I'd tried one more time to talk her into leaving Milwood, but she had adamantly refused. Trying now to reassess the situation, I realized again, as I had the day before, that I could not force Aunt Alice to leave against her will, nor could I ever live with myself if I quit her employment and left on my own, abandoning her to the dangers here. The only answer, I decided, sitting up and straightening my shoulders with determination, was to solve the mystery here and uncover the identity of the person who wished us harm. Once the culprit stood revealed, we could be safe.

I thought of my mother, back in St. Louis, and sent up a prayer of gratitude that she did not have to know what was actually happening here. That reminded me that I hadn't written my letter to her the night before. Seeing how early I'd gotten up, there was a chance that Simon would not yet have begun his trip to Hot Springs.

I left the window seat and padded over to the table beside my aunt's chair, where the writing box still stood open with paper, pen, and ink ready at hand. I dashed off a quick note to my mother, saying that we had arrived safely and that I found "taking the waters" to be a novel experience. That was certainly true, I told myself grimly. I then included individual greetings to my younger brothers and sisters. After addressing and sealing the envelope, I was faced with the problem of getting the letter downstairs to the front desk. I didn't want to risk awakening my aunt by going back into the bedroom to get dressed. Surely no one would be up yet, I told myself. I could slip downstairs in my wrapper and leave the note at the desk, then be back upstairs in no time.

Once I'd made the decision, I arranged my robe more firmly about my waist and tightened my sash. My waist-long hair hung loose about my shoulders, a wanton display that I was glad no one would be around to see. I picked up the key that lay on top of the table and quietly let myself out into the hallway, locking the door behind me . . . a futile gesture, no doubt, since my attacker had a key. Still, it gave me a sense of security, however false, to know that the person couldn't just suddenly burst in upon my aunt in my absence but would have to fumble around at the door. Since I intended to come right back, those few seconds might make a difference.

I hurried quickly to the lift and called it from below, hoping its groaning ascent would not awaken the household. I wanted no one to see me in this state of disarray. But it couldn't be later than five-thirty in the morning, I reassured myself. The lobby was bound to be deserted.

Just to make sure, however, I slid open the door at the first floor and poked only my head out, checking to see that no one was around. The only movement that I could see in the large dim room came from the rustling leaves of the potted palms. I darted across the polished floor to the desk and leaned my letter against the small handbell that sat next to the registration ledger. Congratulating myself on the success of my foray, I turned and ran lightly back toward the open door of the lift.

Henry stepped out from behind a palm and blocked my way. "What are you doing down here at this hour?" he demanded.

I caught my breath with shock at his sudden appearance. My pulse began pounding in my throat while my palms went damp with sudden perspiration. I wiped them on the skirt of my wrapper and was thereby reminded that Henry had caught me in my night clothes with my hair streaming free like a woman of loose virtue. I felt a tide of heat flood my neck and face. Henry's eyes were appreciative as he ran his gaze up and down my body.

To cover my embarrassment, I assumed a haughty air, lifting my chin and peering at him down my nose in an effort to quell him the same way his grandmother had attempted to squash me the night before.

"Move out of my way if you please."

"But I don't please."

He began to grin, the arrogant smile of a man who knows he has a woman at a disadvantage. Flaring with anger over his impertinence, I drew my skirts tight and tried to circle around him to get to the lift, but he kept stepping back and forth to block my path.

"You are being rude."

"Did you know that your eyes flash with little red sparkles when you're angry?"

"Would you let me pass?"

"And your hair . . ." He lifted one hand as though to touch me, and I flinched back. "What *is* that color, anyway? It isn't really red, and yet it isn't brown, either. A dark burnished copper, maybe."

"I will thank you to stop looking at me and to let me go by."

"You're a treat for the eyes. We don't get young beautiful female guests here much anymore."

"I can certainly understand why."

Unable to tolerate his intimate appraisal any longer, I turned from him and swept up the stairs, trying to retreat with dignity. But when I'd crossed the first landing and placed one foot on the risers leading to the second floor, still shadowed in the dim light of early morning, I hesitated, overcome by my fear from the night before. Henry bounded up the steps after me, taking two at a time.

"Joanna, I'm sorry. I was being rude. Come back down and take the lift. I know you don't want to climb those stairs, not after the fright you had last night."

"I could have sworn you thought I'd imagined all that."

"I'm not sure you didn't. But imaginary or not, it obviously seems real to *you*, and that makes the fear real indeed, no matter what the cause."

I glanced toward the shadows in the hallway above, toward Henry, toward the hallway again, and made my decision. Turning, I ran past him and darted down the stairs to the lift before he could again block my path. He strode after me, but I was safe inside with the gate closed by the time he could catch up. I peered at him through the grillwork.

"What were *you* doing up so early?" I countered, echoing his earlier question.

He shrugged. "Someone has to feed the horses and milk the cows. I gather you've noticed the dearth of servants around here?"

I hadn't thought much about it before, but now that he'd mentioned it, I could see that taking care of the book work, the cleaning, the laundry, the cooking, the carriages, the bathhouses, and all the farm animals would certainly require more time and effort than Granny Bennett and Maybelle could provide.

"That's why I had to quit my studies and return to Milwood without getting my doctor's license," he went on. "When my father got hurt . . . well, they needed me here, and I had to come. I thought last fall that I might be able to go back and finish my studies, but then Rhodes died. . . ." His voice deepened, losing the teasing tone he'd used with me. The lines tightened on either side of his mouth while his brows drew together in the middle, giving his face a look of pain. I could see now that he had returned to Milwood at great emotional cost.

"But you haven't given up, have you?" I asked. "You *will* be able to finish your studies one of these days?"

He grimaced, his expression bitter. "Milwood is almost bankrupt. Every one of us here does the work of three or four people as it is. If I were to leave—" He shrugged and cocked one eyebrow. "Well, you see the problem."

I clenched my hands around the bars of the door. "If we could just find that trunk!"

His expression was startled.

"Simon filled me in," I said, answering his unspoken question. "Henry, why didn't you tell me the whole story?"

"What can you do about it?"

"I can help look."

He shook his head. "We're grasping at straws here. There probably isn't anything in that trunk, even if it still exists. We just want to think there is. Besides"—again his face darkened and the lines around his mouth sank even deeper—"maybe you're a hysterical young woman who has imagined these attacks and maybe you're not. If you're not—"

The lift shuddered and began to move.

"Henry, I didn't push the lever!"

I turned and searched the panel beside the door for a button that would stop the lift's progress, but all I saw was the one lever marked "UP" on the right and "DOWN" on the left. Meanwhile, the lift moved inexorably upward with a rattle and a whine. Henry's face peered toward me, a startled blur of white through the grilled door, then vanished from sight. I stepped backward and huddled against the wall of the cage while looking frantically about for a weapon I might use. Nothing. With my heart pounding in my throat, I kept my eyes fixed on the view through the bars as the second floor hallway glided past and I was borne upward toward the third floor— and whoever or whatever awaited me there.

Chapter 8

The lift stopped with a jerk at the third floor. Aunt Alice glared at me through the bars, her hair disheveled, her clothes awry.

"Where have you been?" she demanded in a shrill voice. "I woke up a while ago and you weren't there."

I shoved the door open and emerged into the hallway to the sound of footsteps pounding up the stairs, along with Henry's voice yelling, "Joanna!"

"I'm all right!" I called.

He bounded into view, taking the steps two at a time. The fear melted from his face when he saw my aunt. He stopped his mad dash and walked up the last few steps, but his breathing still sounded labored.

"You had me scared there for a moment," he said.

"Joanna, you're—you're not dressed!" My aunt's eyes widened in horror. "And you, Henry—" She paused, and I saw, by the growing look of alarm on her face, that she thought she'd caught us in an assignation.

Heat suffused my neck and flowed up through my cheeks. No explanation I could give Aunt Alice would excuse such a flagrant display of immodesty. I had been willfully indiscreet. If I'd felt embarrassed before, down in the lobby, I was twice that now, seeing the situation through Aunt Alice's eyes.

"It's not what you think," Henry put in quickly. "She came downstairs to leave a letter at the desk, and I happened to be passing through the lobby."

"I—I didn't want to awaken you by stirring about," I said to Aunt Alice, "and I didn't expect to meet anyone down there."

"A likely story!"

The breeze that wafted down the hallway felt cold against my fevered skin. I looked down at the carpet, unable to meet Henry's eyes.

"If you ladies will now excuse me?" he asked in a neutral tone. Without waiting for spoken permission, he turned and trotted back down the stairs.

That's right, I thought bitterly. *Go off and leave me to face this alone.*

I circled around my aunt and headed for our suite while she tottered after, haranguing against the deteriorating morals of modern youth. When we were both inside our sitting room, I turned and held up one hand to stop her.

"Please—"

". . . never would have thought such a thing in all my born days! Traipsing around in your gown—"

"Aunt Alice."

"—like a wanton hussy! For shame! How could you—"

"Aunt Alice!"

"—behave in such a disgraceful way! What would your poor dead father think?"

I pulled my upper lip in under my top teeth and bit down to keep from letting out a shriek of vexation. It was bad enough to be lectured by Aunt Alice in this manner, but even worse to know that she was right. I fled to the bay window, where I knelt on the window seat and pressed my forehead against the cool screen. I closed my eyes for a moment and took several deep breaths in an effort to still my pulse while Aunt Alice continued her angry discourse. Over the top of her words came the sound of a horse trotting down the lane. I opened my eyes to see Simon disappear around a bend beneath the arching

94

oaks. I had posted my letter just in time.

". . . should send you packing to St. Louis at once!"

Aunt Alice's last statement caught my attention.

"Yes, that's a good idea," I said, twisting about on the window seat, "and you must come with me."

"We're back to that, are we? That's just what you want! Perhaps you planned this whole episode this morning to get me to send you away."

"No, I didn't. If it means anything to you, I am thoroughly ashamed of having been caught outside our room in my gown and wrapper. But I told you, we're in danger here."

"And I told you I'm staying."

I sighed, overwhelmed by the burden of protecting her.

You could leave her to her fate, whispered an antic voice inside my head.

Even as I thought it, I knew I could never live with myself if I did such a thing. Despite my lack of affection for her, she was family. The old phrase *Blood is thicker than water* popped into my mind. Then, too, my nurse's training, with its emphasis on preserving life despite the unpleasantness of a patient, had influenced me to the degree that even had Aunt Alice not been family, I still could not have abandoned her.

The only good answer to all this, I told myself again, was to solve the mystery here as soon as possible and uncover the villain.

"After breakfast," Aunt Alice went on, "I shall do what I came here to do and again take the waters."

Thus it was that I found myself back in that steamy bathhouse several hours later with Aunt Alice. This time she insisted on having Granny Bennett in attendance instead of Maybelle. When I said I thought I could handle the bathing now, she said she doubted it.

Granny proved to be a deft attendant, despite her cataracts and gnarled hands. With my aunt she used a manner I hadn't seen in her before, joking and cajoling and recalling incidents from other summers, which soon had them both cackling with glee.

"Have you taken the waters yet?" Granny asked me after she'd gotten my aunt submerged for the first soak.

"No," I replied. I shifted my body about, wincing at the bruises that were just beginning to surface, and allowed myself to think how good it would feel to soak in a steaming bath.

"Go ahead," Granny said. "I'll sit right here on the bench beside Alice and never take my eyes off her."

Considering Granny's cataracts, I doubted the efficacy of such a promise. Nevertheless, the tug of that water proved irresistible.

"All right," I said. "Just for five minutes."

Granny offered to get me a bathing dress, but I declined. I went to a cubicle several spaces down and turned on the water, filled the tin teapot, then quickly slipped out of my clothes. I tested the water with a toe and found it to be so hot as to barely be tolerable. I had to ease into the tub gradually. At last I lay totally submerged except for my head, which rested against the padded board. The water laved my naked body, drawing out the pain. I closed my eyes, breathing in the vapor that rose from the surface of the water in a misty cloud. Remembering Maybelle's instructions, I sat up to take a long drink from the teapot, then lay back once more as the warmth spread through my stomach to soothe me from the inside. I could feel healing taking place even as I lay there. It was a remarkable sensation. For the first time I understood why my aunt had become so addicted to these summer sojourns in Arkansas.

Within minutes my body relaxed into a painless blob of jelly, lacking bone or bruised flesh, as I floated languidly in the water. How easy it would be, I thought, to drift into sleep and slide, unknowing, beneath the surface. Was that what had happened with my aunt? Had I really misread the situation the day I'd found her facedown in the tub?

But no, I argued within myself, when I'd left her that day, she'd been lying back against the resting board, even as I was now. If she'd fallen asleep, she simply would have slid down into the water on her back or slumped sideways against the edge of the tub. She would not have sat up and fallen forward into the water, as I'd found her those few minutes later, nor would she have sustained that bump on her head.

Still pondering the mystery, I took another drink of the hot water and lay back again, loathe to obey that five-minute time limit I had set for myself. The voices of the two older women echoed through the tiled room, their laughter calling forth images of the witches from *Macbeth*. A picture formed in my mind: I saw myself being boiled in a cauldron stirred by two cackling crones dressed in tatters. My peace dissolved away, floating upward with the vapor, as my fear of this place crashed in on me again.

I'm in danger, I thought. *I'm in danger now. Someone is watching me. . . .*

I sat up and whipped my head around to stare toward the curtained doorway. A puckered wrinkle gave evidence of fingers grasping the curtain from the other side. Peering at me through that small opening, like an evil omen, was one cold gray eye.

"Oh!" I cried, automatically clasping my arms over my naked breasts.

The curtain rings grated over the rod as the owner of the eye enlarged the opening.

"Are you enjoying your bath?" Charlotte asked.

But she didn't smile as she asked the question, and her gaze remained cold. At that moment she resembled a gray rat rather than a mouse.

"Yes," I said, "but it's time for me to get out."

I waited for her to replace the curtain so I could have my privacy, but she stood motionless, still staring at me in a chilling way.

"I'm getting out now so I can help Granny with my aunt." I sharpened my tone, hoping Charlotte would take the hint.

Without speaking or changing her expression, she dropped the curtain back into place. With my relaxed mood now destroyed, I climbed from the tub and toweled dry, then dressed as quickly as I could. I emerged from the cubicle to find that Granny had already helped my aunt from the tub and into a dry one-piece flannel garment.

"It's too bad you've already dressed. I could have given you a massage, too," Granny said.

While Granny helped my aunt to lie facedown on one of the sheet-draped tables, I looked toward Charlotte, who now leaned against one wall with her arms folded over her chest.

"You made several accusations against us yesterday," she stated in a cool tone.

"Yes," I said, "and they still stand."

I got the impression of shadows flickering through her eyes like the passage of cloud shadows over a pond in summer. Even as I watched, her shoulders drooped and her body drew in upon itself, losing strength, while the cold calculation in her eyes changed to the weak mousey look I'd seen her wear that first evening.

"You—you must be mistaken," she said. "Both those incidents . . . they had to be accidents. Yes, they *had* to be, there's just no other answer."

Her voice now carried a note of appeal, while her eyes looked as soft and guileless as a deer's in a forest glade. I could not determine which of the two people I'd just seen was the real Charlotte.

"So there's no need for you to leave here," she went on. "I know everything's going to be all right from now on."

That explained her sudden change in attitude. She might not like me personally, but she certainly didn't want to risk losing our money for the summer, just in case I had enough influence over Aunt Alice to persuade her to leave. Well, I could certainly have set Charlotte straight on *that* score, but I didn't have to—Aunt Alice did it for me.

"What nonsense, Charlotte, of course we're not leaving," my aunt huffed. "Joanna is a spoiled child who wants to go home to her mother."

While keeping my eyes on Charlotte, I rubbed my shoulder where I'd bounced against the wall the night before. I thought I saw the tiniest flicker of a smile touch one corner of her mouth. Perhaps she was reacting with relief to Aunt Alice's announcement but wished to conceal her triumph.

"I'll get back to the kitchen, then," she said. "Since Granny's busy here, Maybelle may need some help with the noon meal."

She scurried away, the folds of her gray skirt twitching behind her like a nervous tail. She would have to work quite hard, I thought, to help keep this place going. It was no wonder she wanted to make sure that we were staying on.

"Watch here now," Granny said to me. "You work your way down, like this, from the scalp to the neck. Takes out the kinks."

"Ouch!" Aunt Alice stiffened and lifted one hand to touch the back of her head. "You hit my sore spot."

"Oh, I plumb forgot about that!"

"Please be careful, that's all." Aunt Alice relaxed once more.

I watched Granny carefully, marveling that she could work so well with her thick fingers, as knobby as tree roots. Demonstrating strength far greater than I would have imagined, she worked her way down the body, front and back, manipulating muscles and applying oils to those areas not covered by the flannel chemise. I could see that the art of massage was a true skill not to be learned in one easy lesson.

When Granny had finished, Aunt Alice announced that she felt so relaxed she wanted to go back to the room to rest. Granny nodded her approval.

"'Tain't good for the vitals to move around much after a treatment," she said to me. "You got to rest to get the good of it."

Accepting their wisdom in the matter, I helped Aunt Alice dress, then took her back to our suite where she soon dozed off. The day promised to become a scorcher. To stay cooped up with my aunt all morning in the growing heat was a prospect I didn't welcome. I went back into the sitting room and pulled up all the sashes in the bay window, then sat on the window seat and opened the neck of my uniform to the breeze.

My body sat quietly, but my mind refused to do so. Questions tumbled about in my head like a roomful of wrestling children: *Who? Who around here would want Aunt Alice and me to die? And why?*

The "who" was not such a stickler as the "why." For that last one I hadn't a clue.

I peered down at the flagstone paving of the courtyard with my head pressed against the screen. There was a faint snap and a stirring as the screen shifted on its hinges. Although I'm not given to vertigo, I did have one tug of dizziness as I pictured falling through the screen to smash on those stones below. I pulled back and lifted my gaze to peer out across the wind-tossed treetops toward the blue rim of mountains beyond. Cotton candy clouds drifted in the azure sky, teased by soaring hawks.

When I heard hoofbeats and saw Simon reappear from beneath the trees, at first I felt surprised that he could return so soon. Then I realized that he'd left Milwood near dawn and that it was now mid-morning, plenty of time for a strong horse to travel six miles into town and return.

The sight of him quickened my desire to search for the trunk. Among its contents, I felt sure, must lie the key to the mystery here. But to search for the trunk meant leaving Aunt Alice alone and vulnerable. I envisioned the days to come. There would be no way to stay with Aunt Alice every minute. Since she chose to ignore my warnings, she would undoubtedly escape from me occasionally to wander around on her own through the hotel and surrounding grounds, as she'd been doing here at Milwood for over thirty years, and there would be nothing I could do about it.

No, the only way to protect her was to get to work at once on uncovering the evil here so that we could walk in safety once more. In the meanwhile, I would just have to trust Aunt Alice to God's care and hope that His plan included keeping her out of trouble.

With that decision made, I quickly scribbled a note to my aunt telling her that I was going for a walk. I leaned the note up against the mirror on the dresser, where she couldn't miss it, and then tiptoed from the room, closing the door behind me. I decided this time not to bother locking the door. What was the use, after all, since my attacker could obviously get into our suite if he so chose?

I hesitated outside our door, debating which way to go—down the center stairs, the side stairs, or the lift? Each of those directions seemed to carry its own possibility of danger.

Remembering the soft sound of blowing leaves that had pursued me through the darkness, I shivered, my skin prickling with horror. For one brief moment I wanted to run back into our room and slam the door.

If you don't watch out, you can become paralyzed by fear, I told myself sternly. *You'll get nowhere if you allow fear to take over.*

I turned and walked swiftly along the path where I had fled the night before, to the end of the corridor and around the corner toward the side staircase where I'd come so close to being killed. How different that hallway looked today, with sunlight streaming in through the tall narrow window at the head of the stairs. The view through the window of the bluffs beyond, with their spill of misty water, their spray-varnished rocks, gave me a quiet moment of pleasure. It seemed hard to believe, in observing that peaceful scene, that evil could lurk at Milwood; but the wicked intent of those hands that had pushed me from behind had been real enough. Quickly I glanced over my shoulder to make sure I wasn't being followed now. The corridor stretched behind me, empty and still, disturbed only by a lazy drift of dust motes.

I hurried down the stairs to the ground floor. My purpose in coming this way was to examine this lower corridor where I'd been told the family lived. I'd hoped everyone would be off taking care of chores elsewhere, but those hopes were dashed when I encountered Charlotte and Nell removing fresh laundry from a cart. Several rooms stood open, including the two that were nearest me. Inside one of those rooms I spotted Amos wheeling about in his chair. I hadn't realized before that he possessed the coordination to operate the chair by himself.

Amos looked up at that moment and met my gaze. His face contorted into a mask of rage. He hurtled over the floor and out the door, yelling, "Catch the thief! Run her down!"

Since he seemed bent upon doing me harm, I darted toward the two women, where I took refuge behind the cart. Meanwhile, Amos continued to shout, "Grab her before she gets away!"

Henry stepped forth from a room at the far end of the corridor. He broke into a lope when he saw what was happening.

"Dad, would you stop that!" he shouted. "Joanna is not a thief!"

"Arrest her! Drag her off to jail!" Amos yelled, paying no attention to his son.

I thought he was going to crash full tilt into the laundry cart, but he braked at the last moment. Thwarted in his attempts to reach me directly, he began wheeling back and forth in front of the cart while the two women blocked his path.

Charlotte held out her hands toward him beseechingly and said in a soothing tone, "There, there, dear, don't excite yourself. Everything is all right. You don't have to worry. Everything is going to be fine, I promise."

Amos ceased his raving. He fixed his wife with a look of appeal. "You do promise?"

"I've told you so many times. Everything is going to work out for the best, you'll see."

I heard desperation in her voice, mixed with compassion and love. The realization that she still cared passionately for her husband despite his infirmities made me view her with new respect.

Henry touched me on the arm. "Are you all right?" he asked in a worried tone.

"Yes," I said, "no harm done."

"That's what you say," Nell put in, her voice hostile. "But the harm *you've* done to us with your malicious lies is something else again."

"I didn't lie," I said firmly. "I may be mistaken about those so-called 'accidents,' but I don't think so."

"Who is this woman?" Amos demanded. "Why is she running around here loose?"

"I've told you, Dad, this is Aunt Alice's grandniece," Henry repeated patiently.

"Alice." Amos spit out the name, then sat brooding while his face contracted into a knot. "Alice malice palace."

Henry's lips drew into a white line as he stared down at his father. I felt a stirring of pity for the injured man. It was obvious, looking at his strong frame, that not so long ago he would have been a match for his two sons, a man past middle-age to be sure, but still in his prime. What a shame to see the waste the accident had made of his life.

"Did you need something? Were you looking for one of us in particular?" Henry now asked, and I realized I needed a quick excuse for having entered their private domain.

"I—uh—"

"Perhaps you wanted to post another letter?" he continued smoothly. I detected the undercurrent in his voice, an unspoken reminder of our earlier encounter when he'd caught me in dishabille. I felt a flow of warmth suffuse my face.

"No, I—uh—I need to do some mending, and I forgot to pack my white thread." I gave him a bright smile to cover my lie and then glanced quickly toward Nell and Charlotte. "If I could borrow a spool of thread—"

"Maybelle can do your mending for you," Charlotte said. "If you'll go get whatever it is that's torn, she can take it home with her tonight. . . ."

"No, no, that's all right, it's just a tiny tear," I said quickly.

"I'll be happy to do it myself."

"Perhaps you tore your wrapper?" Henry asked politely.

I gritted my teeth at this revelation, in front of the others, that he knew the style and color of my nightwear.

"No, it's—it's the hem of a dress that's coming out."

"Oh, if that's all, Maybelle can do it for you this afternoon," Charlotte said, "or I could do it myself."

Was I going to have to go back upstairs and deliberately rip out a hem to cover my tracks? I sighed with chagrin, reminding myself that telling lies does indeed seem to draw one ever deeper into the mire. From the slight grin that now lifted one corner of Henry's mouth, I got the feeling he'd seen right through the ruse.

"I wouldn't think to bother you with such a trifling task," I said to Charlotte. "If you'll excuse me now, I'll go look for Maybelle and get the thread from her."

I set off briskly down the hallway before there could be any more argument. Henry fell into stride beside me.

"Why do you pull that gorgeous hair back into such a tight bun?" he asked. "Why don't you let it hang free, the way you did this morning?"

"A gentleman would not refer to what he saw this morning," I said stiffly.

"A lady would not wander about a hotel in her nightdress," he replied.

He had me there. Since there was no good response, I said nothing. We turned the corner, out of sight of the others, and headed toward the front lobby.

"Tyranny," Henry murmured.

"I beg your pardon?"

He stepped out in front of me and stopped, turning to face me so that I was forced to stop, too. I looked up at him and saw that his eyes had darkened with some kind of strong inner emotion.

"Lately I've been thinking about tyranny," he said. "The different kinds of tyranny that bind us all, particularly you

104

and me."

"What in the world are you talking about?"

"The tyranny of poverty, for instance," he said. "I'm bound here, unable to continue my studies because of poverty, and you're bound in servitude to your aunt for the same reason."

"Well—"

"Then there's the tyranny of illness, which nails my father to that chair and which keeps 'Mr. Lock from Little Rock' away from his business."

The idea began to intrigue me. "Hmmmm," I said.

"Then there's the tyranny of family loyalty," he said. "I could walk away from here, try to finish my studies on my own, abandon my family, which is what I really want to do—oh, God, do I want to do that—but . . ." He paused, and I saw his brows draw together in anguish, watched the lines deepen on either side of his mouth.

Remembering my own impulse to run out on my aunt just a few minutes earlier, followed closely by the knowledge that I could not do that, I now vibrated in sympathy with Henry's dilemma.

"I know what you mean," I breathed fervently.

"I thought you would. Then there's another tyranny. . . ." He paused again, his eyes devouring my face.

"What is that?"

"There's the tyranny of love."

He reached out and clasped me roughly, drawing me toward him.

I gasped, but he cut off my protest by lowering his lips to mine in a hungry kiss that robbed me of breath. For a moment I hung in his embrace, too surprised to resist. He drew me closer until my body was pressed full-length against his own. I felt the strength in his arms, the powerful thudding of his heart against my breast, the touch of his thighs against mine. I'd never been held by a man in this way before. Despite the indignation racing through my mind at such a liberty, I found my body responding of its own accord, beyond my will to control,

105

turning to flame in his arms. As I gasped again, my lips parted and his tongue possessed my mouth at once in hungry exploration. Having experienced only chaste pecks on the cheek from relatives, I had never guessed that there were kisses like that. The fire that now burned in the very core of my body spread outward in pulsating waves.

This is not the tyranny of love, shouted a warning voice inside my head. *This is the tyranny of lust.*

The shock of that realization gave me the strength to place my fists against Henry's chest and shove him away. I opened my hand and slapped it hard across his face.

"How dare you!" I exploded, glaring at him in rage. "Don't ever do that again!"

Ducking around him, I fled down the hallway, running not only from Henry but from the passion he'd ignited within me, emotion so powerful I felt as shaken as though I'd just been through an earthquake.

"No," I whispered to myself. "No, no!"

I dashed through the lobby and veered around the corner into the corridor leading toward the kitchen.

"What's your hurry?" bellowed a deep voice as another set of arms closed about me to stop my forward plunge.

So it was that I escaped from Henry only to run full steam into Simon's embrace.

Chapter 9

Startled, I clung to Simon for a moment, trying to regain both my physical and emotional balance. I also struggled, with small success, to control my ragged breathing. He held me gently, his hands warm against my back.

"Has something frightened you again?"

In no way did I want him to guess what had just happened with his brother. I stepped away from him and lifted my hands to resettle the pins in my hair.

"No, I'm fine," I said, forcing a laugh. "Sorry for almost running you down."

"Why were you running, anyway?"

"High spirits."

Now he laughed. "I can believe that. You impress me as a woman who likes action and adventure."

"Then I chose the wrong profession, didn't I?"

"Maybe not. It's brought you to Milwood, and just look what's happened since you got here."

Those words, uttered in a sardonic tone, had a sobering effect. For a moment our eyes locked and held, acknowledging our secret pact.

"Are you still willing to help me look for that trunk?" he asked.

"Now more than ever."

"We've got an hour until noon. Shall we start?"

I hesitated, remembering my suspicions concerning him the night before. Could I trust him or not? I still didn't know. On the other hand, I could not find answers if I didn't take some chances.

"Yes. My aunt's asleep, so this is a good time."

"All right, we'll begin with the attic. I've already looked there, but maybe you'll see something I missed."

He led the way back into the lobby to the lift. We rode to the third floor, eyeing each other in silence. The small enclosed space created an intimate atmosphere, reminding me of the intimacy we'd shared in the darkened glade the night before. I knew I was compromising my reputation by meeting with Simon alone in secluded spots. As I looked at his full lips, parted slightly to reveal a flash of teeth, I thought of his brother's tongue invading my mouth, and I found my face once more growing warm. I ducked my head, afraid that Simon would see himself as the cause of that blush.

After we emerged into the corridor, I darted quickly down to our suite, followed by Simon, to see if my aunt was still sleeping. She was. When I came back out, Simon said, "This way," and veered at an angle to open a door across the hall from us but several rooms down. I'd assumed all those doors opened into guest suites, but that particular door revealed a steep stairway leading upward.

"The attic's divided into two sections, with a widow's walk between," he said. "The other stairway is down at the far end of the corridor."

What a rabbit warren! I thought as I followed Simon up the stairs. *Any number of people could hide out in this hotel and no one would know.*

I shivered, picturing again that shadowed face I'd seen in the window on the second floor. I had sensed something menacing in the stillness of the figure, as though he or she had been studying me with particular attention and not to my good. The memory now stirred my nerves and sent my pulse skittering as we neared the top of the stairs. I almost expected someone to jump out and yell, "Boo!", the type of stunt one or another of my younger brothers would have delighted in playing on me in order to hear me shriek.

The dim light from the attic filtered down the stairs in a gray mist, providing just enough illumination to help me see the flaking plaster walls and grimy steps. Simon ducked through the opening and walked a few steps away, his steps echoing hollowly on the wooden floor. I followed him into a nightmare world of broken chairs, old toys, dressmaker forms, plant stands, magazines bound with twine, and wooden crates of various sizes stacked about like giant children's blocks. Tools, rusty with age, hung from nails among the rafters, along with tin pails, enamel washpans, and battered old teapots similar to the ones I'd seen in the bathhouses. A large hobby horse with threadbare mane and tail sported a woman's plumed hat set over its ears at a jaunty angle.

Because the dingy dormer windows admitted little light, I could not see into the far corners of the room, which seemed to stretch on and on, gradually dissolving into darkness.

"This is impossible!" I cried. "No wonder you haven't found that trunk."

Simon replied with a wry chuckle, "Wait until you see the attic on the other side. It's just as bad as this, if not worse."

I let out a low whistle of amazement. "I don't even know where to start."

"Now you see why I asked for help?"

I walked over to a pile of crates. "How big is the trunk we're looking for?"

"Not very big. More the size of a valise, actually. Black leather, with brass corners and a brass lock. And a leather handle on either side."

I groaned. "Then it could be nailed up inside one of these crates."

"Could be. I've already pried open most of the crates in the other attic, and I've found stuff you wouldn't believe . . . ledgers and business papers reaching back to the Civil War. I don't think my grandfather ever threw away a thing."

"My aunt has told me many stories about Milwood, but there's still a lot I don't know. Did Rhodes fight in the war?" As soon as I voiced the question, I could have bitten my tongue. For many, the Civil War was still a touchy subject.

Simon regarded me steadily. "You're fishing to find out which side Granddad was on."

When he didn't continue, I finally asked, "All right, did he wear blue or gray?"

"Blue."

"Oh."

"That's a mighty big 'O'," Simon said. "It's almost big enough to fall into and drown."

"My grandfather wore gray," I said. "He was Great-aunt Alice's brother, and that's why my aunt is now so rich. . . . Her family disinherited my grandfather when he fought for the South."

"So now you're poor, too," Simon said.

I shrugged. "Neither my grandfather nor my father was good at business. If it hadn't been for Aunt Alice, my mother would have been in real trouble after my father died."

"Strange, isn't it," Simon said, "how people still get caught up in the old dissensions even though it's thirty-six years now since the war ended?"

"Arkansas's a southern state. How did Rhodes happen to fight for the North?" I asked.

"He grew up in St. Louis, remember? When the war started, he took my grandmother and my father and Uncle William to stay with relatives there, away from the fighting in Arkansas, and then he joined the Union Army. My dad was eight years old then and Uncle William was ten . . ."

". . . and that's where Nell and Rhodes first met Aunt Alice, at a dance to raise money for the North!" I exclaimed delightedly, as one of my aunt's old stories now came back to me. "I remember Aunt Alice said Rhodes looked handsome in

110

his uniform."

Simon shook his head, a bemused look on his face. "They were in their thirties then, just a few years older than I am now. Can't you see it! Grandmother and Aunt Alice decked out in fancy ball gowns—"

"—with bustles." I picked up a wire frame with the ribbon sash still attached, which was lying on top of a nearby box. "What a sight that must have been." Simon grinned at me.

I smiled, too. Thinking of my aversion to corsets, I was glad I didn't have to struggle with such a silly fashion as a bustle. But as I pictured Nell and Alice in their frippery, I remembered my question from the first evening, a question to which I still had no answer. "Simon, why does your grandmother dislike Aunt Alice now?"

"I don't know."

"Did something happen between them ... maybe something when you were little? Do you remember an argument, anything like that?"

His grin widened. "Maybe Aunt Alice flirted with Rhodes, and grandmother got jealous."

I made a face at him. "Of course," I said with exaggerated sarcasm. "Why didn't I think of that?"

"You don't think that's it?" he asked in an innocent voice. "Do you?"

Now he laughed out loud. "No, not really."

I put the bustle down and considered once more with dismay the seemingly impossible task of sorting through all that junk. Perspiration trickled down my face and neck from the oven-like heat that had built up under the rafters, while a musty, mildewy smell assailed my nostrils with the same pungency as the odor from the slime in the stream outside. Simon stepped into one of the alcoves and tugged open a window. The breeze that drifted in helped a little, but not much.

"I don't know how much of this heat I can take," I said. "We'd better get started."

Simon lifted down crate after crate and pried off the lids

while I sorted through the contents. It was a big temptation to linger over old school papers written in boyish scrawls and bearing Simon's, Henry's, or Jeremy's names in the corners.

"That's not fair!" Simon protested when he saw me scanning a story about the possibility of flying, which he'd written while still in grammar school. "You're going to find out how foolish I was as a child, and then you won't respect me anymore."

"On the contrary; I like a person who dares to dream," I said. "First there was Icarus. . . ."

"Well, this Icarus fell off the stable roof and broke his arm," Simon interrupted, pointing toward the rafters in a shadowed alcove I hadn't yet investigated. There, tacked up in dusty splendor, was a trophy that might have been taken from a giant mythological bird.

"Simon, your wings!"

I dumped the papers back into the box, then rose, shaking out my skirts and hurrying to take a closer look. Each wing consisted of a wooden framework covered with stretched canvas, sagging now and gray with dust. Mirror images of each other, the wings sported straps underneath where they could be attached to either arm. "How clever!"

"But not very efficient. I fell like a rock."

"You tried," I said. "You dared to test your dream, and that's the important thing."

"Do you think so? Because now I have another dream—"

"—of finding the trunk and using the treasure to rebuild Milwood."

"Yes. I love this place, I really do. But I'm damned tired of having no money, and I get bored during the slow periods, with no guests coming in. Just to show you how desperate I am . . ." He paused, considering. "Well, no, I'd better not say it."

"Say what?"

He chewed his lower lip while viewing me from narrowed eyes. Then he cocked one brow and lifted his mouth in a sardonic grin containing little humor. "All right, then . . . I've

112

even thought of riding into Hot Springs some dark night and robbing a bank."

Despite his attempt to pass it off as a joke, I sensed that underneath he was halfway serious.

"Simon!" I exclaimed, unable to hide my shock.

"You don't think the end justifies the means?"

"Nothing could justify that! To commit such a crime . . ."

"It might prove a fine panacea for boredom."

"I understand life in prison is very boring."

"If I didn't get caught . . ."

"But you've already told someone your plan. You've told me."

"So I have."

His eyes hardened into dark marbles while the smile left his lips. My quick inhalation stuck in my throat. It was as though the air had changed texture, had thickened with danger, making breathing difficult.

"Of course, I could keep you from talking. I could throttle you and stuff you into one of these crates, and you might never be found," he stated quietly.

My heart hammered in my chest, seeking release. "In this heat, I imagine I'd be found rather quickly," I said.

Our eyes held for a long moment while the room throbbed with tension. Then Simon laughed, breaking the spell. "Thus speaks the pragmatic nurse. Threaten her with murder and you get no hysterics, just the facts. Joanna, you're wonderful, did you know that?"

I certainly didn't know it. He had shaken me to my toes.

"To save you from a life of crime, we'd better find the trunk," I said briskly, surprised that I could speak normally.

I walked away from him and started shifting furniture about in a far corner while he went back to opening crates. I needed time to collect myself, so I was glad he chose to work alone. It took a while for my pulse to quiet to its regular rhythm.

We were interrupted in our labors by the peal of the dinner bell, muffled with distance. Simon straightened up and said,

"Guess we have to quit," just as I had started to move a chair with a broken rocker. It was then that I spotted the corner of an envelope sticking out from behind a loose board down near the floor behind the rocker. Why I bent over and drew the envelope forth and why I concealed that find from Simon is something I can't explain other than to say I wanted to share nothing with him at that moment. I quickly stuffed the envelope into my pocket, covering the action by pretending to stumble against the chair.

"Careful there, Icarus!" Simon called. "You don't want to break an arm, the way I did."

But I was not in the mood for levity. All I wanted was to get out of that attic and back downstairs, surrounded by people.

There's saftey in numbers, I reminded myself.

"Goodness, I'm dirty," I exclaimed, patting my hands against my skirt and watching the dust fly up. "I'm going to have to wash up before I eat."

I hurried across the floor and started to push past Simon, but he reached out and grabbed my arm. When I stiffened and tried to pull away, he said, "Joanna, I'm sorry. What I said a while ago was in very bad taste. I can tell I've offended you, and I want to apologize."

"Some things just aren't funny," I said, "particularly in view of what happened yesterday."

"I am not planning to rob a bank or murder you, surely you know that."

"I certainly hope not," I replied. "Simon, let me go. My aunt is bound to be awake and getting angry by now."

He released me, and I trotted at once down the stairs. After the suffocating heat of the attic, the air in the corridor felt light and cool. Without looking back to see if Simon were behind me, I hurried to my suite where I found my aunt seated before the fireplace with her cane clasped firmly in both hands.

"That must have been a very long walk," she said cheerfully. "A dirty one, too. Your face and hands are smudged."

I was vastly relieved to find her in such a good mood.

"I'll just go and wash up, and then we can go down to dinner," I said.

I hurried into the bathroom and closed the door. I sat on the edge of the tub and drew forth the envelope from my pocket. It was addressed, in a spidery Spencerian script, to Rhodes Hampton in care of a post office box number in Little Rock. That was strange, I thought. Why have mail for Milwood sent to Little Rock instead of Hot Springs? The handwriting looked familiar. Perhaps it was because all school children had once been trained to write in that manner, I thought, removing the one folded sheet from inside the envelope. But when I opened that page, my mouth fell open in a sudden gasp. I *did* know that handwriting. Although there was no signature at the bottom of the page, the elaborately scripted *A* with the tail swirling around to become a bird with outstretched wings, the circles over the *i*'s instead of dots, told me all too clearly who the writer, then young, must have been. The date at the top of the sheet read "August 15, 1850," and the letter began, "My darling Rhodes."

Black spots danced before my eyes, temporarily obscuring the page. That was ten years before my aunt was supposed to have met any of the Hamptons. I blinked until my vision cleared, then read on: "I miss you so I feel sometimes I cannot live. I know we've already said good-bye, and yet I have to say one more time that I love you. I love you. There, I have said it, and yet I must say it again. I love you, Rhodes. I will always love you. I'm well enough to travel now, and my coach leaves tomorrow for St. Louis. My family still thinks I've been away on a long holiday, so our secret is safe. Kiss our son for me, and as he grows to manhood through the years to come, remember me, as I shall remember you. Yours forever, your loving A."

Good God, I thought.

I closed my eyes, breathing hard.

William. The "foundling" that Rhodes brought back from Little Rock to Nell to bring up as her own.

William, Jeremy's father.

William . . . son of Alice and Rhodes.

"Joanna, are you ready?" called my aunt from the next room.

I stuffed the envelope and letter deep into my pocket, then rose and splashed water over my feverish face. I stood for a long moment with my face buried in the towel while questions tumbled through my mind. Had Nell found out, after all these years, about the deception? If so, that could well provide a motive for murder. And Jeremy . . . No wonder my aunt wanted an excuse to keep him near.

"Joanna?"

I hung the towel back on the rack and smoothed my hair with trembling hands.

"Yes," I called. "Yes, Aunt Alice, I'm coming."

Chapter 10

I don't know how I got through the noon meal. I kept watching my aunt from the corner of my eye, trying to reconcile the wrinkled harridan beside me with the passionate, reckless girl revealed in that letter. I remembered the beauty I'd seen in her face that first night when she'd greeted Jeremy in the moonlight, and how I'd thought then that I'd glimpsed the girl she once had been. I tried to recapture that moment, but with little success.

"What's the matter with you, Joanna?" she demanded now in a sharp tone. "You haven't said a word for the past ten minutes. Cat got your tongue?"

I gave myself a mental shake as I tried to dispel the shock that still gripped me.

"She's probably moonin' about some fella back home," Mr. Lock boomed. "Is that it, little lady? You got a sweetheart waitin' for you back in St. Louis?"

"No, I'm just a little tired," I said.

"You probably walked too far and too fast. Did you take a parasol?" my aunt asked.

"No—"

"That's it, then. I swear, Joanna, you'll not only end up as brown as a berry, but you'll get sunstroke, too. Next time you must take my pink parasol."

117

"Yes, Aunt Alice."

I spoke submissively, giving her a weak smile, while my mind raced with carnal thoughts. I saw her, young and naked, locked in an embrace with Rhodes Hampton in their love nest in Little Rock. In my daydream I became my aunt, while the man in my arms was Henry. He pressed his mouth over mine, demanding, seeking. . . .

"See, you *are* sunburned!" my aunt said accusingly. "Your face is just as red as it can be."

I brushed my napkin to the floor, making it seem an accident so I could bend to retrieve it and give my blush time to subside. My mind left the love nest and traveled ahead in time to my aunt as a young woman back with her family in St. Louis, keeping her secret while struggling alone with her grief over the loss of both a lover and a son. No wonder she never married. . . . Her bridegroom would have realized she wasn't a virgin, and she would have been cast out in disgrace. What a terrible burden to carry alone in one's heart.

Then, ten years later, to unexpectedly meet Rhodes again at that fund-raising dance for the Union Army in St. Louis . . . Rhodes—and Nell.

And William.

Ten-year-old William, who would not have known that Alice was his real mother, who probably died in that buggy accident after he was grown, still not knowing.

Tragedy upon tragedy for my aunt. No wonder she had hardened into this tyrant, suppressing warmth and laughter while wearing a mask of cold respectability, who now tried to rule those around her. . . . That was probably the only way she had managed to survive.

Now I knew why Jeremy was the one person who could call forth the remaining bit of softness and love, buried deep inside my aunt. As her grandson, Jeremy would be my . . . what? Cousin twice removed? Wouldn't that make a relationship between us incestuous? I had heard that in most states first cousins could not marry, but what the rules were for second or third cousins I didn't know. I still did not wish to marry Jeremy, but I did find myself thinking of him more kindly, now that I knew him to be kin.

". . . shall take a stroll to settle this meal." My aunt's words broke in upon my reverie.

"Are you up to it?" I asked.

"Yes, my nap this morning has left me quite refreshed. I think I'll ask Jeremy to accompany me."

"That's a good idea."

"And you, too, Joanna. You haven't yet seen the Sapphire Pool. Or have you? Is that where you walked this morning?"

"No, I just strolled about the grounds."

"Then you must come with us! The pool is beautiful, the deepest blue, fed by one of the cold water springs down near the river. It's a lovely walk. And it will give you a chance to know Jeremy better."

I now welcomed the chance to know Jeremy better, although not for the reason my aunt had outlined. She dispatched me to search for him, and I found him at the far end of the front verandah, perched on the railing next to a wisteria vine loaded with lavender blooms. When I came up to him, he was scribbling in his notebook, a preoccupied look on his face, but he closed the notebook good-naturedly enough when I'd explained my mission.

"I'll be happy to walk with you and Aunt Alice to the Sapphire Pool. Indeed . . ." He paused, searching my face with his limpid eyes before continuing, ". . . after all that's happened, I think it's a good idea if you have an escort."

I sat down on the railing next to him. "Jeremy, what did you mean last night about sensing something malignant here at Milwood?"

He looked cautiously about before responding in a low whisper. "I—I hear strange noises at night. Footsteps in empty rooms. The lift going up and down, when everyone is supposed to be asleep. And the ghost . . . I saw that ghost just last week."

"The ghost!" My skin prickled with chill.

"It wasn't that Spanish soldier everyone talks about, but it *was* surrounded by a blue glow."

"Where did you meet it?"

"I didn't meet it, thank God, but I did see it. Up on the widow's walk around ten o'clock at night. Everyone else was in bed, but I couldn't sleep. I went out to sit beside the fountain in the front courtyard . . . seeking inspiration for a poem, you know."

I nodded. "What did it look like?"

"A figure in a long robe, surrounded by a blue light."

"You weren't mistaken?"

He gave me a wounded look. "You're asking if I imagined it? No, I didn't."

I reached out and touched his arm. "Jeremy, I'm sorry, I shouldn't have said that. I know what it's like to have people doubt your word when you're telling the truth."

"The way people doubted that you heard that voice outside the bathhouse, or that someone pushed you down the stairs?" he said.

"Yes. And you're right, there is something malignant about Milwood. I sensed it the moment I laid eyes on the place. What I really wanted to do was turn and run."

"Maybe you should have done just that."

"Maybe so. I've made up my mind, Jeremy, I'm going to get to the bottom of all this. But I'll need your help."

"What can I do?"

"Help me keep an eye on Aunt Alice. I can't be with her every moment if I'm going to play detective, and you're the only person here I feel I can trust."

He put his notebook aside and took both my hands. His eyes were serious, his manner intense. "Then we're in this together."

"Thank you. Thank you, Jeremy."

A rustling in the nearby bushes caught my attention. I twisted about to see Maybelle emerge from the courtyard with a basket of berries on her arm. When she saw Jeremy holding my hands, she stopped as abruptly as though she'd run into an invisible wall. Her face darkened with jealousy and pain, storm clouds covering the sun. I withdrew my hands from Jeremy's grasp and stood up, smiling down at Maybelle in a friendly manner to try to pass off the incident with Jeremy as a casual encounter.

"Hello!" I called. "It looks as though you've been very busy. Are those wild strawberries?"

She turned her head away for a moment in an obvious effort to control her emotions. When she looked back once more, her expression was bland, her voice normal. "Yes. Granny likes to cook with things from the woods . . . berries, greens, mushrooms. . . ."

While she circled the porch to the front steps, Jeremy and I strolled in her direction. She looked fetching, I thought, in her flower-sprigged dress, long white apron, and sunbonnet, the epitome of the bouncing country lass; but Jeremy, who had paused to make a quick entry in his notebook, seemed oblivious to her charms.

"We're going for a walk," I called out brightly, "Aunt Alice and Jeremy and I. Aunt Alice wants me to see the Sapphire Pool."

I'd been trying to make conversation, to fill the awkward moment with cheerful chatter, but I saw at once that I'd said the wrong thing. Her face darkened again as she flicked her glance back and forth between Jeremy and me like the crack of a whip wielded by an angry hand.

"I'm sure Jeremy would rather stay here and work on his poetry, but Aunt Alice is the one who insists that he accompany us," I told her now, trying to let her know that she had nothing to worry about.

But Jeremy unwittingly cancelled my efforts by looking up and saying, with a gallant smile as he slipped his notebook into his pocket, "Dear Joanna, what man could resist spending an hour with you! My poetry can wait until later."

So much for making Maybelle feel better, I thought wryly.

121

She stamped up the steps with a flounce of her skirts and a toss of her head.

"Have a nice walk," she said in a neutral tone as she passed by us and into the hotel.

We followed her in, where we found my aunt sitting in one of the wicker chairs under a potted palm, a copy of the latest *Saturday Evening Post* spread out in her lap.

"I've decided to stay here and read," she said. "You two go on without me. I do so want you to see that pool, Joanna."

"I'll sit here with you," I began, but she interrupted impatiently.

"How can I read if you're here distracting me? I'll stay right here in the lobby until you return. Now go on, please, but do me one favor." She pointed to her pink parasol, which lay on the floor beside her chair. "Carry that to keep the sun off your nose."

"But—"

"Go on. Scoot! Both of you!"

I saw now that she had never intended to walk with us. The whole thing had been a scheme to throw Jeremy and me into each other's company to further our romance. Jeremy cast me a concerned look above my aunt's head, saying as plainly with his eyes as though he spoke the words that he, too, did not think we should leave her alone.

But now she said sternly, "I've started an interesting story in this magazine, and you're bothering me. I insist that you leave me be."

"How far is this pool?" I asked Jeremy in a low tone.

"Not far. Maybe half a mile."

"If we hurry? . . ."

He nodded, then said to Aunt Alice, "Will you promise, my dear lady, that you'll stay right here in the lobby and not go walking around until we get back?"

"Yes, of course, although I don't see why that is necessary." She picked up the magazine and snapped the pages impatiently. "Will you please go?"

"The pool is out back," Jeremy said to me, "down past the stables." He bowed slightly while indicating the corridor leading toward the kitchen.

I curtsied in return, and we headed together down the corridor and out the side door into the kitchen courtyard. There we encountered Maybelle seated on a bench and stemming the strawberries.

"I thought you said your aunt was going with you," she remarked, animosity lurking behind her gaze like a skulking cat.

"She decided to read instead," I replied airily. After all, she had no claim on Jeremy. I could walk with him if I wished.

We crossed the bridge and strode briskly along the path past the chicken house toward the stables. Farm noises echoed around us in a homey chorus: the cluck of chickens, the lowing of cows, the bleat of goats, the nicker of a horse, and in the distance, the call of a turtle dove. The moldy odor from the stream blended with the rich steamy smell of the chicken and stable yards, cooking under the midday sun. In deference to my aunt's wishes, I did raise the parasol, although I would have preferred the sun's direct rays on my face to the filtered light that now bathed me in a pink glow. When we entered the stable yard we came across Simon, who was seated on the log bench mending tack.

"I'm going to show Joanna the Sapphire Pool," Jeremy announced.

Simon threw me a veiled look as though asking if I were still angry over the episode in the attic. Considering the strange things going on at Milwood, I was not prepared to forgive and forget Simon's statement about throttling me, even if it were spoken in jest. Therefore I merely said, as though he were a stranger I'd encountered by chance on the road, "Beautiful day for a walk, isn't it?"

He lifted one eyebrow and replied in a mocking tone, "Yes, beautiful."

Jeremy and I followed the path past the stable and continued along in front of a long carriage house, where a cinder drive made a broad sweep over a rustic bridge to circle through the trees toward the hotel. As we continued past the barn, I remarked, "Five double doors? That carriage house is big!"

Jeremy nodded. "Back when I was young, we used to have a lot of guests. Things were lively then, carriage rides in the afternoon, musicales in the evening. My father used to sing the latest songs to entertain the people, while my mother played the piano. . . ."

His voice trailed off, and for a moment he seemed lost in thought, as though reliving those happier times.

"What were your parents like?" I asked.

He walked for a while along the sun-dappled path without answering. We passed through a grove of gnarled oaks that spread their leafy arms above us, giants straining the light like water through green sieves to spatter on the pink canopy of my parasol.

"My father was quite different from Uncle Amos," he said at last. "Of course, that's to be expected, since my father was adopted. Uncle Amos was always stronger, more domineering, the spittin' image of Grandfather Rhodes, while my father was . . . well, quieter and—and gentler. My mother was very quiet, too, and frail. I don't think Grandmother liked her very much. In fact, I think Grandmother was somewhat indifferent to my father, too. She . . . well, she seemed partial to her own blood son."

"Was Rhodes partial to Amos, too?"

"No, and that's a funny thing. He seemed to love my father very much, different as they were. Of course, Grandfather's the one who found my father abandoned as a baby in that alley, over in Little Rock, and I think that made him believe he and my father were somehow linked by fate."

"A more fanciful notion than I would have expected, from what I've heard of Rhodes," I said.

Jeremy cocked his head and threw me a quizzical look. "My grandfather was a strange mixture of the romantic and the practical. There were times, when I was young, that he took me on his knee and told me stories about the medieval days, and about giants and dragons, and I felt close to him then, as though he were actually my blood kin."

He sounded so wistful that I almost told him what I had learned; but something held me back, a shyness about revealing the sordid details until I knew him better. As sensitive as he was, he just might go into an emotional decline if he learned his father had indeed been illegitimate, although that possibility must have occurred to him by now. But I knew there were still those straitlaced individuals in every community who, despite the broader attitudes toward sexual morality that had supposedly been ushered in by this brand-new twentieth century, would hold Jeremy in disregard if the truth of his background were made known.

"I believe he thought he was doing something wonderful by bringing the baby back to Milwood, since he and Grandmother couldn't have children," Jeremy went on. "But as it turned out—" Again he paused.

"As it turned out, two years later she did have Amos," I finished.

"Yes. And Uncle Amos, so I've been told, was a strong baby, a healthy baby, while my father was sickly and hard to handle, right up into his school-age years. I think maybe that's one of the reasons Grandmother came to like Uncle Amos better."

That made sense to me. And if, after all these years, Nell had finally learned the truth about Aunt Alice and Rhodes and their love child, she might well have gone into a rage, feeling used and betrayed, and could now be seeking revenge. With Rhodes out of the picture, there was little to hinder her from proceeding with plans to harm my aunt. Why she should want to hurt me, too, I couldn't fathom, unless she judged me guilty by association.

While Jeremy and I had been walking, absorbed in our conversation, the path had angled downward, growing steeper and rougher. Now we came to an area so eroded, with washed-out sandy places and guillies snaking through the exposed rocks, that we had to cease talking in order to concentrate on making our way safely to the bottom. We left the shelter of the trees and emerged into a rocky glade at the base of a bluff. Several thin streams of water sprang from the dun-colored rocks to spill into a bright blue pool that fluoresced in the sunlight.

"The Sapphire Pool!" I cried in delight. "Jeremy, it's beautiful!"

"It is, isn't it? I like to come here . . . to get away from the others, and to think and write."

We made our way over the rough ground to stand on the edge of the pool. Here and there bubbles rose to break on the surface, giving evidence of the springs underneath. The water near the surface appeared transparent, yet when I tried to see to the bottom of the pool, all I could focus on was that intense blue, growing darker as the water deepened until it finally became opaque.

"Must be deep," I said.

"It is. Granny Bennett says it's bottomless, but of course that can't be so. Still, these cold water springs sometimes well up out of underground caves, and I've heard you can dive into a pool like this and never come up again."

I shivered, looking into those icy blue depths. I pictured falling in and being dragged down, down, by my water-logged clothing to an underground cavern where I would float forever, hair streaming lazily among the bubbles, eyes staring sightlessly up at that false blue sky. Perhaps it was that disconcerting image or perhaps it was the heat, but the pool suddenly spun before me like a pinwheel.

"You look faint," Jeremy said, directing me to a rough-hewn bench beside the water. "Here, sit down."

"I'm all right," I said, but I found I was glad to sink down upon the bench beside Jeremy. I held onto the edge of the rough wood until my uneasiness passed. We rested together, staring into the hypnotic depths. I became aware of the sound of rushing water, over and above the water splashing into the pool from the bluffs.

"Is the river nearby?" I asked.

Jeremy nodded. "The stream behind the hotel empties into Brushwood Creek, which flows into the Ouachita. Circle on around this bluff, and you'll come to the old mill on Brushwood Falls. The river's just a hop, skip, and jump beyond."

"The name Milwood—"

"A combination of *mill* and Brush*wood*," Jeremy said, anticipating my question. "The mill was here even before Grandfather uncovered the hot springs. He bought the mill from the original owners, but he never did much with it, and now it's fallen into ruin. Come on, I'll show you."

"Do we have time?"

"It will just take a few extra minutes."

My wish to leave the edge of the pool caused me to acquiesce. The path was overgrown but passable, and we soon arrived at the mill, a weather-beaten structure missing some boards and shingles. The waterwheel itself still turned, creaking and splashing, propelled by the falls, a slick torrent pouring over a dam. I noticed thick insulated wires running from one of the windows to a nearby tree. Looping along to the next tree, then the next, the wires disappeared up the hill in the direction of the hotel. From inside the mill, in a section that seemed to have been recently repaired, came the soft whir of machinery.

"Simon's generator!" I exclaimed. "The one that sends electricity to the lift."

"He *had* to have it," Jeremy remarked flatly. "He said it was necessary, to keep up with the hotels in Hot Springs. Now we're even deeper in debt than we were before. Come on, I want to show you the grindstone."

A path had been cleared through a tumble of old boards and matted vines to the entrance of the mill. We picked our way along, keeping a sharp watch for water moccasins, until we stood inside the mill itself. We looked about in silence, awed, I think, by the joining of an earlier era, evidenced by the huge grindstone, with the modern electrical age, represented by the generator. Wind sighed through the rafters, releasing a sprinkle of dust to sift down from the loft above. The building murmured to itself as it shifted and settled on its foundation, infinitesimal movements too small to be seen by the human eye but revealed by the occasional soft snap, the creak of boards adjusting themselves to a more comfortable position. Over and above those sounds flowed the rush of water from outside, the rhythmical squeak of the waterwheel, the continued purr of machinery.

The grindstone was a huge gray thing, covered with small black droppings—signs of the mice, I decided, who had munched on the drift of flour and grain left after the mill shut down.

"The stone's made of novaculite," Jeremy said, breaking the silence. "It's supposed to be the best rock around for making grindstones, and it's quarried right near Hot Springs, on top of Indian Mountain. Maybe I can take you there someday on an outing."

Wouldn't that please Aunt Alice! I thought sardonically.

Actually, the trip sounded interesting. I still could not think of Jeremy as a lover, but I was beginning to like him as a cousin and friend. When he wasn't quoting that terrible poetry or acting like an affected fop, he had a certain boyish charm, an open desire to please, which was quite appealing.

"Perhaps we can do that someday," I said, "but right now we'd better get back to Aunt Alice."

Worry lines appeared between his brows, making him appear suddenly older, closer to his twenty-seven years. "Yes, you're right. I was having such a good time I almost forgot our troubles there for a moment."

We left the mill and hurried back along the path to the pool.

"One more brief delay," Jeremy said, his face brightening. "With that pink parasol, you deserve a bouquet of primroses.

128

They're just up the hillside. Wait on the bench, will you? I'll be right back."

He darted off before I could object, circling up the hill to one side where the bluff wasn't quite so steep. I felt that was wise, for the overhang above didn't look too stable to me. The spill of stones and boulders at the base of the bluff beside the pool showed that rock slides were not uncommon.

"Be careful!" I called.

"I will!"

His answer floated down from the hillside, where his figure flickered in and out among the leaves of the trees and bushes, then disappeared altogether. There seemed nothing to do but to sit on the bench, as he'd directed, and look once more into those bubbling depths. The afternoon sun was now beating down full-strength so, mindful of my aunt's warning, I positioned the parasol above my head to protect my nose from the burning rays. When the rustling sound came from the top of the bluff, I thought that Jeremy had clambered there to perch on the edge in what he would envision as a dramatic pose.

"Jeremy, I said be careful!" I called again as I rose and lowered the parasol, turning to look up at him. What I saw, instead, was a boulder shudder on the brink of the bluff, then break loose and careen toward me. I took an involuntary step backward and flailed my arms, tracing arabesques in the air with the parasol as my feet lost purchase. The boulder struck the bench with a splintering crash, then deflected sideways. I scrabbled my shoes on the crumbling muddy edge of the pool like a hen scratching for worms, but it was too late. With horror blooming in my mind, an unfolding of petals painted with pictures of drowned bodies in deep dark grottos, I toppled into the pool.

Chapter 11

The force of the fall drove me deep beneath the surface. After the heat of the sun, the shock of the cold water against my skin felt like an actual blow. I clawed at the water frantically, trying to climb back toward the air. Although I'd learned to swim with my younger brothers in a creek near our home back in Missouri, I was not a good swimmer, and my layers of clothing did indeed drag against my efforts to reach the surface, just as I'd foreseen. I opened my eyes and looked up through the glassy blue roof of my prison toward a diffracted glint of sun, knowing that there lay air and life. With a dawning of hope I saw the parasol floating above me, buoyed up by its wooden handle. I reached one hand as high as possible, flailing and kicking my way slowly upward until the handle came within my grasp. That frail support gave me enough leverage for a desperate pull, which brought my head above the surface of the water.

"Help! Jeremy, help!" I screamed.

I went under again, still holding onto the parasol. This time, aided by the handle, I sank only an arm's length below the surface and was again able to pull myself upward into the air.

"Help! Help me!"

I snatched a lungful of air before going under once more. This time I took hold of the parasol handle with both hands and flattened my body in the water, using a scissors kick to try to propel myself toward shore. I might as well have been swimming through syrup, for all the progress I seemed to make. Then, when I'd decided my struggles were in vain, I felt someone grab hold of the front of the parasol and begin to pull, dragging me through the water like a hooked fish. Soon I lay gasping and choking on the muddy bank. Jeremy clasped one of my hands and begged, "Joanna! Are you all right, Joanna? Can you speak to me?"

"J—Jer . . ."

"Yes! Thank God you're all right!"

"The ro—the rock . . ."

"It almost hit you. If you hadn't moved—"

"Jeremy?"

"What is it, Joanna?"

I struggled to sit up before answering. He placed an arm around me, supporting my head.

"Did . . . were—were you up on top of the bluff?"

"No." He gestured toward a bouquet of primroses, which now lay shattered on the path. "I picked those on the hillside, then started back down. That's when I saw the boulder. . . .

"You saw it happen?"

"I saw it break loose and fall. I yelled. . . ."

"Did it just . . . did it break loose of its own accord?"

His face turned ashen. "My God, you think someone pushed it."

"Did you see anyone up there?"

"No."

I sighed and leaned my face for a moment against his chest. "I'm getting tired of these accidents."

"Look, before we both panic, it's possible this one really *could* have been an accident," Jeremy said. "That is an unstable overhang, and rocks do fall from there all the time. I almost got hit here by a rock slide a couple of years ago. I should have warned you."

"You're sure you saw no one? Were you looking at the top

of the bluff all the time?"

"Not all the time, but I did glance over there a couple of times while I was on the hill, and I did see the boulder start to totter. Of course, there were bushes on either side. . . ."

"So you might not have noticed if that boulder had been given a little human help."

"I don't th . . . maybe not."

"My aunt . . . we must get back to the hotel!"

I pushed myself forward, away from Jeremy, and struggled to rise. My water-soaked clothing felt as though it were lined with lead. Jeremy jumped to his feet and gallantly helped me to stand. I wrung the water from the hems of my petticoat and skirt, then took the pins from my dripping hair, allowing the bun to uncoil down my back. I shoved the pins into my pocket, where I felt the remains of my aunt's letter to Rhodes, now a disintegrating sodden mess.

Who had known for certain that we were hiking to the pool? I asked myself. Certainly Mr. Lock and Maybelle and Simon. Of course, I'd talked about the proposed outing in the dining room, on the front verandah, in the lobby, in the kitchen courtyard, and at the stables. Anyone could have overheard. It would have been a fairly sure thing that sooner or later I would rest on the bench beside the water, presenting an ideal opportunity for someone to either smash me with a boulder or knock me into the pool or both.

Again I was left with the question *Why?* and for that I still had no answer.

"I'll go up and search the top of the bluff if you want me to," Jeremy said.

Here was another brave offer from a man I'd once pegged as a toad. That should teach me not to make hasty judgments of people's characters, I thought.

"I'll go with you."

I retrieved my aunt's ruined parasol, not wanting to clutter the landscape by leaving it there on the ground. As it turned out, I was glad to have brought the parasol with me, for it

132

proved useful as a walking stick on the steeper portions of the hillside. When Jeremy and I reached the top of the bluffs, we searched the grass and bushes, looking for anything—a broken branch, a footprint, a dropped handkerchief—which might give us a clue as to whether or not someone had lurked up there waiting for us. We examined in particular the spot where the boulder had broken loose, taking care not to go too close, for the raw wound at the edge of the bluff, still bleeding dirt and small stones, looked slippery in the sunlight. The only thing I found, exposed by the slide, was a tiny arrowhead, perfectly formed.

"That's a beauty," Jeremy said, taking it from me to look at it more closely.

"What tribe do you suppose it's from?"

"Could be Caddo, but I'm not sure. The hot springs area was considered a sacred place, a place of healing, and many different tribes used to come here, even warring tribes. This was called the Valley of Peace. Any Indians who met here were automatically at peace until they left the sanctuary."

"The Valley of Peace?" I asked, sweeping my gaze across the view. "Under the circumstances, that seems ironic."

From this vantage point I could see the Ouachita River curling through the valley about a quarter of a mile away, with the blue mountain range beyond. It did look peaceful in the afternoon sun, with birds soaring lazily on the thermal currents. But in the distance toward the southwest gathered a line of dark clouds, harbingers of an approaching storm that might well bring rain before nightfall.

"I wish we could have peace at Milwood," I mused, "but I feel as though we're caught in an unending storm."

"Come on, let's get back to the hotel," Jeremy replied.

As we scrambled down through the trees, we talked again about the accident at the pool, and I had to agree that there seemed to be no evidence pointing to anything other than an unfortunate incident in which I happened to be in the wrong place at the wrong time.

When we arrived at the stable yard I looked about for Simon, but he had disappeared. As we were about to leave the clearing, heading along the path for the chicken house, Simon hurried out of the woods, his shirt plastered to his chest with perspiration, his rumpled hair sporting a couple of twigs. I noticed, my mind quickening with suspicion, that he came from the direction of the pool.

"What happened to you?" he exclaimed as he took in my wet clothing.

"I fell into the water," I said, searching his face for a guilty reaction.

What he did was laugh. "You have a penchant for accidents."

Flaring with anger at his lack of concern, I said, "I'll just have to be more careful."

"Yes, I think you will."

After Jeremy and I had hurried out of earshot, I murmured, "I don't think I like him very much."

"He can be cruel sometimes."

"Has he been cruel to you?"

Jeremy gave me a wry sideways look. "He and Henry both have had their fun teasing me. I—uh—well, it's no matter. There's not a lot going on in the way of amusement around here, so I guess they see me as a source of entertainment."

Right then I didn't like Henry much, either. Jeremy might not be as masculine as his cousins, but that did not give them a license to torment him, no matter how bored they might be at Milwood. I made a resolution that neither Henry nor Simon would ever tease Jeremy in my presence and get away with it.

"Henry says everyone here holds three or four jobs. What are your jobs?" I asked.

"I'm the . . . what am I? The corresponding secretary, I suppose you could say. I write the business letters for the hotel, pay the bills when we have the money, keep two copies of all the books and records, work like that. It still gives me time to write my poetry, for which I'm grateful."

134

I sighed, wishing I could tell Jeremy in a tactful way that his poetry was bad. Now that I was beginning to see depth and richness to his character, to see the gold nuggets that did indeed lie hidden beneath the false glitter of the pyrite, I believed he might be able to write something good if someone would just give him a nudge in the right direction. I could not pursue it then, however, for we arrived back at the hotel where we hurried at once to the main lobby, driven by our mutual concern for my aunt.

My aunt and his grandmother, I added to myself, realizing that the concept of Alice McPherson as "the other woman" still had not sunk in with me.

We found Aunt Alice still seated comfortably in the wicker chair with her magazine in hand.

"Back already?" she asked, looking up with an eager smile. I could tell she was hoping for signs of a budding romance. When she saw my bedraggled clothing and damp hair, her smile changed to a frown.

"You *didn't* fall in?" she asked in a scandalized voice, showing that she knew quite well I had.

"Yes. Jeremy saved me."

That brought back the smile. "Dear boy, how brave! I'm so proud! And so grateful!"

She pushed herself out of the chair to plant a kiss on his cheek.

"I'm afraid I've ruined your parasol," I said sheepishly, holding out the wooden handle with its limp mud-stained rag.

"Oh dear!" she cried in dismay. "That's the only one I brought."

Jeremy took the parasol from me. "She says I saved her, but that's not altogether true. She might have drowned if she hadn't been able to catch hold of this. It's the parasol that deserves all the credit." He put one hand over his heart while holding the parasol dramatically at arm's length before him. "I shall write a poem. It will be called 'Ode to a Pink Parasol.'"

I sighed. The bogus Jeremy had returned. My aunt did not

135

seem to mind.

"Sweet boy, you're so modest, giving the praise to the umbrella. But then, that's the way you are, the way you've always been. Sit here beside me and recite for me again that beautiful poem you wrote in honor of my arrival."

"If you'll excuse me, I must go change," I murmured.

My aunt dismissed me with a languid wave of her hand, her attention riveted on Jeremy's face. Leaving her in the safety of his company, I hurried for the stairs where I met Henry coming down.

"Another accident?" he asked, lifting his eyebrows.

Anger exploded inside me at the amused condescension in his voice.

"No, it's such a hot day I decided to take a swim," I responded airily.

Pushing past him, I continued up the stairs with my chin in the air, pursued by his mocking chuckle.

Chapter 12

The next several days drifted by without incident. The quiet routine of taking the waters with my aunt each morning, followed by a rest period, then by a good meal and leisurely walks about the hotel grounds in the afternoon, lulled me into thinking I had indeed let my imagination run away with me. I began to believe that the "accidents" in the bathhouse and at the Sapphire Pool had been just that, although I still could not explain away those hands that had pushed me down the stairs.

One morning, after my aunt had fallen asleep in our rooms following her massage, I decided to slip down to the kitchen for a cup of tea. Still eschewing the lift, I had just descended from the third floor to the second and had started around the railing for the top of the steps, which would lead me down to the lobby, when I heard a faint groan coming from the west wing hallway. The hairs lifted on the back of my neck as all the fears I had suppressed for the past few days came rushing back upon me full force. It was from a room off that corridor that I'd seen the strange face looking out the window the morning my aunt had collapsed in the bathhouse. It was from the darkness in that corridor that I'd first sensed someone or something following me the night I'd been pushed down the stairs.

With my pulse pounding in my throat I tiptoed down the corridor, trying to pinpoint the room from which the sound had emanated. Automatically I counted off the doors: *One, two, three . . .*

At the sixth door I paused and pressed my ear against the wood. From inside came muffled noises—sliding footsteps, faint clanking sounds as though a heavy chain were being dragged across the floor, grunts and groans that made me think of a soul trapped in Hell's torment.

There were only two answers, I decided: Either the Spanish ghost was walking around in there, or that room housed a prisoner.

My first instinct was to run. If a hollow-eyed ghoul in a coat of Spanish mail opened that door, I suspected I would drop dead on the spot. I inhaled sharply, struggling to control my swimming senses. There could not possibly be a ghost in that room, argued my intellect. Only in tales created by man's imagination did such beings as ghosts exist. Ergo, the chained creature in there had to be a prisoner. Who the poor devil could be I had no idea, but I determined now to set him free.

Cautiously I took the knob in hand and tried to turn it, but the door was locked. Throwing aside all caution, I rattled the knob and called out, "Who's in there? Do you need help?"

All noise inside the room ceased at once. Even as I stood holding my breath in order to pick up any whispered plea, so did I now get the feeling that the same thing was happening on the other side of the door.

After a moment I called again, "Don't be afraid. Who are you? Can you speak?"

The silence beyond the door remained complete. My nerves began to prickle. Why should the person inside that room keep still? Surely a prisoner, hearing that help was at hand, would call out.

Determined to try one more time, I cried, "I'll help you if I can. If you can't speak, if you're gagged, then make a sound in your throat to let me know you're in trouble and need help."

The silence was now so thick it oozed from under the door like pudding. Alarm bells pealed inside my head, telling me in terms not to be denied that I had stumbled once more upon a pocket of Milwood's malevolence. When I heard a harsh, ragged inhalation of breath only a couple of inches away from me on the other side of the door, I took a step backward, no longer wanting to meet the person who lurked there. Turning, I fled toward the far end of the corridor, intending to dash around the corner of the west wing and down the side stairs; but when, behind me, there came the sharp rattle of the knob, I panicked and jerked open the door nearest me, slipping through and closing it quickly. I fumbled for the lock and realized, with sinking heart, that it was broken. Desperately I turned, pressing my back against the door as I looked around the room for a hiding place. The furniture, draped in white dust covers, loomed like snow-covered mountain peaks in a silent landscape.

Under the bed, I thought, then rejected the idea at once, sure that was the first place anyone would look.

That chair?

I lifted the dust cover and peeked underneath but realized that my huddled form would not be disguised, that it would reveal itself, to a searching eye, as being separate from that of the chair. The same would be true of the desk against one wall.

I fled on tiptoe across the room and peeked into the closet. I found it stuffed with feather beds, each stored in its own white covering, a billowy pile of cumulous clouds now condemned to darkness.

The sound of a heavy, measured tread in the corridor outside filled my veins with ice. With the decision forced upon me, I entered the closet and quietly closed the door. It hung slightly askew on its hinges, allowing a faint line of light to penetrate the gloom. Quickly I squirmed in behind the pile of feather beds and crouched down, pulling the top bed over my head. Now I huddled in total darkness, wrapped in a hot stuffy nest that immediately made my temperature soar.

The steps passed by without haste, continued toward the end of the corridor, then came back again. When they paused outside the door of the room in which I was hiding, I drew my body into an even tighter knot inside the feather beds, scarcely daring to breathe.

Go on. Go away.

Mentally I projected the command toward the person outside, to no avail. The knob clicked, and the opened. The footsteps advanced into the room, then stopped. I envisioned the person slowly turning on one heel and searching every cranny, every shadowed corner, through slitted eyes.

My nose began to tickle from the dust and the smell of the feathers, a faint sweet smell carrying a pungent undertone. I closed my eyes and clenched my face like a fist, working my nostrils about in an effort to ward off a sneeze. Tears rolled from beneath my eyelids as the need to sneeze grew ever stronger. Knowing I could not hold off much longer, I finally inched one hand toward my face while praying that I would not scrape against the ticking or disturb the position of the feather bed over my head. Just in time I pinched my nose shut to halt the pending explosion. The heat had built inside my cushioned prison until I felt I might soon burst into flame, a victim of spontaneous combustion. Perspiration sprang from my scalp to soak my hair while my clothing clung to my body in a damp embrace, as sodden as it had been when I'd fallen into the Sapphire Pool. The air inside the small pocket surrounding my gasping mouth grew more humid and stale with each exhalation. *I could suffocate in here,* I thought with rising panic. If the person outside did not leave soon, I would be forced to reveal myself and take my chances against that unknown danger, for the known dangers of my hiding place were becoming all too clear.

Just when I thought I could bear it no longer, the footsteps moved, pacing even closer. With mounting terror, I followed the progress of those steps toward the closet.

Don't move. Don't panic, I told myself fiercely.

The sound of the opening closet door grated against my ears like thunder. It was followed by a long moment of silence. I had the irrational feeling that the feather beds had become transparent and that I stood revealed before those probing eyes. My muscles tightened, my skin crawled as I steeled myself for the feather beds to be jerked away from my body. I remembered times, as a child, when the suspense while playing "Hide and Seek" had become so unbearable that I'd jumped from my hiding place and shown myself to the seeker just to get it over with. I had the impulse to do that now.

Keep still, commanded my inner voice. *Do not move. Do not move.*

Finally the closet door closed and the footsteps retreated, pacing slowly across the room. There was another pause, a rustling sound, and I pictured the person peering under the bed. After another moment of silence, the hall door clicked open and the steps moved through, followed by the sound of the door closing once more. I heard the steps retreat, steadily and deliberately, down the corridor.

Still I waited, telling myself to keep quiet. What if the person had taken off his shoes and crept back to open the door? What if I were to edge out from behind the feather beds and step from the closet, only to find myself staring straight into a pair of cold cruel eyes?

I sucked at the spent air, my brain fuzzy from lack of oxygen. I could not stay covered up any longer. For better or for worse, I had to emerge into the open air where I could breathe once more.

I wormed out of my nest and reached for the closet knob. My hand trembled when the thought struck me that I might find the door locked, but it opened with no problem. Feeling much relieved, I peered around the corner into the room. When I saw no one lurking in the shadows, I stepped forth, shaking out my skirts. My arms and legs felt weak, as though all the strength had washed from my body. It was a good thing, I decided, that I hadn't been called upon to try to defend myself.

I had no desire to go out just yet and chance meeting the hunter in that hallway. I sank down on the edge of the bed, trying to collect my strength. Gradually I became aware that the clanking had begun again, muffled by distance. I'd read that a glass, held to the wall, could sometimes work as an amplifier of sound, but when I rose and searched for such a utensil, I found that this particular room had no water closet. I tried cupping my hands against the wall nearest to the strange sounds, but it didn't work. Of course, I was not in the room adjacent to the noises, so I suspected that had something to do with my failure.

I moved to the window and peered through the curtains toward the bathhouses, pondering again the face I'd seen in the window that first morning. Who could possibly be making those strange sounds, and why? As I stood there, Maybelle came out the kitchen door and rang the bell for the noon meal.

Now what was I to do! I asked myself in dismay. The bell would awaken my aunt and she would get up, expecting me to come at once to prepare her for the dining room. I paced away from the window, clenching my fists at my sides, and stopped to press my ear once more against the wall. The clanking had ceased. Now I heard the low murmur of voices, but I could distinguish no words. Did that mean two people were in the room? I listened again but could not tell whether the voices were masculine or feminine. If they were conversing, perhaps they were not ready to come out into the hall. I moved to the door and opened it a crack, peering cautiously around the edge. When I saw that the corridor stood empty, I slipped through, closed the door behind me, and dashed to the end of the hallway and around the corner. I continued to run until I reached the stairs, where I glanced back over my shoulder. My breath expelled in a huff of relief at seeing no one behind me. I proceeded at a more sedate pace down to the main floor and around to the front lobby. There I found my aunt seated in her favorite wicker chair, her hands planted firmly upon the top of her cane.

"You went off and left me again," she said accusingly. "You look a fright. Hurry upstairs and tidy yourself, or we'll be late to the dining room."

The prospect of going back upstairs filled me with dismay, but I could think of no good excuse to disobey. Wishing to avoid the stairs, I sped to the lift and slammed the door shut with a clang behind me. As the cage shuddered upwards, I began plotting ways to persuade my aunt to abandon our suite upstairs and move to the first floor. I peered nervously through the grillwork as I passed the second floor and started with shock when I caught sight of a tall man striding away down the corridor. He glanced over his shoulder, his face contorted in a scowl, and for one bone-chilling moment I stared full into the baleful eyes of Henry Hampton. As the lift carried me upward, he leapt for the stairs leading to the third floor, and I realized, with my breath catching in my throat, that he was coming after me.

Chapter 13

I arrived at the third floor a few seconds ahead of Henry and slammed open the door of the lift to dash down the hall toward our suite.

"Joanna!" he called in a commanding tone as he topped the stairs.

Knowing that flight was useless, that I'd never make it to our door in time, I turned to face him, trying to present as strong a front as possible. When he saw that I'd stopped, he slowed from a lope to a stride. His eyes blazed toward me like two green stars.

"I've been trying to talk with you alone for days, but you've managed to put yourself always in the company of others. Why do you do that? Why have you been avoiding me?" he demanded.

Anger flamed through me at the memory of his audacious kiss. "Surely you know why!"

He shrugged. "Can I help it if your beauty overwhelms me and tempts me to rash action?"

At his teasing tone my anger increased. I felt insulted, as though I were a servant girl in some cheap novel who was being pursued by the lecherous master of the house. I was not Henry Hampton's servant, nor was I about to become his doxy. If he wanted that kind of entertainment, he'd have to make a trip to

Hot Springs, where I understood such services were readily available.

"If you can't restrain yourself, then I certainly do not wish to be alone with you," I said sharply.

He reached out and touched my arm, his eyes smoldering in a way that sent my pulse skittering. "Are you sure?"

Emotions tumbled through me in full spate like water over Brushwood Falls. To my horrified surprise, I found my knees softening in response to the heat radiating from his body while my lips tingled with the sudden wish to be explored once more by his seeking tongue. Shame, combined with my suspicions regarding his presence just now on the second floor, gave me the strength to break away.

"Do not touch me, sir! I told you that before."

"Yes, you did, but I got the feeling you didn't mean it."

"You were mistaken. Now, if you'll excuse me, I have to wash up and get back to my aunt downstairs."

I marched through the door into our suite and slammed it hard behind me. I hurried to the water closet and bathed the perspiration from my face, then brushed my hair and rearranged it with shaking hands. There was no doubt about it; Henry Hampton possessed the ability to wreck my composure. The fact that a part of me welcomed his attentions was a shocking revelation. I had not known that I could feel so wanton just at the touch of a man's hand. My mother, despite her seven children, had never discussed sexual matters with me. It may seem surprising, in these modern times, that I could have grown up so naive, but the truth is I did not really learn the facts of life until I studied nursing. Then the facts had been just that, "the facts," with no indication of the power that emotion plays in the interaction between a man and woman. I wanted Henry to kiss me again. I wanted him to touch me. . . .

My breathing quickened, misting the mirror. I clenched my fists and closed my eyes, concentrating on blue skies and quiet waters, anything to dispel the desire uncoiling inside my body like a fern frond, which begins as a tight bud, then opens to receive the heat of the sun.

You cannot love him, you cannot trust him!

I struck one fist hard against the side of the sink. The pain that jarred through my wrist dealt the final blow necessary to stem the tide of my emotions. Once more in control, I smoothed the skirt of my uniform and hurried back out into the hall. Despite my resolve, my heart thudded when I saw Henry still there, leaning against the wall with his arms folded across his chest.

"Even when you're flustered, you're beautiful," he said.

I had the uneasy feeling he knew exactly what he was doing to me.

"You are rude and impertinent," I said coldly, then added, deciding to take the offensive, "What were you doing on the second floor just now?"

"Looking for you," he replied.

One corner of his mouth tilted up in a slight smile, while his eyes held mine with that same mocking challenge I'd seen him use so often. His remark, tossed off in a light tone, might have been without hidden meaning, yet I found myself wondering if he had indeed been the person who'd opened that closet door just a few minutes earlier. If so, then what did he have to do with the strange noises in that locked room? What cat-and-mouse game was he playing?

"I can't imagine why you were looking for me there," I said in an offhand tone.

"Maybe it's because you're a young woman who pokes her nose into things which aren't her business."

My spine stiffened and I fixed him with a look I hoped was daunting. "Anything concerning my aunt's safety is my business."

I marched away from him. With just a couple of his long strides, he was by my side.

"Joanna, can we declare a truce?"

"I don't know. Can we?"

"I . . . actually, I like you very much."

"You have a strange way of showing it."

"Some women might think a kiss was a good way of showing it."

I felt a telltale blush spread across my face. "I'm not just any woman."

"So I've noticed. Perhaps you already have someone on the string?"

"Now who's poking his nose into something that isn't his business?"

The fact was I did not have anyone "on the string," as he'd so crudely put it. One of the doctors where I'd studied had once professed a passion for me, but he'd been a sixty-year-old widower, thrice married, with five grown children and four grandchildren, so I hadn't taken him seriously.

At the door of the lift Henry gave me a formal bow while saying, "I'll leave you now, Miss Forester. Please remember, things aren't always what they seem."

With those cryptic words, he stepped back and watched while the lift carried me down out of sight. His statement left me more confused than ever. If he did know something about that locked room and if he'd been trying to tell me so, then why hadn't he come right out with it? Henry Hampton was proving to be a summer complication I hadn't expected. I felt betrayed by my own body and its response to his presence.

I continued thinking about Henry during the noon meal. Jeremy had joined my aunt and me, at her request, and they'd begun reminiscing about a balloon ascension they'd once witnessed in Hot Springs, a story that did not require my participation except for an occasional smile and nod. This left me free to puzzle over that room upstairs. If the person I'd heard had been in there of his own free will, then why the groans? Why hadn't he answered when I'd called? I shivered, wondering who I would have encountered if I hadn't stayed hidden in the closet. Would it have been Henry or someone else . . . perhaps the person who had pushed me down the stairs? I did not know the identity of the person who'd been searching for me, but he knew my identity—I'd revealed that when I'd made the rescue offer at the door.

Henry had said he'd been looking for me. . . . What did he mean, *Things aren't always what they seem?* Just as I'd wondered in the bathhouse about the *real* Charlotte, now I puzzled over the *real* Henry, who seemed friendly at times, hostile at others, sometimes distant, sometimes too close for comfort. Things might not always be what they seemed, but Henry was so complex I couldn't determine how he was supposed to seem or how I could ever sort out the contradictions.

"What's the matter, little lady? You daydreamin' again about that beau in St. Louis?"

Albert Lock's booming voice from the table next to ours all but rattled the dishes. I knew he must be desperate for attention. My aunt had made such a point of excluding him from our mealtime conversation that he was bound to have been hurt by the snub, but he was not one to be put off easily.

"I have no beau in St. Louis," I said, "but you're right, I was daydreaming. How are you today, Mr. Lock?"

"I ain't improvin' as fast as I'd hoped. The old foot's still swole up like a melon. Got to get back out on the road, make the rounds of my regular customers, afore someone else moves in on my territory. Here, I got somethin' for you."

He beamed at me, his face a full moon rising. With the gesture of a magician producing flowers from his sleeve, he pulled from his vest pocket a round tin container with a label pasted on top: *Honeysuckle Salve.*

"Just take a whiff a that, if you wanta smell somethin' good!"

I snapped off the lid and sniffed at the cloying sweetness that wafted up from the slick pink surface of the salve.

"Just one small sample from the fine line of Perkins Products I peddle in these parts," he said proudly. "You can keep that, a gift from me. It's good for just about anything that ails you—sprains, sunburn, poison ivy, seven year itch."

But not gout, I thought.

"Thank you, Mr. Lock, that's very nice of you."

I snapped the lid back on and slipped the tin into my own pocket. He was quite pathetic in his way, I thought, just a fat, crude, aging, lonely man trying to make a living.

"I'm a poet and I know it," he went on, grinning at Jeremy. He proceeded to recite in a singsong voice:

> *Albert Lock from Little Rock*
> *Peddles products 'round the block,*
> *Over hill and over dale.*
> *What you want he's got for sale.*

He burst into a loud laugh as he reached over and slapped Jeremy on the shoulder. "What do ya think, sonny? Can I versify or can't I?"

Jeremy looked pained; Aunt Alice looked incensed. Albert Lock seemed oblivious to their disdain. He forged right on, now addressing me.

"I been talkin' with Granny out in the kitchen. She says she can brew me a potion out of some leaves she finds in the woods that'll help my foot. I think I'll give 'er a try."

"Granny makes her own medicines," Jeremy told me. "She uses roots and leaves and tree bark, and has quite a collection of 'cures' over in her cabin near the old mill. Some of the country people around here come to her instead of going to the doctors in Hot Springs. It upsets Henry."

"Why?"

"He doesn't hold with old wives' remedies. I think he still dreams of becoming a doctor himself someday. He'd like to start a proper clinic right here at Milwood, you know."

I hadn't known that, but I received the news with interest. Here was one more piece to the complex puzzle that was Henry Hampton.

"If her medicine works, I could maybe get the Perkins people to bottle it," Albert Lock put in. "We could call it

149

'Granny's Gout Cure.' What do you think?"

"You'd better test it first and see how you fare."

"Yes, I'm gonna do just that."

Maybelle came in pushing a cart with a steaming cobbler and a glass pitcher holding thick yellow cream. The smell of hot peaches smothered in syrup perfumed the air, making my mouth water.

"Look what I made, Jeremy," Maybelle said eagerly. "Peach cobbler, your favorite."

"Thank you, Maybelle, but I don't believe I'll have dessert today," he replied.

Her shoulders sagged and the joy faded from her face. She blinked back tears as she spooned cobbler into individual bowls for Mr. Lock, my aunt, and me.

"Smells wonderful," Mr. Lock said, smacking his lips. "I just believe I'll probably end up with seconds on this."

As it was, he ended up with thirds, dolloping cream over all three helpings. When he'd finished, he opened his vest while smothering a belch. Then he reached out and took a piece of ham, which he ate with just as much relish as he'd shown for the very first bite of the meal.

"I like to leave the table with the taste of salt in my mouth," he explained.

I thought that taking smaller portions and leaving the table sooner might help Mr. Lock's gout just as effectively as the hot bath treatments and Granny's brew, but it wasn't my place to say so.

"Are you ready to soak that foot again?"

The sound of the deep voice coming from the direction of the dining room door flashed through me like the lightning that was beginning to flicker in the clouds outside the window. I peered sideways from beneath lowered lashes as Henry advanced into the room toward Albert Lock.

"If you say it's time, then I guess it's time," Mr. Lock replied. "But after this good meal, I'm likely to fall asleep in there."

"I'll stay with you," Henry said. "Besides, you can sleep if you want to. It's just your foot that'll be in the water today." Glancing toward me, he asked in a casual tone, "Did you enjoy the meal?"

"Yes, thank you," I replied, my voice sounding stiff even to my own ears. "Maybelle is an excellent cook."

I'd hoped the compliment might placate her, but I was not the one she'd needed to hear it from. With her mouth in a pout, she slid a resentful look toward me, then busied herself removing the soiled dishes from the tables.

While Henry helped Mr. Lock stand and adjust his crutches, the drummer bellowed, "Say, Henry, did I ever tell you about the time I rode on the stage to Hot Springs and we got held up by the James boys?"

"Yes, but tell me again," Henry replied pleasantly enough. "A story like that bears repeating."

That was all the encouragement that Albert Lock needed. As he hobbled toward the door, assisted by Henry, he intoned in the declaratory fashion of a man beginning a long saga, "Back in 1874 it was, when thieves and bushwhackers had this country by the tail. I was a young man then, just startin' out in the trade. Caught the stage at Malvern and we set off on that rocky road, not a good road like we got today. Anyway, there was three conveyances in that caravan—the stage and two wagons that acted as ambulances. We had us some important people along that day, includin' Governor John Burbank of the Dakota Territory. . . ."

His voice faded away as they passed through the door and turned down the corridor. My aunt stared after them, her face filled with indignation. Throwing back her shoulders and lifting her chin, she gave a sarcastic snort.

"Humph! He was not on that stage when the James brothers committed their nefarious deed, but *I* was."

She proceeded to repeat the full story, which I'd heard many times, of how five horsemen wearing blue army overcoats had stopped the vehicles about a half mile beyond a watering hole along the route and had robbed the thirty passengers of their watches, jewelry, and money.

"There was a traveling drummer with us that day, a tobacco salesman from Memphis, but I can assure you we were not accompanied by Albert Lock from Little Rock," she concluded firmly.

Jeremy's glance slid past mine. His smile, so slight and quick as to be almost nonexistent, shared with me a fond amusement over my aunt's desire not to be bested by anyone, even an inconsequential salesman of Perkins Products.

"I shall now sit in the lobby and read some more in the *Post*," my aunt announced. "You two go off for another walk, but be careful, Joanna. Don't fall into any more pools."

She was matchmaking again, which was fine with me. I'd been dying to get Jeremy alone to tell him about the noises I'd heard in that locked room. With Henry out of the way at the bathhouse with Mr. Lock, this seemed an ideal time to do some sleuthing, if Jeremy were willing.

We deposited my aunt once more in her favorite seat in the lobby. Then, seeking privacy, I led Jeremy down the west corridor to the ballroom, which adjoined one end of the dining room. There I drew him inside and quickly closed the big double doors. When I'd finished reviewing my experience, to his exclamations of surprise and horror, he said, "Remember? I've heard strange noises, too! I've heard the lift go up and down late at night, and I've heard footsteps in rooms that were supposed to be empty. Then there was that ghostly figure I saw up on the widow's walk. . . ."

"Could you get a key to that room on the second floor?" I interrupted. "Could we slip up there now and look inside?"

He nodded. "The box with the keys to all the rooms is in the office behind the front desk. I'll get the key and return. Wait here."

He slipped back out through the doors and closed them behind him. I turned and advanced across the vast expanse of wooden floor, dusty now from disuse. I'd only glanced through the doors a couple of times before without coming inside, so I was not really acquainted with this room where Jeremy's father and mother had once performed to entertain the guests. Now I saw with interest that there was a stage at the west end of the room, which still held a huge square piano and ornate gilt chairs for the musicians. Floor-to-ceiling windows, arched at the top with a fan pattern in leaded glass and draped on either side in red velvet fringed in gold, ran along the entire length of the south wall. The room now lay shrouded in air that seemed made of gray gauze, which brightened momentarily as lightning flashed outside, then dimmed again to the tune of the rumbling thunder. The many prismed chandeliers, disturbed by the vibrations, set up a tinkling protest. I saw a drapery move at a window near the east end of the room, where French doors stood slightly ajar, leading into the dining room. Fearing that the window was open and that rain might soon pour in to warp the floor, I hurried across to close it before the storm began. My shoes tapped against the floor, and I imagined women in full-skirted ball gowns, men in frock coats and ruffled shirts, swirling to the music as the violinists sawed away at their strings accompanied by a pianist who swept up and down the keyboard in rippling arpeggios. My plain blue uniform with its prim white collar and cuffs seemed even plainer when compared with that imagined splendor, dresses made of silk, taffeta, moire, velvet. . . .

The drapery before me moved again, a puzzling phenomenon, for a brilliant burst of lightning through the panes showed me that the window was closed. It also showed me something else equally puzzling: The drapery, hanging in regal folds like the skirt of a ball gown, had grown a pair of feet.

Chapter 14

Emboldened by the knowledge that Jeremy would soon be returning, I whipped the drapery aside. There I saw Maybelle huddled against the window frame. Her eyes were swollen, her face contorted, and I decided she'd taken refuge in the ballroom to sob out her grief over Jeremy's spurning of her love offering. As we confronted each other, she burst out, "Jezebel! You can't be satisfied with just Simon or Henry, can you? You have to capture Jeremy, too!"

"Believe me, Maybelle, I am not romantically interested in Jeremy."

"But I don't believe you. I hate you. I wish you'd die!"

She pushed past me and fled, sobbing, through the dining room doors. I started to follow her but paused, realizing that Jeremy would soon be returning with the key and would wonder where I'd gone. I reasoned that even if I were able to convince Maybelle that I had no designs on Jeremy, which I doubted I'd be able to do no matter how much I protested, there could still be no future for her with him. Better, I decided, not to fill her with false hopes.

Thunder shook the chandeliers again, while a sudden rush of rain pounded against the windows. The light dimmed and thickened inside the room, as though night had come at noon. I made my way back across the floor to the stage, where I pushed aside the fringed shawl that covered the piano, then lifted the hinged lid away from the keys. I saw that several of the ivories were missing, leaving those keys dark and rough, like rotting teeth in a long thin smile. Although I was only an average piano player, I did know a few songs, such as "Jeanie with the Light Brown Hair" and "Flow Gently, Sweet Afton", so I now picked out some chords, wincing at the jangly sound. The name stenciled on the face of the piano was Chickering, a fine old name in pianos, but this instrument had been allowed to deteriorate. I was sure that a piano tuner would have been one of the first luxuries to fall by the wayside when Milwood had been forced to economize.

Jeremy reentered and came to join me at the piano.

"What a shame," he said, shaking his head at the discordant sound.

But my mind was now on more pressing matters. "Did you get the key?"

In answer, he held up a long key with a trefoil head, similar to the key to our suite. A tag tied through one loop of the trefoil bore the floor and room number.

"There are two keys for every room, and both the keys to that room were hanging in the box at the office," he said.

"Then someone has returned them. There may have been two people in there this morning. I thought I heard voices at one point, but I couldn't tell what was being said."

We left the ballroom and slipped around to the far end of the west wing and up the back stairs to the second floor. Now that Jeremy was with me to lend protection, my curiosity flamed up, burning away fear. At last some of Milwood's malevolence was about to be opened like a boil. What corruption might pour forth I did not know, but one thing I did know, speaking as a nurse, was that poison had to be drained from a wound before it could heal. The sickness gnawing at Milwood had, until now, remained unidentified, but perhaps I was about to uncover a symptom that could help me make a diagnosis. My pulse quickened as we approached the door. I heard no noises now. If a person was imprisoned there, perhaps he was sleeping. I wondered who brought food, who took care of the sanitation problems that would exist if this were indeed a jail.

Jeremy pressed his ear against the door, then glanced toward me and shook his head. He fitted the key into the lock and tried to turn it. When nothing happened, he jiggled the key and tried again. Finally he withdrew the key and checked the numbers on the tag against the number stenciled on the door. He lifted his eyebrows and shrugged his shoulders, expressing bewilderment. He tried the key once more without success, then bent and examined the lock.

"It's been changed," he murmured.

"When?" I asked in surprise, thinking there would have been no time during the noon meal for someone to change a lock.

He followed my train of thought. "I don't mean today, but sometime in the past few months."

I leaned over and looked at the gouged wood where the old lock had been removed and the new one inserted. Although the area had been revarnished, those scars, combined with the shiny newness of the lock, attested to the accuracy of Jeremy's surmise. Leaning closer, I tried to peer through the keyhole. My field of vision was severely limited, and the gloom created by the storm further hampered my efforts. Still, the area I could see, fuzzy though it appeared, showed me something that I hadn't expected.

"The room is empty!" I said.

"You mean no one is in there. . . ."

"I mean no furniture is in there. No rug. Nothing. The room is empty."

"Let me look."

Jeremy fitted his eye to the hole. After a moment he stood up once more as he said, "You're right! Now why—"

I took it up. "Why would anyone place a new lock on an empty room?"

It was a question neither of us could answer.

"Jeremy, what do you know about the missing trunk?"

"I know that Grandfather kept it locked up inside a larger trunk in his old office, a trunk that was chained to the wall. I used to be frightened by that big trunk and that chain. When I was little, Henry and Simon used to tell me that there was a monster locked up in there that would jump out one day and eat me." He made a wry grimace. "I believed it. It gave me nightmares."

"After Rhodes died last fall, what happened to the trunk?"

"This is the strange part. When Grandfather realized how ill he was, he took the little trunk out of his office and hid it somewhere. It's as though he didn't want anyone to open it. He died not telling us where it was."

"Do you really think it contains money?"

"I don't know. I think it might. Grandfather used to come up with ways to pay the bills when I thought there was no money left. I told you I keep the books. I can show you records, times when we were down to nothing. Then Grandfather would make a trip into Hot Springs and return to tell me there was now money in the bank. He hadn't taken out a loan, so where did the money come from?"

I was beginning to have an idea, although I couldn't tell Jeremy about it, at least not yet. Ever since finding that letter from Aunt Alice to Rhodes, I'd wondered what their relationship could have been all those years following their reunion in St. Louis during the war, for it was after that that Aunt Alice had become a regular guest at Milwood, using "delicate health" as an excuse. I knew now that her real purpose had been to visit her son, and later her grandson, even though it seemed obvious that neither William nor Jeremy had ever suspected who "Aunt Alice" really was. Had Alice and Rhodes met for clandestine embraces during those long hot summers, perhaps in the very suite we occupied now? Was that why that suite, on the third floor away from the regular family quarters, had become so important to her?

Poor Aunt Alice, desperately seeking love. Poor Aunt Alice.

157

But not so poor where money was concerned. Quite rich, in fact, the sole heir to the McPherson shipping fortune . . . rich enough to underwrite her lover's hotel and not even miss the money. She probably brought Rhodes cash each summer, and he stashed it in the trunk; but he could never have told anyone in the family where the money came from, nor why.

It was a scandalous situation, but it did make sense. What didn't make sense was Rhodes's last action. Where had he hidden the trunk, and why? Surely the money itself could not have been traced back to Aunt Alice. Why not let the family find it?

No, I could not tell Jeremy my suspicions; but I felt more anxious than ever to find that trunk before someone else in the family did, in case there was something in it—love letters similar to the one I'd already found or a document of some kind—that could lead to the revelation of Aunt Alice's long-kept secret. I personally did not condemn her, but I knew there were many in her social circle back in St. Louis who would, should the scandal become known.

"Do you think the trunk is in that room, maybe hidden in the closet?" I asked.

"I don't know. If it is, then someone in this household now has access to it but doesn't want anyone else in on it."

"Why the groans? Why the noises?"

He shook his head, his expression indicating he had no answers. We moved away from the door and drifted together toward the center stairs where we paused, equally reluctant, I think, to give up our moments together and resume our duties.

"What do we do now?" I asked.

"I don't know. If I could find out who changed that lock . . ."

The round stained glass window above the stairs, set in a geometrical pattern in red, green, blue, and pearly white, brightened like a flickering lantern slide show as the lightning stabbed through the sky outside. The thunder crashed hard upon the heels of the lightning, rattling the panes. Jeremy and

I leaned against the railing and watched the changing colors in the window, a kaleidoscopic display.

"Joanna . . ." Jeremy paused, rubbing one finger back and forth over the bannister as he searched for words. Finally he looked toward me, his eyes filled with yearning. My heart sank, for I thought he was about to make a declaration of love. Instead, he said, "Joanna . . . what do you really think of my poetry?"

The question set me back, it was so unexpected. I swallowed, looking into those vulnerable eyes, while I debated whether or not to be honest. After all, he *was* a cousin, however distant, and that deserved more than a polite, shallow answer from me.

"Jeremy, I—I think your poetry is insipid and dull."

Pain flared across his face. He reared back as though I'd struck him. I hastened on, wanting to reassure him if I could.

"Look, I'm not a writer, so take what I say with a grain of salt; but your poetry doesn't sound . . . it doesn't sound real to me. It sounds . . . I think the word is *contrived.*"

A cold gleam appeared in the back of his eyes. I'd thought of him in the past as a deer—defenseless and soft. Now I saw the predator that lurked deep inside him—the wolf or perhaps the weasel—slipping silently through the undergrowth. The sudden realization that Jeremy could be dangerous chilled me as completely as though we'd been transported from June ahead to January and were now being peppered by snow. I remembered the boulder that had rolled off the top of the cliff when I'd been sitting down by the Sapphire Pool. Jeremy had been prowling around on that cliff.

I swallowed hard and stumbled on. "Back in St. Louis, I met a poet once, at a soirée given by Aunt Alice, and he said you have to write about what you know, what you really feel, for a poem to be good . . . that you have to actually let people see into your heart, let your own life's blood flow onto the page."

I decided the reference to life's blood had been unwise as Jeremy's glare continued to blast me like an arctic wind from the north.

"I—ah—I don't mean to hurt your feelings," I finished lamely.

He moved several paces away, where he stood with his back to me for a long moment while the thunder rumbled around us. He clenched his hands at either side and lifted his head toward the ceiling. It was another dramatic pose, which I might have discounted in the past as being affected, but this time I got the feeling he was truly struggling to bring his emotions under control. When he turned around, the predator had disappeared.

"I appreciate your candor," he said, "although I am disappointed."

Disappointed in himself or in me? I couldn't tell.

"Jeremy, all that business about the lark and the wren, and comparing Aunt Alice to Helen of Troy. It . . . well, it didn't move me. I didn't feel I was learning anything about you or about myself."

"What do you mean, about yourself?"

"That poet I mentioned—the one in St. Louis—he said a poem has to be so powerful that the reader's life is changed just by reading it, that it makes the reader look at the world in a new way or discover something deep inside himself he didn't know before."

I thought I saw a gleam of interest flicker across his face.

"No one ever expressed that to me before," he murmured.

I shrugged. "As I said, I'm not a poet, so ignore this if you wish. I'm just telling you what that man said. If you asked me to write a poem, I'd be totally lost."

I'd hoped to smooth the waters, but I wasn't sure I'd succeeded. Now that I'd glimpsed the primitive animal that lay hidden beneath Jeremy's soft disguise, I placed myself on guard, watching for danger signals. I felt a sense of loss, for I'd counted on being able to trust him. Now I had to face the fact that the only person I could trust was myself.

Nell appeared at the bottom of the stairs and peered up toward the bannister where I was leaning. She wore a high-necked black dress and an annoyed frown.

"Is Jeremy up there?" she called.

He returned to the railing and looked down toward her. "Yes, Grandmother?"

She advanced up the stairs, her back ramrod straight, her skirts swishing in tune with the rain that hissed against the window. I thought again of how hard everyone in this household had to work, with only two servants to help ease the load. Although Nell was obviously much sturdier than my aunt and still filled with energy—a strong woman for her age—I wondered again if she envied my aunt's life of ease.

She now addressed Jeremy in a voice edged with annoyance. "Have you finished that book work I asked you to take care of this morning?"

It was definitely the voice of command, and I heard an additional undertone, which told me she knew full well he hadn't.

A flush suffused his face as he replied, "I was planning to get to that this afternoon."

She glanced toward the watch pinned to a ribbon on her bodice, then toward him. The look said: *The afternoon is going by and I don't see you taking action.*

Jeremy bowed to me. "If you'll excuse me, I'll get back to work."

I nodded my assent, and he hurried down the stairs past his grandmother. I thought Nell would follow him, but she continued on to the head of the stairs where she confronted me with hostile eyes. I wondered again how much she really knew about her husband's past. I decided to take the initiative in our exchange.

"Your grandsons have been telling me a lot about the past. What an interesting history Milwood has!"

She straightened her shoulders even more as she glanced about at the hotel.

"Rhodes and I built this place together." Her pride in that accomplishment spilled from her like the ringing of a bell. "It

161

was nothing when we started, just the land and the springs. We had to do it all."

"Your first hotel here, before the war, was a log lodge. . . ."

"A lodge that the Yankees burned!" she interrupted fiercely.

Well, well, I thought. Her husband might have fought for the North, but her sympathies had obviously not been so well-defined as his. Of course, she'd grown up in Little Rock in the middle of southern territory, while he'd grown up in St. Louis, an area divided by conflicting political attitudes.

"I understand you met Aunt Alice at a ball in St. Louis during the war," I said, watching her closely to see if she might display a guilty reaction to that, anything that would tell me she knew Rhodes had met Alice before.

She didn't hesitate as she replied, "Yes, that's right. It was a charity ball to help outfit the Union soldiers from the area."

"How did you feel about that?"

Now she did hesitate, her face a study as she looked me over. "You seem to be intuitive."

"If by that you mean that I think you sympathized with the South, yes. My grandfather did, too, you know. Or perhaps you didn't know."

"You're referring to Alice's brother."

"Yes."

"I never knew him. But I do know that your family cut him out, leaving all the wealth to Alice. How do *you* feel about that?"

She'd neatly turned the tide in my direction, away from herself, and I had to laugh.

"That was long ago," I said. "There's nothing that can be done about it now."

"There's always something that can be done about every situation," she said flatly, looking once more about the hotel.

I sensed more meaning there than I could catch hold of.

"It's hard with Rhodes being gone, but I will save this hotel," she went on. "I will not lose what we worked so hard on together. I will find a way."

It was as though she were warning me, although I could not understand about what.

"I certainly hope you do," I replied. "I've noticed how hard everyone at Milwood works."

"How hard some people work," she amended. "I must go now and see what preparations Granny and Maybelle will be making for supper."

"And I must get back to my aunt," I said.

I don't think Nell welcomed my company, but I walked downstairs with her anyway. In the lower lobby we met Henry and Albert Lock, their hair dripping, their coats soaked from their walk from the bathhouse back to the hotel through the rain.

"Hi there, little lady!" boomed Mr. Lock. "Got a real gully washer goin' out there."

I slid my eyes toward Henry and caught him doing the same with me. His expression was closed, hiding his thoughts. His earlier words sounded once more in my head: *Things aren't always what they seem.*

My plans to lance the boil and release the poison that threatened Milwood remained unfulfilled. Motive, that's what I needed—a motive for each person here that would explain why my aunt and I had been attacked. Jeremy had said that Henry wanted to finish his medical studies and turn Milwood into a clinic. To what lengths would Henry go to realize that dream? I wondered. How could harming my aunt and me help him fulfill his wish? Henry claimed to be attracted to me, but I'd studied some cases dealing with criminal or perverted behavior, back in nurse's training, where a man professed love for a woman in order to get close to her for ulterior motives.

Still puzzling over the situation, I looked about the lobby. The rain seemed to have driven everyone inside. At a table near one of the front windows, my aunt and Charlotte sat engaged in a game of cards, watched by Amos from his wheelchair. Simon stood at another window looking out at the rain while slapping his thigh with his riding crop. Through the door behind the front desk that led into the current main office, I saw Jeremy now bent over a table, pen in hand, record books spread out before him.

Simon turned from the window and swept his gaze around the lobby.

"Hail, hail, the gang's all here," he said.

I still tended to shy away from Simon, as I'd done ever since our encounter in the attic where he'd threatened to throttle me. Despite his claim that he'd been teasing, his remark had been in such bad taste that it had colored my attitude toward him. Now, as he strode toward our group, crop clenched in one fist, I involuntarily took a step backward.

"How's the gout, Albert?" he asked.

Mr. Lock shook his head. "Ain't gettin' better. I'm gonna try some of Granny's medicine and see what that does."

Henry frowned at that announcement. "Witches brew," he muttered.

"Maybe not," I said. "Didn't they teach you in school that a lot of modern day medicines are based on old-time recipes handed down through the centuries? Peasant lore, Indian lore?"

He raked me with a scathing look. "They told me that, yes, but I don't take too seriously such palpitations over old wives' brews from the 'good old days.' Don't forget about the old wives who said you could protect yourself from hydrophobia by having oxen dig a trench around your village, or avoid the plague by hanging raw meat from poles in the village square."

Simon snorted with laughter. "The latter might have worked. If you'd been a stranger walking around with the plague, sick at your stomach and feeling terrible, would you have come on into a village filled with the stench of rotting meat?"

"This whole conversation is disgusting," said Nell. "I refuse to stay and listen."

She swished off down the corridor in the direction of the kitchen.

"Jeremy told me you'd like to turn Milwood into a clinic," I said to Henry.

"Good luck to you," Simon put in bitterly, saluting his brother with the crop. "That'll take a lot of money, much more than I've suggested spending for advertising."

"The clinic is something I've thought a lot about," Henry admitted. "The springs here are good, just as good as those in town. I know Hot Springs is a glamorous place, with the gambling and the horse racing, but it's also noisy. I think there might be a number of health seekers who would prefer the peace and quiet we have here to the confusion there. If I could finish my studies, get my doctor's license . . ."

"You're really serious about this," I said.

"I . . . yes, I am. We could turn the west wing of the hotel into the clinic, keep the other wing for regular guests . . ."

"And how," interrupted Simon sarcastically, "do you propose to accomplish all that?"

"I don't know. But I do think about it."

Mr. Lock gave us a beaming smile. "I got an idea. We'll bottle Granny's Gout Cure and sell it on our own. Make a fortune."

Henry shook his head, his mouth set in a grim line. I envisioned the hotel with a big sign over the door: MILWOOD BATHS AND CLINIC, and underneath in smaller letters: HENRY HAMPTON, M.D.

But Simon was right; it would take a lot of money to realize such a dream. The west wing would have to be completely remodeled and special equipment installed. It would be impossibly expensive under the current circumstances. How much money might be in that missing trunk? I wondered. Enough to pay Milwood's debts and still build a clinic?

"Gin!" exclaimed Aunt Alice with satisfaction. I turned to see her slap a card down on the table in front of Charlotte.

"That's three games I've won in a row."

"Gin, pin, win," intoned Amos.

"If you paid more attention to the cards, Charlotte, you'd do better," Aunt Alice went on.

Charlotte's face slowly flushed until it turned the color of a grape. "It depends on the deal," she replied in a choked voice. "Some of us are given better hands in this life than others."

"Don't think I don't catch your innuendo," Aunt Alice replied coldly, "but if you think I feel guilty about my wealth, you're wrong. My family worked hard to make that money, and we deserve it."

"As I recall, your grandfather and father made that money. All you've had to do is spend it."

"Money funny, funny money," Amos said. He swiveled his head about and caught sight of me. "Why aren't you in jail?"

A crack of thunder, as loud as the proverbial crack of doom, made us all jump.

"That was close," Henry said. "Might have struck a tree."

The rain increased with a roaring rush of sound, battering the verandah roof and pounding against the ground. Aunt Alice picked up her cane from the floor beside her chair.

"Rain always makes me sleepy. I think I'll go upstairs and take a nap."

Rain sometimes made me sleepy, too, but a more gentle rain, not the furious storm now shaking the very walls. I was not happy about riding up in that electrical lift with all the lightning flashing about outside, but Aunt Alice didn't seem to give it a second thought. We jerked and creaked upwards while Aunt Alice regaled me with a running commentary: "That Charlotte is a sly one, pretending to be so mousey most of the time, but really greedy as a rat. She hates me for being rich, an attitude I've run into with others, even back in St. Louis. People will toady up to you and pretend to be your friend, but underneath they're seething with jealousy."

"The tyranny of envy," I murmured.

"What?"

"Henry talked one day about the tyrannies that rule us, such as passion or poverty or illness. Envy can be a tyrant, too."

"One of the worst. But I am free from that one, thank God."

Only because you're free from want, I thought.

We arrived safely in our rooms, where I helped Aunt Alice remove her shoes. She lay down on top of the quilt, carefully smoothing out her skirts so as not to muss them during her nap. I then covered her with a shawl and read to her from a book of Emerson's essays until she fell asleep. During that time the rain settled down into a quiet, steady downpour and I found myself nodding, too; but I did not want to sleep the afternoon away. I laid the book down on the table beside the bed and tiptoed into the other room, where I paced, reviewing the disturbing events that had happened since our arrival at Milwood.

Everything seemed to hinge on the missing trunk. If papers of a personal nature pertaining to Aunt Alice were indeed hidden in there, then I knew, with rising certainty, that I wanted to be the first to find them; and if that letter from Aunt Alice to Rhodes had been hidden behind that wall board upstairs, other letters might be there, too, perhaps even the trunk. This seemed an excellent time to look.

I slipped quietly out into the hall and headed for the attic.

Chapter 15

Due to the storm, the stairwell was even darker than when I'd climbed it with Simon. By the time I reached the shadowed room above, I wished I'd brought a lamp. The rain, beating against the shingles overhead, sounded like a train thundering through the sky. Somewhere in the recesses of the attic a drip from a leak in the roof hammered rhythmically on metal, while the dank odor of mildew assailed my nostrils.

I felt my way through the musty furniture and boxes to the place where I thought I'd found the letter sticking out through the crack in the wallboard, but the room was so dark, the clutter so jumbled, I couldn't be sure. Was this the chair I'd pretended to stumble against to hide my actions from Simon? I looked back toward the stairwell, trying to remember just where and how far away Simon had been standing in relation to my position when I'd found the letter. It was difficult to judge, but I decided I must be near the right spot.

I grabbed hold of the arms of a chair that stood against the wall and tugged it aside. Shock drove through me like a spear when I saw that several of the wallboards had been pried off, close to the floor, and that a hole now gaped there like a yawning mouth. I dropped to my knees and tried to peer into the hole, but it was too dark to make out details. A dank smell belched into my face, like an exhalation of bad breath, and I drew back, wrinkling my nose. After a moment I leaned forward again and reached into the hole, praying I wouldn't touch the warm fur of a mouse or the sliding coils of a snake. I patted about in all directions and choked back a sneeze when dust billowed forth, a soft explosion of gray. The hole went much deeper than I'd expected, angling in under the eaves. Plenty of room, I decided, for a small trunk to have been concealed, along with a bundle of old love letters. Rhodes could have taken out the wallboards to make room for the trunk, then nailed the boards back in place. But *why?* If this was the original hiding place, where was the trunk now?

Suspicion rose inside me, an ugly specter which whispered that Simon must have seen me take the letter from the wall and had returned later to search again. If he had found the trunk, why was he keeping it a secret from the rest of the family?

Greed. That's another tyranny which can rule a person's life. Perhaps Simon did find the money and now wanted it all for himself. Although he'd stated that he loved Milwood and wished to renovate it, that desire might have vanished once he actually had the money in hand. Perhaps the gambling parlors and race tracks in Hot Springs now held greater attraction for him than the quiet halls of this crumbling hotel.

But the attacks on my aunt and me had come *before* Simon would have found the trunk, were this hole the hiding place. I was still left with questions I couldn't answer.

The sound of the rain began to slacken. I stood up, wiped my hands on an old quilt that lay across one of the chairs, and tried to put myself in Simon's place. If I'd found the trunk, what would I have done with it? Where could I have taken it without running the risk of being seen by the people downstairs? I might, I thought, choose some other hiding place right here in this attic, or I might carry it to the other attic and hide it there.

I made a quick foray to the back of the room, peering into the corners for evidence of damage to walls or disturbance in the dust, which would reveal a new hiding place. Of course, the truth was that Simon might have noticed the loose board behind which I'd found the letter and removed more boards there but not found the trunk.

The rain drifted away. Quiet descended over the attic, a muffling blanket, disturbed only by the continued drip on metal. I peeked behind an old bureau and saw the source of the noise, a toy metal drum, its red, white, and blue decorations eaten away by rust.

My eyes by now had adjusted to the gloom. I hurried back through the room to the door on the opposite end, beyond the stairwell, which led, I surmised, out onto the widow's walk. The knob on the door was of brass, cold and smooth to the touch. I pulled the door open and peered outside. Gray clouds still scudded overhead while water dripped from the chimneys and gushed through the gutters edging the roof below the widow's walk. A cold wind pushed past me, ruffling my hair.

I decided to cross the widow's walk to the other attic to see if the door there were unlocked. Mindful of securing my retreat, however, I propped this door open with an old flatiron.

I stepped out into the wind and took a deep breath, reveling in the fresh damp smell, like newly washed clothes. To the southwest writhed pendulous gray clouds, pregnant with rain. The puddles on the widow's walk were a dull slate color, reflecting the sky. I hurried along the walk, trying to sidestep the puddles while hanging onto the wrought iron railing with one hand and using the other hand to hold my billowing skirts. The mountains in the distance lay shrouded in mist, giving the landscape the look of dream, as though Milwood were the only substantial thing left in a melting world.

From this vantage point the roof of the hotel was not a dream but an architect's nightmare, with its turrets, dormers, and chimneys, its intersecting ridgepoles marking the different arms in the E shape of the hotel. I looked down into the backyard where the steam from the springs, beaten down by the rain, hung in a flat layer of gray clouds around the bathhouses.

The dampness penetrated my uniform, raising goose bumps

on my skin. Not wanting to remain out here in the wind any longer, I speeded my steps until I reached the door to the other attic. The knob resisted my efforts, as I'd feared it would. Nothing to do, then, but return to where I'd started.

Behind me came the sound of a slam.

Oh no! I thought. I turned quickly to see that the door to the other attic now stood closed, an eyeless barrier, blind and still. Had the wind grabbed the door and shifted the flatiron out of place? I ran, heedless of the water splashing onto my skirts, to grab the knob, which I rattled and shoved but to no avail.

"Help!" I shouted. "Help! I'm trapped on the roof!"

My voice whipped away, borne on the rising wind. A few sprinkles of rain splattered against my back, then increased into a full-fledged downpour as the clouds, writhing in agony, gave birth. I pounded on the door, hoping that the sound of my voice would drift down the stairs inside and awaken my aunt.

"Let me in!" I shouted. "Let me in! I'm out here on the roof."

Above the storm I seemed to hear a laugh from the other side of the door, then the sound of retreating footsteps.

"Don't leave me out here!" I shouted.

The only answer came from the roaring chorus of rain. Even though I knew it was futile, I continued to pound on the door and shout until my fists felt flayed. I drew my skirt up over my head, trying to make an umbrella of sorts, but the water soon soaked through until the material drooped about me like a sagging tent. I ran across to the west wing and pounded on the attic door there, yelling until my voice became a rusty hinge. At last I huddled down inside the door frame, where the wind was less severe, drawing myself into a ball to try to preserve my body heat. By the time the storm finally blew over, I was shivering clear through; but at last the sun came out, weakly at first, then gaining strength until it crowned the retreating clouds to the east with a brilliant rainbow. I rose and stepped into the light, lifting my face. The sun's warmth touched me like a blessing. The mountains gained substance and solidified as the mist drifted away. First one bird began to sing, then another, until the air danced with their thanksgiving. A cow lowed, a goat bleated. I advanced to the center of the widow's walk and looked down into the backyard, hoping that someone would soon emerge. At last Granny limped into view from the direction of the kitchen with a pan of scraps, which she set down on the ground. A couple of cats slunk out of the bushes and hunkered beside the pan.

Granny! Granny, up here!"

She turned and started back for the house, not looking up, and I realized she must be hard of hearing.

"Granny! I'm on the roof!"

When she still didn't look up, I quickly unlaced a shoe and pulled it off. Drawing back my arm as my brother had taught me how to do while playing ball, I heaved the shoe over the roof in Granny's direction, hoping it wouldn't hit her on the head. She had disappeared below the edge of the roof by then, but she quickly hobbled out back into the yard and squinted toward me through her cataracts, one hand held over her eyes.

"Help! I'm trapped up here!" I yelled.

Now her hand cupped one ear. "What did you say?"

"Help!"

She nodded and smiled. "Hello!"

"No, *help!* I'm trapped! The door slammed shut."

"I can't hear you."

I gestured frantically toward the door, then pointed to myself, then back at the door. "Help me. Please!"

She shook her head and frowned to show me she still didn't understand. She picked up my shoe and studied it, then looked toward me again, obviously puzzled as to why I'd thrown it at her. I ran to the door and banged my shoulder against it, rattled the knob, then turned toward her and threw out my hands in frustration while squinching my face into a mask of grief, hoping she'd get the idea. This time she nodded vigorously and waved my shoe at me before limping into the house.

I paced up and down in the sun, absorbing the warmth with

172

gratitude. Such a long time went by that I began to fear Granny hadn't gotten the message after all. Then I heard fumbling at the attic door to the east. It opened and Henry ducked through.

"In trouble again," he stated flatly, shaking his head as though I were an object of wonder beyond belief.

"I—ah—I came up to look around and—and the wind blew the door shut," I said.

"I'll swear, you need a keeper."

His patronizing attitude made my hackles rise.

"I can't help what the wind does," I said testily. At the same time I wasn't sure it had been the wind. For all I knew, Henry Hampton himself had shut that door on me and stomped off laughing while I yelled for help.

"You should have propped the door open," he said.

I started to protest that I had, but decided that such argument was beneath me. With my chin in the air, I brushed past him, secretly rejoicing when my wet skirts slapped against his trouser leg to leave a large damp stain. After the sunlight I had to blink several times to adjust my eyes when I stepped back into the dim attic.

"Look, there's a flatiron you could have used for a doorstop," Henry said after following me in. He nodded toward something with a jerk of his chin.

I blinked again, then peered in that direction. The flatiron now rested on top of a box a couple of feet away from the door. No gust of wind had placed it there.

"You're right," I said, not wanting to tell him the true story. "That would have held the door open nicely."

A crumpled white rag on the floor near the box caught my eye. I stepped to one side as though trying to get out of Henry's way, but what I wanted was a closer look, for the shape seemed familiar.

A dust cap. A white ruffled dust cap, such as the one May-belle often wore to protect her golden curls. I quickly moved away, heading for the stairwell to divert Henry's attention.

"Would you like some help getting out of those wet things?" he asked as he followed me down the stairs.

His voice was innocent but his eyes, when I glanced toward him in the hallway below, danced with mischief. Head still held high, I entered my room without replying and firmly closed the door.

Chapter 16

I'd been afraid I might take a cold, but I awoke the next morning none the worse for wear. This was partly due, I decided, to my robust constitution and partly due to the hot soaking bath I'd taken following my experience on the roof. My recovery might also have been aided by the pot of herbal tea Granny had brought to me in my room the night before, along with my shoe.

"When that shoe come heavin' over the eaves, I thought what in the world, now it's rainin' shoes 'stead a cats and dogs," she'd said, shaking her head. "Then I seen you up there on the widder's walk dancin' around, and it finally dawned on me what was goin' on."

"I'm glad it did. I would have hated to have been trapped up there all night," I fervently replied.

I huddled in a blanket while sipping the tea before a warm fire, which had been started by Simon in the fireplace in Aunt Alice's and my suite. My aunt, seated across from me in one of the upholstered chairs, said, "Joanna, you're getting to be just as flighty as your mother! I would have thought you'd have more sense than to go out on the roof during a storm."

She was still harping on that same theme the next morning.

"Young people these days aren't as mature and responsible as they used to be," she said. "Now when *I* was your age, I knew better than to go out in the rain."

But you didn't know better than to get involved with a married man, I thought cynically.

I studied her through narrowed eyes, wondering again how such a liaison could ever have come about. Could she have met Rhodes in St. Louis when they were both still young, before he headed for Arkansas with his invalid mother? Could they have had an adolescent romance but parted on a quarrel, only to meet and fall in love again after Rhodes's marriage to Nell?

My tongue burned with the wish to ask her straight out about her past; but there she sat in her purple silk dress with its crystal bead collar, looking so regal and so proper that I couldn't bring myself to slap her in the face with my knowledge of her shame. After all, she was no longer young. Shock can bring on a heart attack in the elderly; a confrontation with me could well do her damage. As her nurse, it was my duty to protect her health, not threaten it. Therefore, I held my peace, both with her and later at breakfast with Mr. Lock, who ribbed me unmercifully about my escapade.

Following breakfast, my aunt had her morning mineral water bath and massage, attended by myself and Granny.

"I'm goin' out to the woods pretty soon to look for mushrooms," Granny said to me. "That rain yesterday must a popped 'em up by the droves. Would you like to come with me while your aunty takes her nap?"

"Perhaps I shouldn't leave her—" I began, but my aunt interrupted me with an indignant snort.

"Nonsense! Go with Granny and learn something useful for a change."

Thus it was that thirty minutes later I found myself headed down the path toward the Sapphire Pool with Granny and, to my chagrin, with Maybelle.

"I had another dream last night," she said darkly. "Another dream about death."

Granny nodded solemnly. "I told you Maybelle's dreams sometimes come true."

176

It had been quite a while now since Maybelle's other dream about the white roses and mushrooms, and no one had died, so I decided to take their dire mutterings with a grain of salt.

Nevertheless I asked, "What was this dream like?"

"It had you in it." She flicked me an unsmiling look, her eyes ice-blue marbles. "You and your aunt and Mr. Lock. You were on a merry-go-round, like the one they have in the park in Hot Springs. It went faster and faster until it was just a blur. Mr. Lock fell off, then your aunt and then you. The horses grew until they were as big as the hotel, and they jumped off the merry-go-round and trampled you to death. Then I saw the same thing I saw in my other dream, with the coffin and the white mushrooms, only this time there were three coffins."

Despite my resolve not to take her seriously, I felt a chill frost my arms.

"Did the dream frighten you?" I asked.

"No, but I think it would frighten you."

That's what you want, I thought. *You want me to be so frightened I'll leave here and not come back, and then you can have Jeremy all to yourself.*

"Here's a good place to look," Granny said, leading the way from the path into the woods. "Morels usually grow around here after a rain. Watch out for poison ivy and copperheads."

Tree limbs arched over us, the raftered ceiling of a cathedral decorated in patterns of green, with gold light filtering through to dapple our arms and hands. Taking heed of Granny's warning, I picked up a long stick and tapped ahead of me through the brush to warn away the snakes while keeping sharp watch for the shiny ivy leaves with the five points, which can blister the skin.

"There, Granny," Maybelle said, darting toward a rotting log that lay in a shaft of sunlight.

Her flowered sunbonnet, tied loosely under her chin, had slipped from her curly golden hair to dangle down her back. That hair, which had pulled loose from its bun, now caught the light to create a halo about her face such as the one I'd seen on that first day. A multitude of small white butterflies rose from the log to circle her in a storm of winged snow. It was an idyllic scene of woodland innocence, which I viewed with cynicism.

"Morels! Big fat ones!" gloated Granny. She pointed toward the log, which sheltered several mushrooms with wrinkled caps that looked like brown sponges. "Those'll taste good, fried in my special egg batter." She gathered the mushrooms carefully and placed them in her basket. "Now you know what to look for," she said to me, "so keep your eyes peeled."

She was right; the rain had brought out the mushrooms in droves.

"These are beefsteaks," she said, peeling several fleshy growths from the side of a stump. "They're good, too. But watch out for the Death Angel."

"How can I tell it if I find it?"

"It's snow white and looks pure, but it's deadly. Ask me before you touch any white ones."

Thus guided by Granny, Maybelle and I soon helped fill the basket. We wandered west through the woods, away from Milwood, and at last we came to a clearing with a log cabin in the center. It had a porch across the front where two rocking chairs squeaked gently in the wind. A washtub and scrub board hung from nails beside the front door, while red and white ruffled curtains peeked through the small-paned windows on either side.

"How charming!" I exclaimed. "Who lives here?"

"We do," replied Granny, her face crinkling in a gap-toothed grin. "My husband, he built this cabin long ago. Now he's gone, why it's ours, Maybelle and me."

"Then we're not on Hampton land any more?"

"No, this here is ours, just a few acres, but we got some good bottom land down toward the river."

"Where did you come from originally?" I asked.

"Over Tennessee way. Still got people there. Great-grandpap, he come from England, got hisself some land, then sent for his bride and started his family. Four generations of my folks has lived there now. But me and my husband, we come on here and settled right after we got married. Thought we might go back to Tennessee someday, but we never did. Come on in, I'll make us some tea."

We climbed the steps and crossed the porch to enter through the unlocked door. The interior, with its log walls chinked with white, its plank floors covered with rag rugs, was rustic but homey. A fireplace built of rough stone, blackened with smoke, stood in the center of one wall, with shelves on either side that held crocks and jars, each neatly labeled: *Lavender, Basil, Sorrel, Foxglove, Nasturtium,* along with other names I didn't recognize.

"What do you use nasturtium for?" I asked as I crossed the floor to examine the collection of herbs more closely.

"Lots a things. Sailors, they eat the leaves so they won't get scurvy. The seeds can make a laxative if you know how. And the Injuns . . . well, sometimes they rub the petals on a cut place to keep it from festerin'."

She busied herself at the old iron stove, building a fire and putting the pot on to boil, while I walked around the room. A plank table and benches, homemade but polished to a soft shine, occupied the middle of the floor. Two rocking chairs with quilted pillows sat before the fireplace, while a small marble-topped table between the chairs held an open Bible. Samplers, carefully worked, hung on the walls: *Home Sweet Home* and *God is Love,* surrounded by letters of the alphabet and numbers intertwined with flowers. A door, standing ajar, gave me a glimpse of a second room holding two beds covered with quilts, one in the wedding ring pattern, the other sewn from hundreds of tiny hexagons in bright colors. The thing that really caught my eye, however, was a beautiful old stringed instrument, which lay on a table in front of one of the windows, an instrument inlaid with different kinds of woods and iridescent mother-of-pearl. I'd never seen the actual instrument before, but I had seen pictures.

"Is that a lute?" I asked in awe.

"Yep, it sure is," replied Granny. "My great-granny—the one I mentioned afore—brought that with her across the ocean. Used to sing the old songs, she did, and she taught me. My voice is too cracked to sing anymore, but Maybelle sings." She turned and smiled at her granddaughter. "Honey, would ya sing a song fer us whilst I finish up here?"

Maybelle obediently brought the lute, although I could tell she was not too pleased to oblige. She had removed her bonnet and loosened her curls, which now flowed about her shoulders in golden profusion. When she sat down in one of the rockers and adjusted the instrument in her lap, she looked as though she could have graced an Elizabethan court. She strummed a chord in a minor key and began to sing:

> *My love, he was so wondrous fair,*
> *Lili, lili, O.*
> *Pale his skin and pale his hair,*
> *Lili, lili, O.*
> *He said one day he'd marry me,*
> *And we were happy as could be.*
> *We lay together by the sea.*
> *Lili, lili, O.*

The song went on for many verses, telling of the man's betrayal of the girl's love, of her despair, and of the way she eventually murdered both her lover and his new paramour. Now, reciting her sad story, she waits to be taken to the gallows.

It was a doleful song, and Maybelle sang it with relish . . . sang it well, in a thin clear voice that blended beautifully with the timbre of the lute. I was impressed, despite my uneasiness about her choice of subject matter, which struck too close to home. The pale skin and pale hair made me think of Jeremy,

180

and I imagined she was thinking of him, too. When she finished, she lowered the lute and looked at me with steady eyes.

"Maybelle, you have a beautiful voice," I said, "and what a treasure, all those old songs. . . . You really should write them down before they're lost."

"We don't need to write 'em down, we got 'em in our heads," Granny said. "I passed 'em on to Maybelle, and she'll pass 'em on to her own children."

"But I was thinking of others. . . ."

"Them's *our* songs," Granny said emphatically. "They belong to us."

"Oh," I said, never having thought before of a tale or a song as being a family possession; but if you had little else, then I could see how you might place great store in your own oral tradition.

Granny poured the steaming tea into three sturdy mugs and placed them on the table, along with a squat cut-glass sugar bowl and three spoons. We sat together on the benches and sipped the tea, a pungent brew of Granny's own mix. While we drank, Granny told me how Maybelle's parents had been "carried off" by a fever many years before and how she had then taken her granddaughter to bring up as her own.

"Been a comfort to me, she has," she said, reaching over to pat Maybelle's hand. "Don't know what I'll do without her when she marries and moves away."

Maybelle's face flushed and she looked down at the table, avoiding my eyes.

"Well, I guess we better drink up and get back to the hotel. It's gettin' on toward noontime," Granny went on.

While she put out the fire, Maybelle and I rinsed the teacups in water dipped from the pail that sat on top of a tin-covered washstand. With Maybelle carrying the basket of mushrooms we emerged once more into the morning air. It clung about our shoulders like a hot damp dishtowel, so heavy was the humidity. The very woods seemed to steam as we picked our way back through the undergrowth.

"Oh!" cried Maybelle suddenly. She knelt and pushed aside some grass for us to see. "There they are."

"They?" I asked.

"The mushrooms from my dream . . . the Death Angel," she said. "Eat one of those and it'll put you under the ground. But first you curl up in agony like a worm touched by a match."

Again she fixed me with a steady look. My shoulders jerked in an involuntary shudder.

"Don't touch it," Granny warned. "Might get some juice on your fingers. You'd have to lick 'em, a course, to get the poison in your system, but still it don't pay to mess with them things."

We rose and moved away, no longer chattering casually as we had been doing. I noticed that Maybelle paused and looked back for a long moment, as though memorizing the location of the mushrooms. I swore then that I would never eat a mushroom in the Milwood Hotel, no matter how good Granny's batter might be.

We came at last to the path on Hampton land that led to the Sapphire Pool. A crunching sound, as of feet bearing down on gravel and twigs, preceded Henry's appearance around a bend in the path from the direction of the pool. He carried a half-filled gunnysack in one hand.

"I see you've been out foraging," he remarked, glancing at Maybelle's basket.

"It looks as though you have, too," I said.

He neither opened the sack nor offered an explanation, but continued on in a conversational tone, "Did you see Granny's cabin?"

"Yes, it's cozy."

"Certainly cozier than Milwood."

"Any place would be cozier than Milwood."

He flicked a glance in my direction, as though waiting for me to elaborate, but I said, instead, "I also heard Maybelle sing and play the lute, and she's wonderful. Have you ever heard her?"

His eyes widened in surprise. "No, I haven't! I used to listen to Granny play, but I didn't know Maybelle could. Why have you kept it a secret?" he demanded, turning to the girl who stared back at him with a closed sullen face.

"No one ever asked me."

"Well, I'm asking you now. Bring your lute up to the hotel sometime."

"Maybe."

We passed the barn and carriage house to enter the stable yard where Simon stood currying his horse. I couldn't be sure, but it seemed to me that tension flared between the two brothers.

"Now there's a pastoral scene if I ever saw one," Simon remarked dryly when we appeared. "Been out for a picnic?"

"Not hardly. Been gatherin' mushrooms," Granny replied.

"Four of you to gather mushrooms . . . you must have made quite a haul," he responded.

He slid his eyes across the others to fix upon my face. "I see that you've recovered from your adventure on the roof?"

"Yes, it was stupid of me not to prop that door open," I replied, placing my own attention on Maybelle.

She started slightly and shot me a glance through narrowed eyes. I met her look head-on, my face stiff, my lips drawn tight, to let her know I realized she was the guilty party. She stared back for a long moment, then turned away, pretending to examine a patch of Sweet William that nodded in blue splendor beside the stable wall.

"I hope you'll be careful to have no more such 'adventures.' They could prove harmful to your health," Simon continued in a pleasant tone.

"Yes, you're right. I shall be very careful," I replied, equally polite.

We left Simon to finish currying the horse and proceeded down the path toward the hotel. To make conversation, I asked Henry how long it would take him to actually finish his studies and get his doctor's license, and he said perhaps half a year, no more.

"All my life I've wanted to be a doctor," he continued fervently. "I think I was marked at birth. I'm named for William Henry Hammond, the first doctor who ever came to Hot Springs. Of course my Uncle William was always called William, so I was always called Henry, to avoid confusion. But my full name is William Henry Hampton. If I could start a clinic here, with other doctors . . . and with nurses," he ended, giving me a smile filled with meaning.

A thrill shot through me at the implication. To be a nurse in an actual clinic, helping many people, not just one arthritic old woman, was, to quote Shakespeare, a "consummation devoutly to be wished."

We passed the chicken house and continued along the path past the bathhouses. As we mounted the bridge, I glanced toward that mysterious window on the second floor, checking to see if a face were peering through the curtains. When the window proved to be empty, I peeked from the corner of my eye toward Henry, thinking only to surreptitiously admire his lean craggy face. To my surprise, I saw him also examining that second-floor window. His brows were drawn together, his mouth set in a hard line. He actually paused for one brief moment with his eyes still fixed upon those curtains, as if by staring hard he could make them become transparent. Then, recovering with a slight shrug, he looked away and remarked to me, with a casual smile, "The paint is peeling here on the south side. We must get the money to do something about that soon."

He was trying, I could see, to divert me, in case I'd noticed him looking at the window. I was not deceived. Nevertheless I said, "Yes, you're right, the place is run-down. The longer you wait to do something about it, the worse it will get."

"Money," he muttered. "Always money."

Instead of the love of money being the root of all evil, perhaps the blame should be fixed on the lack of money, I thought.

We continued on toward the kitchen door, where we met Charlotte standing on the porch.

"I was beginning to get worried about dinner, you were gone so long," she said. She came down the steps and peered into the basket. "Oh, you did find mushrooms, and aren't they beauties!"

She went back into the kitchen with Granny and Maybelle while Henry, still clutching his sack, excused himself and headed off across the grass toward the back door of the east wing. I entered the hotel through the kitchen courtyard and went to hunt for Aunt Alice. I found her writing letters in our suite.

"It's going to storm again today," she said, "so stay off the roof."

"The sky is clear," I responded. "Surely, after that big rain yesterday, we'll have good weather for a day or two."

She picked up her cane and thumped it on the floor. "Mark my words, it will rain before nightfall!"

I didn't argue but instead occupied myself by writing another letter to my mother, telling her that the waters were proving beneficial to Aunt Alice's arthritis and again extending my love to my family. As I penned my innocuous note, I kept wondering if my mother knew anything about Aunt Alice's checkered past; but that was not a subject I could bring up in a letter.

By the time the dinner bell rang, my letter was finished and sealed. As I escorted Aunt Alice down to the dining room for the noon meal, I wondered if we'd be served those mushrooms fried in Granny's special batter.

They did not appear at that meal, but they did appear at supper.

185

"What're these?" Mr. Lock demanded when Maybelle set a platter down on the table before him. The fillets, deep-fried in a batter that had cooked to a crispy golden brown, looked like small fish.

"Morels," she said. "They're really good."

He dug in at once, forking one of the mushrooms from the platter and lowering it into his upturned mouth like a huge fat baby bird swallowing a worm. He closed his big yellow teeth over it and chomped a couple of times before practically swallowing it whole.

"Yum," he mumbled. "You're right."

Maybelle slid mushrooms from a second platter onto my aunt's and my plates, then added slices of roast beef and spoonfuls of mixed vegetables. I quickly reached over and picked up my aunt's plate, sliding the mushrooms back onto our platter.

"You mustn't eat those tonight," I told her firmly. "Mushrooms at night are bad for the digestion."

"Nonsense, Joanna! I've eaten mushrooms for supper many times."

"And you've sometimes had indigestion at night, too," I told her. "As your nurse, I'm telling you that you will not eat those mushrooms."

I slid my own mushrooms back onto the platter.

"But—" Maybelle began.

I held up my hand to silence her. "No arguments from you, either," I said, my voice slicing through the air. "We will *not* eat those mushrooms."

"Joanna!" my aunt barked angrily.

"I mean it, and this time I will have my way. No mushrooms."

Mr. Lock had by then finished off his whole platter. "If you're not going to eat yours, can I have 'em?"

"Too many mushrooms will upset your digestion, too," I said firmly.

While I did not think anyone would have put the Death Angel in Mr. Lock's mix, I did not want to take a chance on ours. Still, I felt reluctant to come straight out and say so. I was just reaching toward our platter to "accidentally" knock it off onto the floor when Mr. Lock shot his beefy hand across the space between our two tables and scooped the platter out from under my nose.

"Shame to let 'em go to waste," he said, dumping several of the mushrooms onto his plate.

"That is not a good idea. Send them back to the kitchen," I told him firmly.

When he didn't do so, I started to rise, intending to forcibly take the mushrooms away from him. With a twinkle in his eye that reminded me of a mischievous school boy defying the teacher, he stabbed several of the mushrooms onto the tines of his fork and crammed them into his mouth. Grease dribbled from between his lips as he chewed and swallowed. I watched him in horror, remembering Maybelle's description of a worm twisting in agony around a lighted match. While I knew that poison does not take effect at once, still I almost expected to see Mr. Lock turn purple and fall from his chair. Instead, he belched in appreciation, then proceeded to polish off the mushrooms that were left.

Should I drag him outside and stick my finger down his throat to make him vomit? I wondered. How in the world would I ever explain such an action? I had no proof that anything was wrong with those mushrooms, just an uneasy feeling.

Beside me, my aunt ate her beef and vegetables while glaring at me in indignation. "I had my mouth all set for those mushrooms," she pouted. "Joanna, you have made me very angry."

"Too late now," Mr. Lock put in cheerfully. "They're gone."

"I just hope you don't get sick tonight," I said.

187

"Not me," he replied, patting his belly. "I got a cast-iron stomach."

I pray you're right, I thought as I watched him dig into the beef and vegetables.

Later my aunt and I shared a pot of tea on the verandah with Charlotte and Nell. While we watched the fireflies twinkle around the honeysuckle vines that were scenting the dusk with their heavy sweet perfume, Charlotte remarked, "It's been a beautiful day."

"It certainly has," my aunt agreed. Turning to me, she added in a triumphant voice, "See? We did not have rain, despite your prediction. I *told* you the evening would be fine."

She was rewriting history again. I sighed and bit my lower lip, but decided not to argue the point since I'd won about the mushrooms. Let Aunt Alice have her little moment of triumph over the weather issue. Meanwhile, Nell sat drumming her fingers on the arm of her chair. She had seemed preoccupied when we first sat down, and she still appeared to be thinking of things far away.

"You act nervous tonight, Nell," my aunt observed. "Are you worried about something?"

"Nothing you can do anything about," Nell replied shortly.

"Is it the hotel? I know you're having a hard time. . . ." my aunt began, but Nell interrupted her, snapping, "I don't need your sympathy, Alice McPherson. We'll work this out somehow."

Charlotte shifted about in her chair as though she'd developed a sudden itch. I heard the chair legs scrape against the porch.

"Amos gets all upset," she said in her mousey little voice. "I try to keep his mind off Milwood, but he sits and broods."

"He seems obsessed with that missing trunk," I put in, testing the waters to see if I'd get a reaction.

Nell sighed, the first sign of weakness I'd noticed in her since coming to Milwood. When she spoke, she sounded wistful as well as tired. "Rhodes and that trunk . . . He wouldn't ever let me see inside it, always kept the key hidden away. I sometimes wondered if he had some awful secret locked up in there."

Now it was Aunt Alice who jumped slightly, causing her chair to squeak.

"What nonsense you talk, Nell," she said. "Rhodes probably just had important business papers in there, things he thought no one else would understand."

"He was a strange man in many ways," Nell mused on, almost as though she were alone. "He could be so practical and hardheaded sometimes, and such a dreamer at other times. And sentimental. I don't think he ever threw anything away, not one letter, not even the rose I gave him on our wedding day. He pressed it in our family Bible and kept it until it fell apart."

Aunt Alice started rubbing her hands back and forth on her skirt in an agitated way. I felt sorry for her, wondering if she still suffered from having been the "other woman," the one who could never be publicly acknowledged or listed in the family Bible.

"I suppose I'd better get back to Amos. It's time to get him ready for bed," Charlotte said. She placed her tea cup on the table and pushed herself out of her chair. "Did you enjoy Granny's mushrooms for dinner tonight?"

Aunt Alice sniffed in an offended way. "Joanna wouldn't let me eat them! She said they'd upset my digestion."

"Sometimes they don't set too well on the stomach at night," I hastily put in, "so I thought it best to avoid them this evening. But Mr. Lock certainly enjoyed them. He ate them all, his and ours, too."

"With his weight and bad heart?" Nell exclaimed in disapproval. "He'll end up with apoplexy or a stroke if he's not careful."

Using the excuse that it was our bedtime, too, I coaxed Aunt

189

Alice upstairs and finally got her into bed, where I sat beside her with the lamp turned low while reading an Emerson essay aloud. The flow of words soon lulled her into sleep. I then went to bed, too, but for me sleep would not come. I kept wondering if Albert Lock were all right. I chided myself for not having gone ahead and made a scene over the mushrooms, then argued the other side, telling myself that I was being overly cautious. At last, unable to lie in bed any longer, I slipped into the other room and lit the small rose glass lamp. I read another essay, hoping it would prove to be as soporific for me as it had been for Aunt Alice, but my own base thoughts kept overriding Emerson's elevated ones: In my imagination, Aunt Alice and Rhodes embraced, their bodies intertwining in passion. Then the images shifted. Rhodes changed into Henry and I became Aunt Alice, clasping each other in the hot night, our mouths open to each other's kiss, our hands sliding over damp flesh. . . .

A distant clang echoed through the corridors, bringing me with a start back to the present. I looked at the clock on the mantle. Ten minutes past midnight. I knew then that I had been dozing over the book. I put it aside and stood up, listening. There was a sharp snap as the walls settled above the cooling earth, followed by the lonely hoot of an owl drifting in through the open windows.

I'd begun to think I'd dreamed that clang when I heard a faint anguished cry that lifted the hairs on my arms. I hurried across the floor to our door and opened it cautiously, peeking with one eye around the edge to peer into the darkness. Floating away from me down the far end of the west corridor was a robed figure surrounded by blue light. Even as I watched, it drifted through the open door that led to the attic. The light continued to glow through the door for a few moments, then gradually diminished and faded away until the corridor was left in darkness.

I leaned against the doorjamb gasping for breath while my heart fluttered in my throat like an imprisoned bird seeking release. I did not want to step into that corridor; I did not want to go after that ghostly figure. But if I did not, Milwood might never give up its secrets. I grabbed my wrapper from a chair and tied the sash around my waist. With my pulse still pounding, I slipped from our suite and sped lightly through the darkness toward the far end of the corridor and that open attic door.

Chapter 17

My steps began to drag as I drew closer to the door. All the stories my younger brothers used to tell, trying to frighten "big sister" with shrouded ghouls and grinning vampires, now flew through my mind like a whirling black cloud. I paused at the bottom of the steps, holding my breath as I listened for sounds of movement. My eyes had by now adjusted to the darkness in the corridor, so the pale blue glow above, defining the shape of the attic entrance, seemed almost as bright as dawn.

For a moment I heard nothing. Then a scraping sound, as of a box sliding a short distance over a dusty floor, echoed down the stairwell. That was followed by another moment of silence, then a rustling noise, such as a rat might make rummaging in a nest of papers.

I huddled against the wall, concentrating on additional sounds: a thump; another sliding sound; a faint screech, metal on metal; more rustling; a faint gulp, which might have been a sob.

I crept up the stairs, pausing for a moment on each step to listen again as I prepared to turn and flee should footsteps head in my direction. When I finally reached the top, I knelt on the steps, then edged my body upward, keeping my head low. Gradually, avoiding any abrupt movements that might attract attention, I pushed forward and peeked around the edge of the stairwell. I choked back a cry as a black shape with a misshapen head wavered toward me, silhouetted against the blue glow. Then I realized that the shape was a dressmaker's dummy wearing a feathered hat. It had seemed to move because the light had shifted, an eerie will-o'-the-wisp at the far end of the room, its source hidden by the attic's debris. The door to the widow's walk creaked open, admitting a burst of wind that gusted through the attic to stir the dust and lift papers in the air. A mournful cry rode the wind like an early frost. I felt the chill of it against my skin and pulled back, shivering, to crouch once more against the wall. The glow diminished, admitting the night. I rose to my feet and peered again around the edge of the stairwell. I saw that the door had been propped open. A figure with flapping robes drifted away from me along the widow's walk, headed for the other attic. The blue glow preceded it, casting a luminous edge about the figure. It paused before the closed door and fumbled about there. After a moment the door opened and the figure glided through.

While a closed door obviously could not stop a ghost, I felt driven to put a barrier between us. After edging carefully around the dressmaker's dummy, I felt my way across the room, lifted the box aside, then closed the door and locked it. With that action I lost the small amount of light that had filtered in from the stars outside. Darkness closed in around me, as thick as chocolate pudding. When something light and feathery brushed against my hand, I cried out and stumbled backward, falling against the door while flailing my arms wildly to ward off an attack from whatever it was that had touched me.

Cobwebs!

The realization left my knees as weak as though they were made of butter. With my heart hammering in my chest, I took one step forward, then another, then another, groping my way along with shaking hands. This, then, was what it must be like to be blind . . . to cringe at the thought of being suddenly touched by an unidentified hand, to wonder what evil thing might be standing right in front of you, grinning at your helplessness.

At last I reached the other side of the room, uninjured except for a bruised shin, which I'd barked against a crate. I darted down the stairs and along the corridor until I reached the safety of my own door. Breathless with relief, I started to step inside, then stopped, drawn by an illogical urge to creep across the hall and open the door to the east attic to see if the blue glow were still there. I knew such an action was not wise, yet I found myself moving across the corridor as though pulled by an irresistible force. I opened the door to the stair-well and inhaled sharply to see the opening at the head of the stairs filled with the blue glow. There wafted toward me a sobbing moan.

Go back while you still can! I ordered myself. Still drawn by that force, I paid no attention to my own command but crept up the steps with my pulse hammering in my temples. When I reached the top of the stairs, I once more edged my head around the corner of the opening, hoping to see but not be seen.

A shriek split the air, striking my nerves like lightning.

"Ahh!" I cried out before I could stop myself.

"Who's there?" It was a woman's voice, tense with alarm.

Having reacted instinctively to the scream, I was already halfway down the stairs by the time she spoke. Now I paused and made myself turn around. If I were ever to learn the secrets of Milwood, I had to take some chances. Still, it required all the courage I could muster to mount those steps and expose myself by stepping out into the light.

Charlotte stood several feet away, dressed in a long white peignoir and holding a blue glass hurricane lamp through which the flame of a candle flickered like an azure moth. "You!" she exclaimed, her face a knot of pinched flesh.

"I'm sorry I frightened you, but you frightened me, too," I said. "I thought you were the Milwood ghost."

"How long have you been spying on me?"

"About fifteen minutes, but I didn't know it was you until just now. You're looking for the trunk, aren't you?" It was a question, but I made it a statement, knowing the answer already.

Her hand with the lamp began to tremble, jiggling the flame into mad patterns. The light danced across Simon's wings tacked to the rafters, flickered along the dented tin teapots, struck cold fire from the glass eyes of the hobbyhorse.

Charlotte's knotted face unraveled like an old rope. Tears filled her eyes and overflowed, following the creases in her cheeks.

"I can't bear it . . . to see Milwood go under, to see my husband and sons ruined! It isn't fair. We've worked so hard . . . stayed here through thick and thin. No, it isn't fair!"

"So you do think there is money in the trunk, enough to pull Milwood out of the fire?"

"I think"—she paused and surveyed me bitterly through streaming eyes before finishing with conviction—"I think that Milwood's future lies in that trunk. I'll do anything, *anything* to ensure that future. For Amos, for Henry and Simon . . ."

Her voice had taken on a fanatical ring, which triggered a warning bell inside my head. At that moment she looked quite theatrical and not altogether stable, in her Lady Macbeth robe and holding that blue lamp, with her salt-and-pepper hair springing about her shoulders in a tangled mass.

"Anything." She repeated the word in a harsh whisper.

Pity flowed through me, replacing my earlier fear. The worry over the hotel and her husband's health had obviously driven Charlotte to the breaking point.

"I understand," I said, "but now you need your rest. Come, I'll walk downstairs with you."

"I've searched and searched," she said. "Amos . . . and my boys . . . We—we've got a stone around our necks, a millstone. Yes, Milwood *is* a millstone, and it's destroying my husband

and my sons. I have to save them. I must!"

I stepped forward and took her arm.

"Charlotte, you can do nothing about it tonight. Come on, it's time for bed."

The tears stopped, but the desperate glitter remained in her eyes. "Did you know Henry wants to be a doctor?"

"Yes, I know."

"He'd make a good doctor."

"I'm sure he would."

"And Simon . . . he wants, he needs people around him, many guests. Ambition. Yes, he is ambitious. He envies those big hotels in Hot Springs. He could turn this into a showplace if he just had the money to work with."

"It would take money, that's true."

"Lots of money. A fortune."

"Perhaps. Come now . . ." I guided her toward the stairwell. She shuffled her feet along the floor like a sleepwalker.

"They're good boys. They deserve a chance—a chance to fulfill their dreams. Don't you think they're good boys?"

Hardly boys, I thought. Nor was I as sure as their mother that they were good. But I said, to soothe her, "Yes, they're fine men, Charlotte. You and Amos can be proud of your sons."

I led her awkwardly down the attic stairs to the corridor below. Words continued to pour from her, water gushing from a spring: "Proud. Yes, we are proud. I love my sons. I love my sons so much . . . and my husband. I love them more than life itself. I must help them, I must! Can you understand that? If I can just do something—there has to be a way. . . ."

She kept up the hysterical chatter all the way down to the first floor. Henry, tall and gaunt in his dressing gown, stepped from the shadows at the foot of the stairs into the pool of blue light.

"Mother? Where have you been?"

She pulled away from me and flung herself into his arms,

almost dropping the lamp.

"I want you to be happy, Henry," she cried.

He looked at me quizzically over the top of her head.

"I found her in the attic," I said. "She was searching for the trunk."

He enfolded her tenderly in his arms. "Mother, you'll make yourself sick, all this worry. You must get your rest, you know that. Come, I'll take you back to your room."

Since he had now taken charge of his mother, I turned to go back upstairs. He shook his head in my direction and mouthed silently, "Wait for me."

Surprised, I huddled against the side of the stairs until he returned.

"I got her back into bed," he said quietly. "Joanna, I need to talk with you. Please, come with me to the front verandah."

Like conspirators we tiptoed down the corridor together, past the closed doors where the members of his family were presumably sleeping. Presumably. After finding Charlotte in the attic, I didn't know who else might be up and wandering about. That brought me back to Henry.

"What were *you* doing out of bed?" I asked.

"I've been worried about Mother for some time," he replied. "Lately she's taken to wandering in the middle of the night, and I sometimes get up to check on her when I can't sleep."

"She seems to be trying to carry the burdens of the whole family."

"Back when my father was well . . . I wish you could have seen them together, my mother and father. She worshipped him, still does, I think. She's not physically strong, but she makes up for that in loyalty, fierce loyalty. . . ."

"Almost an obsession," I put in.

"Yes, you could say that."

"The tyranny of love."

"What!"

Although the corridor was dark, I could picture, from the

197

surprise in his voice, the startled look on his face.

"That day when you talked about the tyrannies which rule each of us?" I asked. "Well, you mentioned the tyranny of love. I think your mother is ruled by that, by strong family feeling. It now obsesses her."

"Strange that you should remember that conversation," he said softly.

Oh really? I thought. *That's the day you kissed me, Henry Hampton! Yes, I remember. I remember everything about those moments.*

The fact that we were now passing down that part of the corridor where the kiss had taken place heightened my awareness of Henry's body hovering close to mine in the dark intimacy of the hallway, both of us clad in nightclothes. A suffocating heat rose inside me, a dawning of day inside my veins. My lips softened with desire, with the need to feel the touch of Henry's mouth. His arm brushed against my side, and I inhaled sharply. At the sound he paused.

"Joanna?" he whispered.

I tried to answer, but my voice caught in my throat.

"Joanna," he repeated. His pronunciation of my name caressed the air between us.

I swayed toward him, drawn as metal to a magnet. He swept me into his arms, holding me close against the length of his body. His heart beat strong inside his chest, an engine thrumming against my breast, while his hands, strong and hot, seared along my back. I lifted my eyes, wanting to see his face, to see his expression, but the shadows were too deep. With a low moan he pressed his face to mine, holding me even closer. I felt as though the air were being squeezed from my lungs, so tight was his embrace. He kissed my forehead, my left temple, my right temple, then trailed his lips, a brushing feather, down my cheek. My joints turned to jelly at the touch of his lips against my flesh. My own lips parted in anticipation of his arrival at my mouth. Instead, he bypassed my lips and I felt the tip of his tongue taste my chin. He drew his tongue upwards and ran it lightly around the edges of my mouth. I felt I could not bear to wait another moment and moved my face under his seeking tongue until I possessed his lips with mine. A strange lassitude overtook me. His left hand caressed my breast, his tongue sought out the tenderest recesses of my mouth, while I tangled my fingers in his hair, holding him captive. Never, never had I dreamed that love could be like this. I moaned, and he echoed the sound, lost, I could tell, in his own rapture. Excitement filled me with a white heat that brooked no denial. Again he moaned, and I rejoiced that I could pleasure him so.

Suddenly he pulled back, his arms stiff, his body tense. I tried to draw his face toward mine, but he shook his head under my hand.

"Listen!" he hissed.

The moan came again.

"What! . . ."

"Shhhh!"

Another groan sobbed through the night. Now I knew that the noise I'd thought was the sound of Henry's desire issued, instead, from a room down the corridor toward the front lobby, and it was the sound of pain, not pleasure.

"That's Albert Lock's room!" he said, alarm shrilling in his voice.

"Oh no. Mushrooms!" Guilt washed through me, dashing my passion.

"What mushrooms?" he demanded.

"The ones we had for supper. Two platters of fried mushrooms. Albert ate them both."

Henry gave a disgusted snort. "Stomachache. I thought he was having a heart attack."

He turned and hurried down the hallway, with me stumbling after as I worked to retie my sash.

"Henry, it may be something else!" I called, but he was already pounding on the door and didn't seem to hear me.

"Albert, are you all right?" he shouted.

In response came another groan, then a strangled, "Help me, for God's sake!"

I heard Henry rattle the knob, saw a slight change in the color of the gloom as the door swung open. Henry's footsteps charged into the room toward the sound of retching.

"Sick," Albert gasped. "I'm sick."

I heard a snap, saw the flare of a match. Henry removed the flue and worked with a lamp beside the bed. As the wick flared up, dispelling the shadows, I saw Albert hanging from the edge of the bed with his head over the wastebasket. His back heaved and a green liquid spewed from his mouth, fouling the air with its sour smell. When the paroxysm passed, he rolled back onto the bed, wiping his face with the sleeve of his nightgown.

"Sick," he moaned again.

"After two platters of mushrooms? Not surprising," Henry said sternly.

"Henry . . ." I began again, but he ignored me. He hurried into the water closet and turned on one of the faucets. After fumbling about in there, he emerged with a wet cloth, which he used to wipe Albert's face.

"When did all this start?" he demanded.

"I don't know . . . half-hour ago. Cramps. Getting worse." Albert's usually florid face looked a dirty shade of yellow-green.

"Bad case of indigestion," Henry said to me.

Worse than you know, I thought grimly.

"Henry, I need to see you outside for a moment. . . ."

But I was interrupted by more spasms from Albert, which shook his whole body as the vile vomit poured forth. Henry and I supported the sick man on either side until the retching stopped. We lifted him back onto his pillow where he lay gasping like a beached fish. A thread of saliva dribbled from the corner of his mouth.

"Could be a heart attack after all," Henry murmured in an

200

aside to me.

"Or it could be poison," I whispered.

That got his attention.

"What are you saying?"

I jerked my head toward the hallway. "Outside?" In a louder tone, I said, "We'll be back in a minute, Mr. Lock."

"Don't leave me," he begged.

"We'll be right back, I promise."

Once we were in the corridor, Henry grabbed my arm in a viselike grip. "Poison? What do you mean?"

"The Death Angel . . . what are the symptoms?"

"The Death Angel? My God, you don't think—"

"Maybelle showed me a patch of Death Angel mushrooms in the woods this morning. Mr. Lock ate fried mushrooms for supper."

"Coincidence. Granny knows better than to cook the Death Angel."

"Granny has cataracts. She might not notice—"

"She'd never pick them in the first place."

"Someone else might. Someone who later slipped into the kitchen and crumbled them into the batter, that thick crusty batter Granny prides herself on."

I stopped, stricken by the memory of that gunnysack in Henry's hand. He'd never told me what was in that sack. He displayed no sign of guilt, however, as he exploded, "Who would want to poison Albert Lock? It makes no sense!"

"Not Mr. Lock. Aunt Alice and me. There were two platters of fried mushrooms, one for him and one for us. Ours were the poisoned ones, I'm sure of it. But he ate ours, too." I lifted my hands and covered my face for a brief moment, unable to face either Henry or my own guilt. "I suspected the mushrooms might be unsafe, and I wouldn't let Aunt Alice eat them. But when Mr. Lock reached over and grabbed the platter . . . I could have knocked it from his hand, but I didn't. I thought about it, but I let the moment pass. I just sat there while he ate

201

those mushrooms, and I did nothing."

Henry shook me by the shoulders. "Get hold of yourself, Joanna! We don't know he's eaten the Death Angel. He *does* have a bad heart, and vomiting can go along with a heart attack. It can also go along with indigestion, simple indigestion, and two platters of fried mushrooms on top of a large dinner could make even a lumberjack sick. Don't jump to conclusions."

Another vomiting attack drew us back to Albert Lock's bedside. That the man was suffering horribly could not be questioned. He began to shiver as though he were in a blizzard. We piled on extra covers, but they didn't seem to help. Suddenly his jaw clenched, his eyes rolled back in his head, and his back arched as though someone had given him a jolt of electricity. His arms and legs began to jerk uncontrollably, pounding the bed in convulsion.

"That's not simple indigestion!" I cried as I grabbed hold of Albert to keep him from flailing off the bed. "Henry, something is really wrong! What are the symptoms of Death Angel poisoning? Is there an antidote?"

"I don't know. I don't think so."

"Granny—"

"—is asleep in her cabin."

"Go wake her. Ask her about the symptoms. Ask her about an antidote."

"Old wives' remedies!"

I glanced up to see a sneer curling Henry's upper lip.

"What difference does it make if the remedies work?" I snapped. "Do you want Albert Lock's death on your conscience because you're too snobbish to get help from an 'old wife'?"

Our eyes locked over the sick man's bed. Henry's jaws tightened until his cheeks made dark hollows on either side of his face. His lips were pressed so tightly together that they slashed in a long thin cut above his chin.

The convulsion passed and Albert sagged limply on the bed,

his face ashen and clammy with sweat. I growled at Henry through clenched teeth, "Will you please go?"

Henry looked down at the suffering man and up at me again. Then, saying no more, he spun on one heel and stalked from the room. Albert opened his eyes to stare wildly at the ceiling. He groped for my hand, grabbing it in a desperate grip.

"Pills . . . in the drawer," he gasped, waving his other hand toward the table beside the bed.

I freed myself from his grasp, then tugged the drawer open and pulled forth a small brown glass bottle labeled: "Perkins' Heart Pills." The instructions printed below the name said to place two pills under the tongue at the first sign of a heart attack. Fearing it was futile, I unscrewed the lid and tipped two pills into my palm. I placed the pills under Albert's tongue, but he lost them at once in another fit of vomiting.

"Ohhhh!" he cried, pressing his fists against his stomach. He drew up his knees and hunched his body forward over his belly. Maybelle's writhing worm appeared before me like a picture stamped on glass, its image superimposed over the writhing body of Albert Lock.

"Help me, please," he begged.

He panted for breath, then let out a strangled cry as his body once more arched in convulsion. I had nursed more than one dying patient in the hospital back in St. Louis where I'd finished my training, patients for whom I'd felt great compassion, but I'd still been able to keep my professional objectivity while I worked with them. Now I found tears streaming down my cheeks while I held the flailing man on the bed. He might be crude, but I had sensed his loneliness beneath his salesman's bravado, had known that he'd wanted to be liked and admired. Now he lay here dying in my place. Grief, guilt, frustration, anger boiled up within me like a bubbling pot of gruel, and I wanted to shout, "No! Damn you, Milwood! What have you done?"

It was at least thirty minutes before Henry returned with

Granny. The old woman's petticoat peeked crookedly from beneath her dress, which was buttoned up wrong; her gray hair, usually coiled in a neat braid around her head, now hung down her back in one long, thick frizzy plait. Maybelle, her face pale beneath her tousled curls, trailed along behind the others, her hands clutching a basket loaded with vials and jars. It was the same basket which, just that morning, had held the mushrooms.

"What's the matter here?" Granny said, bustling into the room. "Got the miseries, have you?"

Albert tried to answer, but all he could manage was a harsh croak.

"He's had another convulsion since you left, and he's vomited some more," I said to Henry. "He wanted these, but he couldn't keep them in his mouth."

I handed Henry the bottle of pills. He read the instructions, his brows drawn together in a frown. "I asked Granny about the mushrooms," he said in a low tone. "She denies that anything could have been wrong with them."

Granny sniffed with wounded pride. "Ain't never served bad mushrooms in all my born days," she told me vehemently. "Always been careful, always."

"But someone else could have crumbled the bad ones into small pieces and stirred them into your batter when you weren't looking, isn't that true?"

Behind me, I heard Maybelle gasp. I turned to see her standing wide-eyed with her mouth hanging open in a startled O.

"Do you know something about this?" I demanded.

"Nothing, nothing," she hastily replied. "But I did dream. Tonight, again. About the—you know what about."

She set down the basket and grasped the back of a chair, as though she had gone suddenly faint.

"You'd better sit down," I advised.

She sank into a chair and huddled there, her face a pinched

mask. Could she have had a hand in making this dream come true? I wondered. She'd said she wished I'd die, but did she hate me enough to risk including my aunt and Mr. Lock in a plot to murder me? Could she really be that depraved?

I stepped forward and grasped Albert's wrist. His pulse fluttered lightly beneath my fingertips, as erratic and weak as a butterfly.

"Hurts," he mumbled. "It hurts . . . so bad."

I turned my back to the bed and asked in a low tone, "Granny, how long does it take for a victim to show the first signs of mushroom poisoning?"

"Depends what kind. Fly Agaric, that 'un takes half hour, hour maybe, to hit ya. Death Angel, that 'un takes longer— several hours, maybe eight, maybe ten."

I glanced at the clock on Albert's mantel. "Henry, it's been eight hours now since supper." To Granny, I continued, "What are the symptoms for the Death Angel?"

"Stomach cramps. Pain. Vomiting. Convulsions."

"See?" I said fiercely to Henry. "I told you!"

"But a heart attack can cause those symptoms, too," he replied. "Let's try these again."

He slipped two pills under Albert's tongue and then held one hand under the sick man's chin to hold his mouth shut while talking to him soothingly. "Try to relax, Albert. Just relax and let the pills dissolve. We'll help you all we can."

"Just how long does it take for someone to—to die after eating the Death Angel?" I now whispered to Granny.

"I seen two different people die from it," she replied softly. "One it took two days, the other it took three."

"Three days?" I hissed, aghast. Three days of unbearable torment; it was a death I wouldn't wish on the worst villain in the world. "There must be something we can do!"

"Ain't no cure," she murmured darkly. "Not if it's that."

"Henry, we've got to send for a doctor from Hot Springs."

"You're right," he said, then added bitterly, "If only I had my license, we'd have a doctor on the premises right now."

"Well, you don't, so we need someone who does," I said. "Do you want to go, or do you want to send Simon?"

"I'll go. There's no point in waking up everyone in the household."

He stood for a long moment staring down at the bed. "Albert, I'm sorry," he said at last.

His apology startled me. It was almost as though he were claiming responsibility for Albert's distress. Again I thought of that gunnysack.

"Six miles each way. It will be dawn before we can get back here," he now said to me.

"Do the best you can."

He reached out and touched me on the arm. His face softened as he looked at me, losing for a moment the tense bitter expression that had etched deep lines around his mouth. "You, too. I hate to leave you alone with this."

Despite my uneasiness about the gunnysack and my suspicion of all those around me, I found myself melting at Henry's touch.

Don't go! I wanted to cry. *Stay and help me.*

But I was the one who'd suggested the Hot Springs doctor. My mind said, "He must go," even as my heart cried for him to stay.

"Be careful," I murmured. "Roads can be dangerous at night."

"It's a long time since the James brothers terrorized this area," he replied, giving me a crooked smile.

"Rocks, chuckholes for the horse to stumble into," I said. "Just be careful, that's all."

He turned and patted Albert's shoulder. "We'll get back as soon as we can."

Albert clutched his arm for a brief moment. "You—you—" But although his mouth worked, he could say no more.

Henry hurried from the room. About twenty minutes later I heard the clop of the horse and the rattle of the buggy receding down the lane into the night. Time faded into a blur as Granny and I worked together over Albert, assisted by a whimpering Maybelle. Dawn had just begun to pink the sky when Albert, racked by more convulsions, went into cardiac arrest. Henry and the doctor arrived soon after, but by then it was too late. Albert Lock from Little Rock was dead.

Chapter 18

The Hot Springs doctor announced that Albert had died of a heart attack brought on by acute indigestion. While he filled out the death certificate, I tried to discuss the possibility of mushroom poisoning with him, but he dismissed my questions with a wave of his hand, obviously annoyed that a nurse would dare to try to influence his decision.

"I can tell this man was a glutton," he said. "I'm sure, with that bad heart, he'd been warned not to overeat. But some people are ruled by their stomachs. You can't tell them anything."

Another tyranny—gluttony. Poor Mr. Lock. I believed, for all his crudeness, he'd never meant anyone any harm. Now he himself had fallen into harm's way, the harm intended for my aunt and me.

It's strange how convention, another tyranny, can hold a person in thrall. I knew I should demand that a sheriff come out to Milwood to investigate Mr. Lock's death, yet the idea of defying the doctor, of creating a scene and making a fool of myself when I had nothing but supposition to go on, made me back down after the doctor's pronouncement. Henry, too, continued to discourage any attempts to discuss the similarities between a heart attack and mushroom poisoning. When all was said and done, what could I prove? The kitchen would long since have been cleaned and the evidence thrown away.

By now the sun was up and the whole household awake, except for Aunt Alice. I let her sleep. So long as she stayed in bed, she was one less problem with which I had to cope. I helped Henry wrap poor Mr. Lock's body in blankets for the trip to the mortician. Simon and Henry carried him out to the wagon and laid him carefully in the back. Henry had copied down Mr. Lock's Little Rock address from the register. He told me he'd send a wire to Mr. Lock's family, once he got to town. Now he and Simon climbed into the front seat, along with the doctor, and headed down the lane. I stood on the verandah and watched them depart. Then, feeling exhausted and drained, I sought out a quiet spot on the bench by the fountain in the rose garden, where I sat pondering the night's events.

"Joanna?" Jeremy slipped through the rose bushes and paused before me. "Are you all right?"

"I don't know."

The water in the fountain arched in thin streams from a perforated central core, creating a pattern like a willow tree, which shimmered with rainbows in the morning sun. I slumped on the bench, held captive both by fatigue and by the mesmerizing display. Jeremy sat down beside me.

"Mr. Lock dead—I can't believe it," he murmured.

"If you'd been there, you'd believe it." I began to shiver, picturing my aunt and myself writhing in the foul grip of the Death Angel. It could have happened. It could have happened so easily. . . .

"What happened?" Jeremy's question, echoing my thoughts, jarred me back to the present.

I told him about the mushroom hunt the previous day and about my fear of the fried mushrooms at dinner. I mentioned no names but did say I suspected someone had slipped into the kitchen and crumbled poisonous mushrooms into Granny's fry mix, which Mr. Lock later ate.

"No!" Jeremy stared at me, his pale eyes wide with horror. "Who would do such a cruel thing? Surely the doctor is right.

It must have been a heart attack."

"It was, in the end. Yes, a heart attack killed him, mercifully so if Granny is right about mushroom poisoning taking two to three days. But I have no proof about the mushrooms, just this cold, uneasy feeling. I do know who your ghost was, however."

I told him about Charlotte and the blue hurricane lamp.

"The blue light reflected off her white gown and made her appear to glow," I told him. "It startled me, too, at first."

He gave me a sheepish grin. "You had the courage to investigate, something I didn't do. My imagination . . . it runs away with me sometimes."

I wrapped my arms about my body, trying to control my shivering. "Is that what's happening with me, Jeremy? Am I allowing my imagination to run away with me, too? Because Henry and the doctor could be right. Mr. Lock's symptoms could have been caused by acute indigestion and cardiac arrest, although I've never seen anyone else convulse the way he did. But it wouldn't be impossible. People do sometimes go into convulsions when they're under extreme physical stress."

"I still feel that evil has taken over Milwood," Jeremy replied. "That may be imagination, too, but it's a feeling I can't shake. I—ah—" He paused and gave me a shy look before drawing a folded sheet of paper from his pocket. "I—I've been thinking about what you said, about my poetry, about making it stronger. Would you like to hear?"

I did not want to hear, not at that moment, but I could think of no good excuse for putting him off when all I was doing was just sitting there.

"All right."

I closed my eyes and lifted my face to the warmth of the morning sun, musing that Albert Lock would never see nor feel the sun again. Jeremy began to read:

> Cringe before the ruthless god of Fear.
> Whimper when his knife lays bare the soul.
> Shiver while he jeers and laughs and mocks,

Mouth ajar, eyes like dead black coal.
What a fiend, this Fear. He twists the blade,
Draining strength away in scarlet streams.
"Is there, then, no help?" The victim's cry
Echoes through the torture hall of dreams.
But wait—a light so bright it rivals day!
Within that light Fear loses form and scope.
Amazed, the victim stands, his strength restored,
Touched by the healing hands of dawn-robed Hope.

I had by now opened my eyes to stare at Jeremy in surprise. He returned my look with pathetic eagerness.

"Do—do you think it's any good?"

"I don't know poetry, I told you that before. But with all the fear I'm feeling now, that poem, good or bad, speaks to me more strongly than anything else of yours I've ever heard. Why did you write it?"

He laughed, a low bitter sound. "Because of my own fear. I spend my nights consumed by doubts, wondering what's going on here. If you're right about the mushrooms . . ."

"I just don't know. I do know I wish we could leave here and go back to St. Louis. I wish we could go today."

"Joanna, is that you down there?" My aunt's imperious voice fell like a stone from the sky.

I looked up to see a shadow against the window screen of our sitting room, three stories above.

"Be careful, that screen's loose!" I called. "Don't lean on it!"

She did not acknowledge my warning but demanded sharply, "Why aren't you up here helping me dress? And why hasn't the bell rung for breakfast? It's already past eight o'clock."

"She doesn't know," I murmured to Jeremy. "I decided to let her sleep. Well, I can't put it off any longer. She has to be told."

I pulled myself wearily to my feet and walked with flagging steps back into the hotel. The day stretched ahead of me like a

211

black tunnel without end. I wanted to collapse in that darkness and drift into oblivion, free of Jeremy's "torture hall of dreams."

Such was not to be, however, for my aunt had rested well and was now full of vinegar, ready to face the day. When I said that Albert Lock had just died, she replied, "I'm sorry to hear that, of course, but I'm not surprised. His weight and florid complexion spelled apoplexy, right from the start. And the way he stuffed down all those mushrooms last night . . . It's a wonder he managed to live this long, with an appetite like that."

"He did not die of apoplexy," I said. "The doctor has pronounced it a heart attack, but I have my own ideas."

"Oh? You know more than doctors now, do you?"

"I think those mushrooms last night may have been poison."

Her mouth fell open and for once I saw her speechless. Her silence did not last long.

"Poison? Granny, cook poison mushrooms? Never!" She thumped her cane on the floor.

"Not Granny, but someone else who sneaked into the kitchen and added bits of fried Death Angel to the platter intended for you and me."

"Joanna, I think your mind is going, all these strange ideas. First you claimed someone tried to drown me, and then you said someone pushed you down the stairs. Accidents, just accidents, yet you've built them into big stories. Now an overweight sick man dies of a heart attack, cause of death confirmed by a doctor, but you say it's poison intended for us. Your imagination is running away with you, young woman. I am not pleased."

"I try to tell myself that it's imagination, but I'm not sure. To be on the safe side—"

"No, we are not leaving! I have never met such a conniving, scheming young woman as you are! You'll make up any kind of tale to get your way."

212

You're a conniver, too, I thought. *You and Rhodes. How many schemes did you dream up through the years to get your way?*

We were interrupted by the bell announcing that breakfast would be served in fifteen minutes. I hastened to help Aunt Alice finish dressing, then stripped out of my soiled clothing and took a quick dip in a tub of steaming water to cleanse myself from the horror of the night before, donning fresh underclothing and a simple everyday dress of blue muslin. A few tendrils from my damp hair, hastily combed and coiled into a bun, escaped to curl about my face in a red halo. When I glanced into the mirror for a last check of my buttons, I winced at the pallor of my skin, the dark circles under my eyes. I looked haggard and old beyond my years. When I emerged into the sitting room, Aunt Alice rose and inspected me critically.

"You look terrible," she said. "Jeremy will not find you attractive if you let yourself go like this. Remember, I expect to see you married before the summer ends. Twenty-five thousand dollars, Joanna, twenty-five thousand dollars to your mother on your wedding day to Jeremy!"

I writhed inwardly at her reminder, thinking how much my mother needed that money. I'd had a letter from her telling me that one of my younger brothers might need surgery on a broken leg that hadn't healed properly.

The tyranny of poverty. How right Henry was!

"Have you ever asked Jeremy how he feels about your wedding plans for us?" I asked.

"Of course not! These little things must be arranged quietly by the woman, so that the man thinks everything is his own idea."

"Is that how it's done, then? Is that how relationships come about?"

I knew my question was cruel, given the knowledge I had about her past. She dropped her eyes and stood for a moment with her head bowed. When she looked up at last, her expression was subdued, her eyes dark with pain.

"I can hardly pass for an expert, can I?" she commented

quietly. "I'm just a dried-up old maid who never married. It's lonely to grow old like this, Joanna. Lonely. I—I hope you never know this loneliness."

My heart squeezed in my chest. Impulsively I crossed the room and hugged her, a liberty I'd never dared before. She reared back and huffed through her nose.

"Really, Joanna! Come, we're going to be late."

When we arrived in the dining room, I blinked back tears at the sight of Albert Lock's empty chair. The loneliness of Albert's life and death, followed by my aunt's admission of loneliness, had opened a door deep inside me to reveal, lurking there like a small dark demon, my own mortality. Usually I kept it locked out of sight, but now it leered at me from the shadows, its beady eyes glowing with triumph. *You will die someday,* said those eyes. *Your aunt will die. Your mother will die. All those you know and love will someday die.*

With morbid thoughts like that, I did not expect to be able to eat breakfast; but when Maybelle arrived with the squeaking cart and I saw the boiled eggs in their protective shells, rising like blank-faced Humpty-Dumpties from the egg cups, my appetite returned. Boiled eggs would be safe, boiled eggs would be nourishing. The coffee smelled good, too. Suddenly I was ravenous and could hardly wait for Maybelle to serve so that I could eat.

She moved slowly, however, sighing when she glanced toward Albert Lock's table.

"Are you tired as I am this morning?" I asked her quietly.

She turned toward me in frank surprise at my concern.

"Thank you for asking," she replied. Her gratitude sounded sincere. "I—I don't think I'll ever sleep again. I don't want to dream. I never want to dream, not ever. When I think of that robed figure and that coffin . . ."

A shudder shook her from head to toe, so that the egg she extended to me rattled in its cup.

"Your dreams weren't the cause of Mr. Lock's death," I said, taking the egg. "You can't blame yourself in any way."

Or can you? I added silently. *Did you go back yesterday and harvest that patch of Death Angel mushrooms after we finished our walk?*

"What dreams?" demanded my aunt.

"Maybelle has had dreams about death, about a coffin covered with white roses and mushrooms," I said.

"So *that's* where you got your strange idea about mushrooms!" she exclaimed.

"I—I heard you questioning Granny." Maybelle kept her eyes averted while serving us toast and rashers of bacon. "It can't . . . I don't . . . Granny is very careful. She would never have cooked and served the Death Angel."

"Who else was in the kitchen yesterday afternoon?" I asked.

Maybelle flicked her eyes toward me, then looked away again. "Let's see. Both Miz Nell and Miz Charlotte. Henry came in, in the middle of the afternoon, and ate a piece of pie. And Simon . . . he stopped by to drink a cup of coffee. Mr. Amos?" She frowned, thinking, then nodded. "Yes, he was there for a while with his wife. She'd taken him out in his wheelchair for a trip around the yard. And"—she paused, and her pale face flushed a becoming pink—"and Jeremy. You, Miz McPherson, you were there."

"You, Aunt Alice? You didn't tell me!"

"I didn't think it was important. I was looking for Jeremy, that's all."

Everyone had been in that kitchen but Mr. Lock and myself. The place had, indeed, been a veritable train station, everyone coming and going in a confusion of activity. I sighed and concentrated on breakfast, finding that the coffee, the soft-boiled egg, the thick slices of bread spread with butter and honey, brought back the strength I'd lost due to lack of sleep. That was a fact I'd noticed before: With plenty of sleep, I needed less food; but lose a night's sleep, and I always had to eat more to keep going. Perhaps that's why some of the senior nurses I'd worked with back in St. Louis had been fat. Doctors, too. For illness is not polite. Illness does not wait for daylight but often comes in the middle of the night, bringing with it a demanding knock on the nearest doctor's door.

Despite the hearty breakfast, I would still have welcomed a few hours of sleep. Aunt Alice wanted her morning bath, however. Usually she preferred the ministrations of Granny, but this morning I did the honors in the bathhouse after I found Granny, gray with fatigue, snoring away in the kitchen rocking chair. Later I nodded off, too, while sitting on the bench beside the tub in the hot steamy cubicle, where Aunt Alice soaked in the healing waters and sipped from her teapot. My nap lasted only about twenty minutes, but it served to greatly refresh me.

That's why, after I'd deposited Aunt Alice back in our suite for her post-bath rest, I did not collapse on my own bed but headed downstairs once more to see if Henry and Simon had returned. When I reached the second floor, I paused, arrested by the scraping, clanking sounds that echoed once more down the corridor. All my fear, grief, and frustration now welled up inside me, a hot bubbling spring of anger. I marched down the corridor to the door and beat my fist against it, shouting, "Who is in there? Open up this instant!"

The noises stopped abruptly, even as they had before, but this time I did not back away. I grasped the knob in a white-knuckled fist and turned it sharply. To my surprise, the tumblers clicked and I realized the lock was not engaged. Still supported by anger, I pushed the door all the way open and banged it against the wall. The momentum carried me a full stride into the room before I slammed to a halt against an invisible wall of ice, a shock barrier through which I gaped with my mouth hanging stupidly open.

The center of the room was empty, even as Jeremy and I had seen when we'd peeked through the keyhole. The walls of the room, however, were lined with equipment: a wooden bar about waist height along one wall, supported on metal brackets and standing out about four inches, such as one finds in dance

216

studios; a strange stationary bicycle with the back wheel removed, the seat supported by a strong metal pole bolted to the floor, and the front wheel suspended in a metal brace, which allowed one to pedal without going anywhere; two trapeze bars suspended on chains from the ceiling, one waist-high, one the height a man could reach with arms extended; a set of shallow steps with metal bannisters going up to a platform and descending on the other side; a set of waist-high parallel bars bolted to the floor, about a body's width apart, with a walkway between.

The sight that knocked the air from my lungs and froze me to the spot, however, was the person who stood on the platform at the top of the steps. He glared at me, his eyes wild, his gray hair springing about his face in disordered tufts.

"Where is the trunk?" he demanded. "What have you done with it?"

As I stood there immobilized, he swung himself down the bannisters, his arms as strong as an ape's, and lumbered toward me with jerky steps, shuffling, staggering, but walking nonetheless, his calloused hands and sausagelike fingers extended toward me in a strangler's hold. A groaning sob welled from his throat.

"Joooo . . ." he cried in a drawn-out wail. "Jo . . ."

He stopped, staring at me, his brows drawn together in a puzzled frown.

"Joanna," I said softly. "Amos, it's Joanna."

"Jo . . . Joanna," he repeated. His gaze cleared briefly, the sun from which obscuring clouds had parted. "Joanna. Go. Go, Joanna. Go away. Leave Milwood. Take Alice, malice, palace, take Alice. Go."

The clouds returned, along with tears, which coursed down his cheeks like rain.

"Danger," he muttered. "Danger."

He turned and lurched back to the steps, past his parked wheelchair, as though he'd forgotten I was there. While he pulled himself painfully up to the platform, groaning with exertion, he continued to mumble to himself, "Danger. Go away. Go away."

I did go away, backing from the room and softly closing the door. Once outside, I leaned against the wall and breathed deeply to still my pounding heart.

Amos could walk. That was the astounding fact I struggled to absorb. Amos could climb steps. Who knew what else Amos could do? And who had installed all that equipment in that room, equipment designed to help an injured man regain his strength?

To the second question, I was sure I had an answer: Henry had started, on a small scale, to build his clinic.

Chapter 19

Henry and Simon did not get back to Milwood until late afternoon. When I heard the wagon rattling along the lane, I hurried out onto the verandah and down the steps to meet it.

"Hello! You're back at last!"

"Whoa!" Simon pulled back on the reins. "Hop aboard."

He scooted over into the middle of the seat while I scrambled up beside him. Henry, his face haggard, greeted me with an almost inaudible grunt from the other side. Simon shook the reins and we clopped on toward the stable.

"Did you wire Mr. Lock's family?" I asked.

"Yes," Simon replied when Henry didn't answer. "At least we sent the wire to the one address we had. Albert had no wife or children, just one older brother that we know of."

"You left the body at the mortician's?"

He nodded. "If the brother doesn't come to escort the body to Little Rock, then we may have to go back into town and put the coffin on the train. Actually we have to return to town anyway, to ship Albert's personal belongings."

I shivered. "Poor man. It was a terrible way to go."

I leaned forward to look toward Henry and caught him sliding his eyes in my direction. I wondered if he were having second thoughts about the mushrooms. If he were, he gave no sign but merely faced forward again, hunching his head

219

between his shoulders.

Simon sniffed. "What's that smell?"

I laughed, a little embarrassed. "Mr. Lock gave me a tin of his honeysuckle salve. I rubbed some on my hands a while ago, in homage to him. Rather silly, I guess."

Simon glanced toward me in a sympathetic way. "Not silly at all." He began in a gentle, singsong voice, "Albert Lock from Little Rock—"

"—peddles products round the block." I had to stop for a moment, swallowing hard, before I could go on. "Poor Albert Lock. He wanted so much to be liked."

We clattered around the bend and over the bridge. The steam from the springs drifted through the trees in thin wisps.

"Now we have one less guest," Simon said wryly. "But I don't wonder no one wants to come to Milwood. You should see Hot Springs right now, all bustle and excitement. Getting ready for the Fourth of July picnic, that's what they're doing. It's going to be quite a shindig this year—band concert, bicycle races, fireworks . . ."

After the horror of the night before, it seemed shameful that I could want to go to a picnic, but right at that moment the idea of being surrounded by laughing, happy people sounded most attractive.

"So what do you say?" Simon asked. "You want to go to the picnic with me?"

I swallowed, wondering if he had read my mind.

"Thank you, but let me think about it," I replied. "This hardly seems the time. . . ."

He sobered. "You're right, it is disrespectful to think of fun right now. Albert was a man who meant well, and we owe him a time of mourning. Of course, the picnic is three days off, so maybe . . . well, maybe . . ."

He gave me such a hangdog look of appeal that I couldn't help smiling.

"Perhaps. We'll see."

Henry glanced toward me again, his expression shuttered. I

thought of my wanton response to his embrace the night before and felt my face grow warm.

Why have you kept that room upstairs a secret? I wanted to shout. *Why haven't you told people your father can walk?*

Our arrival at the stable interrupted my mental confrontation with Henry Hampton. I'd thought I might be able to corner him alone somewhere on the walk back to the hotel, but he leapt from the wagon and stalked off, leaving me behind with Simon.

"He seems to be in a bad mood," I commented.

Simon quirked one eyebrow, watching the stiff-backed retreat of his brother. "He's been like that all day. Albert's death has really upset him. Why didn't you wake me up last night to help?"

"Granny and Maybelle were there, and Henry, and myself. There was really nothing you could have done."

"I could have gone for the doctor and left Henry to help you. Or vice versa. Actually the vice versa would have been better." He looked me up and down with open admiration. "You're not only a brave, competent woman, you're very beautiful. Did you know that?"

I laughed. "How am I supposed to answer such a question? 'Yes, I know,' sounding conceited, or 'No, I didn't know,' sounding coy? Thank you, Simon. I appreciate the compliment, particularly on a day like this when I feel both unbeautiful and incompetent."

While he unhitched the horse, I perched on a nearby bale of hay. He began to curry the horse, and for a while I watched in silence.

"Have you searched any more for the trunk?" I asked at last, thinking of the hole in the wall in the east attic where I'd found the letter.

"Some. No success, though."

"I've looked, too, but I haven't had any success, either. Your mother is also searching. I found her up in the attic last night, close to midnight, in her white gown and carrying a blue hurricane lamp. I thought at first she was the ghost."

Simon's jaw tightened and a line deepened between his brows. "Mother worries about Milwood, worries more than any of us, I suspect. Ever since my father lost the use of his legs . . ."

A shock ran through my body. *Your father can walk!* I shouted mentally, but bit back the verbal revelation of that fact just in time. There had to be a reason for Amos's secrecy, and until I knew what it was, I felt I should keep silent.

"I—I want to show you something," Simon continued, a note of shyness in his voice. He went to a tack box over by the wall and returned with a handbill. "I've had a thousand of these printed. I plan to hand some of them out in Hot Springs during the picnic and also to give out some more at the train station to incoming health seekers and to send the rest to Little Rock to put up in shop windows there. What do you think?"

He held up the bill for my inspection. It was a lurid thing in three colors, black and red ink printed on yellow paper. The name MILWOOD HOTEL crawled in fancy letters across a banner held by an eagle at the top of the bill. Below the banner was a paragraph, bordered by a floral design, which extolled the virtues of the hotel and listed the springs as providing a cure for everything from corns to weak lungs.

"Advertising," he stated with satisfaction. "I've said all along that we need to advertise. People aren't going to come to Milwood if they don't know we're here."

His reasoning made sense, although I personally would have preferred a more tasteful design for the poster.

"Those . . . should attract attention," I said, trying to be diplomatic in my choice of words.

"That's what we want, isn't it, to attract attention? And if we can attract some customers? . . ."

"Does Henry know about your handbills?"

Simon's face tightened like a fist. "I asked him about the idea, but he said we didn't have the money. Well, it takes money to make money."

"Then how—"

"I charged them. At the printer's. I said we'd pay in four weeks. We should have guests by then, brought in by the handbills."

More debts for Milwood. I saw the desperate gleam in Simon's eyes, the hard set to his mouth, and wondered what he would do if those guests did not materialize.

"I'm tired of being poor," he went on in a vehement tone. "I'm tired of scrimping to make ends meet while Milwood falls apart. Jeremy moons about with his poetry, and Henry is just as bad, whining because he doesn't have his doctor's license. Someone has to take the bull by the horns around here if Milwood is to be saved. If that means taking chances, so be it."

His reckless anger fried the air between us. I drew back, startled by his intensity.

"I hope the handbills work," I said.

"They must." He shook the bill in the air as though to infuse it with his own strength of will. "They must!"

He put the bill back into the box with the others. I took advantage of that moment to rise and move quickly toward the door.

"My aunt will be wondering what's keeping me," I called over my shoulder. "I'm going on back to the hotel now."

But he foiled my escape by saying, "I'm finished here. I'll walk with you."

He turned the horse loose in the stable yard, then joined me on the path.

"I hope we can keep the story of Albert's death quiet in Hot Springs," he said with a worried look. "Things like that are bad for business, for the reputation of Milwood. Of course, Albert brought that bad heart with him, along with his gout, but you know how people talk. They might say the minerals in our springs here aren't as powerful as those in town, just when we need good publicity."

You don't know how bad your publicity could get! I thought sardonically. *If I were to go to the police and suggest Albert was murdered? . . .*

But Time had worked its little miracle with me again. As the hours had crept by during the day, I'd found myself becoming less and less sure that Albert had died of mushroom poisoning. *It could have been plain indigestion and a heart attack*, a small voice kept arguing inside me.

For my own peace of mind, I wanted it to be that.

All the events of the past few weeks now paraded through my mind, waving flags of doubt: *Perhaps you did imagine that a voice called you out of the bathhouse*, murmured my teasing inner voice. *Perhaps you really stumbled and fell down those stairs. After all, your groaning "prisoner" in the west wing has turned out to be Amos taking physical treatments. Your "ghost" was Charlotte with a lamp. How many of these other things have logical explanations?*

"A penny for your thoughts," Simon said, reaching out to wave his hands before my eyes.

"They aren't worth a penny. Save your money for the handbills."

At that reminder of his debt, his face once more turned grim. "Why should the hotels in town have all the luck? Milwood is a good place. All we have to do is build it up again."

Would an influx of guests, bringing in new life, new influences, dispel the darkness that now hovered over the hotel? I wondered. I envisioned polished carriages with high-stepping horses clopping to a halt before the front steps to discharge women in frilly summer dresses and wide-brimmed flowered hats, men in striped blazers and white pants, their laughter echoing over the lawn. There would be dancing in the ball room, banquets in the dining hall . . .

"The Fourth of July celebration should be exciting," Simon said. "Have you decided? Will you go with me?"

"I—we'll see. I'm not sure I could leave Aunt Alice alone all day."

"That presents no problem. We'll take her along," he announced cheerfully.

I paused to look at him in wonder. "Simon, do you mean it?"

"Why not? The trip to town might do her good."

I chewed my lower lip, sorely tempted by his offer. "Let me speak to her about it, all right? Maybe if I introduce the subject gradually . . ."

He laughed. "She's not an easy person to manipulate, is she?"

"She definitely has her own ideas."

That proved, later, to be all too true. When I brought up the subject of the trip to town, she said, "I've told you, Joanna, I don't like the confusion in Hot Springs. Those crowds on the Fourth of July will make things even worse. No, I don't care to go."

Disappointment drove through me like a cold rain. She didn't seem to notice but continued in a decided tone, "It would just be noisy and dusty there, Joanna. You wouldn't like it either, believe me."

I was still nursing my disappointment during supper, a meal I ate with some trepidation, testing every forkful for bits of mushroom. When we'd finished, I trailed after my aunt into the lobby, where we encountered Jeremy emerging from the office, his soft hair more rumpled than usual.

"I'm just trying to get all our creditors appeased and the books brought up to date," he said when he saw me glancing at his ink-stained fingers.

I wondered what he would say if he knew Simon had just incurred a new debt for Milwood.

"Dear boy, you look tired. Come out on the verandah and sit with us for a while," my aunt said, laying her hand on Jeremy's arm.

"All right, then," Jeremy replied as he gave her a fond smile.

They drifted together through the door out onto the porch. Before I could join them, Henry came striding into the lobby and grabbed my arm.

"Come with me," he said coldly.

Still holding onto my arm, he half led, half dragged me down

225

the corridor to the ballroom. Once we were inside, he firmly closed the door. I jerked away and stood rubbing my arm, which I felt sure would soon display a bruise.

Deciding to get in the first word, I demanded, "Why have you kept that room upstairs a secret? Why haven't you told the people around here that your father can walk?"

He towered over me, his face taut. "Dad told me you barged in on him this morning."

"Why didn't you warn me about what was going on? You must have been in there with him the day I knocked on the door."

He shrugged. "It's my father's secret, not mine. He wants it to be a Fourth of July surprise for Mother and Grandmother, the fact that he can walk."

"All that equipment—"

His tense expression softened a little as he asked, "What did you think of it?"

"That bicycle . . . I've never seen anything like it!"

He nodded, and I saw a touch of pride dawn in his eyes. "I designed that and got a man in Hot Springs to build it for me. It's done wonders, helping Dad regain the use of his legs."

"Is that the kind of thing you'd like to do with your clinic?"

"Yes. Many of the health seekers who come to Hot Springs . . . well, some of them are partially paralyzed, and they need exercise, special exercises designed for their individual needs. I'd be good at that."

I admired his lack of false modesty. Still, I bristled, thinking of the fright I'd had that day when I'd retreated to hide in the closet.

"You must have laughed when I pounded on the door and offered to rescue the 'prisoner,'" I said curtly.

"It was Dad who motioned for me to keep quiet, but I had second thoughts and went to look for you. Where did you disappear to, anyway?"

"In that spare room, behind the feather beds in the closet."

He snorted with sudden laughter. "It would have served you

226

right if I'd locked that closet door."

"The possibility occurred to me."

"Or, better yet, I should have joined you in there. The two of us together, in that steamy closet with all those feather beds?"

His eyes darkened and he took a step toward me, his fingertips brushing my arm. My skin sang under his touch while my knees softened into bread dough. For one mad moment I pictured myself in the closet with Henry's hand on my breast, our moist breath intermingling. Heat flamed from my neck into my face. I had the uneasy feeling that he could read my face as clearly as though the words "I want you" were stamped across my forehead.

Such forwardness in us both shocked me. I knew that decorum demanded a more subtle courting pattern. I should have remained demure and chaste, peering coyly from behind a fan, while Henry should have postured and bowed like a strutting bird, hands gloved to avoid touching my bare skin. Our speech should have consisted of trite phrases about the weather, the latest fashions, the upcoming taffy pull or Sunday school picnic. The overtures he'd been making to me ever since the morning he'd caught me downstairs in my wrapper should have resulted in my dismissing him from my presence, never to allow close contact again.

But I wanted that close contact. I wanted his arms around me once more. I wanted his body pressed against my own.

"God, what a passionate woman you are," he whispered in a husky voice. "I've never desired anyone as much as I desire you."

The fact that he had desired others at all dashed me from the cloud on which I'd been floating. Of course, he would be an experienced man, I told myself. He must have made many trips into town to visit willing women in back alley rooms. I stepped away from him, once more in control.

"Henry, that's enough. We've gone too far already, you know that."

227

"Last night in the corridor—"

"Exactly. It's not your fault, it's mine for not having called a halt sooner. We've behaved shamefully."

"Yes, indeed," he agreed with a wicked chuckle.

I shook my head. "It mustn't happen again. I know that nurses have a reputation for being loose, and I may seem to you to be the example that proves the rule; but I refuse to become your plaything. There are too many dangers. . . ." I paused, thinking of my aunt and all the problems she'd encountered by loving too freely.

"You speak plainly," he said.

"There's no point in being coy, not after the liberties I've already allowed you to take."

"I've enjoyed those liberties." His eyes gleamed at the memory.

"The shocking thing I must now confess is that I've enjoyed them, too. If lusting in one's heart is a sin, and the Bible says it is, then I'm a sinner."

He reached for me. "And I am, too."

I scurried away from him and up onto the stage, putting the piano between us. "Lust is not enough, Henry. There has to be love, as well."

"Don't you love me?" he asked in a teasing voice. "Am I not the most lovable person you've ever met?"

The light way in which he was treating the whole matter told me that he certainly did not love me. Perhaps his casual experiences in Hot Springs had hardened his heart to true love. That was a waste, I thought sadly, admitting to myself for the first time that I'd been harboring a dream of marrying Dr. William Henry Hampton and helping him run his clinic. A dream only, since he was not a doctor, nor was there a clinic.

"I don't care to discuss this any further," I said in a firm tone. "What I *do* want to know is why your father has chosen the Fourth of July to make his announcement."

"He picked that day as his goal, back when we first started doing the exercises. They're painful, and he had to have something to look forward to to give him the courage to go on. I think he sees that as his own 'Independence Day,' you see."

"Yes, I can understand that setting a goal gives one an incentive to work harder." My words sounded stilted and prim. I hurried on. "The other thing I want to ask is why you refused to even consider the possibility of mushroom poisoning last night. We should have had Albert's death investigated by the law."

The anger rekindled in his eyes. "Are you still harping on that? You tend to take the extreme view in any situation, Joanna. That's the sign of an overzealous imagination, not a good characteristic in a nurse. You need to watch that."

The condescension in his voice sparked my own anger. "A closed mind such as yours is much worse! A doctor, a true doctor, should look at every possibility before making a diagnosis. It seems to me that you're the one who has a lot to learn. Don't forget, I have my medical certificate. You don't."

His face congested with fury, turning a dark red, while thick cords stood out in his neck.

"No, I don't forget that. I never forget that. And if I should forget that, I'm sure you would remind me."

He turned and strode from the room, his long legs quickly covering the distance, his boots thudding on the bare wooden floor. I stood with my fists planted against the top of the piano. He did not look back but slammed the door behind him, leaving me alone.

My anger had sustained me during his departure, but now I sagged into one of the ornate orchestra chairs, regretting my harsh words. I knew the lack of a license was Henry's most vulnerable point. Still, he'd hurt me, too, with his arrogance and patronizing attitude. Better to pull back and keep distance between us, I decided.

I waited for several minutes before leaving the ballroom. I looked nervously around as I stepped into the corridor, not wanting to encounter Henry again. Fortunately, he'd had the good sense to take himself elsewhere. I proceeded back to the lobby and peeked through the front door to see if my aunt was still sitting out on the verandah with Jeremy. She was, and she spotted me at once.

"There you are! We wondered where you'd disappeared to. Come out and join us."

For once I was glad to do so, welcoming the chance to be with others in case Henry showed up again.

Jeremy gave me a bright smile. "Aunt Alice mentioned that you asked to go into Hot Springs for the celebration on the Fourth. Look, I have no desire to go, and I think you need a day off. I'll keep Aunt Alice company if you want to go."

I peered sideways toward my aunt, expecting her to insist that I remain on call, too. To my surprise, she leaned forward and placed a hand on Jeremy's arm, delight softening her face. "Dear boy, you are so thoughtful and unselfish. I'd love spending the day with you."

"Good, it's all settled," Jeremy responded, gently covering my aunt's hand with his own. "We'll have a wonderful time together. Perhaps we'll even go for our own little picnic out under the trees."

"And you shall read your latest poetry to me," my aunt said. "I'd like that very much."

The next morning after breakfast I ran into Simon in the lobby.

"Jeremy says he'll stay with Aunt Alice, so I can go with you to Hot Springs on the Fourth if you still want me to."

His face broke into a wide grin. "Joanna, that's wonderful! You can help me pass out the handbills."

That set me back a little. The idea of accosting people on the streets and thrusting handbills at them made me uncomfortable. Still, it would be a day in town, away from the tension at Milwood.

Away from Henry Hampton.

"Oh, by the way, I found this in your box this morning," he went on.

He took an envelope from a cubbyhole behind the desk and

handed it to me. I turned it over in my hands, expecting to see my mother's handwriting on the front, although I realized that Simon was the one who usually rode into town for the mail and should have known if I'd received a letter. The envelope was sealed and had my initials scrawled across the front in a shaky hand. A shiver ran through me, a premonition of dread, as I looked at that handwriting.

"Thank you, Simon," I said, smiling to conceal my fear. "I'll read this upstairs."

I stepped into the lift and rode past the second floor before removing the one sheet of paper. When I unfolded it, a shock thudded through me at the word printed there: "DANGER," in the same shaky scrawl, with the *N* and the *E* reversed. It might have been the handwriting of a child . . . or of a sick man not yet in total control of his faculties.

Amos? Was Amos warning me again, or had this cryptic message been left for me by someone else, someone who had taken great pains to disguise his or her handwriting?

I left the lift and hurried to our suite, where I hid the note and envelope in the drawer containing my underclothing. Later that day I caught Jeremy alone in the courtyard and told him about the note, although I did not reveal that Amos could walk nor did I say that Amos might have been the one who wrote the warning, not wanting to spoil the Fourth of July surprise.

I did say to Jeremy, "Maybe I shouldn't leave you with the burden of protecting Aunt Alice on the Fourth. Maybe we both should stay here together."

"Look, it'll be all right," he said. "My grandmother and Charlotte will both be here, as well as Uncle Amos. And then there's Granny and Maybelle . . ."

Since I didn't know whom to trust and whom to distrust, I was not reassured by his statement.

"You forgot Henry," I said. "Henry will be here."

"No, Henry will be going into Hot Springs that day for the band concert. Didn't you know Henry plays a trumpet in the band there?"

Henry would be in Hot Springs? My heart squeezed with dismay at the news.

All the next day, thinking of the warning in the note, I debated whether or not I should go to Hot Springs; but everyone around me seemed so calm and Milwood, for a change, seemed so peaceful that I talked myself into believing things would be all right.

Thus it was that I got a good rest the night before the pending trip, and thus it was that I awoke refreshed to don my very best dress of white lawn, with leg-of-mutton sleeves, white lace jabot, and pink silk sash, on the bright and sunny morning of that fateful Fourth.

Chapter 20

It was just after breakfast that a trumpet fanfare drew my aunt and me from the dining room out into the lobby. There stood Henry at the foot of the stairs, resplendent in a blue band uniform with red piping, blowing on a silver trumpet that flashed white fire in the morning light.

"Henry! What are you doing?" Nell demanded as she strode in from a side corridor, her black silk skirts hissing like an angry kitten. "That's enough to wake the dead!"

He slid his eyes at her, a gleam of excitement shining in their green depths, but he did not stop playing.

Others came dashing in from various directions: Jeremy from the office; Simon, Granny, and Maybelle from the direction of the kitchen; Charlotte from the downstairs east wing.

"Henry?"

"What's this?"

"What's that racket?"

"Henry, what's going on?"

The questions blended together in a raucous babble that Henry ignored as he continued to play. When we had all gathered in a milling group around him, he lowered the trumpet at last.

"Laaadies and gennntlemen!" he announced, sweeping one

hand out in a dramatic gesture. "If you will step back, please . . . there, that's the way, just line up there . . . yes, that's it. Laaadies and gennntlemen! Today is the Fourth of July, the day of our nation's independence. In honor of this day, I present to you . . . the hero of the hour!"

He stepped aside with a bow and pointed toward the staircase.

"What—" Charlotte began, but Henry stopped her with a finger to his lips.

"Shhhh. Just watch."

From the landing above came the sound of sliding footsteps. Then Amos appeared, clinging to the bannister and moving like some kind of stiff-jointed mechanical man. Nell gasped and put her fingers to her mouth while Charlotte, standing beside me, let out a squeaking cry like a wounded bird. I quickly scanned the faces of the others, taking in their looks of surprise or disbelief.

"A miracle!" cried my aunt.

"No," I announced. "The result of hard work—Henry's and Amos's. Wait until you see their exercise room upstairs." Jeremy gave me a quizzical look and I nodded, remarking in a lower tone, "That's right. Our mystery room."

But everyone else's attention remained focused on Amos as he painfully but bravely descended the stairs. Charlotte rushed to meet him, tears streaming down her cheeks. She threw her arms around him and sobbed, "Amos, Amos, my darling Amos, I never thought—I never dreamed . . ."

"Dad, I'm so happy." Simon stepped forward to embrace both his parents.

I surreptitiously watched the play of emotions over Henry's face. He looked proud, but I also saw tension there, deepening the lines on either side of his mouth. He glanced toward me; our eyes locked and held. All expression left his face, as though it had been wiped clean by a blackboard eraser. He did not smile but gazed long and deep, then looked away again, leaving me with the uncomfortable feeling that he no longer liked me.

Despite my former anger with him, I felt an emptiness in the center of my being at the loss of his friendship. But had we been friends? Not really, I was forced to admit. No, our relationship had been something else, an animal attraction that seemed to bring out the worst in each of us.

As I pondered these things, Nell stepped forward to congratulate her son. My aunt followed suit, along with Jeremy. But when I moved toward Amos to do the same, he shrank back, his face blanching.

"Da—da—danger," he gasped, lifting one hand to cover his eyes.

"You're upsetting him!" Charlotte hissed. "You've upset him right from the beginning."

Not wanting to do anything to cast cold water over the family's present joy, I quickly backed away and stepped behind a palm, out of Amos's sight. Jeremy joined me there.

"When did you find out about the room?" he asked.

"Three days ago. The door was unlocked, so I walked in. I found Amos standing at the top of a set of steps."

"Why didn't you tell me? I thought we were in this together." Both his voice and his eyes reproached me. I could tell I'd hurt him by keeping my discovery a secret from him.

"Henry asked me not to say anything. He said his father wanted this grand entrance to be a surprise for everyone."

"Well, he certainly succeeded! When Amos appeared on those stairs . . ." He stopped and shook his head to show that mere words could not express his astonishment.

"Jeremy, about today . . . is it still all right? For me to go, I mean."

"Yes, don't worry about a thing. I'm going out now to set up a picnic spot for us in a clearing in the woods, a place with lots of wild flowers. Then I'll come back and spend the rest of the morning with Aunt Alice before taking her there for our luncheon. If the weather stays fine, we should have a pleasant day."

"This is generous of you, Jeremy. I really appreciate it."

"Say no more, my dear friend. And I repeat, don't worry. I'll keep her safe."

Sensing someone watching us, I glanced around to find Simon lurking nearby, his expression one of curiosity. He cocked an eyebrow at me as though to ask, "What is that all about?"

"Simon!" I smiled, putting on a casual air to divert him from attaching any importance to Jeremy's and my conversation. "Are you ready to go now?"

"Not quite. When I started to hitch up the buggy a while ago, I found that the seat had come loose. I'm going out now to put in new bolts, so just relax in here where it's cool until you hear me pull up in front. I'll hurry as fast as I can."

As Simon strode away, Jeremy murmured to me, "Actually, that's a bit of good luck. You'll be able to stay here with Aunt Alice until I get back. I'm taking a small table and a couple of chairs to the clearing now, in a wheelbarrow, to set up a special surprise for her. We're going to have all the trimmings—white linen, crystal, a bouquet of roses on the table."

"Jeremy, she'll love it! I'm almost tempted to stay here and hide in the bushes to watch her expression when you lead her into that clearing at noon."

"No, you go on into Hot Springs and have a good time. We'll see you this evening."

He gave me a courtly bow, then hurried away, too. I stepped from behind the palm to see Charlotte and Nell, on either side of Amos, strolling down the corridor into the east wing. Maybelle and Granny had already disappeared, headed back, I assumed, to the kitchen. Aunt Alice was still there, however, talking with Henry. My heart jumped in my chest like a stranded fish at the sight of him, looking so important and military in his uniform.

". . . can't believe what you've accomplished!" my aunt was saying.

"Without Dad's determination . . . well, he's worked very hard, that's all I can say."

I could not avoid Henry Hampton forever. After inhaling deeply, I threw back my shoulders and stepped out to join them as though nothing were wrong. If I'd hoped for a truce, my hopes were soon dashed.

"I see you've now taken to hiding behind the potted plants," he commented in a cool, sarcastic tone.

"Yes, I like to spy and eavesdrop," I replied, equally cool.

"So I've noticed."

"It's amazing what one can discover if one just keeps one's eyes and ears open."

His brows pulled together in a dark line, shading his eyes and turning them into emerald pools. "What have you discovered?"

"Many things of interest. You might be surprised."

"Do you think so?"

I took a step backward and deliberately looked him up and down as though he were some kind of strange display. "Perhaps not. Perhaps you already know all of Milwood's secrets."

"What's going on, you two?" my aunt demanded harshly. "What's this all about?"

"Why, nothing," I said lightly. "There's nothing going on, is there, Dr. Hampton?"

"Absolutely nothing." His eyes stabbed through me like two green swords.

"My, it's warm in here," I said, fanning my face with my hand. "If you'll excuse me, I'm going in search of a breeze."

I swept past the two of them and stepped out onto the verandah. The air was already scalding hot and so humid that it lay across my forehead like a fever cloth. I hoped Simon would hurry with the buggy so we could be on our way. I looked forward to the breeze that would be set up by the horse's pace. But Simon was a long time coming. I finally reentered the lobby and found it empty. Guilt flowed through me when I remembered that I was supposed to keep my aunt company until Jeremy's return. By the time I'd run up the stairs to the third floor, my corset, donned in respect for the proprieties of town, felt like the steamy interior of a bathhouse. I wished I could roll up my sleeves, but to go into town with bare arms would also be scandalous.

The tyranny of fashion.

The most foolish tyranny of all. Why couldn't a person be comfortable? I wondered. Bare arms, bare legs, short skirts, no corset—but such a prospect made me blush even as I thought it. To be so exposed before the eyes of men . . . no, indecency like that could not, would not, ever be condoned.

My aunt was not in our suite. Now I *did* feel panicked. I ran back down the stairs to the kitchen. My breath expelled in a sigh of relief when I saw my aunt at the kitchen table listening to Maybelle who sat nearby strumming her lute. Even as I entered the kitchen, she began to sing:

> *The wind, it came down from the north,*
> *And it did cruelly blow.*
> *My love, he came on bended knee*
> *And gave to me a crow.*
> *The crow did sit upon my hand.*
> *I loved it from the start.*
> *Its eyes were cold, its eyes were black,*
> *As black as my love's heart.*

I was not in the mood for a song like that. Nevertheless, I waited as patiently as I could until Maybelle finished all sixteen verses. She then lowered the lute and looked at me through veiled eyes. I could see she'd been transported to some dark land of her own.

"You do sing well, Maybelle," I said briskly. "Aunt Alice, is everything all right with you?"

"I'm perfectly fine," she replied, "but where's Jeremy?"

"He'll be back soon." At that moment I heard the whinny of a horse and the crunch of wheels on stone. I stepped out onto the back porch and peered in the direction of the stable.

Through the trees I caught the flickering movement of the buggy, heard the clatter as it rattled over the bridge. I hurried back into the kitchen. "Simon's ready now. If I go on, will you be all right until Jeremy gets back?"

"Of course," my aunt replied. "I'll go wait in the lobby until he comes."

She rose and accompanied me back to the front of the hotel, where she settled herself in her favorite chair beside an open window overlooking the verandah. I gave her a quick peck on the cheek and started to leave when she called sharply, "Aren't you forgetting something?"

She pointed to another chair where I'd earlier left my hat, a wide-brimmed straw decorated with pink and white flowers.

"Since you have no parasol, Joanna, the least you can do is wear your hat," she added querulously.

"Yes, Aunt Alice. You and Jeremy have a nice day."

I departed quickly, before she could give me any more instructions. Simon was waiting for me in the driveway. He wore a blue suit, white shirt, and red bow tie, with a straw boater perched at a rakish angle over one eye. There was a red, white, and blue hatband around the boater and a small American flag stickpin in his lapel.

"You look very patriotic," I said. "You also look warm."

He took a handkerchief from his pocket and wiped his flushed face. "I'll bet it hits a hundred degrees today."

"Don't stand on ceremony with me. Go ahead and take off your coat."

"That suits me just fine."

He slipped the coat from his arms and I saw he was wearing red, white, and blue striped suspenders. I began to laugh; the tension that spilled out with my giggles left me lighthearted and giddy for the first time in days.

"I'm so glad you asked me to go with you today," I said. "I needed some time away."

He flashed me an engaging smile while reaching over to pat my hand. "Just settle back and I'll give you the grand tour.

239

We'll make this a day to remember."

As we traveled along he pointed out the various kinds of wild flowers, which nodded in clusters beside the road or carpeted the meadows in colorful profusion: pinks, verbenas, phlox, violets, golden coreopsis. He went on to name the different trees in the woods and on the hillsides: oak, hickory, pine, elm. We passed one section of gray bluffs.

"That's novaculite," he said, "the best stuff around for making grindstones and millstones."

"Jeremy told me about that. He showed me the millstone in the old Brushwood Mill."

He grinned at me again. "Then you saw my generator?"

"Yes. I was impressed."

"Everyone in the family argued with me about installing that lift, but we'll soon be getting many guests, not just your aunt, who can't climb those stairs. I've got the handbills in a box under the seat, by the way. Today we begin to advertise!"

His optimism was infectious. I still cringed at the thought of handing out those lurid flyers, but I told myself it was for a good cause.

The Milwood road soon merged with a larger, busier road, where other buggies and wagons carried families through clouds of dust toward town. A man on horseback trotted by. He briefly touched the brim of his blue band cap as he passed us, and I found myself looking for one heart-stopping moment into Henry's sardonic gaze. A small black case attached to his saddle held what had to be his trumpet. He flicked his reins and the horse broke into a gallop, soon carrying him out of sight around a bend.

"He doesn't seem to want our company," I commented lightly.

A frown darkened Simon's face, eclipsing his previous merriment. "Henry gets in strange moods sometimes."

"Yes, I've noticed that."

But I had little time to brood about Henry's moods. The closer we got to town the more the crowds increased. Everyone seemed to be in his or her best holiday garb, and the shouts and laughter of the children hanging over the sides of the wagons made me laugh, too.

"Simon, what're those?"

I pointed toward a roadside stand where a man, woman, and three small children offered crystals for sale, huge clear multi-faceted gems that looked like something out of a fairy tale. Simon immediately pulled the buggy over to the side of the road and stopped near the stand. The man ran toward us, holding out in both hands a cluster of the transparent crystals, which protruded at different angles from a milky base.

"Those are Arkansas diamonds," Simon said seriously, but I saw the twinkle in his eyes.

"Real diamonds?" I gasped. "Diamonds that big? They must be worth a fortune!"

Now the twinkle spread to his mouth and he grinned, showing he'd been teasing me. "No, they aren't really diamonds. Those crystals are quartz, but the quartz around here is so clear, so pure, that people have taken to calling it 'Arkansas diamond.' It makes up into beautiful jewelry."

When the man heard Simon say that, he darted back to the stand and put down the cluster. He returned with one tiny crystal no bigger than the end of my little finger but perfectly formed, every facet so slick it looked as though it had been sliced by a knife. It was attached to a delicate chain so that it could be worn around the neck.

"Perfect!" Simon exclaimed. "I'll take it."

"Simon, you mustn't . . ." I began, thinking of the debts he'd incurred already; but he paid no attention to me. He pulled some coins from his pocket and paid the man his asking price without even haggling. There was nothing to do but graciously accept. When Simon fastened the clasp behind my neck his fingers lightly brushed my skin, sending a shiver of delight through my body. His gentle touch, combined with the unexpected gift, pleased me greatly. As I peered down at the crystal, nestled in the folds of my jabot, it winked at me, dancing with light in a magical way.

"Simon, thank you. I've never had a lovelier present."

I could tell he was pleased by my words. We pulled back out into the flow of traffic and proceeded on into town. Simon went first to the train station, where a puffing steam engine had just arrived with several passenger cars behind. The station was gaily decorated with red, white, and blue bunting, as was the train itself.

"We might as well get started!" he exclaimed, excitement thickening his voice.

My pulse began to race as he helped me from the buggy. I did not want to accost that throng of strangers with handbills. Still, Simon had warned me that this was one of his reasons for coming to town, and I had not demurred. It would seem petty, after accepting his gift, to back out on him now. I stood to one side, refastening my hat pins, while he dragged the box of handbills out from under the seat. He picked up a fistful and gave a few to me but, to my relief, kept most of them for himself.

I realized now that we were not alone in this endeavor of touting hotels and bathhouses. A number of men, some white, some black, walked about with handbills or signs, shouting out the virtues of their particular establishments.

"Milwood Hotel!" Simon shouted, holding up one of the flyers. "Milwood Hotel is the place to go! Healing waters, quiet surroundings, pleasant rooms, good food! Milwood Hotel! Here you are, sir . . . come to the Milwood Hotel. Here you are, madame . . . we'd appreciate it if you'd consider our baths, the best in the valley. . . ."

I hovered in the background, unable to push myself forward as he was doing. I decided that Simon had more than a little of Albert Lock's brash salesman's personality.

"Milwood Hotel! Mineral waters to cure all your ailments!" Simon yelled.

A portly middle-aged man in an expensive suit with a gleaming stickpin in his lapel now sidled up to me and whispered,

242

"Where is your room, my dear? I'll come to visit you later."

I gasped and quickly stepped away. "You mistake me, sir! I am not—I am not a—" I couldn't say the word. My face flamed while tears stung my eyes.

He had the good grace to look ashamed. "I *am* sorry," he murmured. "I thought—"

"I know what you thought."

"Then why—"

"I'm with him," I said, pointing toward Simon. "We're from the Milwood Hotel."

To prove the validity of my claim, I held up a handbill. To my surprise, he reached out and took it from me.

"The Milwood Hotel? I've never heard of it." He quickly scanned the text. "Sounds good. Perhaps we'll consider it."

He moved along, joining a group of men and women farther down the platform. I leaned against the wall of the station, all the strength gone from my knees. Simon continued to walk up and down the platform, shouting the attractions of Milwood and giving out the handbills until all the new arrivals had dispersed. At last he rejoined me, looking pleased.

"An excellent beginning," he said. "How did you do?"

Weakly I held up my handbills. "Simon, I'm not very good at this."

"That's all right. Come on inside, I want to check with the telegrapher to see if we've had any word from Albert Lock's brother."

There was indeed a message waiting: WILL ARRIVE TRAIN HOT SPRINGS 2:00 P.M. JULY FOURTH. It was signed: HERBERT LOCK.

"This is a stroke of luck!" Simon exclaimed. "I've got Albert's trunk with all his things behind the buggy seat. Brought it with me, thinking to ship it today. I'll be able to turn it over to Herbert instead."

Poor Albert Lock, I thought. How he would have enjoyed this picnic! The reminder of his untimely death put a damper on my spirits for a while, but I found it impossible to remain

243

unhappy for long in Simon's company. After he had tacked up a couple of handbills in the lobby of the train station and given some more to a porter he knew to put up in Little Rock, he sought out the livery stable, where he left the horse and buggy—but not before hanging a handbill there, as well. He gathered a large sheath of the bills and tucked them into a carpetbag, along with his small tool kit containing tacks, hammer, and sticking plaster.

"I'm going to put up these flyers all along bathhouse row," he announced cheerfully when we'd left the stable and begun our stroll down Central Avenue.

My heart sank at the news, but I told myself we'd get through it somehow. I was soon distracted from my self-consciousness by the town's well-deserved "clamor and glamour." The bathhouses were lined up in a row at the foot of Hot Springs Mountain. They were elaborate structures built in a variety of materials, with peaked roofs, cupolas, towers, dormers, and porticoes. In honor of the festivities on this day, each one flew an American flag, and some were draped with red, white, and blue bunting. It made a colorful sight, with steam from the springs rising behind and drifting on the welcome breeze that had at last sprung up. As we strolled along, I read the names of the individual bathhouses: Lamar, Rammelsburg, Ozark, Magnesia, Horse Shoe, Palace, Independent, Old Hale, Superior, Rector. Every now and then Simon stopped to tack a handbill to a tree. I always stood to one side, trying to look as inconspicuous as possible. My attention was drawn to the end of the street where I saw the towers of an impressive hotel.

"That's the Arlington," Simon said when he noticed the direction of my glances. "It's one of Hot Springs's best known hotels." Envy ate like acid through his voice.

If I'd thought the bathhouses were elaborately decorated, they were nothing compared to the Arlington. It was built in an exotic Moorish style, in three sections and five levels. I couldn't begin to guess the number of rooms that hotel contained or the size of the staff that would be required to maintain it. Bunting was draped along every one of its levels, and large flags flew from both towers. Crowds of people, beautifully dressed, drifted in colorful array along the front verandah, where the pillars were connected by Spanish arches. Black servants dressed in livery circulated among the guests with trays of food and drink.

An electric trolley rolled toward us down the street, its bell clanging. Passengers hung from the open windows waving little flags.

"Come to the Milwood Hotel!" Simon shouted as he jumped from the sidewalk to thrust a handbill into one man's hand. He ran for a small distance alongside the trolley while continuing to shout, "The Milwood! Come to the Milwood!"

"Simon!" I gasped, my heart pounding against my stays for fear he might slip and fall under the wheels. He kept his footing, however, and soon returned to me, his face flushed with triumph.

"This is going to work, you'll see," he said with great satisfaction.

"Simon, do be careful," I couldn't help saying. "If you should fall . . ."

"Would you miss me?" he asked, grinning at me like an eager school boy. "Would you shed a tear or two if I should get run over?"

Looking into his impish emerald-green eyes, I found that I would grieve indeed.

"Don't give me chance to find out, would you please?" I begged.

He bowed over my hand and kissed it lightly, then tucked my hand under his arm as we proceeded down the sidewalk.

"The Hot Springs creek used to run right down the middle of this road," he said, "but it often flooded and caused all kinds of problems, so just a few years ago the town confined the creek to a channel and built this street and sidewalk over the top of it."

"You mean the creek's still there, flowing under our feet?"

I asked, amazed.

"Sure is."

We came to Fountain Street, which intersected Central just south of the Arlington. The traffic here was thick, with men on horseback weaving in and out among the decorated carriages with their gaily dressed, excited passengers. Two boys in knickers and shirt sleeves bounced by on burros.

"There's an amusement park called Happy Hollow up Fountain Street. Come on, it's another good place to put up handbills," Simon said, tugging me out of the way as a bicycler rolled past with red, white, and blue paper woven through the spokes of his wheels.

The street quickly narrowed into a wooded valley curving around the base of Hot Springs Mountain. The activity here continued unabated, with more people of all ages riding about on burros rented from a concessionaire, men popping away at targets in a shooting gallery, and a photographer, head shielded by a black cloth, taking a photograph of a giggling boy and girl who had their heads stuck through holes in a wooden flat painted with a barroom scene.

After the quiet of Milwood, the noise and dust, combined with the heat, was almost overwhelming. Aunt Alice had made the right decision in staying at Milwood, I decided—the right decision for her. As for me, I wouldn't have missed this for anything.

Simon left me on a bench under a tree while he posted handbills at all the booths. He finally returned carrying two frosty glasses filled with a pale pink drink. I hadn't realized how thirsty I was until I saw those glasses.

"Oh, Simon, pink lemonade! With *ice!*"

"There's a public fountain around here where you can drink the hot spring water, but somehow that doesn't seem very appealing today," he said.

He held his glass up to me in a toast, which I returned. The lemonade, winter-cold and laced with flecks of tart pulp, seemed at that moment to be the most refreshing drink I'd ever tasted. When we'd finished, he returned the glasses to the lemonade stand, then picked up his carpetbag and once more tucked my hand under his other arm, a familiarity that was beginning to feel perfectly natural to me. We made our way back down Fountain Street to Central, strolling casually along and chatting in an amicable fashion.

"I have another surprise for you," Simon murmured, his green eyes dancing with merriment.

By now I was ready for anything. Or so I thought. Simon led me north past the Arlington and west down a side street into another park.

"There," he said, gesturing along the path. "What do you think of that?"

I gasped and clutched his arm with my free hand. Trotting toward us was a huge long-necked bird with strong legs and a plumed tail. It was pulling a cart holding a woman and a boy. *A bird pulling a cart.* I am telling the truth!

"Is that—is that an ostrich?" I asked, afraid to believe my eyes.

"I thought you'd be surprised!" Simon exclaimed, obviously delighted by my astonishment. "A man here has imported three hundred ostriches and is raising them for the plumes. Ah, women and their hats! What a strange and wonderful thing is women's fashion."

"You, criticizing women's fashion? A man wearing red, white, and blue suspenders hasn't a leg to stand on," I responded tartly.

Simon's laughter pealed through the air like a bell. "Touché. You have me there."

We stepped out of the way as the cart trundled past. The boy in the cart waved to another boy who was hanging by his knees from a tree limb.

"Hey, Hill! You wanna come and ride?"

That boy dropped lightly from the tree and ran to join his friend. Simon opened his bag and tacked a handbill to the tree just vacated by the boy. I turned slowly on one heel, taking in the colorful flow of people beneath the trees, the women in their frilly summer pastels, wearing hats or carrying parasols, the men in their summer suits. Once in a while I glimpsed a blue suit trimmed with red and realized I was viewing another band member. That caused me to wonder where Henry was and what he was doing. Had he stopped to visit one of his Hot Springs ladies? A twinge of jealousy jabbed me at the thought. *You have no claims on Henry Hampton,* I reminded myself sternly, *nor has he any claims on you.*

Hearing the sound of rollicking music, I peered through the trees and caught the flash of a merry-go-round, its brightly painted horses bearing a troop of shouting children. Simon and I proceeded toward that source of fun, pausing frequently to post the handbills. At last we emerged into the sunshine near the carousel. Beyond I saw the sprawling wooden structure of a grandstand.

"That's where the bicycle races are being held today," Simon told me. "Maybe we'll take in a race or two."

We'd started to move on when my heart clutched in my chest at the sight of Henry striding around the merry-go-round. He planted himself in front of us, legs apart, handbill clutched in one fist. His face was so red I feared he might be headed for a sunstroke. Shaking the handbill under Simon's nose, he demanded in a furious tone, "Just what the hell do you think you're doing?"

Involuntarily I stepped behind Simon. I could see, as Henry swept his angry gaze across my face, that I had, by that action, aligned myself in his mind with Simon.

"A fine pair you are, making an exhibition of yourselves! Cheap, that's what these are. Cheap!" He uncrumpled the handbill and held it up in the light where the garish colors looked even worse than they had in the dimly lit stable.

"Not so cheap," Simon replied dryly. "Fairly expensive, in fact."

"How did you pay for these?"

"Charged 'em. We have a month to pay."

"God." Henry's hand dropped limply to his side. "You've done some stupid things in your time, but this is the worst."

He surveyed us both for one long moment, his face tight with contempt. Then he turned and strode away as though he could no longer bear our company.

"As I said, he gets these strange moods," Simon commented lightly.

But when I stepped forward and looked into his eyes, I saw that the bitter shadowed look had returned, the look I'd seen on his face that first night in the buggy on the way to Milwood.

"I *am* going to save Milwood," he said vehemently. "I am going to save it, no matter what it takes or who I have to step on."

Despite the heat, I shivered with apprehension. For me, at that moment, the light left the day.

Chapter 21

I tried to enjoy the rest of the day for Simon's sake, but the effort took every ounce of will power I could muster. I became increasingly nervous as he continued to post the handbills, his jaw tight, his manner determined. It was as though Henry's protest had hardened Simon's resolve, forging it into steel. We took time out for the free picnic in the park, eating fried chicken, watermelon, and chocolate cake, but to me the food tasted like cardboard. Simon's former mischief, which I'd found so endearing, had vanished. He made no effort to talk while we ate but stared into space, his brows drawn together in a tight line. I was afraid to ask what he was thinking.

While we were finishing our lunch, I heard the band begin playing inside the grandstand, a rousing Sousa march. Simon stiffened when the trumpets blared. Earlier I'd thought of suggesting we join the crowd to listen to the concert, but now I quickly abandoned that idea.

"Let's move along," Simon said at last. He rose and carried our scraps to a barrel under one of the trees, then returned to help me up. "I think we'd better walk to the mortician's to see if everything is ready for Herbert Lock's arrival."

My depression deepened when we reached the funeral home. We entered a carpeted hallway, where candle stands guarded either side of an archway leading into a long chapel with pews

250

on either side. A body lay in state in a coffin before the altar at the end of the chapel. Two weeping women dressed in black hovered nearby, handkerchiefs held to their eyes. I could barely see the profile of the man inside the coffin, but his sharp-tipped nose and tuft of white hair were enough to tell me that this was not Albert Lock.

A tall lean man dressed in black, his hair parted in the middle and slicked down, wire-rimmed glasses sliding off the bridge of his nose, appeared from a doorway to one side.

"Good afternoon, Mr. O'Malley," Simon murmured.

Mr. O'Malley peered nearsightedly over the top of his glasses while whispering, "Are you friends of the deceased?" He nodded discreetly toward the chapel.

"No, we've come to inquire about Albert Lock," Simon replied. "His brother is coming in on the train this afternoon to escort the body back to Little Rock. We just picked up our wire. . . ."

Mr. O'Malley had by now straightened his glasses on his nose. Recognition dawned on his face and he interrupted to say, "Oh, it's you, Mr. Hampton! Yes, I also received a wire, two days ago, with the brother's instructions and the date of arrival. Everything is in readiness. Come, I'll show you."

He motioned for me to go first through the side door, then followed with Simon, directing us with discreet gestures toward a waiting room at the back. There we entered to find a polished wooden coffin resting on a trestle to one side. I sagged with relief against the wall when I saw that the lid was already sealed. Simon did not notice my distress but walked stolidly forward to examine the coffin.

"The brother spared no expense, I see," he said.

A pleased smile spread across Mr. O'Malley's face. "That's our very best line—birch, with brass handles."

Panic rose inside my throat like bile. Suddenly I felt a desperate urge to get back to Milwood. I'd been foolish to leave my aunt, I thought, foolish to suppress my earlier fears and allow myself to be talked into believing everything was all right. Everything was *not* all right. The sight of Albert Lock's coffin convinced me of that.

"Si—" The syllable burst from my throat in a hoarse croak. I tried again. "Simon, can we go home?"

He turned a surprised face in my direction. "Go home? Now?"

"Yes, now."

"We have to meet the train at two o'clock. You know that."

"I want to go home. I want to get back to Milwood."

He stared at me as though I'd suddenly lost my mind. "What's the matter? Are you feeling ill?"

Later I wished I'd lied and said yes. Instead I said, "No, but something is wrong."

"Wrong? What do you mean?"

"I don't know. I—I have this uneasy feeling that something is wrong at Milwood."

He shook his head, obviously disgusted. "Women's intuition. I thought you were too modern for that."

"I'm really worried, Simon."

"It's the funeral home atmosphere, Albert's death . . . that's enough to take the edge off anyone's joy. You're reacting to that, Joanna, nothing more."

"But—"

He held up one hand to stop me while saying in a firm tone, "We can't leave until after the train comes, and that's all there is to it."

"Just as soon as you've talked with Herbert Lock . . . can we leave then?"

"Don't you want to stay for the fireworks tonight?"

"No, Simon, I don't. I'd leave this very minute if you'd let me. I'd walk—"

"You can't do that!" he interrupted sharply. "I *have* to stay until that train comes, and it's much too hot and too far for you to walk home. Joanna, please be sensible."

There was nothing to do but comply, despite my increasing uneasiness. By the time the train puffed into the station at two o'clock, my nerves were twanging inside my body like discordant guitar strings. I paced the platform, unable to stand still. Simon, missing no opportunity, passed out handbills to the new arrivals until a florid man in a pin-striped suit descended from the train and stood looking questioningly about. There was no mistaking his kinship with Albert Lock. Simon marched forward at once to introduce himself. I hung back until Simon turned and summoned me with a wave of his hand.

"This is Joanna Forester, the nurse who attended your brother that last night," Simon said.

Herbert Lock took my hand in his two beefy paws.

"A heart attack, was it? That's what the wire said."

"He—he had an attack of indigestion which led to the heart attack," I replied, sliding my eyes toward Simon, then back again to Herbert's earnest face. "We sent for a doctor from Hot Springs, but he arrived too late."

Herbert mournfully shook his head. "Our doctor at home warned him. 'Albert,' our doctor said, 'you mustn't eat so much rich food. Temperance, Albert, temperance, or the old ticker's going to give out.'" He shook his head again. "Looks like he was right."

"We're certainly sorry, Mr. Lock," Simon said in a solemn tone. "We did all we could."

"I'm sure you did. No, it's not your fault, it's Albert's, for not paying attention to our doctor's warning. If our doctor said it once, he said it a thousand times. 'Temperance, Albert, temperance is the key to health.' That's what he always said. But Albert wouldn't listen."

Looking at Herbert Lock's portly form, I thought he also needed to heed the doctor's advice; but it wasn't my place to say so.

Still, this confirmation of Albert Lock's precarious state of health made me wonder again if I had been mistaken about the mushrooms. Maybe I *was* overreacting to the whole situation. Maybe I did indeed have too much imagination, as everyone

253

claimed. If so, then this premonition about Milwood might be imagination, too. I tried to curb my impatience, tried to tell myself that all was well with my aunt, yet worry continued to gnaw like a hungry rat at the edges of my mind.

The whinny of horses and the crunch of wheels on gravel drew my attention toward the road beside the station. A polished black hearse pulled by black horses driven by a black man in black livery, accompanied by Mr. O'Malley, rolled slowly toward us. The hearse had glass windows on either side, etched with a feather design, which exposed the coffin to view. On the four corners of the hearse's roof nodded clusters of tall black plumes, while similar plumes bobbed above the horses' heads, attached to their harness. It was a solemn sight. The men on the platform removed their hats and stood quietly to one side as Mr. O'Malley climbed down and walked with dignified tread to join us, where he conferred in low tones with Simon and Herbert Lock. There was much discussion of papers, certificates, general business, to which I paid little attention.

Simon and I had already stopped by the livery stable to retrieve our buggy with Albert's trunk. Simon now got the trunk and we all moved inside to the shipping desk. The men talked with the clerk there, making arrangements for shipping the body and trunk back to Little Rock. At last everything was finished. Simon solemnly shook the hands of Herbert Lock and Mr. O'Malley while I nodded my good-byes, murmuring appropriate platitudes.

"Thanks for everything ya done, little lady," said Herbert Lock.

His voice was so like his brother's that I felt my eyes sting with sudden tears. A sense of urgency, of pending doom, struck me again with such force that my stomach turned over. I clutched Simon's arm.

"Please, let's go home."

"All right, if you insist. But I'd have liked to have seen those fireworks." He sounded as disappointed as a child deprived of candy.

Nevertheless, I finally managed to get him into the buggy and headed back for Milwood. We rode in silence toward a line of thunderheads, which towered higher and higher until their anvils spread across the sky, ready for the strike of Thor's hammer. The clouds thickened underneath and advanced inexorably toward us, pushed by the rising wind.

"It looks to me as though your fireworks are going to get rained out," I remarked, glad that Simon would not now be able to hold his loss of fun against me.

He scanned the clouds while worry lines deepened the cleft between his brows. "We may get rained out, too, if we don't get home pretty soon."

He flicked the reins, coaxing the horse into a trot. We traveled through a gloom that soon deepened into twilight, even though it was still the middle of the afternoon. The rain struck just as we reached the turnoff into Milwood's lane. Simon drove straight to the stable, where he pulled the buggy in under the protection of some trees.

"Get inside," he said, nodding with his chin toward the stable as he helped me down from the buggy. "I'll be in as soon as I get the horse unhitched."

I ran for cover, darting through the open doors into the center lane between the rows of stalls. The air inside smelled dusty but sweet, combining the odor of horses and clean hay. Simon soon joined me, leading the mare with one hand while carrying his precious carpetbag in the other. While he dried and curried the horse, I paced nervously back and forth in front of the stable doors, peering out at the downpour.

"Simon, I can't wait any longer. I have to find out if my aunt is all right."

He shook his head as though my foolishness were beyond all bounds of comprehension. Nevertheless, he pulled a blanket down from the rails on one side of the stalls and handed it to me.

"If you feel you have to go out in the rain, then take this. I'll be in as soon as I finish here."

I hung my hat on a nail beside the door, then opened the blanket and draped it over my head. Clasping it under my chin with one hand, I gathered up my skirts with the other and darted out into the torrent. A crack of thunder seemed to split the very sky above my head, causing the rain to gush even harder, like blood from a severed artery. By the time I reached the kitchen porch, the blanket was soaked. Once I was under the protection of the roof, I pulled off the blanket and dropped it in a soggy heap beside the door. I stepped into the kitchen to be met by an anguished wail from Maybelle. The sight of her red eyes and disheveled hair filled me with such fear my knees went weak.

"What is it?" I asked, scarcely able to utter the words.

"It's—it's—"

"It's what?"

"I, ah . . . it . . . ah . . ."

I rushed across the room and grabbed her by the shoulders. Shaking her, I cried, "Maybelle, what has happened?"

"It's Jeremy."

My breath caught in my throat.

"Is he? . . ." I couldn't bring myself to say the word.

"I don't know! We can't find him."

"You . . . can't find him?" I repeated stupidly. "You mean he's missing?"

"Since this morning. He went out with the chairs in the wheelbarrow, and he never came back."

My joints turned to mush at the news. Maybelle collapsed into a chair beside the table and laid her head on her arms, sobbing uncontrollably.

"Where's my aunt?" I demanded.

When she didn't answer, I ran from the kitchen and down the corridor to the front lobby. There I found Nell and Charlotte hovering on either side of a chair where my aunt sat with her face in her hands. Amos rocked back and forth on his heels nearby, looking distressed.

"Aunt Alice!" I cried.

She dropped her hands and looked toward me with desperation in her eyes. Her face was ravaged with weeping.

"Joanna. Oh, Joanna." She pushed herself up from the chair and did something she'd never done before—she held out her arms to me. I rushed forward and enfolded her in a tight embrace, stroking her hair and murmuring, "Don't cry, we'll find him. He has to be all right. We'll find him."

Even as I spoke the words, I knew they were a lie. Nothing in this world, nothing said that Jeremy had to be all right. Still, I continued to whisper, "Don't worry, everything will be all right," while she sobbed into my shoulder.

Chapter 22

When I tried to question my aunt and the others, they all babbled at once, speaking in disjointed sentences; but at last I managed to piece together the story: Jeremy had left with his wheelbarrow that morning while I was still at the hotel. He'd trundled past the kitchen and headed off down the path past the stable and barn. Maybelle had watched him go, and so had Granny. Later Simon and I had left for Hot Springs, and Henry had followed a few minutes after that. No one at the hotel had thought too much about Jeremy's delay in getting back, no one except Aunt Alice and not until mid-morning; but by then the others started getting worried, too. Finally Maybelle went out to search for him. She found the wheelbarrow overturned in the clearing, with the chairs and table spilled out among the flowers, but no sign of Jeremy. She'd hunted frantically all around the glade, but he did not answer her cries. She finally returned to the hotel and enlisted the aid of Charlotte and Granny. They'd searched, too, on and off through the day, returning often to the hotel to see what the others had learned until a short time before when the storm had become too threatening. They'd just been debating sending Maybelle into town to find Henry and Simon, despite the storm, when I'd walked into the lobby.

"My Jeremy, my dear sweet boy! What can have happened?" Aunt Alice asked me now, her eyes imploring me to give her a hopeful answer.

"I don't know. But Simon will be here in a minute, and he'll help us look. We'll find him, I promise."

I continued to pat my aunt's shoulder while looking at the other three in the lobby. Nell's face had aged since morning. Her skin had turned a yellow-gray, and she looked as wrinkled as a prune.

"Mrs. Hampton, sit down, will you please? I'd like to take your pulse," I said softly.

I disengaged myself from my aunt's embrace and settled her back in her chair. Then I turned my attention to Nell. Her hands were cold, her pulse thready and fast.

"You'd better go lie down," I advised. "Today has been a shock to your system. Do you want me to help you to bed?"

"No, no, I don't want to go to bed. My grandson . . . my poor grandson . . ." Her voice died away to a whisper and she closed her eyes, almost as though she were praying. Tears slipped from beneath her eyelids to run down her furrowed cheeks.

My aunt turned slowly and fixed her gaze upon Nell. Knowing what I did, I could almost see the thoughts racing through her head: *Nell, he's my grandson, too, my own flesh and blood. Mine. Mine and Rhodes.*

I watched her hands tremble on the arms of her chair. Slowly, slowly, she extended one hand toward Nell, hesitated, drew back, reached again. At last she touched the other woman's arm.

"Nell? Nell, I'm so sorry!"

The fervor of her apology astonished me. I wondered if she were trying to make amends, with those few words, for all the years of pretense. Nell opened her eyes and stared dully at my aunt. Now that the dam of reserve had broken, my aunt leaned forward, placing her other hand on Nell's arm as well.

"You—you've had a hard life, Nell, harder than I can even imagine. But you—you had a fine husband and you have a fine family and . . . I've envied you that. Yes, I've envied you that, despite all my money. I've come to look upon your children . . . upon your children and grandchildren . . . as my own." She gulped and lowered her gaze to her lap, breathing hard. I could see the struggle within her as she tried to couch her words carefully, revealing some but not all of the truth. "I—I love Jeremy, too. I know you can see that. I . . . oh, Nell, what are we going to do? How are we going to? . . ."

She broke off her anguished wail without finishing the question, but I finished it for her in my mind: *How are we going to bear it if he's dead?*

Before Nell could respond, Simon came striding quickly into the lobby from the direction of the kitchen.

"Maybelle just told me. I'll go out and start looking immediately. Tell me where you've already searched."

"The . . . all around the glade," Charlotte said.

"What glade?"

"The one with the big pine tree on the west side and all those flowers."

"Near Granny's cabin?"

"Yes."

"Have you searched near the Sapphire Pool?"

My breath caught in my throat when I remembered my struggle in that icy blue spring. Jeremy had mentioned underwater caves. . . .

"Maybelle looked there," Nell said.

Charlotte nodded. "And I searched all around the mill."

"Why? Why did he wander off?" my aunt cried, still clinging to Nell's arm.

I'd been wondering that, too. I thought of the voice that had called me out of the bathhouse that first morning. Had a voice lured Jeremy out of the glade? If so, where was he now?

"I want to come with you," I said to Simon.

He shook his head. "Look, it's pouring out there! I have boots and a slicker I can wear. . . ."

"And I have a rain cape. It's upstairs. I'll go get it."

Before I could do that, however, I heard hoofbeats thudding

and splashing down the lane toward the hotel. I ran to the front door and looked out.

"Henry's back!" I cried.

I turned in time to see Simon's mouth tighten at the news. My aunt dropped her hold on Nell's arm and struggled once more to her feet.

"Henry's back!" She repeated my words with a new note of hope in her voice.

"He—Hen—Henry," stammered Amos. He lurched to a window and peered through, squinting his eyes. "Hen—Henry."

Simon's face grew even darker at the enthusiasm with which everyone greeted his brother's arrival.

"Hurrah, everything's going to be just hunky-dory now that Henry's back," he muttered sarcastically.

His jealousy of his brother, coming at that moment, did not set well with me. "The important thing right now is to find Jeremy," I said firmly. "If he's lying hurt and helpless out there in this rain . . ."

"Danger," Amos murmured. "Danger manger."

My aunt once more began to sob. I saw Nell reach out in a manner just as tentative as my aunt's previous gesture, but she finally managed to finish the movement by patting my aunt's shoulder. Henry did not stop at the front steps but galloped on toward the stable.

"I'll get my slicker and go tell him what's happened," Simon said, giving me a veiled look that I couldn't read. I sensed, though, that he'd been angered by the imperious tone I'd just used with him.

I refrained from any kind of placating gesture or smile, merely replying, "I'll go up and get my cape, and I'll meet you both at the stable."

Once upstairs, I stripped out of my white lawn dress, putting on one of my serviceable blue uniforms and a stout pair of shoes. My rain cape, as voluminous as an Indian teepee, also had a hood, so I was much better protected on my way back to the stable than I had been by the blanket. It helped that the rain was slacking off. I saw, scanning the sky, that the storm was drifting away from us toward the northeast and that only its southern edge had passed over Milwood. As I neared the stable, a shaft of sunlight broke through the receding clouds to brighten my path.

". . . behaved like a jackass!" Henry's angry voice thundered through the open door.

"I was just doing what should have been done a long time ago!" Simon shouted back.

I stepped into sight in the doorway. "If you'll both stop behaving like jackasses, maybe we can find Jeremy!"

They stopped and turned toward me as one, their faces shocked by my language. It was the old double standard, I told myself sardonically. Words considered strong and proper for a man were "unladylike" in a woman.

"The rain's over and the sun's coming out. If we hurry, we might be able to find him before dark," I added, stripping off my rain cape and dropping it over a hay bale. Without waiting for either of them to answer, I left the stable and splashed off down the puddled path toward the barn.

"Joanna, wait, we need a plan!"

Henry's voice. I turned to see him standing in the doorway of the stable. I stopped and waited for him to continue speaking, but made no move to return.

"Come on, Simon, she's right. And we do need a plan," he called over his shoulder.

Looking sulky, Simon emerged from the stable and followed Henry to join me on the path.

"They say they've searched around the glade and down by the pool and also by the mill," I said. "Where else do you suggest we look?"

Henry tightened his mouth in a grim line. "There's always the river. But if he fell in and drowned . . . well, we may not find him for days."

Grief constricted my throat. Until now, I had not realized

how fond I'd become of Jeremy. He might only be a distant cousin, but he was kin nonetheless, and now he might be lying hurt somewhere or even dead, caught in the web that had entangled my aunt and me ever since we'd arrived at Milwood. He'd sensed the evil, too, yet he'd tried to help me all he could.

"Wait up, wait for me!"

Maybelle came running toward us from the direction of the hotel. Her face was so swollen with weeping that she looked as though she had the mumps.

"I want to go out again, too. Please, please let me go," she begged.

"All right, then, you go with Simon. Joanna, you come with me," Henry commanded. "Simon and Maybelle, you two hunt again around the pool and mill. We'll search along the riverbank."

I bristled at his military tone. His uniform had gone to his head, I decided.

"Is there some other place he might be, some place no one has thought of?" I asked. "What else is near that glade? Are there bluffs he could have fallen from?"

"There are some bluffs down by the river. . . ." Maybelle began.

"Wait a minute, I've just remembered something," Henry interrupted. "The old sinkhole."

"Sinkhole?" I asked.

"It's a place a few hundred yards away from the glade, back in a section of thick woods. There used to be a cave under there, but now the ground has fallen in, leaving a deep, narrow hole."

Simon shook his head at Henry while giving a snort of laughter. "I don't think so. Remember when we told Jeremy that hole was full of rattlesnakes, back when we were young, and he believed us? He grew up terrified of that sinkhole, never went near it again."

"You're both going to have a lot to answer for on Judgment Day," I said angrily. "What a mean pair of brats you were!"

Henry had the good grace to look ashamed, but Simon continued to grin. I could have struck him.

"Hurry, oh please hurry! Let's all go there now," Maybelle begged.

Henry shook his head. "We should split up as planned in order to cover more territory before dark. Joanna and I will check the sinkhole before heading for the river. You two go look again around the Sapphire Pool. You know how unstable the rocks are on top of the bluff there."

We obeyed Henry's command, although I could tell that doing so rankled Simon. He cast a dark glance or two back over his shoulder toward his brother as he and Maybelle hurried off in the direction of the pool.

"This way," Henry said to me, leading me at an angle through the woods over a path so faint I hadn't noticed it before. As we struggled along through the wet weeds, Henry asked in a sarcastic tone, "Did you and Simon have a good time passing out those handbills today?"

"No matter how you or I may feel about those handbills, he *is* trying to do something constructive," I retorted. "He says that advertising is the key to saving Milwood."

"I know what he says. I suppose you took in the bicycle races and did a little shopping after your strenuous advertising chores?" He continued to sound sarcastic. I decided he needed to be taken down a peg or two.

"As a matter of fact, we went to the funeral home and then to the railway station, where we met Herbert Lock who came in today to pick up Albert's body."

That stopped Henry in his tracks. He turned and looked at me accusingly.

"You should have told me! I should have been there, too."

"We didn't find out about Herbert's arrival until we got to town this morning, and you didn't exactly give us the chance to tell you anything later in the park, now did you?"

We glowered at each other while water dripped on our heads from the leaves above.

264

"Right at this moment I don't like either you or Simon," I continued, spitting out the words. "You're both self-centered and stubborn as mules; but I do like Jeremy and if—if he's—" I paused, swallowing a sob. My throat ached as though it were bruised. Unable to speak, I pointed a commanding finger for Henry to once more lead the way.

He turned without further comment and strode along the path with the weeds whipping his pants legs. I followed behind, trying to hold my skirts folded against my legs to avoid some of the water, but without success. The path widened and spilled into an open space where I saw first a tall pine tree to the west, then the wheelbarrow lying tipped on its side among the rain-beaten flowers. A delicate table with a round top no bigger than the head of a keg lay like a dead bird with its thin legs pointed toward the sky. Beside it were two matching chairs with needlepoint seat covers, soaked by the rain. This sight forcefully brought home to me the fact that something terrible had indeed happened to Jeremy. Never would he have abandoned that fine furniture unless he'd been attacked or threatened in some way.

"Where's the sinkhole?" I demanded.

"This way."

Henry continued through the clearing and entered the thick woods on the other side. I followed and soon found myself in twilight, so dense were the leaves overhead and the brush between the vine-covered tree trunks. The area made me think of a jungle. If I'd been Jeremy, I too would have believed the story about the snakes. When my sleeve brushed against some poison ivy, I sent up a quick prayer that the thick material of my uniform would protect me.

"Over here . . . I think," Henry called, hidden by the foliage ahead. "I haven't been here for a long time."

Was that true? I wondered. Both Simon and Henry had taken their own sweet time getting ready that morning. Either one of them could have slipped away to the glade to do Jeremy harm before heading for Hot Springs.

"No, this way," Henry amended, thrashing off through the brush in another direction.

As it was, I was the one who located the sinkhole, and almost to my hurt. I edged sideways between two tangled elderberry bushes, which had grown almost together, and found myself suddenly teetering on the edge of a dark, narrow cleft, an opening with grasses and pale stringy roots dangling around its lips like whiskers around an open mouth. I grabbed hold of an elderberry limb but it bent under my weight, tilting me into space.

"Henry!"

I flailed my other arm about and grabbed another branch. Scrambling and pulling, I worked my way back from the edge.

"Henry! Over here!"

He came crashing through the undergrowth, making as much noise as a horse.

"Where?"

"Here, over here!"

At last I saw his face peering through the bushes on the other side of the cleft.

"This is it, all right. I might not have found it, the way things have grown up around here."

"How deep is it?" I clung tightly to the branches while peering down into the darkness. The damp odor of leaf mold filled my nostrils, a rich loamy smell.

"Fifteen, maybe twenty feet. We used to swing in on a rope."

I cupped one hand at the side of my mouth. "Jeremy, are you down there?"

Silence.

"Jeremy, can you hear me?"

"If he's down there, we're going to have a devil of a time getting him out."

"Jeremy? It's Joanna. Answer me!" My cries were swallowed up like worms by the cleft's loamy lips.

"He wouldn't have come here, Joanna. Simon's right. There's no reason for Jeremy to be in this sinkhole."

"Unless he was hit on the head and dumped in," I replied.

Henry sighed and shook his head at me admonishingly. "There you go, Joanna, imagining things. It's your 'voice' at the bathhouse all over again."

"You're right, it is the same thing. My aunt was deliberately attacked, and Jeremy has been, too."

"You're jumping to conclusions."

"Oh really? Then where has Jeremy been all day, answer me that?"

"I don't know. Until I do know, I see no reason to believe he's been hurt by human hand."

"Inhuman," I said. "Inhuman hand."

Now he did look disgusted. "You're not suggesting the ghost is the culprit?"

"I'm saying whoever hurt him is, in my opinion, inhuman. Because it's bound to be the same person who poisoned Albert Lock."

At that he snorted derisively, but I chose to ignore his pigheaded response. I got down on my knees, still clinging to the bushes, and peered more closely into the hole. Green light filtered down through the tangled leaves and vines that arched above my head, seeping past my shoulders to barely penetrate the gloom inside that pit. I blinked my eyes, trying to adjust to the dimness. As I did so, a faint moan drifted upward from the bottom of the hole.

"Henry! Did you hear it?"

He knelt across from me and leaned his head forward, searching the gloom. He sucked in his breath sharply and muttered, "Oh my God, he is down there."

We both reared back on our knees at the same moment and stared at each other across the cleft. Henry's face, corded with tension and tinged by the green light, looked like some strange tribal mask. I felt the tightness in my own jaw, the accusation in my eyes, as I projected toward him the silent rebuke: *I told you so!*

Another moan, almost inaudible, drifted like a wisp of vapor from the pit.

"At least he's alive," Henry said quietly. "Joanna, go get the others. Bring ropes, bandages, a plank for us to lash him to. If his back is broken . . ."

Before I could respond, he grabbed hold of a long limb from a bush on his side and, twisting his body lithely about, slid on his stomach over the lip of the cleft. The limb bent, thin but resilient, its thick sap and fresh wood supporting his weight for some distance into the hole. There was a pause, and then the limb whipped upward, singing through the air as he let go. I heard the patter of pebbles and dirt sliding down the side of the hole, heard the thump of his landing.

"Are you all right?" I called.

He went into a paroxysm of coughing, apparently choked by the dirt he'd released. "Y—yes."

I leaned forward again, straining my eyes to see while listening to the rustling sounds as Henry maneuvered about below. I could barely discern his movements in the gloom.

"He . . . I think he has a broken arm," he called.

"What about his back?"

"I can't tell. Blood . . . there's blood on his face. Wait a minute—a scalp wound, yes it's pretty deep."

"Hit on the head," I stated flatly. And now I could not resist rubbing it in, "I told you he'd been hit on the head!"

"He may have hit his head falling in, but we still don't know that someone else hit him." There was an unmistakable edge to Henry's voice.

Why? I wondered. Why did Henry keep trying to rationalize everything away in the face of such evidence?

But the evidence is all circumstantial, I admitted reluctantly to myself.

"Joanna, what are you waiting for? Go get help!"

Still I hesitated. Filled with distrust of Henry, I did not want to go off and leave Jeremy alone with him.

"Joanna, I told you, we need ropes and a plank. Now hurry!"

Silently I consigned Jeremy to God's protection, then scrambled backward, away from the hole, and pushed myself to my feet. I turned and ran as fast as I could through the woods, holding my arms in front of my face to deflect the vines and branches. The trees began to thin, admitting more light, and soon I emerged into the clearing where the dripping grasses sparkled in prismed splendor, touched by the sun's magic wand.

To my surprise, I saw Granny limping into the clearing from the other side with a coil of rope in one hand.

"We've found him!" I yelled. "Over here, the old sinkhole. Hurry, Granny! We've found him!"

I turned and scrambled back into the woods. "Henry, Granny's here!" I shouted. Fervently I thanked the good Lord for having answered my prayer so quickly. Now Henry would not be alone with Jeremy. "Granny's here, and she's got some rope!" I yelled again as I approached the sinkhole. "She can go bring more help while I stay with you."

"You go bring more help," Henry called back. "You can run faster."

He had a good point there, I decided. I dashed back to Granny and guided her through the trees to the edge of the cleft.

"Be careful," I said. "Don't you fall in, too."

"I know ever' inch a these woods like the back of my hand," she retorted curtly. "I ain't about to fall in." She sat down on the ground and grasped a bush with one gnarled hand. "All stove up, is he?" she yelled.

"He's pretty bad, all right," Henry called back.

I heard a faint moan that made my heart sing, for it told me that Jeremy was still alive.

"Joanna, are you still here?"

"Yes . . ."

"Well, get the hell out and go find Simon! It'll take both of us to lift him out of here. Don't forget the plank."

269

This time I did not pause at the clearing but plunged on across the glade and through the woods on the other side. As I neared the fork in the path that led toward the Sapphire Pool, I began to yell, "Simon! Maybelle! We've found him! Simon!"

I veered in that direction, since they would be searching the pool and the mill. As I ran, I continued to cry, "Simon! Can you hear me? Simon!"

There was no response until I got almost to the pool. Then I heard an answering cry from the path beyond.

"This way! We've found him!" I shouted again, cupping my hands around my mouth to make a megaphone.

Soon Simon and Maybelle appeared, running toward me around the foot of the bluff.

"He's at the bottom of the sinkhole. He's hurt," I started but got no further, for Maybelle picked that inauspicious moment to faint.

Chapter 23

"Brandy. Drink it," Simon demanded.

Maybelle straightened in the kitchen chair where we'd deposited her after helping her back to the hotel. She coughed and gagged getting the amber liquid down, but it brought the color back to her cheeks. Consequently we were soon on our way once more. Maybelle carried the lantern and another coil of rope, Charlotte brought blankets, I carried my nurse's kit, and Simon brought up the rear of the procession with a plank we'd found in the barn. As we made our way toward the sinkhole, the rays of the descending sun slanted in ruddy shafts through the trees.

At last we reached the site of the accident and began the difficult chore of getting Jeremy lashed to the plank and lifted from the hole. By the time we finally struggled back through the woods to the hotel, with Henry and Simon lugging Jeremy's unconscious body, we needed the light from Maybelle's lantern. We carried Jeremy to his room off the lower east wing corridor, where Henry and I went over him carefully, checking his wounds. Although his back seemed to be all right, his left arm was indeed broken and his hair was soaked with blood. We pried open his eyelids and peered into his expressionless eyes, noting, from the disparate size of his pupils, that he did indeed have a concussion.

"Could be a skull fracture . . . I can't tell," I said. "We're taking a chance handling him now, yet I think we'd better try to tend his other wounds."

Maybelle had passed through her earlier hysteria into a cold calm. Now that there was something concrete to be done, she hovered at my side, helping sponge the blood from Jeremy's scalp. While I shaved the hair from around the gash, disinfected it, and stitched it closed, she handed me the proper tools before I even had to ask. The broken arm was so swollen that it took Henry's and my combined strength to straighten it and put on the splint. Even in Jeremy's unnatural sleep, he cried out when Henry and I jerked the bones back into place. I welcomed that response, considering it a good sign that Jeremy's spirit was still in there fighting.

My own spirit had smouldered into a rage as I'd worked over Jeremy. Someone had done this to him; someone had tried to kill him. Whoever it was, I wanted to hurt that person back. Jeremy stirred fretfully in the bed, flinging his head about on the pillow. He opened his eyes and stared wildly at me without recognition. "Who—who is calling?"

I bent over him at once. "Jeremy, what is it? What do you hear?"

"Voice . . . who are you? Help? Yes, I'm coming."

"Jeremy, whose voice do you hear?"

At the same time I flashed an accusing glance toward Henry. *See? I told you someone called him out of that glade!*

"What is he talking about?" Maybelle asked anxiously.

I shook my head. "Jeremy? Did someone call to you this morning from the woods? What do you remember?"

Henry glowered at me, his face twisted in the lamp light. "Let him rest. You shouldn't be disturbing him now."

I straightened and planted my fists on my hips; my face burned from the heat of my anger. "How can you keep pushing the situation here under the carpet? You know as well as I do

272

there's a murderer at Milwood. You can't ignore that any longer!"

Beside me, Maybelle whimpered, clutching Jeremy's good arm.

Henry did not back down. "Jeremy's raving. Hallucinating. People who've been badly hurt . . . well, they imagine things, have bad dreams. You can't take what they say seriously."

"I do take this seriously. I take it very seriously."

Henry stalked from the room, and I was glad to have him go. Jeremy closed his eyes and slipped once more into unconsciousness.

"Maybelle, we'll have to take turns watching him all night. If his breathing begins to fail—"

"To fail? Then he—he still might—?" She could not frame the words. Her eyes beseeched me to reassure her.

"I'll do everything I can for him, believe me. The first twenty-four hours are the most dangerous after an injury like this, but he's already survived through more than half that, even without help and in spite of blistering heat this morning and rain this afternoon. He has to be stronger than he looks. If you and I work together—"

"Anything. Just tell me what to do."

She proved to be as good as her word. She refused to sleep and insisted upon sitting beside Jeremy all through the night. When he slept, she quietly held his hand; when he roused to babble incoherently, she stroked his arm, crooning to him in a soothing voice. I rested in a chair nearby and kept watch, too, rising at regular intervals to check his condition. His breathing was thready, his pulse a fluttering bird beneath my fingertips; but still he fought for life, his face drawn, even in sleep, by the fierceness of his battle.

Others from the household tiptoed in from time to time during the night to ask about his progress. My aunt would have remained in the room with us for the all-night vigil had I not been particularly firm with her.

273

"It will do Jeremy no good if you get sick so that I have to leave his side to tend you," I reminded her.

She still refused to go upstairs but did allow me to put her to bed in a room across the hall. I left her door ajar, so I could keep an eye on her, too. Finally toward dawn I began to nod, drifting, without being aware of the change, into a bizarre world where grinning mushrooms the size of people capered around a pirate's chest. The lid stood open, revealing a treasure in sparkling jewels.

"The trunk," whispered a voice in my dream. "The answer lies in the trunk."

I whirled to find Henry staring at me, his eyes dancing with mockery. Slowly he lifted one hand, his finger pointing like the finger of doom.

"Look in the trunk," he commanded. "Look, if you dare."

I turned away from him and fastened my gaze on that beckoning treasure. When I took a step forward, it was as though the ground dissolved beneath my feet. I toppled, screaming, into the gaping mouth that had opened in the face of the earth. . . .

I jerked awake, my hands gripping the arms of the chair, my heart leaping in my chest from the terror of the nightmare. I took several deep breaths, trying to dispel the fear. Near me, Maybelle held Jeremy's hand while crooning a lullabye: ". . . sleep and dream, my love, my love. Sleep and dream 'neath stars above."

Look in the trunk.

Even though the command had come in my sleep, I felt as though I had received an order that must be obeyed. I sat up in the chair, still gripping the arms, and tried to put myself in old Rhodes's shoes. I'd been told more than once that he had a sentimental streak, which had caused him to save mementos. I now felt sure that the trunk had already been found by someone around here, probably even before my aunt and I arrived at Milwood, and that something in that trunk,

274

something, had motivated that person to try to kill my aunt, Jeremy, and me. Still I was left with the question, Why? The fact that the three of us were blood kin didn't seem a strong enough reason for murder. There had to be something else, some way that the killer could profit from our deaths.

But if someone had already found the trunk and rehidden it, where in the world could it be? Simon and Charlotte had both searched the hotel without finding it. There were so many other places it could be that the list seemed endless: the bathhouses, the stable, the barn, the wash shed, the root cellar, the chicken house, even the bottom of a sinkhole. There was even Granny's cabin to consider. Could either she or Maybelle have secreted the trunk there, perhaps under the porch?

That made me wonder again about Granny's appearance, with a rope in that clearing, the evening before. She'd said, when we'd questioned her later, that she'd come looking for us and had brought the rope just in case it was needed. But she'd also mentioned to me, I recalled, that she knew "ever' inch a these woods." If that were so, why hadn't she thought of the sinkhole and mentioned it to the other searchers during the day? What had been her real intentions when she'd entered that clearing with that rope? Had she been returning to the sinkhole to make sure Jeremy was dead? She might be old, but she was tough, from a lifetime of tramping the woods; I felt she might be perfectly capable of climbing in and out of that sinkhole by herself.

Too disturbed to sit still any longer, I rose and padded to the window, where I looked out at a gray dawn swathed in mist. Behind me Maybelle's soft voice continued to croon: "Morning breaks on distant shore. Wake, my love, and dream no more . . ."

As I stood watching, Granny glided out of the mist with a basket over her arm. She did not see me but headed on around the hotel in the direction of the kitchen. In that moment I was captured by a wild resolve: With Maybelle and Granny both

275

occupied here at the hotel, and the rest of the household still asleep, I would go right now and look under that cabin porch.

I returned to the bed and checked Jeremy's pulse. It still felt weak, but some of the stress had left his face. Maybelle stopped singing to watch me anxiously.

"How—?"

"We still need to watch him. Maybelle, will you stay here with him, and also keep an eye on my aunt across the way? I need to leave for a while to take care of some personal business."

She did not question me but simply said, "You go on. I'll stay right here."

Filled with urgency, I slipped from Jeremy's room and fled down the corridor, through the lobby, and along the far corridor to the side door at the end of the west wing. As I ran I kept glancing anxiously about, remembering how I'd met Henry in that lobby before dawn the morning I'd mailed my letter. I wanted to meet no one now and to reach the cabin unobserved.

I stepped out into the thin fog that drifted above the dew-drenched grass. The silence had substance, as though the whole world lay muffled in cotton; no birds sang, no rooster crow greeted the dawn. I welcomed the mist, for it lessened my chances of being observed by someone from the hotel. Still, just to make doubly sure, I did not take the regular path past the bathhouses but instead slipped through the woods to the carriage lane. The fog floated around me in tattered wisps, ghostly figures capering in a silent dance. As I crossed the bridge a vaporous shape in the form of a woman brushed past me, leaving a clammy dew on my face and hands along with a vague uneasiness, as though the encounter with the shape had been a warning.

Go back to the hotel, wake up your aunt, and get out of here! commanded my inner voice.

And leave Jeremy behind? countered my conscience.

No, I couldn't do that, not when he lay helpless and at the mercy of the malevolent forces lurking here at Milwood.

The carriage house loomed out of the mist, a gray windowless building with those five big double doors across the front, each section individually latched and locked. I'd started to slip on past, on my way to Granny's cabin, when I stopped, staring at that carriage house with narrowed eyes. That would make an excellent hiding place, too, I thought, since the only two people ever to go in there were Simon and Henry, and then only to bring out the buggy or the wagon. It wouldn't hurt to take a quick look inside, I decided.

I started at the east end and worked my way along, hoping that Simon would have left at least one section unlocked. I was just beginning to give up when, at last, a couple of the doors responded to my efforts and creaked outward on their hinges, revealing the dark outlines of the buggy and spring wagon waiting in the shadows. My breath quickened when I stepped inside and realized how dark it still was in there. Only a faint pearly glow filtered in through small ventilation grills up under the eaves, giving some illumination but not much.

I blinked, trying to adjust my eyes to the gloom. Gradually my vision sharpened and I saw that there were three other conveyances in the carriage house besides the buggy and spring wagon. One was a surrey with a leather roof, its fringe tarnished and hanging in uneven strips. Beyond it, partially covered by a tarpaulin, sat a barouche, giving mute evidence of the hotel's better days. In the eastern corner of the building, so shadowed as to be almost indiscernible, sat an actual stagecoach, big and unwieldy. Rhodes's family was obviously right when they said the old man had never thrown anything away; but why he would have kept a stagecoach, a bulky thing taking up valuable room in his carriage house, was beyond me. Nevertheless there it sat, a relic worthy of a museum.

I began my search with the dusty bins and cabinets along the west wall. They proved to contain tools for carriage repair,

spare parts in all sizes and shapes, oils for polishing leather, old
rags, leaves and sticks, animal droppings, half-eaten nuts—the
detritus of many years. I jumped back, smothering a shriek,
when a pink-eared field mouse suddenly jumped from one of
the shelves onto my hand and then leapt to the floor to scurry
away.

I moved on to the barouche. When I pulled off the tarp, it
released a cloud of dust that seemed to indicate it hadn't been
disturbed for some time. More animal droppings, along with
deposits from sparrows, seemed to substantiate that supposition. I walked all around the barouche and then climbed up
inside, searching beneath the seats for the elusive trunk.
Nothing.

The surrey came next, and again I found nothing. It was
possible, of course, that the trunk, if here, could be buried
beneath the dirt floor. I zigzagged back and forth as I made my
way toward the stagecoach, searching the floor for signs of
disturbance. There was more debris piled along the back wall: a
soft slope of drifted dust, leaves, sticks, discarded tools and
rags, which might cover a trunk. I selected a large stick and
began poking into the dirt as I walked along, pausing once
when the stick struck something solid. Eagerly I scraped away
the dirt only to uncover a rusty spade with a broken handle.

I left the spade where it lay and moved on to the stagecoach.
Faded letters above the door, barely discernible in the dim
light, read: MALVERN AND HOT SPRINGS. The stage had to
be really old, then, since that line had long since stopped
running. It was a conveyance that did indeed belong in a Hot
Springs museum, and I touched it reverently, envisioning it
jouncing long ago over the rocky mountain road that had
connected Malvern with Hot Springs before the advent of
"Diamond Jo" Reynolds's narrow gauge railroad. Perhaps this
was the very stagecoach that had been attacked by the James
gang.

I opened the door and climbed inside, hanging onto the edge

of the door as the stage creaked and rocked beneath my weight. The leather seats had split with age, releasing tufts of straw stuffing, along with a musty smell. I tried to brush aside a thick cobweb but it tore loose and clung about my hand. While I worked to pull away the tenacious web, another mouse darted from beneath one of the seats and scrambled to safety, leaping from the doorsill to the step and down to the floor. This time I was more prepared and did not cry out when it darted over my feet. Nevertheless, my skin did crawl a bit as I poked about under the seats and in the storage slings overhead. I found more dust and debris but no trunk.

Finally I climbed out again and circled to the back of the coach, remembering that the passengers' luggage had been carried not only in the rack on top but also in the boot. Finding the lid to the boot locked, I hurried back across the floor to retrieve the spade. The shadows had brightened a bit with the rising of the sun. I glanced out through the one set of open doors and saw that the fog was beginning to lift. Driven to get on with the job before the others at Milwood awakened, I attacked the lock with the edge of the spade. The *thunk* of each stroke reverberated through the carriage house, and my heart began to race for fear the noise would carry to the hotel. At last, with a splintering sound, the wood split from around the lock. I pried with the spade until the lock pulled free. Then, with trembling hands, I dropped the spade and lifted the lid to the boot.

There sat the trunk, black with leather handles and trimmed in brass, just as Simon had described it.

With my pulse pumping like a race horse, I stood and stared, almost afraid to believe my eyes. Perhaps the trunk would waver and vanish, pulled back into the nether regions by that mad genie I'd once envisioned as living beneath Milwood's foundation. When the trunk continued to sit there, a solid black reality, I extended one hand and tentatively touched its dusty surface. Smudged fingerprints along its lid showed me that someone else had touched it not so long ago. I pushed an errant lock of hair back from my eyes while inhaling deeply to still my racing heart. Pandora's petulant face rose before me . . . Pandora, a woman in Greek mythology who was told not to open a certain box; but she did open it, thereby releasing all the ills that have since plagued mankind. When I opened this trunk would a chittering cloud of demons pour forth?

Mustering my courage, I took hold of the clasp and tugged upwards. The lid flipped open more easily than I'd expected, falling backward on its supporting chain with a clatter. What rose to greet me was not a cloud of spirits but the mildewed smell of paper and cloth stored too long in an enclosed space. Instead of a pirate's hoard in gems and gold I saw a pile of old letters, lying in jumbled disarray. There, too, torn from its tissue paper wrapping, was a baby's dress, once white, now measled with rusty spots. I picked up one of the letters and opened it. There I saw that familiar old-fashioned handwriting with circles over the *i*'s instead of dots and the initial *A* for a signature, elaborately swirled and ending in the scripted bird. "My darling Rhodes," the letter began.

I snatched up one letter after another, scanning them swiftly, absorbing the references to Alice's pregnancy, the birth of William, the conspiracy between Rhodes and Alice to pass the baby off as a foundling for Rhodes to take home to Nell. If Nell was the person who had found this trunk and examined its contents, how painful that must have been for her. It might indeed have been enough to push her over the edge into a murderous rage.

I dug deeper, looking for further clues, something that might have provided others in the hotel with a motive for murder. I found a silver hairbrush, tarnished almost black, with Rhodes's initials engraved on the handle, perhaps a present from my aunt. I found a faded miniature painted on ivory, a picture of a pretty young woman wearing a rose in her hair and a pink ball gown that revealed her soft shoulders and delicate arms. When I looked at the portrait more closely, I realized that the girl was my aunt and that she had probably been no older than eighteen or nineteen at the time she was painted. I wondered again if Rhodes and my aunt had loved each other in St. Louis when they were young, and if they had parted on a quarrel only to meet again later after Rhodes had already married Nell.

Then I picked up an envelope that temporarily stopped my breath. Written across the face of the envelope were the words: LAST WILL AND TESTAMENT OF ALICE McPHERSON.

My hands began to tremble again as I removed the contents of the envelope. A note written in the slashing script of my aunt's later years was attached to the first page. It was a straightforward message, without the passion of the younger Alice, telling Rhodes that this was a copy of her latest will, which she had signed and placed on file with her lawyer in St. Louis. When I began to read the will, I let out a cry of surprise: In the event of my aunt's death, one third of her fortune was to go into a trust for the upkeep of the Milwood hotel; one third to her "beloved grandson, Jeremy Hampton"; and one third to her "beloved niece, Joanna Forester." In the event of either Jeremy's or my death before these wishes could be carried out, then half the estate would go to the survivor and half to the Milwood trust. But if both Jeremy and I were to die, then all of my aunt's estate would go to Milwood.

I dropped the will from nerveless fingers back into the trunk. I did not know how large my aunt's fortune was, but I'd heard from others back in St. Louis that she was one of the ten richest women in town. Whoever here at Milwood had found and read this will did indeed have a strong motive for murder.

Love of money . . . the root of all evil.

Was the murderer Simon, driven by his desire to turn Milwood into a showplace once more? Or was it Henry, dazzled by the prospect of being able to convert Milwood into a full-fledged hospital? It could still be Nell, armed now with a double motive—greed plus revenge. And what about Amos? He could walk, had been able to walk since before our arrival at Milwood. I recalled the dislike on his face when he'd looked at my aunt, and the way he'd pretended to be more daft than he really was. He had evidenced a fierce gratitude to Henry and would be willing, I felt sure, to do almost anything to help him build that clinic. Was he capable of resorting to murder to do so?

Then there was Granny. She had lived under the protection of Milwood all her adult life and might see her own security, as well as Maybelle's, tied in with the prosperity of the hotel. She could indeed have picked and cooked those poisonous mushrooms, intending them for my aunt and me.

The trunk had given me a strong motive for someone to plot murder but no clue as to who the actual villain was. I thought of Jeremy, lying helpless in bed, and of my aunt, equally vulnerable in her arthritic state, both of them at the mercy of the killer whenever he chose to attack again. I noticed I'd said *when* to myself, not *if*. My scalp tingled with such dread that my hair seemed to lift from my head. I *had* to get them both away from Milwood as soon as possible. It complicated matters that Jeremy could not yet be moved. Still, a plan began to form in my mind. I would push the buggy outside and hitch up the mare. I would then force my aunt to come with me, carrying her bodily to the buggy, if need be, and driving her into Hot Springs where I would go at once to the sheriff. I would leave my aunt in the protection of the law and return with the sheriff to Milwood to rescue Jeremy.

It might not be the best plan in the world, but it was the only one I could come up with on the spur of the moment. At least my aunt would be safe.

I stuffed the copy of the will into my pocket and slammed the lid on the trunk. At the same time another slam echoed through the carriage house and the light disappeared. I whirled and dashed through the gloom toward the carriage house doors, but I was too late. By the time I got there, they were already locked. I threw my body against them, trying to force them open, but to no avail.

"Let me out of here!" I yelled, pushing on the doors with all my weight. "Whoever you are, let me out!"

The only answer was a flurry of movement back and forth along the front of the building, a rustling noise. Then I heard a splash, and a dark liquid oozed beneath one of the doors, along with the smell of kerosene.

"Oh my God," I whispered, backing away.

I ran to the stagecoach and snatched up the spade, then darted to the east end of the carriage house, closest to the hotel, where I began beating on the wall, hoping that the sound would alert someone in time.

"Help, help! Please, someone, help me!"

I was making so much noise that I didn't hear the strike of the match, but I did hear the windlike *whoosh* when the lighted match struck the kerosene. Panic rose in my throat, bringing with it the taste of gall.

"Fire! Fire! Help, the carriage house is on fire!"

Smoke oozed around the cracks in the doors, gray ghosts reaching, seeking, with wispy outstretched fingers. An acrid smell filled my nostrils and seeped into my lungs as the roar outside increased, a waterfall of sound. My eyes began to smart and I looked up to see more smoke pouring through the ventilators under the eaves.

I could not wait for help. I was going to have to get out of here by myself or die. How? My mind cast frantically in all directions, seeking for a way. Would there be time to tunnel out under the foundation with the spade? I didn't think so. What about the carriages? Could I use one of them as a battering ram to break open the doors? I examined the lay of the floor, hoping that it sloped toward the doors. It did not. If anything, it sloped slightly downhill toward the back of the building. For a moment despair threatened to erode my strength. Smoke was now billowing into the carriage house like the onset of night. There was a chance I'd suffocate before I burned, I thought grimly.

The stagecoach was so heavy there was no chance of moving that, but I might stand a chance with the buggy. I realized, however, that the fire had its strongest hold on the doors there. Already they were beginning to blister around the edges, giving off heat like a stove. I turned to the surrey and removed the blocks that had been braking the wheels, then got behind it and braced my arms against the framework. Taking a deep breath, I pushed and grunted with all my might. It edged a few inches forward, paused, then rolled backward into place. The slope of the floor was working against me, I could see. I braced my feet against the floor and leaned with my full weight against the vehicle while pushing again.

It edged a little farther forward that time before it stopped, trembled, then rolled backward again. I jumped out of the way just in time as it gained momentum, traveling all the way back to slam against the wall. It did not even make a dent in the building, but just rested there, beyond my ability to budge. I moved at once to the barouche.

"Ugh!" I grunted, pushing with all my strength. To my joy the barouche rolled forward with more speed than had the surrey, and I saw that it would actually hit the doors. Hit it did, with a thumping sound, but the doors held. I tried again, putting, I thought, more strength into the effort. The doors bowed slightly, then snapped back into place, latch intact.

Sooner or later those doors have to give, I thought.

Despite my efforts, however, the doors held. At last, exhausted, I dropped to the ground where the air was fresher and huddled there, gasping for breath. A thudding explosion came from the far wall where the cabinets were. I saw the sudden leap of flames and realized that the fire had eaten through the wall there to ignite the pots of leather polish.

When I'd fallen into the Sapphire Pool, I'd pictured myself drowning and sinking into the underground caves. At the time that had seemed like a frightening death. Now I would have welcomed the coolness of that water. Burning was supposed to be the most painful of deaths, I'd been told, and I could believe it, having treated burn victims back in St. Louis.

"Please, Lord, please," I prayed. "Don't let me burn."

In answer came the flame's cackling laughter.

Chapter 24

The will to survive, even against seemingly impossible odds, is one of mankind's strongest drives. It's another tyranny, in fact . . . the tyranny of self-preservation, a force that can cause animals and men, caught in traps, to sever their own limbs in order to escape. I did not cower on the floor for long but rose to my knees, searching for another avenue of deliverance. I bunched my skirt up over my mouth to protect my lungs from the searing heat while I cast frantically about for a new tool to use in battering through the walls. What I saw instead, from the corner of my eye, was a flickering glimpse of trees as the fire burned an ever widening hole in the second set of doors to the west. Longingly I viewed that haven of safety, only a few yards away yet totally out of reach. The heat from that direction was so intense that I felt my skin begin to blister. If I were to try to dash through the hole in those burning doors, I knew my hair and clothing would be ablaze by the time I reached the outside while the slightest breath of that superheated air would fry my lungs. I scuttled away, wanting to avoid that fate as long as possible, but ran into the tarpaulin that I'd earlier dropped in a crumpled heap on the floor. It now tangled about my feet, halting my progress. Instinctively I scrambled about and pulled the tarp over my body, shielding myself temporarily from the heat.

That gave me an idea. I'd once attended a circus, back in St. Louis, where I'd watched a lion jump through a burning hoop. I knew my unprotected body could not make it through that burning door, but what if I used the tarp as a cover?

The roar of the fire helped me make the decision. If I stayed where I was, I would certainly soon be buried beneath the collapsing roof. Better to take a chance on the flaming door than sit here waiting for death.

I crawled along the back wall, keeping close to the floor while dragging the tarp with me. When I came opposite the doors with the hole, I again used the tarp as a shield while peering cautiously around the edge to assess the situation. Sparks beat through the air like wind-driven snow. I hesitated, clinging desperately to those last precious moments that might mark the end of my life. Then a feeling bloomed within me, a swelling of resolve, which overwhelmed the fear and set my body in motion. Quickly I judged the distance to the doors, the position of the hole, then pulled the tarp completely over me like a tent and knelt for one moment, thrusting my head toward the floor where a few inches of cooler air still existed beneath the heated upper layers. After inhaling deeply to fill my lungs, I rose and charged awkwardly forward inside the stiff tarp, my body now the battering ram that would either carry me through the doors to safety or topple me into the flames.

Even through the heavy canvas, I felt the heat grow until it rivaled the fiery lake of hell. The flames howled, a predator in pursuit of prey. The air inside my chest grew stale, begging for release, but I forced my lungs to continue their hold on that used-up store while willing my feet forward in their flight. The journey seemed to take forever. Somewhere in the distance a bell tolled, gleefully rung by the Devil himself whose laughing face danced on the inside of my eyelids. I ran and ran, trapped forever in the fire. Then the Devil reached out and grabbed me, pulling me forward. I fell, screaming, into the lake from which there is no return.

"Joanna!"

The Devil called me by name, claiming me as his own. He pulled the tarp away so that the cruel flames might roast my flesh.

"Joanna, are you all right?"

The pent-up air in my lungs exploded in a fit of coughing. I leaned my head against the Devil's chest, knowing he was not a safe place of refuge yet welcoming, however briefly, the illusion of safety in his arms.

Another voice bellowed harshly from one of the Devil's henchmen. "Come on, Simon, I need more water!"

Still coughing, I pulled away to look wonderingly into Simon's soot-smeared face.

"Thank God you're all right!" he exclaimed. "How did you get locked up in there, anyway?"

I tried to answer but could not force the words through my toasted throat.

The voice yelled again, and now I knew it to be Henry's. "Simon, come on, maybe we can save the wagon or the buggy!"

Simon swept me into his arms and carried me away from the fire to a mossy spot near the stream.

"Stay here out of the way," he commanded. "I'll be back as soon as I can."

He grabbed up a bucket and dipped it into the water, then hurried toward the blazing carriage house. As I peered after him through watering eyes, I saw Henry grab the bucket out of Simon's hands and throw the water onto the flames. A hissing explosion of steam blasted a white cloud into the dark smoke. Simon rushed back to the stream to refill the bucket while Henry darted up to me and grabbed away the tarp. He dipped the whole thing into the water, then dragged it, a heavy sodden mass, back to the carriage house where he began using it to flail the flames. I crawled to the edge of the stream and splashed the warm spring water over my face and arms. Compared to the fire, it felt cool.

The bell from Hell continued to toll. It was, I now realized, the bell in the backyard. That meant others from the hotel would be streaming down here to help fight the fire. Desperate to get back to Jeremy and Aunt Alice, I forced myself to my feet, then held onto a tree while the world circled giddily, a flame-colored carousel. Henry ran by with the steaming tarp to douse it once more in the stream.

"When there's trouble, you always turn up in the middle of it," he snarled.

Anger made me reckless. "I've noticed that about you, too. For all I know, you're the Milwood killer."

He did not answer but dashed back to the fire. I took advantage of his and Simon's preoccupation to stagger across the stream and through the woods back to the west wing of the hotel. By that time my dizziness had passed and I could move without stumbling. As I started to enter through the side door, I realized that the bell had stopped ringing. I glanced toward the bathhouses but saw no one on the path, a strange thing, I thought. . . . I would have expected most of the Hampton household to answer that bell's urgent summons.

Once inside the hotel, I quickly made my way to Jeremy's room. Shock jarred through me when I found him alone. Maybelle was the one person I had not expected to respond to the fire bell; I didn't think she would leave Jeremy's side for any reason. I hurried to his bed and leaned over him anxiously. His face was so pale that for one heart-stopping moment I feared he was dead. Then I heard his gentle inhalation, saw his eyelids flutter in sleep. His long golden lashes lay like moth antennas against his cheeks. I pressed my fingers against his wrist and felt for the first time a strong pulse beating steadily against my finger tips.

Reassured by that, I hurried across the hallway to awaken my aunt. Her bed was empty and her cane was gone. I turned on one heel, searching the corners of the room.

"Aunt Alice? Aunt Alice, are you here?"

"Jo—Joanna?" Jeremy's voice, so weak that I almost didn't

hear it, was the only answer I received.

I ran back to him at once. He looked up at me from the pillow, his brows drawn together in confusion.

"What—what happened to me?"

"You were hurt."

"When?"

"Yesterday morning. Jeremy, can you remember anything about—"

"A voice."

"You tried to tell me about that voice last night, but you were too confused. What voice?"

"It said—it said Aunt Alice was hurt. . . ."

"Was the voice male or female?"

"I . . . don't know. I followed it into the trees."

"Then what happened?"

He lifted his good hand to his bandaged head, his face wincing with pain. "Headache."

"Jeremy, concentrate. What happened?"

"I—I can't remember."

The inability to remember is not an uncommon side effect from head injuries. Aunt Alice had not been able to remember very much, either, following her clout on the head.

"Where's Maybelle?" I asked.

"Maybelle?"

"She's been with you all night, but she's gone now. Where is she?"

"I . . . don't know."

"Where's Aunt Alice?"

"Upstairs?"

That could be so. I gnawed my lip, wondering what to do. On a curio stand in the corner of Jeremy's room I saw an Indian tomahawk, its stone head lashed to the handle with leather thongs. I picked it up and handed it to him.

"Jeremy, I'm going to run up to our suite to see if my aunt is there. Someone in this hotel wants all three of us dead—you,

Aunt Alice, and me. I'm not sure you can defend yourself, as hurt as you are, but hang onto this until I return, all right? I'll hurry as fast as I can, and when I bring Aunt Alice back down, I'm going to get all three of us out of here, that's a promise!"

Even as I pronounced those defiant words, I remembered that the buggy in which I'd planned to escape had probably burned by now.

"Where's your key to this room?"

"In . . . the desk."

I opened the drawer and removed the key. "Jeremy, I'm going to lock you in. That won't stop a murderer for long, but it might delay him a trifle."

Jeremy pushed himself to a sitting position against the headboard of his bed, the pain on his face replaced by determination. He lifted the tomahawk and waved it feebly in the air.

"If he comes in, I'll bash him a good one."

I doubted he could carry that out, but I felt heartened by his spirit.

"All right, then. I'll get back as fast as I can."

I stepped from the room and locked the door, then dropped the key into the pocket with the will. I sped back to the lobby and up the stairs, eschewing the lift. What if the murderer had cut through the cables, making the lift a death trap? Even as I had that thought, I discarded it. Everyone in the hotel used that lift; the murderer would have no way of knowing he would catch the right person. No, the lift would be safe, but I still didn't welcome being cooped up in that little cage. One thing the murderer could do would be to stop it between floors and trap me there while working his will on my aunt and Jeremy. The stairs had to be safer. Still, I kept a sharp watch in all directions as I ran, not wanting to be caught off guard by someone lurking around a corner.

I reached our suite and burst in, calling, "Aunt Alice! Are you here?"

"Of course I'm here!" came her angry response from the direction of the bay window. "You deserted your post beside Jeremy and went traipsing off God knows where! I came to find you. How dare you leave your patient!"

I ran toward her, holding out my hand. "Come, we have to get back downstairs. Hurry!"

She looked me up and down with disgust. "You're filthy, Joanna. Where have you been?"

"Someone locked me inside the carriage house and set it on fire. There's a murderer loose here, Aunt Alice, and he's after you and Jeremy. Me, too. Come on, we have to get out of here!"

"Murderer? You and Jeremy?" she repeated stupidly. "Why—?"

"You should know!" I interrupted. I took the will from my pocket and shook it under her nose. "You're the one who started this whole snowball rolling. Now your grandson is in danger because of you, can't you understand that?"

Her face turned as white as the lace curtain billowing beside her. Still, old habits die hard. She drew herself up with an air of injured dignity.

"Grandson? What are you talking about? I swear, Joanna, you're as flighty as your mother, all these strange ideas you keep coming up with!"

At her condescending reference to my mother, something snapped within me. I grabbed the cane from my aunt's hand.

"You're a deceitful old woman!" I cried. I thumped the cane upon the floor. "All those lies, all those years! You've turned into a tyrant, using your money to manipulate people, but now you've gone too far!"

Thump.

"You rewrite history to suit yourself, but this is history you can't deny!" Again I shook the will in her face. "You talk against my mother, you criticize me, as though you're the original paragon of virtue. Well, go look in the mirror, Aunt Alice! Look at the adulteress, look at the mother who gave up her child!"

Aunt Alice let out a cry and hunched down as though to ward off a blow. Before my eyes she seemed to wither, even as a doll carved from an apple shrivels into old age. A small amount of pity for her stirred within me, but not enough to stop my outburst now that I'd begun.

"I'm telling you right now that you can take your twenty-five thousand dollars and throw it away, for all I care. I don't need your help, and neither does my mother. I'll go back to St. Louis and get a job in a hospital. We'll do just fine on our own."

Thump.

"But right now I'm going to save you in spite of yourself! You're getting off that window seat and coming downstairs with me *now*, do you hear me?"

Thump.

"If you don't, your grandson may die, and you and I may die, too. This will! Do you see it? This copy of your will! Someone found it, someone read it. Because of all this, now someone wants the three of us dead!"

"That's right."

The voice behind me was as cold and quiet as the knell of doom. When I heard it, I went cold, too. I turned slowly to find myself looking down the black eye of a pistol barrel.

"When did you find the trunk?" I asked.

She shrugged. "Just before you came to Milwood, behind some loose boards up there in the attic. I took it out and replaced the boards, then hid it in the stagecoach."

"But you continued to look. . . ."

"To throw others off the track. But I knew, when I saw that will . . . I knew—"

"—that you were going to kill us."

"I told you, I'd do anything, *anything*, to help my husband and sons." The corners of her eyebrows twisted together in the middle, revealing her frustration. "But murder is not so easy,

293

did you know that? You make your plans and think you have it all worked out, but things go wrong. . . ."

"You can't kill us now, Charlotte. You'll be discovered."

"I don't care about that anymore. If you're dead, you're dead, and the money still comes to Milwood. That's all that matters."

My skin chilled as I saw her finger tighten on the trigger.

"Stop!" The command boomed through the doorway like a cannon shot.

Startled, Charlotte whirled toward the sound, and the gun jerked in her hand, discharging its deadly missile. What happened then is a strange phenomenon I can't explain. It was as though time itself ground to a halt, slowing all action. Henry fell forever, falling, falling, falling, twisting slowly in air as thick as cold honey. Charlotte shrieked, and her cry stretched down the halls of eternity, forever, forever, stretched forever, never to cease.

Then Henry struck facedown on the floor and time returned to normal. Disbelieving I watched a trickle of blood edge out from beneath his body, a creeping red worm. Charlotte dropped the gun and clapped a hand to either side of her head, backing away from Henry in horrified denial.

"No," she whispered. "Nooooo."

The last word rose in pitch and became a high keening wail. She turned toward Aunt Alice and me, her eyes burning with desperation.

"You! It's your fault!" she screamed.

Before I realized what she was about, she hurled herself at my aunt and grabbed her by the throat. I dropped the cane and leapt forward, trying to pull Charlotte away, but she proved to be stronger than she'd looked. Gone was the mouse; in its place was a tiger. She wrestled my aunt about on the window seat, pushing her back against the screen. I let go of Charlotte and grabbed up the cane once more, trying to find a moment to strike when I wouldn't hit my aunt, but the threshing bodies

294

rolled about on the seat as though they had somehow grotesquely become one. Then, displaying more agility than I would have supposed possible, considering her arthritis, my aunt twisted about and placed both hands against Charlotte's shoulders, giving her a shove. Charlotte flew backward against the screen, which popped outwards with a sharp crack. She scrabbled desperately with both hands for a hold on the window jamb but could not fight against the pull of gravity. I lunged toward her, grabbing for her skirt, but it ripped through my fingers. For one brief moment her terrified eyes looked full into mine, and then she was gone. A moment later I heard the bone-crunching thud of her body against the flagstones.

"Oh my God," I gasped, leaning forward to peer through the gaping window. From the distorted position of Charlotte's body, sprawled in the courtyard below like a broken doll, I knew at once that she was dead.

My aunt huddled, whimpering, on the floor beside the window seat. With dread freezing my veins, I hurried across the room and knelt beside Henry. The flow of blood had widened into a small pool. Gently I eased him over on his back, trying to steel myself for the sight of his dead face. Anguish squeezed my heart like a vise.

I love you, I cried silently. *Why didn't I tell you? Why did I wait until it was too late?*

Pride can be tyrannical, too, a cruel ruler who exacts happiness as his toll. I had allowed pride to still the admission of my love, and now I had to live with the consequences for the rest of my life. At least I could say it aloud just once.

"I love you," I whispered, stroking the hair back from his cool, pale brow. "Henry, I love you."

My tears dropped unchecked, splashing on his face. A faint sigh escaped his lips and his eyelids fluttered.

"Henry?" Hope dawned within me like sunrise. "Henry!"

I ripped open his blood-soaked shirt and examined the place where the bullet had grazed his ribs. It took only a moment to

295

determine that one rib was broken but that nothing vital had been damaged.

His eyes opened, and I gazed into their green depths, dark with pain but with another emotion, too. His voice was weak, but the words were unmistakable. "Say it again."

"I love you."

Bending, I lightly brushed his lips with mine.

"Is it love or lust?" he murmured.

"Both."

As I touched his lips again, I knew it to be true.

Chapter 25

"A beautiful day for a wedding," the Reverend Jasper Huntington from Hot Springs murmured to me while gesturing toward the bright blue autumn sky, "and such an unusual location."

I glanced about at the group gathered near the edge of the Sapphire Pool: my aunt and Nell seated together on the log bench with Amos; Granny and Simon standing nearby; Jeremy and Maybelle, arm in arm, their faces radiant as they smiled at each other; and Henry, my beloved Henry, looking stiffly proper in his black suit and pleated white shirt.

"This whole area around here is called the Valley of Peace, did you know that?" the Reverend Huntington added. He chuckled. "But then, I'm sure it's always peaceful here. What could ever happen to disturb the peace at Milwood?"

I slid my eyes toward Henry but kept silent. Charlotte's death four months before had been pronounced an accident by the county coroner, and all of us at Milwood, by mutual consent, had allowed that ruling to stand. There was no need, we had decided, to reveal Milwood's secrets to the public. Doing so would not bring back poor Albert Lock nor would it bring back Charlotte. It would only hurt the living, and the living had been hurt enough. What we had to do now, we'd all agreed in a family conference, was to bury the past and

297

start anew.

The amazing thing to me and to the others, too, I think, was how quickly that plan got implemented. For Simon's flyers worked! Reservations began pouring in within the first two weeks after the Fourth, and by the end of the summer we'd had almost more business at Milwood than we could handle. By then, too, Jeremy's heart had been captured by Maybelle's repertoire of Elizabethan ballads, and so, on this golden October day, we had gathered at the Sapphire Pool for a double wedding.

"Let's get on with it!" my aunt demanded, thumping her cane against the bench.

Henry met my sideways glance and gave me a quick wink. Perhaps he was envisioning, as I was, the day when the sign on the west wing would read: ALICE MC PHERSON CLINIC, HENRY HAMPTON, M.D.

My aunt had said that putting her name on the clinic was not necessary, but Henry and I argued that since she was sponsoring it, she should indeed get the credit. Despite her protests, I could tell that she was pleased. We were already packed to return with her to St. Louis after the wedding, where Henry would complete his studies and I would take additional training. Who knew, I told myself, perhaps someday I might become a full-fledged doctor, too. Was this not the start of a brand-new century when opportunities for women were bound to flourish?

As I glanced about once more, I caught sight of a patch of pokeweed, said by Granny to be good for rheumatism, and I had to laugh to myself, thinking of Henry's gunnysack and the secret he had sheepishly revealed. Pride. Yes, pride is indeed a tyrant; for Henry, after all he'd said against Granny, had not wanted to admit he'd been gathering herbs on the sly and experimenting with medicines made from "old wives'" recipes.

"I agree with Alice," Amos now put in. "Let the wedding proceed!"

I was glad to hear strength in his voice. Of all those at Milwood, he had taken Charlotte's death the hardest. He'd suspected what she was up to, but because of his love for her, he hadn't wanted to betray her. Therefore he'd tried to frighten me into leaving with Aunt Alice. Nevertheless, the tragedy he'd hoped to avert had still taken place.

But all that was now in the past, I reminded myself firmly. This was my wedding day, and I refused to let any bad memories obscure the joy that warmed me like the sun. The Reverend Huntington produced a small Bible from his vest pocket and cleared his throat; but before he could begin, Jeremy held up one hand.

"Just one moment, please. I'd like to recite a sonnet I've composed in honor of this day."

My spirits sank at the news. Aunt Alice, however, clapped her hands in delight and cried, "Oh, Jeremy, dear boy, how wonderful! A wedding sonnet."

He stepped forward and turned to face us all without assuming his usual melodramatic pose. Instead, he recited in a simple, straightforward manner:

> *Some men seem bent to walk this world alone.*
> *They show no need for family, hearth, or field.*
> *They seek out ruins, crack old tombs long sealed,*
> *Taking pleasure not in flesh but bone.*
> *They wander far to lands as yet unknown,*
> *Swords and picks, not plows, the tools they wield.*
> *Their hearts are hard and not inclined to yield*
> *To lure of tropic clime or temperate zone.*
>
> *But now and then, to hide from jungle's din,*
> *The worn explorer finds a sheltered place*
> *Where Adam's rib, though bone, wears warm soft skin*
> *And welcomes him with eyes that light the face.*
> *She leads him to the fire to meet her kin.*
> *He finds his home at last in her embrace.*

When he had finished, he glanced toward me with a question in his eyes. I nodded slightly to show that I liked the poem and thought he was improving. Only then did he smile and turn to receive Maybelle's adoring embrace.

Perhaps it was a trick of the light, or perhaps an uninvited guest had decided to attend the wedding . . . I'll never know; but for one brief instant the air shimmered on the other side of the pool and I saw, in the midst of that wavering glow, the translucent form of a Spanish conquistador in full armor. He, too, was looking toward Jeremy and I saw him nod as another shadowy form appeared and shyly took his hand, an Indian maiden dressed in beaded buckskins.

"Dearly beloved, we are gathered together . . ."

In solemn tones the Reverend Huntington began the service that would join my life with Henry's. The sun glanced off the surface of the water in a dazzling flash that filled my eyes with dancing red dots. When my vision cleared, the conquistador and his maiden were gone, and in their place floated two vaporous shapes, the drifting mists of Milwood.

GOTHIC ROMANCE
By Zebra Books

SAPPHIRE LEGACY   (1979, $2.95)
by Beverly C. Warren

Forced into a loveless marriage with the aging Lord Charles Cambourne, Catherine was grateful for his undemanding kindness and the heirloom sapphires he draped around her neck. But Charles could not live forever, and someone wanted to make sure the young bride would never escape the deadly *Sapphire Legacy*.

THE SHADOWS OF FIELDCREST MANOR   (1919, $2.50)
by Casey Stevens

Alleda had no recollection of who she was when she awoke at Fieldcrest Manor. But unraveling the past was imperative, because slowly but surely Dr. Devean was taking control of her mind . . .

SHADOWTIDE   (1695, $2.95)
Dianne Price

Jenna had no choice but to accept Brennan Savage's mysterious marriage proposal. And as flickering candlelight lured her up the spiral staircase of Savage Lighthouse, Jenna could only pray her fate did not lie upon the jagged rocks and thundering ocean far below.

THE BRIDE OF FAIRCHILD ABBEY   (1660, $2.95)
by Veronica Smith

Within two weeks of Emily's marriage, the happy bride had become a grieving widow. Emily became afraid of what she hardly dared suspect. And—most of all—afraid of the very man whose dark passions ignited a fire of love in her heart.

THE MASTER OF BRENDAN'S ISLE   (1650, $2.95)
by Marion Clarke

Margaret MacNeil arrived at Brendan's Isle with a heart full of determination. But the secrets of Warwick House were as threatening as the waves that crashed upon the island's jagged rocks. There could be no turning back from the danger.

Available wherever paperbacks are sold, or order direct from the Publisher. Send cover price plus 50¢ per copy for mailing and handling to Zebra Books, Dept. 2074, 475 Park Avenue South, New York, N.Y. 10016. Residents of New York, New Jersey and Pennsylvania must include sales tax. DO NOT SEND CASH.

MYSTERIES
by Mary Roberts Rinehart

THE DOOR   (1895, $3.50)
Elizabeth Bill was about to discover that the staid and or-
derly household she had presided over for years in peaceful
isolation harbored more than one suspect with a motive for
murdering poor Sarah Gittings. And, unfortunately, more
than one victim. . . .

THE HAUNTED LADY   (1685, $3.50)
When wealthy Eliza Fairbanks claimed to have found rats
in her bedroom and arsenic on her strawberries, Miss Pin-
kerton was promptly assigned the case. But apparently,
someone else was watching too. For the old lady's worries
were over, but so was her life.

A LIGHT IN THE WINDOW   (1952, $3.50)
Ricky was forced to live with her husband's family when he
was shipped off to war. But she could not know the depth
of their hatred, or the lengths to which they would go to
break up her marriage—even if it meant destroying her in
the process.

LOST ECSTASY   (1791, $3.50)
When Tom was arrested for a not-so-ordinary murder,
Kay's life turned upside down. She was willing to put her
own life in danger to help Tom prove himself, and to save
him from those out to silence him or those after revenge.

THE RED LAMP   (2017, $3.50)
From the mysterious lighting of the red lamp to the slaugh-
tering of local sheep, Professor William Porter found this
case hard to crack. Either the ghost of Uncle Horace had
developed a bizarre taste for lamb chops . . . or someone
was manipulating appearances with a deadly purpose.

*Available wherever paperbacks are sold, or order direct from the
Publisher. Send cover price plus 50¢ per copy for mailing and
handling to Zebra Books, Dept. 2074, 475 Park Avenue South,
New York, N.Y. 10016. Residents of New York, New Jersey and
Pennsylvania must include sales tax. DO NOT SEND CASH.*

THE BEST IN REGENCIES FROM ZEBRA

PASSION'S LADY   **(1545, $2.95)**
by Sara Blayne
She was a charming rogue, an impish child — and a maddeningly
alluring woman. If the Earl of Shayle knew little else about her,
he knew she was going to marry him. As a bride, Marie found a
temporary hiding place from her past, but could not escape from
the Earl's shrewd questions — or the spark of passion in his eyes.

AN ELIGIBLE BRIDE   **(2020, $3.95)**
by Janice Bennett
The duke of Halliford was in the country for one reason — to fulfill a promise to look after Captain Carstairs' children. This was
as distasteful as finding a suitable wife. But his problems were answered when he saw the beautiful Helena Carstairs. The duke was
not above resorting to some very persuasive means to get what he
wanted . . .

RECKLESS HEART   **(1679, $2.50)**
by Lois Arvin Walker
Rebecca had met her match in the notorious Earl of Compton.
Not only did he decline the invitation to her soiree, but he found
it amusing when her horse landed her in the middle of Compton
Creek. If this was another female scheme to lure him into marriage the Earl swore Rebecca would soon learn she had the wrong
man, a man with a blackened reputation.

DANCE OF DESIRE   **(1757, $2.95)**
by Sarah Fairchilde
Lord Sherbourne almost ran Virginia down on horseback, then
he silenced her indignation with a most ungentlemanly kiss.
Seething with outrage, the lovely heiress decided the insufferable
lord was in need of a royal setdown. And she knew the way to go
about it . . .

*Available wherever paperbacks are sold, or order direct from the
Publisher. Send cover price plus 50¢ per copy for mailing and
handling to Zebra Books, Dept. 2074, 475 Park Avenue South,
New York, N.Y. 10016. Residents of New York, New Jersey and
Pennsylvania must include sales tax. DO NOT SEND CASH.*

FIERY PASSION
In every Zebra Historical Romance

WILD FURY   (1987, $3.95)
by Gina Delaney

Jessica Aylesbury was the beauty of the settled Australian Outback. She had one love; her childhood friend Eric. But she could never let him know how she felt — and she could never let anyone but him teach her the smouldering pleasures of womanhood . . .

CAPTIVE SURRENDER   (1986, $3.95)
by Michalan Perry

Gentle Fawn vows revenge for the deaths of her father and husband. Yet once she gazes into the blue eyes of her enemy, she knows she can never kill him. She must sate the wild desires he kindled or forever be a prisoner of his love.

DEFIANT SURRENDER   (1966, $3.95)
by Barbara Dawson Smith

Elsie d'Evereaux was horrified when she spilled wine on the pants of the tall, handsome stranger — and even more shocked when the bold Englishman made her clean it up. Fate drew them together in love and passion.

ECSTASY'S TRAIL   (1964, $3.95)
Elaine Barbieri

Disguised as a man, Billie Winslow hires on as a drover on a trail herd to escape a murder. When trail boss, Rand Pierce, discovers that the young tough is a nubile wench, he promises to punish her for lying — and keep her for his loving.

PROUD CAPTIVE   (1925, $3.95)
by Dianne Price

Certain that her flawless good looks would snare her a rich husband, the amber-eyed lass fled her master — only to be captured by a marauding Spanish privateer. The hot-blooded young woman had gone too far to escape the prison of his arms.

Available wherever paperbacks are sold, or order direct from the Publisher. Send cover price plus 50¢ per copy for mailing and handling to Zebra Books, Dept. 2074, 475 Park Avenue South, New York, N.Y. 10016. Residents of New York, New Jersey and Pennsylvania must include sales tax. DO NOT SEND CASH.